OPTION ZULU

MAELSTROM RISING BOOK 9

Peter Nealen

COMBINED ARMS

The lead elements of the PLA assault took their time approaching the university. Hank was up on the top floor, all too aware that he was a lot higher up than he wanted to be if the shelling started in earnest, watching as the first armored vehicles edged out of the trees and began spreading out across the fields to the north of the campus. Mostly painted in the weird blue, green, and gray PLAN marine camouflage, the first ZBD-2000 light tanks and ZBD-05 amphibious assault vehicles crept out onto the open ground, PLAN marines using the vehicles for cover as they advanced.

They were moving more slowly and cautiously than Hank had expected. Maybe they'd taken more losses on landing than they'd anticipated.

That slow, cautious advance wasn't going to help them as much as they might have hoped.

A tank's main gun thundered off to his left as one of the dug-in M60A3s opened fire at what amounted to point-blank range for a tank.

The Taiwanese had been upgrading their aging M60 and M48 tanks over the last few years. That particular M60A3 down there was covered in reactive armor and sported a 120mm main gun, instead of the 105mm gun that it had originally been built with, decades before. At that range, it was more than enough punch for the lightly-armored ZBD-2000 trundling across the muddy fields to the front.

The angular light tank blew up with a spectacular fireball as the penetrator round slammed into it just at the turret ring. The turret itself tumbled skyward on a column of flame and smoke as the tank's magazine brewed up.

Part I

Chapter 1

Approximately 13 hours before Grex Luporum Team X, assigned PSD duties for Wenzeslaus Gorman, takes contact on the bridge over the Ochtum.

The *Jacqueline Q* might have changed her digital identifier so that she now appeared to any nautical tracking programs as the *Maureen*, but there hadn't been the time nor the available equipment to change the lettering on her bow. They didn't *know* that the PLAN had fingered her as the privateer she was, but as things stood, it wasn't a great idea to take chances. So, she was well out at sea, south of Taiwan, while Hank Foss and his section rode the Zodiacs toward their target.

Hank had essentially pulled rank as the section leader and had appointed himself coxswain. That was normal, but there was an added benefit on a long transit like this. He was still taking a beating, and he'd been soaked to the bone for the last two hours, but he wasn't getting knocked around nearly as badly as Brule and Carrington up in the bow. Riding the bow in a Zodiac Combat Rubber Raiding Craft for a three-hour over the horizon transit to target was beyond miserable.

The ocean around them looked all but empty, aside from a handful of ship's running lights on the horizon. It was a startlingly low amount of traffic for one of *the* primary sea lanes in the world but, given the events of the last couple of weeks, the sparse numbers of ships weren't all that surprising.

The Western Pacific had become extremely non-permissive lately, though this particular shift in nautical traffic didn't even have much to do with the maritime guerrilla warfare that Hank and his fellow Triarii had been waging against the PLAN and her proxies in the South China Sea for a couple of months. A lot had happened since a Triarii drone swarm had devastated the carrier *Shandong* and the Triarii infantry sections had smashed the infrastructure on several of the Chinese' artificial islands in the Spratly Island chain.

One of those events had led directly to this night's mission.

The wreckage of the bulk carrier CSC *Victor*, sunk by PLAAF J-16s, was still drifting only a few dozen nautical miles away. She'd been heading for the Port of Taipei, and that sinking had finally given the Triarii the green light to wreck house.

If the ChiComs were going to play hardball, so would the Americans and the ROC.

They were getting close to their planned staging point, if his navigation was on, and he was pretty sure it was. He throttled back, slowing and finally letting the Zodiac bob on the waves in place as the other boats closed in.

Scanning the darkened horizon beneath the stars and broken clouds, he looked for running lights. He could see a few to the north and west, but none that looked like their target. He checked his watch. They were in position on time, but the target was late.

He was as sure of their position as he could be without GPS. The Triarii flotilla in the Western Pacific *had* set up something of a mesh navigation network, which allowed anyone with a terminal to use the bigger ships' stellar navigation computers and relative positions to determine their own coordinates. That required a screen, though, and Hank wanted to avoid showing *any* light out on the water that night.

The Chinese had to know that their fighter jocks had escalated the already dangerously tense situation in the Taiwan Strait to the breaking point. Not that it had needed too much of a push. The accelerating mobilization of PLA ground and missile forces on the mainland had been hard to miss.

With the Korean peninsula blowing up over the last week, it looked like the PRC was about to make a play for all the marbles.

Which was what brought Tango India Six-Four out onto the water tonight.

"Contact. Port side, third set of lights from the left."

Keith was on the gunwale, just ahead of Hank, scanning the water through his M5E1's scope. He'd spotted their target.

Hank lifted his own rifle, letting the engine idle. If not for his gloves, he'd probably have had a hard time holding onto the weapon, given how much silicone spray he'd doused it in to keep the salt water off. That rifle had been through hell since they'd left the States, but it was still running like a champ. He wanted it to stay that way.

He had a feeling that it was going to have a lot more work to do soon.

Finding the lights, he cranked up the magnification. Sure enough, that was the *Hong Yun*, the letters standing out in white on her red and black bow. She was a few minutes behind schedule, but she might have slowed down based on the maritime security warnings for the Strait.

It was a good thing Hank was a patient man.

Lowering the rifle, he twisted the throttle again, slowly bringing the Zodiac back up to speed. He was still keeping the speed low, avoiding too much noise or too much of a wake, slowly stalking their prey. They'd let the tanker get past, then the boats would move in from her stern.

Brule and Carrington would have to be on the ball during the next few minutes. Intel hadn't received any *reliable* reports that the PLAN marines had put security teams aboard any of the ships moving into Xiamen or through the Strait to any of the other ports along the eastern seaboard, but it was probably a decent possibility. Given the advantage of height, a handful of men on the fantail could easily lay waste to men in combat rubber raiding craft on the water below. Thanks to the amount of noise a tanker makes on the move, though, and the suppressors every man had mounted on his M5, there was a chance, if they were on the ball, that they could eliminate any security before they were spotted.

Both men adjusted their positions as they got closer, getting down into the boat itself instead of riding the gunwales. Brule tried lying on his belly, his rifle resting on the gunwale, for about thirty seconds before he reconsidered and followed Carrington's lead, getting into more of a sitting position with his boots up on the gunwale, leaning back against the assault packs stacked in the middle of the deck. He could shoot at a higher angle a lot more easily that way.

Still keeping their speed low, Hank closed in on the massive ship. The other boats trailed behind in a loose wedge, keeping well behind the lead craft, trying to hide in the darkness. Hank's boat would be the first to make contact, and if they could avoid being spotted too early, so much the better.

The boat rocked on the massive tanker's wake as they closed in. The running lights were on, but the crew and the security detail—presuming there was one—weren't using floodlights. Hopefully, they thought they were still far enough out at sea that they didn't have to worry about such precautions.

The tyranny of distance has its advantages, provided you can avoid some of its traps. Time and thousands of miles of open ocean can erode even the most intense watchfulness. Nobody can be switched on all the time, no matter how hard they try. And if the Chinese security "contractors" thought that they were now close enough to the mainland that they'd be under PLAN protection… They might have gotten sloppy.

Hank hoped so. He hadn't planned on it, but he could still hope.

The rails were deserted as the boats closed in, Hank steering his Zodiac up right next to the steel cliff of the hull. Jim

Shevlin brought his own boat in alongside Hank's so he could cover the gunwale while Hank and his element started their boarding operation.

Handing the throttle over to Keith, Hank got ready to move. Carrington and Brule had abandoned their earlier positions, and Carrington was hauling the boarding ladder out, extending it as Keith held the boat against the tanker's hull.

The hook went over the steel almost soundlessly. The Triarii of Tango India Six-Four had gotten a lot of practice at boarding operations since they'd sailed through the Timor Sea and into the Philippines with havoc on their minds. The next months of disruption and asymmetric warfare against the Communist Chinese had been instructive. The section was as good at maritime ops now as any dedicated naval commando unit.

Slinging his rifle across his back, Hank grabbed the ladder and started up. He was the section leader. He'd be the first one on deck. There'd been a time, especially back when he'd been a platoon sergeant and then a Company Gunny, that he would have let the younger guys go first. They were all Triarii here, though. There were billets, but no real ranks. And he wasn't willing, after the losses they'd taken from Phoenix to San Diego to Texas to the Philippines, to let another of his guys take the chief risk.

A tiny voice in the back of his head wondered as he climbed, careful not to move so quickly that the ladder bounced against the hull and made noise, if he wasn't halfway *hoping* that he'd get smoked.

Then he might not see a dead kid, torn apart by .50 caliber machinegun fire, every time he closed his eyes.

He shook the thought off as he neared the rail. Not the time. He needed to be focused, entirely in the moment.

He could worry about his mental health when his boys weren't in harm's way anymore.

Just before he reached the rail, he held on with one hand and brought his M5 back around, tucking the buttstock under his arm with the suppressor pointed up toward the top of the ladder and the superstructure that loomed overhead, the white-painted steel bathed in a handful of floodlights.

It took a little more doing to get up and over with only one hand, but as he lifted himself over the lip of the gunwale, he saw no one on deck. They had gotten sloppy. Probably figured that they were close enough to the mainland that they were home free and didn't have much to worry about anymore.

After all, most of the pirate activity was in the Straits of Malacca and the South China Sea. Hank had, himself, had something to do with the specific targeting of China-bound freighters by Indonesian pirates. He couldn't take credit for the idea, though. After all, the Chinese had been pointing pirates at the Australians for months.

When you change the rules in a war, don't be surprised when those changed rules get turned back on you.

He got over the rail and onto the deck, dropping as lightly to the steel as he could. The ladder behind him shifted and creaked slightly as Brule mounted it, clambering up fast so that Hank wouldn't be by himself on the deck for very long.

Meanwhile, the second boat had pulled up in front of them, and LaForce was even then clambering over the rail himself. But Brule wasn't the type to move slowly when his section leader was already in harm's way.

The engines chugged under him, but the deck was otherwise weirdly quiet. Either the tanker was running with a skeleton crew, or they really had gotten dangerously complacent.

He held his position, watching the hatches and portholes just over his weapon as the rest of the section, minus the coxswains, climbed aboard. There were some unavoidable noises as the ladders tapped against the hull and boots went over the rails, even the occasional clack of a rifle against the steel hull, but for the most part, the boarding was quick, smooth, and quiet.

Turning to make eye contact with LaForce, Hank pointed down, getting a slightly exaggerated thumbs up in reply. LaForce and the rest of 2nd Squad quickly vanished into a nearby hatch, leading below. They'd secure the engine spaces while Navarro took 3rd Squad forward to sweep the decks.

Hank, along with Lovell's 1st Squad and their attachment, a short, wiry man in the same green fatigues but carrying a QBZ-191 that the Triarii had captured in the Spratlys, would take the bridge.

On paper, Xu Guang was a retired ROC Army *Shàoxiào*, or Major. In reality, he was an off-the-books contractor for the ROC's National Security Bureau. Officially, he wasn't there, nor was he going to do anything that night.

With Lovell and Carrington taking point, Lovell practically shouldering Hank out of the way as if to say, *this is our job, boss,* they flowed into the superstructure.

This was hardly the first ship they'd had to clear, but this was going to be a little different. This was a "Capture" mission. They didn't want to kill anyone if they could help it. Since they appeared to have achieved complete surprise, they needed to reach the control points and secure the ship as fast as possible before the crew even knew what was happening.

They still moved carefully, soles rolling on the deck as they covered each opening with a rifle muzzle, flowing across the deck and up the ladderwells toward the bridge. They hadn't encountered any resistance yet, so they'd move quickly instead of systematically clearing every compartment.

That part would probably have to come later, but for now, they would bypass what they could to seize control of the ship first.

Hank was right behind Lovell and Carrington as they reached the bridge. So far, so good. No alarms, no security. Carrington put his hand on the handle of the hatch, looked at Lovell, who had his rifle leveled at the opening, and yanked it open.

They went through fast, half of 1st Squad flooding into the bridge with Hank and Xu in seconds.

In fact, they moved so fast, and so quietly, that it took a second before the captain—or maybe he was just the watchstander—turned to look over his shoulder to see who'd come onto the bridge. His eyes widened as he suddenly found himself staring at men in wet green fatigues, helmets, plate carriers, "horse collar" flotation devices, and NVGs, pointing suppressed battle rifles at him and the other two men on the bridge.

One of them, wearing khakis and a black polo shirt, with a QBZ-95 in his hands, very slowly held one hand out, holding the bullpup rifle's forearm with the other, slowly and gently lowering it to the deck. So, there *were* security contractors aboard, but they had gone down to a skeleton crew for the night. This guy might even be the only one up. And he didn't want any piece of the certain death that had just entered the bridge like ghosts.

Xu moved then, stepping up to the captain. Getting a better look at the man, noticeably older than the other two on the bridge, Hank was now pretty sure that this guy was the captain. The hard little Taiwanese officer kept his voice low and calm as he carefully explained to the captain just what was going to happen next in Mandarin.

Somewhere down below, a gunshot echoed through the superstructure. "All stations, this is Six. Status?" Hank kept his own voice down as he keyed his radio, letting his M5 hang as he left security to the other Triarii infantrymen on deck.

"This is Two. Had one of the security guys get froggy. One bad guy down. No friendly casualties."

"This is Three." Navarro sounded almost bored. "Deck is secure."

"Copy." Hank looked up at Xu, who nodded. Everything seemed to be under control. He switched channels. "Juliet Quebec, Tango India Six-Four. Objective secured. Will rendezvous in six hours." He nodded to Xu. "Let's get things going."

Chapter 2

Xu immediately set out instructing the captain to shut off all the running lights and disable the ship's transponder. That drew some protests, but Xu wasn't having it. While the ROC had become somewhat more conciliatory toward the PRC over the years since they'd been broadcasting Nationalist propaganda across the water at Xiamen from the island then known as Quemoy, it was clear enough that Xu was not of the kinder, gentler generation. He lifted his QBZ-191, and the captain visibly crumpled, switching off every external light on the *Hong Yun*, then shutting off the electronic transponder that allowed other ships to track her.

It wasn't foolproof. Chinese satellites had *mysteriously* not suffered as much as the Western constellations in recent years. They would be able to spot the ship eventually. It probably wouldn't take long for someone to figure out that she was moving away from her charted course and that something was wrong. Hank glanced at the weather outside the bridge windows, hoping that the clouds continued to thicken. It was just about monsoon season, which would provide some much-needed cover.

In peacetime, what they were doing—and almost a dozen other Triarii infantry sections and Grex Luporum Teams across the Straits and the East China Sea—would be piracy. In wartime— which this very much was, however murky the actual governmental stances were—it was simply privateering.

With the lights off and the transponder dead—LaForce was already looking for the transponder itself to smash it—Xu gave the captain his new course. Slowly, ponderously, the *Hong Yun* turned south, away from the mainland and Taiwan both.

They'd circle back around, once they were far enough in the clear to avoid any potential PLAN response, and once they were far enough out that it didn't look like the tanker had been seized and sailed straight to Taiwan. They still needed to maintain *some* subtlety here.

From the latest intel reports, the day when subtlety went completely out the window was coming up fast, but with most of the remnants of the US Pacific Fleet and the Japanese Maritime Self Defense Force currently focused on the Korean peninsula, since the DPRK's latest "missile test" had "accidentally" blown a ROK base at the now considerably less-fortified DMZ off the map, the Triarii and their Taiwanese allies had to be as circumspect as possible. They weren't going to get a lot of help at the moment.

So, even though everyone *knew* that they were going after the supply of petroleum going into the coastal ports, as long as they kept it as deniable as possible, they'd have some maneuvering room.

By that point, no one had any doubt, given the effective loss of the de facto control the ChiComs had asserted over the South China Sea, that the move on Taiwan was coming, sooner or later. Judging by the reports of movements of missile and ground combat units into Fujian Province over the last several weeks, Hank's money was on sooner, rather than later. But they still had to play the game and do what they could to hurt the PRC without giving them an obvious excuse to invade.

Every day, every hour that they slowed the attack and gave the ROC time to harden their positions still more and mobilize their reserves to meet the inevitable was going to be increasingly valuable as the situation continued to develop.

Hank wondered, as they steamed south in the dark, paced by the Zodiacs that would be taken back aboard the *Jacqueline Q* when they made rendezvous, if this was going to go all the way.

He didn't see why not. After all, he and his section had volunteered, almost as to a man, to head out into the Pacific in an attempt to take the fight to the Chinese. They'd known for almost a year that Beijing had been instrumental in a cyber attack that had brought down sixty percent or more of the US power grid, enabled the terrorists that had made a bad situation worse, and then tried to use the collapse of a good chunk of the country as cover to attempt to take over the West Coast ports under the guise of "humanitarian assistance." He knew that the first shots might have been fired in Europe—and he had some good friends over there, fighting the would-be totalitarian technocrats of the European Defense Council—but it was the People's Republic of China that had been behind the greatest damage to his country.

Hank might have some serious beef with the US government. Every Triarius did. That was why they were Triarii, members of a military NGO that had effectively set up parallel governance and security apparatus where the powers that be had determined that the law was politically incorrect—or its enforcement, potentially to the benefit of their political enemies, was undesirable. But he was an American, and he'd joined the Triarii after his decidedly bittersweet retirement from the Marine Corps *because* he was an American, and he detested what his country was being turned into.

The PRC had attacked *his country*. He was going to make them pay. That outweighed any discontent with DC he was carrying around.

The Navy hadn't exactly made it easy since they'd come out here. The official line—doubtless dictated by bank accounts and stock portfolios fattened with Chinese money—had been that rogue elements who just happened to be Chinese had been involved in the attacks and the takeovers. The DC establishment wasn't willing to hold the Chinese Communists responsible for blatant acts of war.

That, once again, left it up to the Triarii.

He watched the captain. Xu was hovering near the man and hadn't taken his hand off his QBZ-191's pistol grip since they'd boarded. He wasn't giving the man an inch of leeway, and he was going to make sure that the captain knew it.

Was the captain a committed Communist? Probably not. Hank had been kicking around long enough that he knew that the majority of people, even those who willingly aided and abetted tyrants, technocrats, and even terrorists, weren't true believers. They did what they could to protect themselves and get what they wanted. The former was certainly more admirable than the latter but, given what Hank had seen over the decades of his career, his sympathies for either were pretty limited.

"Tango India Six-Four, Juliet Quebec." While the *Jacqueline Q*'s transponder had been changed, they hadn't changed callsigns. The radios were supposed to be encrypted, anyway.

Hank switched his radio over to the ops net. He'd had it on scan, so it had picked up the transmission from the big fishing vessel turned Triarii raider while he'd still been set to transmit on the section net. "Send it, Juliet Quebec." The signal was a little weak, but they'd already moved about twenty nautical miles closer to rendezvous.

"Be advised, drones have picked up what appears to be a Chinese Coast Guard cutter moving toward your last known position. They must have noticed when the tanker went off the grid. You should be over the horizon by now, but you can probably expect them to have drones and possibly helicopters up to look for you."

Hank cursed silently. The tanker wasn't exactly speedy. In fact, he'd tend to call it a hog on the waves. There was no way they were going to be able to outrun a Chinese Coast Guard cutter, even with most of the big "mega cutters" severely damaged or at the bottom of the South China Sea. Bring helicopters, possibly with PLAN marines aboard, into the mix…

"Roger." There was nothing to do about it. He had the bulk of a section aboard, and they were packing enough heat that they could repel a heliborne assault. And if it really *was* a coast guard cutter, it probably didn't carry more than one helo. Probably a Z-9 or a Z-15. Worst case, if the ChiComs did send a Z-15, they could be facing as many as eighteen PLAN marines. A stiff fight, but they had the advantage of positioning, numbers, and firepower.

The game would be up, then, though. There'd be no hiding the fact that they'd hijacked a Chinese-flag tanker and were taking it south. Then the real heat would come down on them.

That *was* why he'd had the boys setting charges down in the hold. If this went pear-shaped, he'd scuttle the ship and they'd run for it.

It was still going to get hairy, but they'd have a better chance at escaping by bombshelling away in the Zodiacs than they would trying to defend a lumbering oil tanker against a determined assault.

Presuming the Chinese didn't simply decide to send a sub or a missile destroyer to just sink her, in order to keep her out of Taiwanese hands.

He switched back to the section net. "Be advised, we've got a Chinese Coast Guard cutter en route to the tanker's last known position. Somebody noticed when she went dark. Everyone stand to, be prepared to repel boarders if they come after us."

It felt like he should be doing more, but they'd already worked out their stand-to positions as soon as they'd taken the ship, the squad leaders assigning security posts around the deck and up on the superstructure. Provided everyone was on the ball, they'd be ready long before any attackers could get close.

Hank really didn't want to scuttle the ship. For one thing, it would get awfully crowded aboard the Zodes while they made their way back. He wasn't going to murder the Chinese crew, never mind that their PLAN marine counterparts probably would not show the same courtesy, but he wasn't going to leave them aboard to tell the PLAN about the round-eyes in greens who'd taken the ship in the first place.

Again, there were a lot of things that were known in an unspoken sort of way that hadn't been acknowledged, and the longer that went on, the more breathing room they had.

It's a strange sort of war when everyone directly involved knows exactly what's happening, but as long as it's done quietly, nobody *quite* acts on it. Not fully.

Of course, given the sheer resources necessary to try to take Taiwan, it wasn't a huge surprise to Hank—especially after what he'd seen on the island over the last two weeks—that the PRC was taking its time. If they were going to have a hope in hell of a decisive victory, without it turning into a bloody meat grinder, they'd need overwhelming force.

That was going to open a whole other can of worms in the process, but he suspected that was why that fat bastard in Pyongyang was getting squirrelly all of a sudden. It had sure drawn an awful lot of military power and attention north.

Restless, despite the lack of sleep the night before, Hank headed out of the bridge and turned to climb the ladder to the top of the superstructure. He wanted to take a good look around, even though he knew he wasn't going to see more than the *Jacqueline Q* could tell him about from her drone feeds. He just needed to get out and *see*.

The wind was whipping a bit, and he could see the storm coming up from the south. It was still going to be summer monsoon season for a few weeks yet. He was going to get wet, but he'd been out on the water enough over the last few months that he was getting used to it.

As he scanned the ocean around them, he could see little but water, sky, and clouds. They were well out to sea, and even from his elevated position, most of the ship traffic—not to mention both the Chinese mainland and the island of Taiwan— was below the horizon. The Zodiacs were keeping pace, thanks to the extra fuel bladders they'd loaded before splashing the night before. A pod of dolphins skimmed through the water off to the starboard side.

Where are you? He turned north, away from the oncoming monsoon, seeing only more bands of clouds and seemingly endless water. *This maritime guerrilla warfare thing requires a lot more patience than I have anymore.* But they hadn't gotten the call to go Option Zulu on the PRC yet, so he was going to have to play the cards he'd been dealt.

He knew that it probably didn't say much of anything good about where his personality had gone over the last couple of years. Amos Lovell had even taken him aside and tried to talk him into bedding one of their Philippine intelligence allies, not long before, just to try to get him to mellow out.

Instead, he just stared off to the north, waiting for the next fight.

***

He headed back below after less than half an hour. The ocean is big, even in the relatively crowded confines of the Taiwan Straits, something that presented the PLA with some serious issues for their war plans. Issues that the Triarii and the Taiwanese both intended to take full advantage of.

There were still three more hours left before they were supposed to rendezvous with the *Jacqueline Q*. The squad leaders had already put their squads on rest rotation. Hank realized, as he came back down onto the bridge and saw Doc Travis and Jim Shevlin asleep against the bulkhead that he might be the only one not on security who was still up.

Cole Spencer was leaning against the aft bulkhead, his rifle slung in front of him, his arms crossed, rubbing his salt-and-pepper beard with one ebony hand as he watched Xu and the captain. Hank joined him, and his assistant section leader gave him an appraising glance as he leaned against the steel wall beside him.

"Are you gonna rack out for a bit, boss?" Spencer was black as the ace of spades, but he was also a Tennessee redneck, and he talked like one. He was also a hell of a professional, which occasionally surprised people who didn't know him and jumped to conclusions just from looking at him and hearing his drawl. Once they got over the shock of a black guy who liked nothing more than talking about deer hunting. Well, except for deer hunting, itself.

Hank jerked his head toward the deck. "You go ahead." Partly, he didn't want to sleep while one of his team still hadn't gone down for a rest. He was also a little too keyed up, waiting for the inevitable hammer to fall.

Spencer eyed him for a moment, then shrugged. He'd long been Hank's voice of reason, the calmer, more measured devil's advocate to Hank's often hot-headed wrath. But since Texas, he'd backed off a little. Even more so lately.

Hank thought about it as Spencer found a spot on the deck and sat back against the bulkhead, his helmet and rifle next to him, still wearing his plate carrier. He'd long thought that his reaction to Arturo's death had been his alone, but Spencer had been a little more hard-edged, a little less likely to counsel a quieter course of action since then.

The kid hadn't just been the son Hank had never had. He'd been the whole section's little brother. That had been part of the reason he'd gone to his death in the first place, in defiance of Hank's strict orders. Maybe his death had hardened many of the original section almost as much as it had Hank.

He turned his attention back to the ship's captain, who was still at the helm, Xu still watching him like a hawk. If he didn't know better, he'd have thought the former ROC Army officer had a personal grudge against the captain. He knew it was just that hard-core dislike for all things ChiCom, but all the same, the former *Shàoxiào* hadn't slept since he'd boarded the *Jacqueline Q*, at least, not that Hank knew of.

Hank mused on the possibility that he might have to say something. Hate can fuel a man for a long time, but lack of sleep catches up with the hardest of the hard after enough time.

He waited and watched, silently, while they continued to steam south. His eyelids were getting heavy, his eyes stinging with fatigue. It had been a long night.

He was about to wake Spencer and take a nap himself when he got the call from the *Jacqueline Q*.

"Helo is coming your way. They must have a drone up. You've been spotted."

Chapter 3

Hank checked his watch as he nudged Spencer awake. "Full stand to. The cutter got eyes on us somehow. We've got a helo inbound."

Spencer was wide awake in a moment, grabbing his helmet and his rifle as he sat up, rubbing his eyes briefly to get the sleepy out. "How long have we got?"

Keying his radio, Hank called the *Jacqueline Q*. "Solid copy on all. Estimated time to intercept?'

"Maybe fifteen minutes." It sounded like Captain Smythe himself, the *Jacqueline Q*'s skipper. Unlike most Triarii, he wasn't a veteran of any branch of the US military. He'd been a lifetime commercial sailor before his recruitment, but he'd stepped up as a Triarius when the call had gone out. He'd seen a lot since they'd first crossed swords with pirates in the Timor Sea, and he was every bit the hardened veteran now as any of the infantry Triarii aboard his ship.

"Good copy."

Spencer had heard. He just nodded shortly and accepted Hank's hand to haul himself to his feet. "Plenty of time."

Hank keyed his radio on the section net. "Stand to, stand to, stand to. We've got an inbound Chinese helo." He sighed. It would have been nice to get the tanker to Taiwan. They could probably use the oil over the next couple of weeks or months. But there was no way they were going to get all the way there now.

"Two, make sure the charges are ready to go. We'll repel the PLA, then scuttle this tub and RV with the *Jacqueline Q* on the Zodes."

"Roger that." LaForce's voice was clipped and businesslike, as it always was over the radio. He was probably torn between disappointment at not being able to make use of the oil and being glad they still got to use the explosives.

Hank glanced at Xu, got a nod indicating that he knew what was happening and was ready for it, then headed topside. He didn't want to be hanging out on the bridge when things popped off.

Clattering up the ladderwell toward the top of the superstructure, he strained his ears for the growl of helicopter rotors.

Back when he'd been a Lance Corporal, the idea of being under enemy air attack or air assault had been almost ludicrous. How times had changed. They'd been under enemy helicopters more times than he could count at this point.

Reaching the roof, he got down on a knee and scanned three hundred sixty degrees, around the radio and radar masts. The ship's smokestack wasn't far behind him, but it didn't present much of an obstacle.

He knew he was exposed if he stayed up there, but he wanted a good look around before things went loud.

The clouds were getting thicker and darker. That would give the Triarii an advantage, though it was also going to make it harder to spot the incoming bird. If the weather turned nasty in time, though, they might be able to ambush the PLAN marines, scuttle the ship, and disappear into the monsoon. Hell, if the storm got bad enough, the Chinese bird might have to abort.

There. It was still only a speck, black against the darkening gray of the clouds, but that was definitely not a sea bird. Bracing his rifle as best he could, he put his eye to the scope and searched for the oncoming helicopter.

It was a Z-15. That meant most of a platoon. They were going to have to hit them hard and fast, before they could unass the helicopter.

If he could see the helo, that meant they had less than five minutes. He just hoped he could predict their potential landing zone with enough accuracy that his guys weren't running to get into position while the ChiComs were within visual range.

He got to his feet, staying low, and headed below. Finally deciding that there wasn't time to try to get everyone on the bad guys at once, he keyed his radio as he went through the hatch and started back down toward the bridge. "I want Three on the bow, One on the superstructure, and Two covering the fantail. We've got a Zulu One Five on the way in, so figure anywhere from fifteen to eighteen shooters. Get the forty-eights up and be ready to make this count. I don't want them getting a foothold on this ship." He broke squelch, then reconsidered as he reentered the bridge. "If we can drop that helo in the drink, let's do it."

It was a *bit* of a long shot, but enough machinegun fire on a helicopter's vulnerable engine housing or into the cockpit might well be enough to make it crash. If it went down, it might—*might*—slow the response down a bit more.

He'd just reached the bridge when one of the crew decided to try to be a hero.

One of the crewmen who'd been corralled on the top deck suddenly lunged at Xu. He was just a little too far away, though, and something in the captain's expression tipped Xu off.

Xu pivoted as the man grabbed for him, lifting a knee and driving it into his assailant's solar plexus. The crewman doubled over with a *whuff*, and Xu twisted, kicked him in the chest, and knocked him sprawling.

Without hesitation, Xu snapped his QBZ-191 to his shoulder and shot the man in the head.

The report was deafening in the enclosed bridge, and the man's head bounced under the impact, just before he went completely limp. Red puddled under his skull and dribbled from the puckered hole right beside his left eye.

The captain had flinched badly at the gunshot, and now he was staring at Xu with some terror. Hank could understand the sentiment to a certain degree, but if an unarmed man jumps an armed man, he's probably planning on trying to take the weapon away and use it.

"The political officer, probably." Xu sounded downright bored, now that the excitement was over. "I wondered why he didn't try something before."

Hank looked down at the body. Without uniforms or ranks, he had no way of knowing just who the dead man had been. He might have been one of the security contractors, but then again, Xu was probably right.

Even civilian ships working for the CCP had political officers, it seemed. At least under the current conditions. Given some of the intel reports—hazy as they were—about unrest in mainland China, that might not be that surprising. Can't have the crews transporting your fuel suddenly decide to try for a better life elsewhere.

Not that most of the rest of the world was looking too much better than China, these days. Maybe that was the point of all the destruction in the first place.

"Keep an eye on the rest of 'em." Hank wished they'd just stay nice and scared and docile, because he needed every gun available for the helo. But it was what it was.

He moved up to the windows, but he couldn't see the bird. The first spatters of rain hit the glass as the wind picked up. With a grimace, he turned back toward the stern. LaForce and his boys were probably going to get the first shot.

Hesitating a moment, he swept the bridge with his eyes. Doc Travis, Xu, and Jim Shevlin were all on deck, Xu hovering just out of reach of the captain and watching him like a hawk, while Doc and Shevlin watched the other crew and the hatches.

Will it be enough if they get squirrelly? He saw that Shevlin especially was positioned where he could shoot everyone in the compartment *and* watch the hatch. Hank nodded shortly, then turned to the hatchway. "Gonna go join Etienne."

Nobody responded, except Shevlin nodded slightly. Xu didn't even look at him.

It was a short movement to the fantail. LaForce's 2nd Squad was spread out across the stern, all down below the lip of the gunwale, ready to rise up and take the helo under fire as soon as it got close enough.

Hank moved to join LaForce, who was on a knee behind one of the girders that supported the cables and machinery that penetrated the deck from below and extended up into the superstructure. Hank had spent a lot of time at sea over the course of his career, but he wasn't sure what that stuff was for; he'd never become an expert in tankers.

Not that it mattered. In the next few minutes, either they'd be speeding south aboard the Zodiacs while the *Hong Yun* headed for the bottom, or else they'd be dead.

He braced his M5 against some of the machinery and looked for the helo. It was considerably closer, still cruising at about two hundred feet, now almost within rifle range. Easily within range of one of 2nd Squad's two Mk 48s.

Still, he didn't order anyone to open fire. He didn't want to blow this.

"Everybody stay cool." If they opened up too soon, and didn't kill the bird in the first fusillade, this was going to get real ugly, real quick. Right at the moment, the enemy didn't *know* that the tanker had been taken. As soon as they figured it out, they'd come in hot and loaded for bear.

The helo didn't come straight in, to his frustration and some chagrin. Instead, still holding at about two hundred feet, the bird started to circle the ship. A loudspeaker started to blare in Mandarin.

Hank had learned a little bit of Mandarin over the last few months. His knowledge of the language still wasn't enough to understand what was being said, though, with all the distortion and the ambient noise. He could still guess.

Without knowing for sure that the ship had been taken—they'd stormed it before a message could be sent; the *Jacqueline Q* had been listening in on the maritime radio freqs and had confirmed it—the Chinese Coast Guard was investigating rather than coming straight in to assault the ship. In one way, it meant they weren't going to be quite as keyed up and ready for an ambush, but it also wasn't bringing them in close enough, fast enough.

Somewhat to his surprise, a voice responded over the *Hong Yun*'s loudspeaker. He recognized Xu after a moment, and he hoped that the Taiwanese spook was trying to set the PLAN Marines' minds at ease.

Hopefully, he's telling them that there was just an equipment malfunction, and we've drifted. Don't know if they'll believe it given how far *we've "drifted," but there's always a chance.*

There was no response from the helo, which continued its long, slow circle around the ship. Fortunately, Xu had had the presence of mind to tell the captain to cut the engines, and now the tanker really was drifting.

"He's coming in on the bow." LaForce cursed.

Hank could sympathize. He'd picked the wrong spot. He, however, could move. "Looks like Tomas gets the first shot."

"Fuckin' new guy." Fortunately, LaForce kept his irritated mutter low, or Hank would have had to say something beyond punching his 2nd Squad leader in the shoulder with a half a grin before he turned and headed forward. He couldn't have his squad leaders openly at each other's throats.

They'd already been through that with Faris, not to mention the constant bickering between Lovell and LaForce, which had fortunately settled down some over the last few months. Navarro had been through the Spratlys with the section, but he was still the "new guy," along with most of his section. He hadn't seen the really bad times in Phoenix, California, Texas, and Mexico.

Hank was sure that Navarro had seen plenty of bad shit since he'd joined the Triarii. Possibly beforehand, too. But there's a dynamic within a small unit that sees any outsiders who didn't go through the really hard stuff as just that: outsiders.

He really didn't need that kind of thing coming up now.

Moving alongside the superstructure, he got up next to the cargo control room, one deck below the bridge, and got down prone on the deck. He didn't have much cover, but hopefully he wouldn't need it.

He couldn't see Navarro's squad where they were hunkered down in the bow. He didn't worry about it. They were pros. They knew what to do.

It was nice, sometimes, working with guys who'd been there, done that before they'd joined up. It wasn't usually the same as trying to herd privates, PFCs, and Lance Corporals.

The Z-15, a Chinese clone of the Airbus Helicopter H175, flared and slowed as it moved in toward the *Hong Yun*'s bow. There really wasn't a place for the bird to land; it was going to have to hover while the marines—or whoever the react force was—jumped off or fast-roped down.

If it got too close, they were going to have a problem. Fortunately, Navarro was thinking the same thing.

The helicopter had leveled off at about sixty feet, still almost a hundred yards off the starboard bow, and was now drifting in toward the starboard side of the forward crane. Painted a light gray with the red star and bars of the PLA on its tail, it already had its side doors open.

And those side doors were currently exposed to both of Navarro's belt-feds.

He almost couldn't hear the suppressed machinegun fire as both Mk 48 gunners opened up. One poured fire into that open side door as the helicopter sidled up to the tanker. The other concentrated on the cockpit.

Bullets tore through thin aluminum skin, Plexiglas, flesh and bone. Through his scope, Hank saw the copilot take a burst through the side of the cockpit and slump, blood spattering the pilot and the inside of the cockpit.

He realized that Navarro's squad didn't have an angle on the pilot himself. The man was clearly fighting to keep the aircraft under control, the shock of his copilot's sudden, violent death keeping him from thinking about getting away, at least for a few seconds. Hank let his breath out as his finger tightened on the trigger.

Crack. Just before the pilot tried to bank away from the ship, pulling for altitude, Hank's bullet smashed through the windscreen and punched through his throat. Suddenly choking and aspirating blood, the man tried to bank to port but he was already dying, along with everyone else aboard his aircraft, and he overcorrected.

The helicopter flipped over and crashed into the water. It floated on the surface for a few seconds before it disappeared beneath the waves, leaving behind little more than a few bits of floating debris and an oil slick.

Hank let out a deep sigh, even as the first sheet of monsoon rain swept over him and the ship. It had worked.

As he heaved himself to his feet, he keyed his radio. "Everybody back to the boats. Four, get the crew moving. I want charges smoking and everyone off in the next ten minutes."

***

Fortunately, they'd been able to use the boarding ladders to get everyone off. It got a little close, as some of the crew clearly weren't comfortable with heights, and it took longer than he'd hoped to get everyone off the ship and into the Zodiacs.

The boats were sitting extremely low in the water as they motored away from the *Hong Yun*. It made for slow going, and Hank was getting a little nervous as the seconds ticked away. He did *not* want to be too close when the tanker went down. Getting sucked into the whirlpool of a sinking oil tanker was not his idea of a good way to go out.

The *Hong Yun* shuddered, and shockwaves rippled out from her hull as the charges went off, tearing holes in the hull and the structure underlying it. It took a lot to sink a tanker, but this wasn't the first time they'd had to do it. The *Hong Yun* had been in much better shape than the old chemical tanker MV *Brilliant Titan* had been. Still, big enough charges in the right places in the engine and pump rooms had done the trick.

The ship began to creak and groan under the stresses put on the hull as she began to settle at the stern. It wasn't going to take long.

The outboards labored to get the Zodiacs clear of the *Hong Yun* as she sank. Hank turned back forward.

One more incident. One more step down the road to the big one.

Now to get back to the *Jacqueline Q* and get clear before the cutter came to investigate what had happened.

Then, provided they'd successfully broken contact, they'd circle back to the north and look for more targets.

The war went on.

Chapter 4

"I think we're clear." Captain Reggie Smythe was watching the plot, his eyes riveted on the coast guard cutter's transponder. The transponder code was just an alphanumeric, but Triarii and Taiwanese intel assets had managed to ferret out most of the codes used by the PLAN and the Chinese Coast Guard. The Maritime Militia was a little trickier, since they used all ostensibly civilian fishing boats, but that just meant that *any* Chinese flag fishing boat—or any other seagoing vessel, for that matter—was considered to be Maritime Militia or otherwise hostile.

"He's circling the tanker's last position, and there's plenty of debris and oil for him to look at, but there's nothing else there." Smythe straightened with a sigh. "There he goes. Turning north again."

Hank was watching the screen over Smythe's shoulder. "Here's hoping. That was a little closer than I wanted to get." He stifled a yawn. "Let's hang out down here for a little while, let the heat die down, then we can head back north and look for our next target."

"Should we really be pushing our luck like that?" Smythe had been through a lot since they'd sailed from Port Arthur, Texas, but he was still a thoughtful man, and given to perhaps somewhat more caution than some of the Triarii infantry he was carrying aboard his ship. He worried about his ship and his crew, and truth be told, the *Jacqueline Q*'s primary defense *was* her stealth. Not that she was invisible, but since she still appeared to be a commercial fishing vessel, she could disappear into the noise of the rest of the maritime traffic around her. She did have weapons, aside from the Triarii infantry she carried, but she still wasn't much of a warship.

Hank clapped him on the shoulder. "The ChiComs haven't stopped moving units this way, and most of the PLAN that isn't facing off with the Navy, the Koreans, and the Japanese up in the Yellow Sea is here. Sooner or later, the hammer *is* going to fall."

He turned toward the hatch, yawning again. It had been a long thirty-six hours without sleep. "The more we can keep them off balance, the more we can delay that fall. Which means there's no rest for the weary." He stepped out through the hatch before someone could tell him that the phrase was, "No rest for the wicked."

"Wake me up if anything blows up."

***

Hank came out of a deep, hard sleep as somebody shook him. It hurt to open his eyes. "What blew up?" He was kind of surprised that he was cognizant enough to remember he'd said that. He squinted at his watch.

Michael Chan, the other section leader aboard the *Jacqueline Q*, stood over him. "Nothing yet. But you need to come see this."

With a groan, Hank levered himself out of his rack, shoved his feet into his boots, and ran a hand over his face and the thickening beard there. He'd been clean shaven for decades, but the war in the Pacific had finally broken him of that habit. Grabbing his rifle, he got to his feet, narrowly avoiding cracking his skull on the rack above him.

"What's going on?" The rest of the section was asleep, several of them snoring loudly, the racket practically echoing off the steel bulkheads. Everybody was exhausted after the *Hong Yun* op.

"We spotted a small craft moving toward Penghu." Chan kept his voice down so he wouldn't wake anyone up. Hank suspected he was wasting his time. It would take a JDAM going off in that compartment to wake some of those guys up. "The weird part is, it's about the size of a Zode, but it's *way* out to sea. A lot farther out than I'd want to take a boat that size."

Hank was groggy enough that it took him a second to think that through as they climbed the ladderwell toward their op center. "You think it's PLAN marines that inserted by sub?"

"I think it's more than likely. Especially since they're only about thirty nautical miles from shore. And Penghu is a hell of a target."

Hank could only nod as Chan led the way into their op center, a compartment just off the bridge that the infantry sections had been given as the nerve center for their operations. All the radios were set up there, cables running out the hatch to antennas mounted atop the bridge. Several charts, studded with pushpins and little post it notes to keep track of what they could see—since none of the Triarii *entirely* trusted the tech they had, while they'd use it as long as it worked—stood on easels, backup for the tablets and the big plot screen that mirrored the display Smythe had up on the bridge.

The rest of the detritus in the room was made up of notebooks, targeting profiles, weather reports, and all the other various odds and ends that go into mission planning.

The plot was currently zoomed in on their target. Hank would have to say something about that. They could have zeroed in with one of the tablets, instead of getting target fixated on this one anomaly. Still, for the moment, it was Chan's show, and Chan wasn't a slouch. If he'd gone ahead and zoomed in, he must have had reason to.

The other section leader pointed to the screen. "They're moving at a pretty good clip and making a dead straight line for Shanshui Beach. I doubt they'll *actually* land there, but it'll be about an hour after sunset by the time they get in close, so they'll be able to pick a better beach landing site."

Hank eyed the plot, fighting to get his sluggish brain in gear. There was a lot going on here. "Get Xu up here."

Chan nodded to Regis, one of the current watchstanders, who got up and headed below. Xu had been snoring even more loudly than Evans, and that had taken some doing.

"Do you think we should just warn Penghu?" Chan had generally deferred to Hank on operations since they'd headed out to the Pacific. He was a vet in his own right, but Hank had been in the business longer. "That's a lot of ocean and a really small boat. We only spotted it through sheer, dumb luck."

"I'm thinking that we need to approach this carefully." Hank scratched his jaw. The beard itched. The humidity of always being out on the water probably had a lot to do with that. "Those commandos are a threat, sure, and we need to either warn Penghu and/or get out there and intercept them. What worries me is that if they inserted by sub, that means there's a submarine out there, and while they might not immediately identify us as a threat, once we move against that boat, they will." He looked at Chan, whose eyes had widened a little. He hadn't thought about that angle. "This boat ain't exactly an ASW destroyer."

Anti-submarine warfare wasn't something most of the Triarii flotilla was really well-equipped to handle. They had *some* tools, including depth charges that were glorified beer kegs crammed with explosives and equipped with a pressure switch that was right out of World War II. *Early* World War II. Some of the ships had sonar, but it was crude, essentially what could be built with limited resources and off-the-shelf components that had never really been meant for military applications. Against a state-of-the-art military sub—not that the Chinese really had "state-of-the-art" by American standards—it wasn't going to be enough.

And the *Jacqueline Q* didn't have more than the bare-bones gear needed to hopefully keep out of trouble.

"That's a point." Chan scratched the back of his neck as he stared at the plot. "Without knowing where that sub is…"

"We could get close to the infiltrators and take a torpedo up the ass." Hank scowled at the plot. They were still well out of range to engage the small craft from there, which meant they'd have to change course. Moving over to the intercom, he rang the bridge. "Captain Smythe, can you join us in the ops compartment for a moment?"

Xu came up from the berthing at that point, disheveled, bleary, and yawning. "What's going on?"

Hank filled him in. Xu just took it in, nodded, and went to the radio, setting in the channel that they'd been assigned to communicate with the ROC Army and Navy, picked up the handset, and started speaking in Mandarin. The word was getting passed to Penghu.

Meanwhile, Smythe came down and joined them. "What's up?"

"That small craft that we spotted heading toward Penghu? We're pretty sure it's full of commandos out to pull some dirty tricks, but we're also pretty sure that they inserted by submarine, and we don't want to tangle with a Chinese sub, whether it's a Shang class nuke boat or some ancient Ming class diesel." Hank moved to the plot and squinted at the islands, rocks, and shoals that made up Penghu County, tracing a line with his finger. "If we head back in toward the main island, like we're sailing toward Budai Port, then turn back in, could we get ahead of them?"

Smythe eyed the plot with narrowed eyes, thinking. He made no bones about not being a tactician, but Hank had pointed out, after learning it a long time before, that tactics largely boil down to common sense and enough patience to put it into action, just faster than the other guy.

He shook his head. "I think, if anything, that might be more obvious than just continuing north like we're doing. We haven't changed course or speed since the lookouts spotted that boat. To anyone who might be paying attention, it looks like we're just steaming our way north, and Longmen *is* a fishing harbor. It makes sense that a fishing vessel—which we are—would be going there. We *could* speed up a little bit, which just might mean we'd pass within six or seven hundred yards of those infiltrators, just about... here." He pointed to a spot on the plot just north and east of Wangan. "We might be able to do it without raising a sub skipper's suspicions, provided he's still hanging around here. With the *Fong Yang* just a few nautical miles to our south, he might have beat feet." The ROCS *Fong Yang* was a Taiwanese guided missile frigate, formerly the USS *Brewton*.

"I don't want to bank on 'might have.'" Hank eyed the plot and then nodded. "Let's try it."

***

While the *Jacqueline Q* was quite a bit faster than a Zodiac, or whatever the Chinese equivalent was, their intercept plan depended on maintaining the appearance of a commercial fishing vessel. That limited her maneuvering options while she was still trying to keep up the charade.

And even though they'd done all they could to make the *Jacqueline Q* seem harmless, at least from a distance, there was still the factor that the bad guys would want to avoid compromise, if they really were PLAN *Jiaolong* commandos.

"They're veering off. We're getting too close, and they don't want to be observed." Navarro was taking his turn up on the lookout post, on top of the bridge, reporting by section net radio.

"Damn it." Hank was on the bridge itself, watching the horizon through high-powered optics. He didn't have quite the field of view that Navarro did, which was *why* they'd placed a lookout up there. The heavy-duty binos bolted to the deck were probably a little more stable, but they were lower to the water.

"Now what?" Chan asked.

"Now, the ROC Army steps in." Xu had just come through the hatch and onto the bridge, joining the two section leaders at the port side. "We provided the warning, now the hunt is on." He nodded. "I think we can expect several helicopters to start a grid search of the nearby ocean soon."

Hank pivoted his binoculars toward the island to the north. "There's one. Make that two." He focused the binos on the oncoming dark dots against the dying light of the sky. "Looks like a two-ship group of SuperCobras." He still found it somewhat amusing that the Triarii had slightly more advanced versions of

34

those helicopters, having obtained a small fleet of AH-1Z Vipers through channels he didn't want to know about.

He could only watch as the birds flew over the water in a staggered formation, followed by a single UH-60 Blackhawk, the military version of the Triarii's own S70s. Apparently, the ROC was hoping to get some prisoners out of this.

They must have had a drone out, because the SuperCobras hardly hesitated, going straight for the small raiding craft's last known position. Or maybe they had just gone by Xu's reports and were counting on thermal sights to pick up the enemy once they were in the vicinity. That was probably more likely.

It didn't take long. The two attack helicopters began circling and the Blackhawk moved in, its searchlight stabbing toward the ocean. Hank couldn't hear from that distance, but he suspected that the Blackhawk was issuing an ultimatum over a loudspeaker.

Whatever they said, the guys in the boat weren't having it. Hank couldn't see exactly what happened, but a moment later the Blackhawk veered off and the two SuperCobras swooped in, their 20mm rotary cannons spitting fire.

No inflatable raiding craft was going to stand up to that. A moment later, the SuperCobras were pulling back, and the Blackhawk came in low and slow, playing the spotlight over the water, looking for survivors.

It wasn't long before all three helicopters were pulling away, winging their way back toward Penghu.

"Well, hell. Two ops and not a shot fired." Chan shook his head.

Hank clapped him on the shoulder. "Not necessarily a bad thing, brother. Enjoy the quiet while we have it."

He looked toward the horizon, beyond which lay the Chinese mainland. He was pretty sure that a good number of the ship's running lights he could see on that horizon belonged to PLAN vessels.

The relative quiet was going to end. Sooner or later.

Chapter 5

With the distinct possibility that there might be a PLAN submarine on the hunt behind them, the section leaders agreed with Smythe, and they kept moving in toward Longmen Fishing Harbor. Hank resisted for a little bit after Doc Travis badgered him about it. He resisted at first, figuring they really needed to get out there and find some more targets, but he eventually surrendered without *too* much of a fight. He was as tired as the rest of them, and a day or two ashore might not go amiss. Besides, it would provide an opportunity to liaise with their ROC counterparts and get some updated intel.

Things had been moving fast since the Triarii had wrecked the PLAN's airfields in the Spratly Island Chain, effectively crippling much of their stranglehold on that end of the South China Sea. While the PLAN had largely pulled back from the massive swathe of territory that they had claimed was historically Chinese, running from Hainan clear down to Indonesian territorial waters, the probes of Taiwanese airspace, "naval exercises" right at the edge of Taiwanese waters—not that the PRC recognized any such thing—and "missile tests" lobbing ballistic and cruise missiles into the waters to north, south, and east of the island had picked up. A lot.

Combined with the DPRK suddenly getting froggy, Hank had a really, really bad feeling about what was coming.

***

Xu managed to get them a meeting with *Shàoxiào* Jian Shu-Chen, an intel officer stationed on Penghu. He was a small, slightly-built man, kind of the picture of an intel geek. Hank didn't let his appearance affect his impression of the man. From what Xu had told him—he knew Jian personally—Jian could have been a tenured professor in a couple of different disciplines, but he'd chosen to stay active with the ROC Army instead. He was committed.

"Gentlemen, I appreciate the warning last night. We don't know for certain what the commandos' target was, but there are certainly enough possibilities here. The Penghu Islands are considered vital to Communist war plans for securing the crossing to Taiwan." Jian's English was impeccable, which it should have been, considering he'd lived in the States for almost a decade. "We intercepted two more such raiding parties, though we believe that a fourth made it ashore." He smiled coldly. "They will not make it far."

Hank nodded and sank into a chair in the small briefing amphitheater where they'd met. "Good to hear. Does that mean things are about to kick off, though? Commando raids seems like a pretty strong indicator that they're getting ready to make their move. Pretty major escalation."

"It's possible, but we don't think so. Not a full-scale invasion of the island of Taiwan, at any rate. Not yet. There are still too many assets out of position. They are moving, but it will be some time yet, I think."

Chan eyed the map projected on the briefing screen behind Jian. His eyes narrowed as he pointed to the top of the screen. "What's all that movement up north?"

Jian followed his gaze and nodded thoughtfully. "There has been a lot of activity around the Three Gorges Dam over the last month. Judging by a reconnaissance overflight we conducted last week, it appears there is a great deal of construction equipment being brought in, along with several battalions of the 127th Light Mechanized Infantry Division and the 162nd Motorized Infantry Division. We suspect that the haste and corruption that went into the construction of the dam is finally coming home to roost. It was already damaged after record monsoon rains nearly overflowed the reservoir in 2020. The current monsoons have been nearly as heavy." He looked pensively at the map. "If it does crack, we might not have so much to worry about."

"Or entirely too much. How much do you want to bet they'll blame it on Taiwanese 'separatists,' and push the war that much harder to direct the people's energies against an external threat instead of their own malfeasance and incompetence?" Hank knew a bit about Three Gorges Dam. It was one of the vital strategic elements that had to be considered whenever dealing with the People's Republic of China. It was one of several ticking time bombs in the middle of Communist China.

Construction had begun in 1994 and finished in 2003. The story of that construction was more full of corruption and cut corners than just about any mob-associated front project anywhere else in the world. Experts had been worried about the dam's structural integrity from the beginning, given how many millions of yuan intended to finance the project had instead disappeared into Party officials' and Party-aligned construction companies' pockets. The displacement of millions of people and the flooding that followed the dam's commissioning only made things worse.

If it collapsed—*when*, not *if*—the flood that followed would be one of the biggest humanitarian disasters in history.

"That's possible." Jian didn't seem comfortable with the idea. He was probably still hoping that the invasion could be headed off. As prepared as the Taiwanese were—and Hank had seen enough since coming north from the Spratlys and the Philippines that he knew they were *very* prepared, dug in like ticks all over the island, half of which was dominated by the highest mountains in East Asia—a full-blown PRC invasion was going to be a bloodbath.

"Even so, it still appears that the necessary minimum forces will not be in position for some time yet, and *if* the dam cracks, our analysts suspect that the forces they are already moving into the area will not be sufficient to maintain order and deal with the humanitarian crisis." He shrugged. "Beijing might well attempt to scapegoat us for it, but it will still buy us time if it happens."

Chan and Hank traded a glance. "And of course, there are no contingency plans to give the dam a little tap, are there?" Hank knew that even if there were, and even if Jian knew about them in any kind of detail, he wouldn't tell the Triarii. That was deep, dark state secret sort of stuff.

Given the millions of people who would die in the flood, it was borderline genocide. It was an atrocity that would make the firebombing of Dresden look tame. And yet...

Faced with the utter hell that the Chinese Communists would bring to Taiwan if they won, Hank couldn't say he'd blame them for planning to blow the dam and flood the Yangtze River valley. It would tear out the mainland's heart, and when it's survival on the line, all sorts of ugly potentialities begin to look workable.

Jian looked uncomfortable. Hank felt a little bad for bringing it up. Jian wasn't a combat soldier, he was an intel weenie, and he wouldn't have been the man who would have drawn up such a contingency plan, provided it existed.

"While it doesn't look like an amphibious invasion of Taiwan is going to happen just yet, there are indicators that Kinmen and Matsu might become targets within the next forty-eight hours." Jian had apparently decided to ignore Hank's comment, and Hank decided to let it go. Again, he was probably getting into stuff Jian couldn't talk about, anyway. "Which brings me to *why* I was allowed to meet with you."

"I take it you've got targets for us?" Chan leaned forward on the table. "Targets that you can't necessarily hit yourselves, at least not deniably?"

Jian nodded. "We have target parameters." He pointed to the map again and used the remote in his other hand to zoom in on Kinmen, a small island archipelago right in the middle of Xiamen Harbor, within three miles of Communist China at its closest. The Communists had tried to capture the islands in 1949 and again in

1958, but both attempts had failed. The Kinmen and Matsu island chains were the tripwire for Taiwan's defenses. "We believe that the initial assault, if it comes, will be aimed here, at the Kinmen Shui Tou Commercial Port. It would be easiest to offload troops and equipment there.

"If possible, given your capabilities, we would like the channel to that port blocked if hostilities commence in earnest."

Hank traded another look with Chan. "So, you're hoping we can capture another freighter, sail it into the harbor, and scuttle it right there in the channel?"

"It is a technique." Jian seemed uncomfortable with making suggestions. He was passing on what he'd been told to pass on.

Hank mused on it. It was doable, provided they moved fast enough and maintained their cover. He didn't *think* the *Jacqueline Q* had been compromised, no matter how many ops they'd run in the South China Sea. They'd been careful, maintaining the façade of a commercial fishing operation whenever possible. Most of the Chinese military or militia personnel they'd clashed with hadn't survived the experience to pass on news of a fishing vessel that wasn't what it appeared.

The Chinese had to be getting suspicious, after some of the strikes that had sunk or wrecked PLAN vessels, though. And Hank wasn't willing to risk the *Jacqueline Q* if there was another way to do it. She was Smythe's ship, not his, but she was home, or as close as at this point.

"Any chance you have some local fishing boats we could use? The sort that the Maritime Militia uses?" They'd used that sort of Trojan Horse in the South China Sea, and it had worked reasonably well.

"We might." Jian looked uncertain. "What would you need them for? You have your own fishing vessel turned raider, don't you? Shouldn't it be more capable than a Communist scow?"

"Capable, yes. Low profile, no." Hank pulled out one of their secure tablets and started fiddling with it, trying to pull up the shipping schedules. They'd want another Chinese-flag freighter. Better to hurt the enemy logistically while also denying them an attack vector. "They're going to be getting jumpy with all the ships we've been disappearing. It'll be easier to get close if we look like one of their own."

Jian still looked a little uncertain. After all, it was hardly according to the rules of war that he was probably used to. Unfortunately, Hank had seen those rules used against them for long enough that he no longer gave a damn. Sooner or later, unless someone takes it upon themselves to really *enforce* the laws of war—and that can be far more brutal than most people have the stomach for—then those rules cease to have any meaning except as a noose to stick your own neck in.

"We might have a few captured fishing trawlers that the MSS was using to spy on us." That alone was probably a considerable admission, given to a foreigner, even if the Triarii were allies. Allies on the downlow, but allies, nevertheless. "I cannot authorize handing one of them over to you, though."

"Wasn't thinking about handing it over to us." Hank pulled his notebook out of his cargo pocket and dropped it on the table next to the tablet. There was some preliminary planning to do, and he didn't think they had a lot of time to do it in. "I was thinking about one of *your* crews. We can't spare one." When Jian raised an eyebrow, he shrugged. "We've got limited numbers out here. The Triarii have been running on a shoestring since Day One. All of our actual sailors are manning our ships."

Jian had to nod at that. He tapped out a note or a message on his phone. "I will see what I can do."

Just then, his phone rang. He frowned, looking down at the screen, and answered it. He listened, his frown deepening, and the color started to drain from his face. He acknowledged the message in Mandarin, then hung up and immediately started looking for a contact to make another call.

"What happened?" That *something* had just clacked off was obvious to Hank. Chan was watching Jian like a hawk. He'd picked up on it, too.

Jian found the contact he was looking for, tapped the screen, and then held the phone to his ear. "The Communists just started launching air and missile strikes on Kinmen and Matsu. It's beginning." He listened for a moment, said something short in Mandarin, then looked back up at them. "I'll do what I can to get you that trawler. But we have little time."

Chapter 6

Hank didn't know where the National Security Bureau had dug up the grizzled old man named Pan, but he'd clearly been on the sea for a *long* time. He didn't talk much, and from what Hank had heard so far, he wasn't sure Pan even spoke English. Even his Mandarin, judging by the short, monosyllabic sentences he'd spoken in that language, sounded weird. Hank knew that there were several dialects throughout Taiwan and its island territories, but he couldn't identify any of them by sound. Still, Pan was short, grumpy, and uncommunicative, but he clearly knew his way around the trawler.

His crew knew him and respected him, too. Or at least they feared him. They sure jumped when he spoke, even when Hank couldn't recognize the noise he'd made as an actual word.

Xu hadn't been particularly helpful there. He could barely understand Pan, himself. Hank worried a little about that.

Still, even if Pan's speech was borderline unintelligible gibberish, he seemed to understand Mandarin just fine. They were heading in the right direction, at least.

Hank watched Pan at the helm from his position down in the hold. They *had* Maritime Militia cammies, but they were going to be up close all too soon, and therefore it was going to be obvious that most of them were roundeyes, especially Spencer, who was black. The disguise wasn't worth the trouble. They stayed in greens and stayed out of sight and off the deck.

They'd drilled getting up and out quickly before leaving, while Pan and his crew watched, bemused. Once they made contact, they'd have to move fast, though, so he'd let Pan watch and scratch his head.

Hank was getting too old to worry much about strange looks from people who didn't know what was going on.

Pan barked something, and Xu looked up with a frown. He muttered something under his breath in Mandarin, and while Hank's understanding of the language was considerably less than fluent, or even halting, he knew a curse when he heard one.

"*Hé?*" Xu raised his voice. *What?*

Pan repeated himself, slowing down but still sounding slurred and stammering. Xu sighed, then turned to Hank. "We've got a target. A bulk carrier named the *Luck Genius* is presently about five nautical miles away, off our port bow."

"Any idea what she's carrying?" They'd narrowed down a list of viable targets based on known payloads. Someone in Taipei had made it clear that they didn't want to sink a ship full of toxic chemicals right outside a tourist port.

Chan had rolled his eyes at that, and Spencer hadn't been much better at hiding his disdain. Hank had stayed impassive, but at the same time he hadn't had the heart to point out that if this went down, the odds that Kinmen was going to go back to being any sort of tourist destination within a generation were pretty long. Hell, he doubted that the Taiwanese were going to get it back anytime soon if it fell, even if they won the war and maintained their independence, and from what he'd seen and heard, they were *expecting* it to fall if the ChiComs came at them with everything they had. Kinmen was a tripwire and a delaying action, not an ironclad line in the sand.

"Iron ore from Africa," Xu replied. "We shouldn't have to worry about the environmentalists complaining."

"Oh, they'll find something to complain about. I doubt anyone's listening at this point, though." They'd gotten some more intel about the Korean situation while on Penghu, and it wasn't looking good. North Korean troops had crossed the DMZ, and missile strikes had hammered several major cities. The massed tube artillery just north of the DMZ, thick enough to reduce Seoul to sand, hadn't started in yet, but things were picking up.

Environmental concerns would be relegated to the back burner for all but a very sheltered few in very short order.

"Everybody get set." Hank grabbed his binoculars out of his pack and started up on deck, getting a glare from Pan, who apparently thought that his passengers should stay hidden until it was go time. That was all well and good, but Hank wanted to get eyes on before they made contact. While he climbed out on deck, Shevlin popped a smoke grenade and tossed it on the fantail.

He still stayed low, below the gunwales, and found a spot that allowed him to stay mostly concealed behind the boom and other fishing equipment in the bow while he braced his binos and looked for the *Luck Genius*.

There. It was definitely the closest, a floating mountain of steel painted red, black, and white, with four huge cranes standing almost taller than the superstructure at the stern, in between the enormous holds. The name *Luck Genius* was painted in tall white letters near the bow, in both English and Mandarin, leaving little to no doubt as to who owned the ship.

So much the better. He'd have felt somewhat bad about sinking a third party's ship for this. Not that there were as many neutral third parties in this war as appeared on the surface.

Chinese Communist money had bought an awful lot of influence all over the world.

Putting his eyes to the binos, he started to scan the ship. It was so big that it would be easy for a target the size of a man to disappear in the forest of cables and machinery along the top deck and the gunwales. And they were still a good distance away, too.

For a long time, he just kept watching the big freighter. He was reasonably sure that he was well concealed from any observers aboard the *Luck Genius*, even as Pan got on the radio and shouted his garbled Mandarin, repeating himself about three or four times, since the crew of the *Luck Genius* apparently couldn't understand him much better than anyone else. Hank only knew what he was saying because it had been the plan all along for the trawler to feign an emergency and ask for help.

Hank couldn't hear the radio traffic from where he sat, watching the bulk carrier, but he could hear Pan's explosive ranting in response to whatever the reply was. He shouted and raved, still sounding slurred and garbled even to Hank's unschooled ear, until finally there came a somewhat louder reply.

Hank glanced down into the hold to see Xu looking up at him with a wry look on his face. "They are slowing so that we can catch up. I don't know whether it's because they have decided to be charitable, or just because they think that Pan is a witch."

Hank snorted and returned to his scan. He'd heard a few things from Xu about superstition in the supposedly atheistic Communist China. It seemed that the more the Chinese Communist Party clamped down on religious belief and practice, the stronger the belief in spirits and witches got.

He wasn't terribly religious himself, but it was an interesting juxtaposition. It made a man wonder.

The bulk carrier was slowing, though it took a lot to slow down something that big once it got going. Still, the wake at the bow and flanks was getting lesser, and the trawler was beginning to close the distance, though Pan was keeping the throttle to a minimum to back up their assertion that they were having engine trouble.

Running his binoculars along the gunwales of the massive carrier, he stopped and backtracked. There, just aft of the bow. They were still far enough away that it was hard to be absolutely sure, but he was reasonably certain that he'd seen a man with a rifle.

"Looks like we've got some security to deal with, gents."

They'd planned for that. They always planned for it. To assume that your objective will be undefended or will fall easily is to plan for failure. The seizure of the *Hong Yun* had surprised Hank at how smoothly it had gone.

War *never* goes smoothly.

Of course, the *Hong Yun* capture *had* eventually unraveled, but at least he hadn't lost anyone. That wasn't a given this time. Especially if the security was more on the ball than they'd been aboard the *Hong Yun*, and it appeared that they were.

"Is the jammer up?" There had been some argument about whether or not to use one of the RF jammers that the Triarii had brought out with the raider fleet. There were concerns—valid ones, Hank had to concede—that blanket jamming radio frequencies might give the game away. However, since their timing was severely constrained by the fact that the bombardment had already started, they couldn't risk word getting out that the freighter was under attack. They'd be targeted by Chinese anti-ship cruise missiles and sunk before they got anywhere near their target.

"It's running," Spencer replied. "I just hope we got the right freqs."

"It's set for the right frequencies," Xu assured him. "We made sure of that before we left."

Hank just nodded as he continued his scan while they drew closer. He didn't entirely share Xu's confidence. He'd seen intel turn out to be bad far too many times for that. Finally, when he was pretty sure he was about to get spotted, he slipped back down into the hold. "Looks like they've got at least four lookouts up on deck. I saw two on the fantail and one in the bow, but we need to assume that there's a second in the bow." He slipped his rifle sling back over his neck as he stuffed the binos back into his assault pack and swung it on over the sling. "If we figure a crew of twenty, that leaves room for about ten to fifteen security personnel." That was going to make this alarmingly close to a fair fight.

That just meant that they had to move fast and concentrate their assault where they could overwhelm the bad guys.

"We'll go in at the stern. I'll take Xu and 1st Squad to the bridge, Spencer and 2nd Squad takes the engine room, Shevlin and 3rd sweep the forward deck. Move fast, and anyone with a weapon gets shot." They'd already gone over the plan before they'd even boarded the trawler, but a reminder as the adrenaline set in before contact wouldn't go amiss.

He glanced up at the gunwale as they got closer. They hadn't gotten close enough to see the bulk carrier from inside the hold yet. But those two shooters on the fantail worried him.

If they engaged too soon, the security would be alerted, and the fight to clear the ship would be that much harder. If they waited too long, they'd be caught trying to get the drop on the bad guys at close quarters and potentially give them a chance to hold the boarding point while they warned the rest.

Fighting up a ladder was never a good idea.

Xu was ahead of him, though. While they hadn't had a solid plan for dealing with security on deck when they'd set sail, they'd had a few options in mind. Xu, with a megaphone in his hand, had apparently decided that one of the scenarios they'd briefly gone over was going to work best.

Hank wasn't sure of that, but he only had so much control over Xu. The man was attached to them, but he wasn't in Hank's chain of command. Which meant that Hank had little recourse if Xu decided to go off plan.

Fortunately, Xu wasn't going to just take matters into his own hands. He hefted the megaphone and looked at Hank. "I don't really want to try to 'take the hill' from down here. Do you?"

Hank shook his head. They would have to conceal themselves carefully to make this work, without getting so deeply buried that they couldn't quickly get up onto the bulk carrier's deck afterward. But it really did seem like the best option, since it appeared that the security contractors aboard the *Luck Genius* weren't asleep at the switch.

The Triarii rapidly found hiding places around the interior of the hold, mostly against the outer hull and mostly on the port side, closest to the target. They'd have to rely on angles to keep them out of the enemy's sight.

Xu climbed back up on deck with the megaphone. Addressing the *Luck Genius* as smoke continued to billow from the trawler's stern, hopefully convincing the men aboard the bulk carrier that there was, in fact, an emergency, he rattled off what sounded like an urgent plea in Mandarin.

Hank couldn't see what was happening from his position near the bow, under the overhang of the hold, behind several crates and hung fishing nets. The funny part was that the forward compartment, as cramped as it was, wasn't full of fishing gear, but instead a considerable amount of electronic espionage equipment, the MSS gear that the trawler had originally been tasked to carry and use.

A voice floated down from above. Xu responded somewhat more stridently, waving at the smoke rising from aft. After a moment, a faint reply floated down from above, and then a cable ladder slammed down onto the deck.

Get set. It was past time to say anything. Hank leveled his M5 and waited.

The ladder rattled as men came down, and boots banged on the deck. A slightly contemptuous voice barked in Mandarin.

Hank took the risk, easing out until he could look up out of the hold, his rifle at the ready but not quite aimed in. He saw two men in the typical khakis and polo shirts of security contractors, neither wearing body armor, with spare mags on their belts and QBZ-95s in their hands. One of them was approaching the pilothouse while the other stayed by the ladder and looked bored.

There were no other faces up top, on the bulk carrier's deck. They had no overwatch. The two men on rear security had come down to see what was wrong with the dumbass fishermen and left their post empty. If Hank believed in luck, he would have said that the Lady had smiled on them all.

Timing was going to be everything in the next few moments. He made eye contact with Xu, who gave no sign aside from meeting his gaze. Xu was on it.

Hank waited until the first man was within arm's reach of Xu, already bitching at him in Mandarin, then he leaned out and shot the man by the ladder through the skull.

At the exact same time, Xu lunged for the first man, trapping his rifle against his body as he kneed the man in the groin, wrapping one arm around his neck when the shocked contractor doubled over, while he drew a short knife with his other hand. As he twisted his arm around into a headlock, he started stabbing the man in the side, his arm moving fast and sharp, punching the steel deep into the contractor's chest while he choked off his air and kept him from yelling.

A moment later, he eased the body to the deck, soaked with blood.

Hank was already out of the hold, up on deck and heading for the ladder. Reisinger was just a little bit faster. There was no squad order for the boarding. It was just a matter of who got up on deck fastest. They could sort things out and move to clear their designated target areas once they got a foothold.

With Winkler and Bishop covering him, Reisinger swarmed up the ladder. He was still fast, hardly into his thirties. Hank felt old and tired just watching him clamber up the side of the ship.

Just like Hank had when they'd boarded the *Hong Yun*, Reisinger paused just before reaching the top, brought his rifle around, and led with his muzzle as he went over the gunwale. Hank didn't hear any gunshots, which was a good sign.

Faris was already on the ladder, climbing fast, with LaForce right behind him. Hank shouldered his way in front of Evans and Huntsman. He was *not* going to let an entire squad get on deck before him.

The ladder swayed under his boots as he climbed, and he heard the harsh *crack*s of suppressed rifles above him. The boys were already getting stuck in, which meant the security guards had already figured out something was wrong and were responding.

Hank got to the top of the ladder and almost got his head taken off as a three-round burst went past his ear with a crackling series of *snap*s. Going back was not an option; he wasn't the only man on the ladder. He threw himself forward and onto the deck, landing hard as Reisinger shot the man who'd almost killed him, blowing a hole through his upper chest and dropping him to the deck.

Scrambling out of Huntsman's way, Hank struggled back to his feet, dashing across the deck to join Reisinger at one of the big cable spools mounted on the stern, a few yards from the nearest hatch.

The body of the man Reisinger had shot lay in the hatchway, but there was movement behind him. "We've got at least two barricaded forward. There are two more on the port side, using the corner for cover." Reisinger was watching the hatch and the corner forward, though he could give it up quickly as Huntsman and LaForce clambered over the rail and moved to secure that part of the deck.

"Moving!" Evans dashed behind him and Reisinger, heading for another spool to get a better angle on the man behind the corner. More gunshots *crack*ed forward, as LaForce dropped yet another man in khakis and a dark blue polo shirt. Another QBZ-95 clattered to the deck.

More gunshots. Hank leaned around the side of the spool just in time to see one of the last security contractors vanish from the hatchway, disappearing into the darkness of the superstructure.

"Moving." He tapped Reisinger and got up to move, keeping his rifle up and leveled, ready to engage in a split second.

More of his Triarii were spilling over the railing as fast as they could climb, but the earlier plan was just about defunct. The shooting had started already, and that meant there wasn't really time to wait until they were all up and assembled to split into squads and neatly move to their objectives. They had to push the fight.

"On me." Hank led the way toward the hatch where the body was still sprawled over the coaming, half inside the superstructure and half on the aft deck. Reisinger was right behind him, with Carrington and the Rodriguez brothers joining up as they moved.

The immediate hatchway was clear, except for the body. The man was obviously dead, red soaking through his shirt from the exit wounds in his back, but Hank kicked the bullpup 5.8mm rifle away from his hands anyway. It pays to be cautious.

Pushing into the narrow corridor, he tried to get his bearings. The superstructure of a big cargo ship could be a maze, and they needed to get to their targets as quickly as possible. He was still heading for the bridge.

That last shooter had made himself scarce. Hank could hear shouting from somewhere forward and above. No more shooting, though, at least not at the moment.

He found a ladderwell leading up and started to climb, the clatter of boots behind him assuring him that the others were keeping up. He took his hand off his rifle's forearm just long enough to key his radio. "This is Actual. Moving to the bridge."

"Five, moving to engineering." Spencer had gotten on deck and was making do with what he had, just like Hank.

"Four, heading forward." Shevlin had gotten on deck fast. Considering he was one of the oldest and slowest of the section, that was impressive.

Hank kept climbing, getting to the top of the ladderwell and waiting just long enough to make sure that Reisinger was with him and ready to move before he popped out into the corridor, his back exposed for a few precious seconds until Reisinger could get through to cover him. "On me."

He still waited until he felt a hand squeeze his shoulder. Just going for it without knowing there was a man on his heels was asking for trouble.

It took a few more twists and turns before he found his way to the main ladderwell leading up to the bridge. The crew seemed to have hunkered down as soon as the shooting started. The corridors were deserted, which was actually making Hank even more keyed up. That meant that anyone could pop a corner and send a withering burst of automatic fire down a corridor without worrying too much about hitting a crewman.

As he pied off the hatchway, he saw movement out of the corner of his eye, and threw himself backward across the corridor, snapping his rifle to the right just as a head and another QBZ-95 came out of the hatchway at the far end of the hall. One of the contractors had been expecting them to move on the bridge and had set up an ambush.

The bullpup spat flame with a ringing *boom* in the narrow corridor, but Hank had moved too quickly. He heard a grunt behind him, just as he put his offset red dot right on the contractor's head and squeezed the trigger. His own suppressed shot was almost as loud in the enclosed steel box of the superstructure, but he didn't miss. The bullet tore across the QBZ-95's optic and smashed through the man's eye socket. He dropped like a rock.

Hank moved on the hatchway, just in case. Behind him, he heard Reisinger gasping. "I'm good. Took it right in the plate."

The man he'd shot lay across the hatch, leaking blood and other fluids onto the deck. The compartment beyond was small and empty.

Turning back to the ladderwell, he had to fall in behind Juan Rodriguez, who had taken the number one spot, his weapon aimed up the ladder.

Rodriguez drove up the ladder, Hank on his heels, while Carrington finished checking Reisinger over and Marco Rodriguez fell in at the rear. The ladderwell was steep, but they moved up fast.

At the top, Hank and Juan repeated the pause then pop the hatchway maneuver that he and Reisinger had made at the top of the first ladderwell. Making sure no man had his back to a danger area longer than necessary was something that they'd all had pounded into them for years, and all the practice they'd had raiding ships in recent months had only reinforced the lesson.

They were only a few paces away from the bridge hatch. Even as they moved toward it, Hank knew it was probably going to be locked. They'd lost the element of surprise, and there had been plenty of time for the crew to secure the hatch.

Sure enough, it was shut and dogged. "Breachers up."

That took a few minutes. When the shooting had started immediately it had screwed up the breachers, and both BROCO torches were still below.

All the while, Hank held on the hatch while the Rodriguez brothers covered the corridor behind him. Reisinger and Carrington had joined them, covering down the ladderwell, just in case. The whole time, Hank could hear yelling from inside the bridge. It sounded like somebody was trying to get the radio to work through sheer volume alone.

He hoped that the jammer held, at least for the next few minutes.

What might have been distant gunshots reverberated through the hull, though there was a lot of steel between him and the noise, so he couldn't be sure. He could feel the throb of engines increasing momentarily, and he realized that the ship's captain was trying to pull away from the trawler and escape. He felt a hollow dread in his gut. Had some of his boys gone overboard while still trying to board?

"This motherfucker!" Amos Lovell came charging up the ladderwell with one of the torches. He was already slinging his rifle and getting the cutting rod prepped. "Oh, I got something for you, bitch."

"Did we lose anybody?" Hank didn't take his eyes off the hatch.

"No, but it got close. Lee Nakato was hanging onto the side of the ship for a minute with nothing under him but the water." Lovell sparked the torch to life and Hank stepped back. "Fortunately, Pan was apparently waiting for them to try something like this, and he corrected right away. No bulk carrier's gonna get away from that weird little old man." Bending to the work, he started to cut through the hatch. Sparks flew as the metal was superheated, the copper plasma slicing through steel like butter.

It took a good deal longer than an explosive or even mechanical breach would have but using a ram or a Halligan usually didn't work all that well against a steel, dogged hatch. That was why they'd brought the torches.

Hank couldn't hear the yelling from inside over the roar of the torch, but he was sure it was there. Nobody was going to watch their last line of defense dissolve into molten metal and flying sparks and take it calmly.

Lovell was almost finished. "Stand by!"

Depending on who had made it to the bridge, the next few seconds could get awfully hairy.

The last bit of metal sagged, Lovell dropped the torch, extinguishing it in the process, turned, and donkey-kicked the hatch in.

It hit the deck with a clang, and then Hank was going through, ducking and praying he didn't peel his skin off on the still-smoking steel edges.

Juan had dived through the opening after him, even as he almost stumbled trying to get the hell out of that fatal funnel before he took a burst of 5.8mm fire. No gunfire sounded, no bullets plucked at his body armor or his hide.

Pivoting, he swept the bridge with his muzzle. Crewman, crewman, the captain still yelling into the radio, another crewman. No threats. No guns.

Xu came through the slowly cooling hatch, looked around the bridge, and moved quickly over to the captain, kicking him in the back of the knee and driving him to the deck. He spoke quickly and harshly in Mandarin, his rifle still in his hands. The captain, wide-eyed and clearly terrified, only nodded.

"This is Actual. Bridge secured." Hank was slightly proud of the fact that he sounded normal, and not like he'd almost just died, or probably would have if anyone on the bridge had been armed and waiting while the hatch had been cut through.

"This is Five. Engine spaces secured. We've got a couple guys hit down here."

"On the way." Doc Travis didn't identify himself, but Hank recognized the voice. Doc had never been much for radio procedure.

"This is Three." Navarro sounded a little tense. "Four is WIA. We've got two shooters barricaded in the bow."

"I'm on it, bossman." Juan Rodriguez headed out the hatch, which had been opened all the way, with some difficulty since the heat had made the metal expand. Hank nodded.

"Three, this is Actual. Keep your heads down."

About five minutes later, as Xu was on the radio to the trawler—they'd deliberately picked ops frequencies that shouldn't get more than a little spillover from the jammer—a harsh *crack* sounded from overhead. A moment later, a second report echoed across the deck.

"This is Three. Bad guys down. Tell whoever that was, 'nice shooting.'"

Hank nodded. Juan Rodriguez had turned out to be a hell of a squad designated marksman, and the M5s, equipped with magnified optics, many of them personally chosen by the men themselves, could reach out really well.

Xu looked over at Hank. "Pan is taking the trawler away. We are clear and heading to our target site."

Hank returned the nod. Now came the hard part.

Chapter 7

They could see the smoke rising above the Kinmen Islands well before they got close.

A dark gray pall hung over the islands, and even as the *Luck Genius* steamed into Xiamen harbor, another flight of cruise missiles screamed in low from the north, hammering the north end of the larger island, "Big Kinmen," with a series of ugly black fountains of smoke and debris.

Xu stood on the bridge, watching impassively as the bombardment continued. So far, the ship appeared to be out of harm's way. The bombardment was surprisingly focused, and Hank hadn't seen anything hit out to sea. The islands were the target, and while Hank had little faith in Communist target discrimination, based on just what he'd seen in the South China Sea, they seemed to be leaving the sea lanes relatively clear. The *Luck Genius* wasn't the only ship moving through the channel toward Xiamen.

He had to wonder a little at that. "Some of these ship captains have balls."

"They have their instructions." Xu's voice was low and hard. "Most of them probably have families on the mainland, and they have been threatened with repercussions for those families if they don't deliver their cargoes on time." He nodded toward the distant line of Xiamen itself, yet another island in the middle of the harbor, barely two and a half nautical miles from "Little

Kinmen." "Especially now, they need all the materiel they can get. Your operations out to sea have them feeling the pinch, as it were." He looked over his shoulder toward the bridge hatch. "No doubt the crew of this ship have had similar threats leveled against their families and loved ones."

Hank shrugged. He might have been sympathetic, once upon a time. Not so much after what he'd seen in the Southwest. "War is hell."

He knew that most of the Chinese people weren't responsible for what had been done to the US. Nor were they particularly benefiting from it; that was the nature of Communist China. Despite their rhetoric, a Communist Party always works for the benefit of the Party, not those it rules over.

But he also knew that while they would be blamed for any consequences leveled against the crew's relatives, *they* weren't the ones doing it, and they couldn't allow the worries about it to paralyze them. The enemy would attempt to push that narrative, but it was manipulation, nothing else.

The radio squawked as they turned northeast, heading for the strait between Big and Little Kinmen. Hank couldn't make out the Mandarin, but Xu listened, snorted, and ignored it. "They are warning us away from the islands. It is too dangerous, they say."

Hank scanned the horizon. It was unlikely that they'd face air attack, unless the missile units got wise and turned a cruise missile on them. With the sheer volume of shells and missiles howling through the air, flying a helo or even a fixed wing aircraft into the airspace over the islands would be borderline suicide. A missile was more likely, but he doubted it would come before they were committed. That would require a degree of initiative that he didn't expect from the PLA. Not that it was impossible, but he expected that it would take time for requests and orders to go up and back down the chain. That was time they could use to get into position.

He just hoped that they had the hour or so that it was going to take to reach the target site, get clear, and set off the charges. The bulk carrier wasn't exactly a speedboat.

It wasn't just aircraft and missiles that worried him, though. With the majority of the sea lanes—at least to the west of the islands—still clear, they could be intercepted and interdicted by coast guard cutters or even one of the PLAN destroyers from the base next to Xiamen itself.

There. Even as the radio squawked again, he spotted a low, angular shape turning toward them. Interdiction was on the way.

Now it was a race.

"How far do we have to go?"

"Seven nautical miles." Xu was watching the destroyer as well. "Most of another half hour."

"They can open fire on us at any time. That tin can is only about ten miles away." Hank wasn't nervous, exactly, but he was starting to wonder just how workable this really was.

"They could, yes, but do they want to risk it? This is one of their ships, carrying strategically important cargo. And there is a lot of noise out here right now, which should make their targeting difficult." From the tone of Xu's voice, though, he wasn't nearly as sure of that as he was trying to sound. Optimism came hard to men in their line of work, and Xu had been around long enough that he had to know better.

Still, while the radio continued to bark out warnings in Mandarin, they didn't take fire. The explosions and fountains of smoke and dirt continued to rise in the distance as the shore batteries and missile units kept hammering the islands. The destroyer was moving toward them, but even as it became clearer that the bulk carrier was sailing directly for the Kinmen Islands, it didn't appear that the destroyer was picking up much speed. The captain was probably hesitant about putting his ship into harm's way over a single wayward freighter, especially given the losses the PLAN had already taken in the South China Sea.

For the next half hour, all Hank could do was watch and wait. He hated this part. Hated being a passenger, just along for the ride. It made him feel helpless.

Helplessness didn't agree with him. It reminded him too much of the feeling of watching Arturo and his friends get cut to ribbons, not to mention all the other times over the years he'd been unable to do anything while good people, innocent people, got killed.

There was nothing he could do about it, though. He'd done his part, at least up to the evacuation and triggering the scuttling charges. Everything was in place, the last charges set and prepped only about fifteen minutes before they'd entered the outer limits of the bay. That had been a tough job. The *Luck Genius* was a double-hulled bulk carrier, which had meant they'd needed to do some extra work to make sure that when the charges went off, she really sank.

A cruise missile screamed over the bow as the *Luck Genius* steamed past the southernmost tip of Big Kinmen. That was probably the other reason that the PLAN destroyer captain wasn't taking his ship closer. The radio calls continued, warning them to turn aside and get out of the "exclusion zone," but that destroyer still wasn't getting any closer.

They probably not only didn't want to risk the cargo, but they also probably thought the bulk carrier's captain was just being retarded. Nothing they'd said or done so far indicated that they knew the ship had been taken.

Apparently, that jammer had worked just fine.

"Ten minutes." The captain was still running the ship, just with Xu right at his elbow with a rifle. Most of the crew was in the same position.

Hank nodded and keyed his radio. "All hands on deck, prepare to abandon ship."

The next part would have been tricky, if Xu hadn't been coordinating with ROC Navy and Marine Corps units on the island. What came next was going to be risky, but they didn't have much else in the way of options.

Fortunately, the ChiComs hadn't started trying to land yet. Things might get even riskier if they were close enough to see what was happening.

The captain, at Xu's instruction, brought the *Luck Genius* around the point, past the Tashan power plant, and into the entrance to the port. The engines began to throttle down, and the ship slowed as she moved into the middle of the channel, turning to extend her length across it.

Big as she was, the *Luck Genius* still wasn't *quite* long enough to block the entire channel, but she could cut off access to the bulk of the port. Mines and missiles could handle the rest.

A small, fast boat had come out to meet them, braving the artillery and the missile fire, and was now alongside as the massive cargo ship slowed and backed water to come to a halt right where the Taiwanese wanted her. Hank stayed on the bridge with Xu and the captain as Spencer got the rest of the crew and the section on deck and started lowering the ladders to reach the boat that was there to take them off.

"We're here." Xu barked something at the captain, and the man flinched, then turned away from the helm, clearly struggling to keep his expression stoic. His livelihood was about to be sent to the bottom of the ocean, and he knew it. But he was more afraid of the guns at his back than he was of the consequences of losing his ship.

Letting Xu and the captain lead, Hank took one last look around as another flight of cruise missiles roared overhead, then headed down to the deck.

Spencer was waiting at the top of the ladder. "We're the last ones off. Fuses are burning. We've got about ten minutes."

Hank nodded, and Xu prodded the captain onto the ladder.

Even as the captain descended toward the boat, the bombardment dwindled, then ceased altogether. Hank and Spencer both looked at the sky, then at each other. "Not sure that's a good thing."

"Probably not." Hank shrugged, trying to stave off the feeling of dread. They were a long way from the *Jacqueline Q*, and he suspected that things were about to get very, very hot on Kinmen. "Get ready for one of two things."

"What's that?" Spencer swung a leg over the rail and started down the ladder as the captain reached the deck, quickly taken into custody by two men in ROC Marine Corps uniforms.

"Either we run like hell in the next hour, or we dig in and fight next to the Taiwanese." Hank looked up at the sky, spotting a flight of dark arrowhead shapes already winging toward the island from the north. "Either way, the next hour is gonna get *sporty*."

He hustled down the ladder as soon as Spencer hit the deck. The ROC Marines had the crew covered, and the boat's skipper started them moving away as soon as Hank hit the deck and Xu shouted at him. Understandably, the man didn't want to be anywhere near when a ship the size of the *Luck Genius* went down, even if she probably wasn't going to end up completely submerged.

They chugged into the harbor as the *Luck Genius* shuddered, gouts of white water blasting up from her waterline as the charges went off. The dull *booms* were muted by all the water and the sheer size of the vessel, but it was clear enough that the charges had all gone off, especially as the thunder of the heavy bombardment of the island had ceased, at least for the moment.

At first, it almost looked like the scuttling charges hadn't worked. The bulk carrier was still sitting at anchor, still afloat, just outside the entrance to the port. Then, as agonized creaks, groans, and pops echoed across the water, she started to list to starboard, as her bow began to sit lower and lower in the water.

A few minutes later, it was clear she was going down. Settling steadily, the list to starboard getting progressively worse, with a final, echoing groan, just as the first bombs began to fall from the aircraft high above, the *Luck Genius* rolled onto her side and settled to the bottom of the channel.

The harbor was blocked, except for a narrow slot that no full-sized troopship was going to get through.

If the PLA was going to invade Big Kinmen, they were going to have to do it the hard way.

Chapter 8

Several more ROC Marines were waiting for them dockside, and a relatively tall man with boyish features stepped forward to speak to Xu.

Hank took in the Marines and their gear. Their cammies were vaguely reminiscent of the old jungle tiger stripe, but their body armor looked like loose-fitting Interceptor vests, with butt packs attached at the rear and mag pouches on the front. They had clearly seen hard use; every single rig was far more faded than the men's camouflage utilities. Most of them were carrying T91 rifles, though the young man—whom Hank took to be an officer, just judging by his demeanor—was carrying an old MP5N with a lot of the bluing rubbed off.

The young officer and Xu spoke for a few moments, then Xu turned back to Hank. "We need to get to cover." More black clouds were billowing into the sky behind him, and the distant *krump*s of bomb impacts reached them a few seconds later. Kinmen was not a large island. "This is only the first wave of airstrikes. It will not be safe to try to get off the island for a while. They will be targeting any ship attempting to leave."

Hank nodded. It was about what he'd expected when he'd first spotted the incoming aircraft. "Let's move." This was no time to stand around in the open and dicker. He didn't know what the targets were, which made it all the more urgent that they get to cover. It was doubtful that the ChiComs would want to bomb the port, in case they could use it. The sinking of the *Luck Genius* was far too recent for it to have entered into their targeting loop. But staying out without cover while bombs were falling didn't agree with him. He looked at the young officer. "Lead the way."

They moved off at a run. Apparently, the ROC Marines didn't want to be out in the open under an airstrike any more than he did.

The bunker entrance was a lot closer than he'd expected, and almost completely concealed. Kinmen still had a lot of the old concrete bunkers from the Chinese Civil War days on its coasts, but they were now tourist attractions. The real bunker network was carefully hidden, and it wasn't something that was shown to the tourists—far too many of whom were from the mainland.

They hustled into the darkened tunnels while the ground shook faintly as the bombing to the north continued, the Chinese bombers hitting presumed military targets, and possibly a few civilian ones just to sow terror.

Maybe both, by default. While they had come a long way in the technology department, Hank didn't think he was alone in doubting the precision of ChiCom targeting systems.

They had to split up, different squads going to different bunkers. There wasn't enough room for the whole section, reduced as it was, to fit in one, and the tunnels were too narrow to accommodate a large number of men and weapons hanging out in the corridors. Xu accompanied Hank.

They found that they actually had a bit of a view of what was going on. This bunker was one of the main defensive works, set back from the old and crumbling, tourist-trap fortifications, with firing ports that looked out toward Jiangongyu Islet. It wasn't much of a view, but it was a view.

"Now what?" Lovell leaned against the concrete and rock wall, peering out through the drifting smoke at the water and Xiamen beyond. "Are we stuck here for the invasion?"

"I guess we'll see." Hank glanced at Xu, who was watching the bay impassively. "If we get a break in the airstrikes, I'll see if we can get comms up and see about getting us out. I don't think Vetter wants us boxed up on Kinmen when the balloon really goes up. But if they move fast enough, we might not get the chance." He looked around at 1st Squad. "Be prepared to dig in for the long haul here."

It wasn't a comforting thought. They were a long way from support, and they all knew that Kinmen and Matsu were intended to be tripwires, not solid lines of defense. Sooner or later, if the ChiComs were truly determined about it, they *would* fall.

Kinmen—then called Quemoy—had held against the PLA before. Twice. This time felt different, though. The PLA had come a long way since 1958.

They'd have to see. And pray they survived, one way or another.

***

The airstrikes lifted after about an hour. It didn't mean peace broke out, though.

More artillery barrages began to hammer at Little Kinmen, off to the west. Xu got a radio call, and after a moment he looked up, a strange look in his eyes. "There are landing craft moving from Xiamen to Little Kinmen." His stare moved out through the firing ports at the water beyond. "It's beginning."

***

The next hour crawled by.

There wasn't much to see from their positions. The fighting was happening on the other side of Little Kinmen, and a second wave of airstrikes was hitting Big Kinmen, which precluded getting out and moving to a better position, even if that had been doable under Taiwanese command. Reporting was sporadic and unclear, though the thunder of the fighting was faintly audible, since they were less than five miles away.

It sounded like the PLA *had* gotten a foothold on the island. The Kinmen garrison had been pared back considerably since the 1958 crisis, and there were only so many men to go around. Little Kinmen was putting up a hell of a fight from the sounds of it, but it was still going to be little more than a speed

67

bump. Hank would be surprised if the smaller island held for more than a day.

Xu's radio started up after a while, and he listened closely, then turned to Hank with a deep breath. "There are more landing craft moving toward the north shore of this island. Can you assist with the defense?" He wasn't demanding. He was asking. The Triarii were technically contractors, rather than a part of the Taiwanese chain of command. He really couldn't *demand*, not officially.

Hank didn't doubt that he would, though, if things got desperate enough.

It was something Hank had been thinking about over the last hour, as he'd listened to the sporadic reports and the continuing bombardment. "We're here, and we came to help out." He got a bit of a look from Lovell at that. They had, after all, been running what amounted to fast, mobile, sneaky guerrilla operations for the last several months. Hardly the same thing as hunkering down in the trenches and trying to hold the line. The Triarii were all hardened combat soldiers, especially the guys in the Pacific at this point, but this wasn't their mission set.

But what else were they going to do, if the ChiComs were landing and they were stuck?

"Come with me." Xu started out of the redoubt and back into the tunnels.

"Hold up." Hank turned back toward the other bunkers where they'd dropped off 2nd and 3rd Squads. "We'll all go."

It was only a few paces back to where 3rd Squad had gone to ground. The bunker wasn't part of the overall defenses, so it didn't have any firing ports. It was a blank-walled concrete hole, half-filled with supply crates. Navarro's 3rd Squad was awkwardly sitting or lying on the cement floor, in between the crates. They started to get up as Hank loomed in the doorway. There wasn't much light in there, only a couple of bare lightbulbs in fixtures overhead.

"We've been asked to assist with the defenses in the north. We've got reports of PLA landing craft coming in." He looked around at the other men in green, their body armor and helmets still on, every one with his M5 or Mk 48 still slung and still in his hands. "I said we'd do it. Whatever our status is here, we came out to assist the Taiwanese and hurt the ChiComs."

He felt a little strange, justifying his decision to the men in his section. He was the section leader, after all. And they'd already readily followed him into some pretty hairy places. There was just something about this situation that seemed to call for it. Seemed to make an explanation more important than just saying, "I decided, so we're going."

Of course, while Navarro and his squad had fought with them through the Spratly Islands, they were still relatively new to the section. They hadn't been through Phoenix, San Diego, or Texas and Mexico. That made them slightly different, even though on an intellectual level, Hank knew that they'd seen some pretty bad stuff themselves.

There weren't any Triarii on the Pacific flotilla who hadn't. It was a good part of why they were Triarii in the first place.

Navarro was on his feet, his M5 in his hands. Tall, dark, hawk-featured and dark eyed, he'd been a Ranger once upon a time, and that meat-eater, killer man was still there. "Shit. What are we sitting around here for?" He looked around at the rest of his squad. "I'd rather kill a few of those bastards before I get buried when a bunker-buster gets lucky. Let's go get stuck in." He looked at Hank with a faint, feral grin that Hank could tell was partly there just to cover the fact that he was all too aware of how precarious their position was. Hank had been there before, but even Mexico hadn't *quite* been like this. The consciousness of the sheer numbers and the massive firepower out there, bearing down on them, had to be weighing on every man there.

Hank jerked his thumb up the tunnel. "Go meet up with Xu and Lovell. I've got to go bring LaForce and Spencer up."

It took a little bit of looking to find the rest. LaForce had apparently wanted a room with a view, so he'd gone looking for one of the coastal defense redoubts, and had wandered off the beaten path. Hank finally had to resort to the radio, as iffy as that was in the tunnels.

"Two, this is Actual."

"This is Two." The transmission was weak and scratchy, but he could make it out anyway.

"Where the hell are you?" It wasn't proper radio procedure, but Hank didn't especially care at the moment. He'd just been through two bunkers looking for them.

"We're in Bunker Seven." There was a pause, then LaForce stepped out into the tunnel right in front of Hank, just before the next turn. He looked up and saw his somewhat irate section leader and waved a little sheepishly. "We wanted to be in position if things got weird. The other bunkers couldn't see anything."

"Great. Get up the tunnel and join the rest of the section. We've got work to do." Hank wasn't particularly happy about the delay, and he wasn't shy about letting LaForce know about it.

With LaForce in the lead, still looking a little sheepish at his failure to let his section leader know where he'd set up, 2nd Squad hustled down the tunnel to where the rest were waiting.

Spencer brought up the rear. If anything, he looked even more chagrined than LaForce. Hank let it go with little more than a raised eyebrow. Spencer nodded. Coming from him, that was as good as an apology. *Won't happen again, boss.*

They moved quickly up the tunnel, Xu now in the lead. He was less a partner and more a liaison officer now. Even given his somewhat irregular status as a National Security Bureau officer, rather than a ROC Army officer.

Hank was wondering if the tunnels went all the way around the island, but they soon came out onto a camouflaged motor pool with three trucks under the thick foliage that had been deliberately grown into the overhead screen.

Xu went immediately to one of the trucks. "The keys should be in the ignition." Clearly, this was a secure area that the tourists weren't allowed in.

Hank climbed up into one of the cabs and found that the keys were, indeed, in the ignition. He started the truck without difficulty. He didn't doubt that they were started and run almost daily, just to make sure they were ready for just this eventuality.

Xu's voice came over the radio. "We will have to drive quickly. We may come under fire on the way. I am calling ahead so we do not get stopped or engaged by friendly forces."

Hank listened over the rumble of the truck, but he couldn't tell if the distant thumps of artillery, missile, or bomb strikes were close or far away. Either way, this was going to get interesting.

Spencer was suddenly clambering into the cab. "We're all up. Everybody's in."

Under different circumstances, Hank would have told his assistant section leader to get in another vehicle, but he understood why Spencer had jumped in with him. He'd needed to let Hank know they were good, and there wasn't time to go running between vehicles.

Xu led the way out, Hank falling in behind him. They'd only needed the two trucks, which meant the beds had to be pretty jam packed back there.

This was not going to be a comfortable drive.

They moved relatively sedately at first, but that was only because there were a few sharp turns as they headed around the Marine Products fish farms, around the inlet that fed the ponds, and then headed north along the west side of Jincheng. There was a lot of smoke above the town, and while Hank couldn't see that much from the cab, he was pretty sure the old barracks in the center of town had been hit, just in case.

Another airstrike was coming in. He could see the dark specks in the sky through the drifting smoke to the north. "Oh, shit." Spencer buckled his seatbelt. Not that it was going to do any good if they took a 1000-lb bomb to the roof.

Xu stomped on the accelerator and started to pull away. Hank accelerated to follow.

The road apparently wasn't a primary target, though the bombs still fell close enough to increase the pucker factor by an order of magnitude as they went screaming up the two-lane road, past elegant brick-and-plaster row houses and carefully manicured hedges and lawns. Some of the manicuring had already been wrecked by fire and bomb impacts.

Hank's assessment of the precision of the enemy's bombing was proving true.

Xu suddenly swerved, and Hank thought for a second that he was about to get hit, but then he saw the crater blasted in the road and corrected just before he went straight into it.

Then they turned off the coastal road and ducked into another covered mini-motorpool just on the south bank of Ci Hu. Xu was already out of the cab almost before the engine had died.

Hank and the rest of the section followed as he hustled down into the underground command post. There wasn't room in the CP itself, so the section spread out along the tunnel, pressed back against the wall to avoid getting in the ROC soldiers' way.

After a few minutes, Xu came out, looking somewhat calmer. "We have some time, it seems. The initial reports were in error. They appear to be massing landing craft—or else civilian boats pressed into service as landing craft—across the bay, in the port of Autoucun, but they have not started moving yet."

"Why not, I wonder?" Hank looked up the tunnel, though he couldn't see anything of the water or the enemy from there.

Xu might have smirked. "It seems that someone successfully struck the petroleum station at Xiao'aoutou Tsai. I do not know if it was our airstrikes or your arsenal ships, but the station is burning. It seems to have given the Communists pause, at least for now.

"Now we can get into position and prepare. Follow me."

Chapter 9

It didn't take long to get situated. Each squad was placed in a bunker along with a ROC Marine fireteam. Seeing how few Taiwanese troops were holding the north end of the island was sobering. Hank had known that the ROC had reduced their garrison on Kinmen, but he hadn't realized how much they'd cut back. The Taiwanese forces were spread way too thin along the northern shores.

Still, the assault on the east island still hadn't quite materialized by the time the sun went down. Hank was pretty sure he'd seen some drone swarms heading *north*, which meant that either the Taiwanese had a few more tricks up their sleeves than he'd expected—though he *knew* there had been Taiwanese cruise missiles winging their way into the mainland—or else one or more of the Triarii arsenal ships, still disguised as freighters or bulk carriers, had sailed north to launch in support of the Kinmen garrison.

It had worked against the *Shandong*, though the targets at the moment were far more spread out and numerous.

Hank made the rounds as it got dark. The bunkers were a little crowded, but they'd been built with much larger defensive forces in mind. Most of his boys were either on watch or chatting with their Taiwanese counterparts, several of whom spoke English to some degree. It seemed that there were fewer Taiwanese who understood the language than he might have expected. Still, there appeared to be at least one English speaker per bunker. He figured that their commander had arranged that deliberately as soon as Xu had shown up, bringing along twenty-eight roundeyes with guns.

LaForce was leaning against the wall, peering out through the camouflaged firing slit where two of the ROC Marines and Evans were also on watch, the ROC Marines each behind a T75 5.56 light machinegun, the homebuilt Taiwanese version of the FN Minimi. "So, how much time do you think we've bought?"

Hank shrugged, eyeing the Taiwanese machineguns. The Republic of China had been building their own munitions and weapons manufacturing capability for a long time, something that the Triarii were only recently getting into. "Who knows? I'm surprised they've held off as long as they have." He peered through the slot, but even on NVGs, he could see only water and the lights of Xian'ang across the way.

Those lights could be a problem. They washed out NVGs and made it harder to see anything moving on the water. It was likely that an attempt to storm the beaches would be big enough that they'd be able to see it despite the glare behind it, but a raid might be another matter.

A distant rumble reached them through the ground. More bright streaks roared through the night sky overhead as another round of missile strikes came in from the mainland.

He could still hear, if faintly, the sounds of artillery and small arms fire from off to the west. The fighting on Little Kinmen hadn't slowed down much, even with the descent of darkness. Maybe the bulk of the PLA's attention was on the smaller island, intending to systematically take first one, then the other.

That didn't fit with what he'd read about Chinese war plans. They must have hit something that had slowed things down. He peered carefully across the strait between the island and the mainland. He thought he could see fires amid the lights out there.

The question was, were the ChiComs too badly hurt to kick off the next phase of the offensive, or was there something else going on?

He turned away from the firing port and headed for the next bunker, where Lovell was holed up with Shevlin and Doc Travis. He needed to be able see more.

He was restless, and he knew it. He'd never been fond of defensive operations. Even when their assignment had been helping the folks down on the border defend their town and ranches, he'd tried to be as proactive and offensive as possible. He didn't like just sitting there, waiting to get hit.

Unfortunately, there wasn't much more to be seen from Lovell's position, either. Lovell had put about half the squad down, since there wasn't much happening yet, and they'd need to be fresh when it did drop in the pot. Smart. Hank nodded his approval, got a report from Lovell—which pretty much just confirmed that while the bombardment continued, there'd been no movement across the water just yet—and moved back out into the tunnels.

Doc Travis followed him. "Hank, have you set a rest schedule for yourself?" He knew that the squad leaders would have, as soon as it had become apparent that they weren't going to get hit immediately. Doc also knew that Hank was chewing nails and pacing like a caged tiger, and the section leader's welfare was as much his responsibility as the most junior Triarius's.

"I'll get to it." Hank knew what Travis was getting at, but he didn't want to face it right now. He was too keyed up.

"I'm not kidding, Hank. None of us are exactly young bucks anymore." When Hank turned a baleful eye on Travis, even in the dim light of the tunnel, the section medic didn't even flinch. "Not least yourself. If you're going to be making tactical decisions, you can't be staying up all night pacing the tunnels while we wait for the ChiComs."

"I said I'll get to it, Doc." This wasn't a conversation he wanted to have, especially since he knew Travis was right, but he loathed the idea of going to sleep when the assault could come at any moment.

Travis wasn't having it, though. He tilted his head to one side and stared at Hank, unblinking. "Do I need to get Huntsman over here to *make* you go to sleep?"

Hank glared at him, but it wasn't an empty threat. Huntsman was a *big* dude, and even if he wasn't the best grappler on the face of the planet, he could still wrap Hank up easily enough, just through sheer muscle power.

Travis wasn't the type to use drugs when he could just get a section mate to choke somebody out.

There *would* be repercussions, but Travis was also the kind of doc who'd deal with them when he knew he was right. And right then, he *was* right, and Hank knew it.

"Fine, you fucking kneebreaker. I'll go down for a while." He glared at Travis, who only smirked. There wasn't much else he could say, so he just shook his head and growled as he turned away and headed back toward LaForce's bunker.

He didn't expect to be able to sleep much, but Travis was right. He had to try.

***

It was still dark when Xu shook him awake.

"Are they coming?" Hank hadn't slept deeply, though he'd still fallen asleep far more quickly than he'd expected. Exhaustion has its effects, even over adrenaline. Now, though, he was immediately awake.

"Not yet. Soon, we think. There is movement on the far shore. But your commander is on the radio, and he has word from my own superiors, as well." Xu seemed fairly ambivalent in his tone, but Hank thought he sensed some conflicting feelings in the man.

Hank just nodded, though, and rolled to his feet, taking his rifle from where he'd leaned it against the wall and slinging it before putting on his helmet and following Xu back toward the command post.

He didn't like it when people tried to pry into his head, so he wasn't going to do it to Xu. Even though a part of him kept whispering that he *needed* to know what it was that was bugging their liaison officer.

The CP was buzzing when they got there, though all the chatter was in Mandarin, so he couldn't make out what was happening. From some of the red dots on the map on screen in the middle, though, he could guess.

It looked like the PLA had a foothold on Little Kinmen, and the ROC Marines were steadily falling back toward the causeway that linked the two islands. Hank didn't doubt that they had charges in place to collapse the causeway as soon as they were across.

More red icons blinked malevolently around the outside of the bay, on the south side of the islands. That wasn't good. That meant that a full naval blockade was being put in place.

Getting off Kinmen before it fell might be difficult. To put it mildly.

Xu pointed him toward one of the desks, where a handset sat next to an Army radio. When he and Hank walked up, the watchstander looked up, saw Xu, turned his eyes to Hank, and held the handset out without a word.

"Tango India Six Four Actual." It was a mouthful, but it was the identifier they had. He'd quashed several suggestions for individual or squad callsigns. Not because they weren't entertaining, but because Vetter hadn't established them as SOP for the flotilla. He knew that the Grex Luporum Teams used individual callsigns, but they operated slightly differently.

"Six Four Actual, this is Tango Charlie Actual." Vetter didn't even sound tired, which Hank was pretty sure was purely a matter of iron discipline. "What's the situation look like on your end?" Vetter probably had access to far more intel than Hank did, but he was the kind of leader who always wanted to hear from the man on the ground. Ground truth was his bread and butter, and Hank had learned early on that Vetter wouldn't make a decision until he had as much of that ground truth as he could get. He was a former Delta operator, and he knew the value of reconnaissance and on-the-spot reporting over old intel reports and the TOC game of "telephone."

"We're still under sporadic bombardment, but right now it appears that the PLA is concentrating on Little Kinmen first. We're set into the ROC's bunker system, just waiting for the other shoe to drop."

"Are your bunkers under fire, or is the bombardment still hitting farther inland?" Vetter wanted all the details.

"Still farther inland." Hank thought about it for a second. "I suspect they're still trying to knock out the air defense system." Most of what they'd been able to see since descending into the bunkers had been more missiles and long-range artillery.

"Probably. They lost a few birds yesterday, we know that. I'm told that the ROC Marines are tearing apart what's left of a couple of J-16s that crashed near the southern shore of the big island." Vetter paused a moment, and Hank could almost see him studying the map. "Where are you on the island right now?"

"We're stationed up by Ci Hu." He didn't need to tell Vetter that that was probably one of the more likely first attack points.

"I'm trying to get some RHIBs in to get you off, if we can get past the blockade before the assault hits." Vetter paused again, as if waiting for Hank's response, but Hank didn't really have a response at the moment. Getting off the island might free the section up to move and raid, hitting the ChiComs where they lived, and hopefully gaining the ROC Marines more time than they could by simply digging in and fighting off the landing. All the same, the thought of leaving those kids—and on average, his Triarii were a good five to ten years older than any of the ROC Marines they were sharing the bunkers with—to face the PLA landings on their own stuck in his craw. "We've got a couple of the torpedo boats moving to try to tear a hole in the blockade. I think you boys can do more good as raiders than dug-in defenders. That's not our job here. If you can get to the beach at Chi Shan before the sun comes up, we should be able to get you off."

Hank checked his watch. "It's gonna be tight. Especially if we have to go to ground to avoid another wave of bombardment."

"I know. But there's a lot going on right now, and this is the earliest we could get assets into position." Hank suddenly thought of the strike on Xiao'aoutou Tsai. "Move as fast as you can. I don't know how much time you've got left."

"Roger." There wasn't much else to say. "We have observed movement to the north, across the water. Don't know if it means the hit is coming yet or not."

"Good copy. Get moving. Boats will be on the beach in seventy minutes. Charlie Actual out."

Hank handed the handset back to the watchstander and turned to Xu. "My command wants us off the island. Pickup at Chi Shan beach in seventy minutes." He kept his voice level, emotionless.

Xu's nod was every bit as emotionless. Of course, he was going with them, unless he had orders otherwise. He'd been attached to Hank's section for the duration, at least that had been the way Hank had understood it. That might have been what he'd been talking about when he'd said that Vetter had word from his superiors, too. Vetter sure hadn't said anything like that to him.

Maybe Xu was fine with getting off Kinmen before it all went up in smoke. Or maybe, like Hank, he was thinking of those kids in ROC Marine tiger stripes, facing an amphibious landing with 5.56.

"Let's go. We've got to move fast if we're going to be in position by the time those boats get here."

***

The bombardment had lifted, just a little. Hank didn't know if they had just run short of munitions, or if they were attempting to run a Bomb Damage Assessment from the air, to see if they'd properly neutralized their targets.

Or maybe the bombardment had lifted just to make sure that the PLA landing force didn't accidentally get bombed or shelled by their own batteries.

It had taken almost forty minutes to get everyone loaded up and drive the just over seven miles to the south. Now the section, along with a quiet and brooding Xu, was in another bunker complex overlooking the Chi Shan beach. It wasn't prudent to hang out in the open at the moment, whether the bombardment had lifted or not.

The bunkers were manned, mainly because the ROC Marine commander for the islands, a *Siōng-hāu* named Tsai, didn't want to chance some PLAN *Jiaolong* commandos getting into his rear area. They were still only lightly manned, however, because even with the civilian reserves being called up, the Kinmen garrison was still awfully small.

Hank held out his hand for the binoculars, and the young man on watch handed them over. Scanning the water in the growing light of dawn, red as it was from all the smoke that still hovered over the islands, not to mention the next band of monsoons on its way, he started picking out the gunboats and frigates on the outer blockade.

There were an awful lot of them. As thoroughly as the Triarii, Philippine Navy, and even the Vietnamese People's Navy, had hammered them in the South China Sea, the People's Liberation Army Navy still had more ships than even the US. Numerically, it was the largest and most powerful navy on the face of the planet. Especially after that LNG tanker "accident" in Hawaii.

It was arguable that both the US and the Japanese were *stronger*, but that becomes an academic exercise when staring at that much floating steel and firepower. Especially when extract was on the other side.

He checked his watch. There was still some time left. Most of twenty minutes. Still, as he watched the fleet out there on the water, he wondered. It was going to take some seriously sketchy timing to get the RHIBs in and back out under cover of darkness, no matter how big a hole the raiders blew in the blockade.

Muzzle flashes flickered out in the dimness, and a moment later the *pom-pom-pom* report of a 30mm floated across the water to the bunker.

Something exploded out beyond the frigate—Hank thought it was a Type 056, judging by its silhouette—and then another burst of fire arced out over the ocean, toward the south. A few seconds later, a massive explosion lit up the frigate's flank, and the ship rocked as a gout of white water spewed dozens of feet into the air. A moment later, the ship was burning.

More fire was stuttering out from several nearby ships, though, and even as one of them took another hit—Hank hadn't seen a drone or a missile, so he had to suspect a torpedo— something else went up in a fireball farther out to sea. Then another.

Hank couldn't be sure, but he had a sinking, crushing feeling that he was watching the torpedo boat assault get torn to pieces.

Time crawled on. Those ships out there were just outside the range of what shore batteries the ROC Marines had. Hank started to wonder why an arsenal ship hadn't been brought in to aid the torpedo boat attack, but he realized that there were probably only so many assets Vetter could spare to break out one section.

The fire out at sea died down. Extract time came and went. The sun came up, as the dark clouds began to move in. At least the invasion, if it came today, wouldn't have air cover.

"Jim, get comms up, if you can." Hank had a feeling he already knew what had happened, and what was coming, but he had to check.

That took a while. The oncoming weather was no small part of it, but Shevlin also had to go outside and get the antenna up. Hank just hoped that their HF could get through the haze of jamming all over the Taiwan Straits, never mind the monsoon.

The view outside, at sea, became deceptively peaceful again, except for the PLAN frigate still burning and starting to settle at the stern. At least the boys in the torpedo boats had gotten one hit in.

Finally, Shevlin came back down, pulling the antenna with him. His face was grim.

"Extract's off. The torpedo boats got spotted by a drone on the way in and got fucked. Two down, one severely damaged."

That was better than Hank had assumed, given what he'd seen out to sea.

"The RHIBs aren't coming. They can't get through." Shevlin looked around at Hank, Xu, and Spencer. He'd kept his voice down because he hadn't wanted the rest of the section to hear it yet. "Looks like we're here for the duration."

"Or until Vetter comes up with a new plan." Hank looked around and saw that several of the section had heard the news despite Shevlin's low tone. "We're not dead yet."

Shevlin looked a little uncertain. An older man, he'd joined the section later, replacing Tony Velasquez as the "Gear NCO." He hadn't been in San Diego. Hadn't seen just how bad it could get.

Granted, Hank wasn't sure this wasn't going to make San Diego pale in comparison. The ChiComs had been working with limited resources then. They had a *lot* more numbers and a *lot* more firepower here.

Xu's radio chattered, and he listened closely for a moment, going absolutely still. All eyes suddenly locked on him, the loss of their extract momentarily forgotten.

He acknowledged, then looked up at Hank. "The landings are starting in the north. Several hovercraft and at least a battalion of ZBD-05s. They are making for Nanshan and will be on the ground within the next ten minutes."

Chapter 10

"Where does Colonel Tsai want us?" Hank was already shifting his mindset from dread and disappointment at missing extract to the task at hand, which was survival. He had to, if only to make sure that his boys saw him do it. They were pros, but even professionals get strung out, and it had been a long war so far, with very few breaks. Eventually, everyone hits their snapping point. He wasn't going to drag his Triarii any closer to that point than need be.

Xu barked into his radio, listening for a moment, then sighed slightly. Hank couldn't read the man quite well enough to know what to make of that sigh.

"He wants us back up at the command post, in order to act as a mobile reserve." Xu's voice was flat and emotionless. He was already bracing himself. This was going to get ugly, he knew it, and he wasn't sure exactly what the Americans were going to do. Even after the time they'd already worked together, the fact that the Triarii had already tried to pull them off the island had brought that question freshly to mind.

It was something that Hank suspected that the Taiwanese had been worried about for a long time. Would the Americans *really* stand with them when the metal met the meat? The degree to which DC had played both sides, distancing itself from Taiwan in order to appease a Communist China that already had its claws deeply into American pockets—and dominating manufacturing and strategic materials markets in many sectors—had made it a legit concern.

Hank gripped Xu's shoulder. "We're in the same boat here, brother. And we came here to kill PLA. Just let us know where you need us."

Xu nodded. "We should get back north, before the roads are cut."

***

The drive back north was fast and harrowing. The ChiCom's fire support hadn't ended, it had just shifted inland. Hank didn't know what all they were shooting at but given how deeply dug in the ROC Marines were, he suspected that the bombardment hadn't been nearly as effective as the PLA hoped.

The People's Liberation Army command apparently thought that they'd probably knocked out the heavy-duty air defenses, because even as the trucks roared up the road, dodging bomb craters and piles of rubble where air and missile strikes had knocked civilian buildings into the street, another flight of JH-7s roared overhead.

Less than a minute later, the Taiwanese demonstrated that the PLA had far from knocked out their air defense network.

Four streaks of fire and white smoke arrowed up from a patch of trees, one of them intersecting one of the JH-7s with an ugly black puff of smoke and fire. The Chinese strike fighter's wing came apart in a shower of debris, and the aircraft heeled over and dropped, heading for the ground or the sea beyond, trailing fire and smoke as the canopy blew off. One man ejected. The other didn't.

They'd just passed the northern edges of Jincheng when a wave of rockets hammered down across the road with a rippling series of explosions, rocking the lead vehicle and showering both with flying debris, even as that lead truck practically disappeared in a cloud of smoke and flying dirt. The trail vehicle was already backing up before the smoke cleared, revealing that the road itself had been cut, smashed into a series of rubble-strewn craters.

84

"Gonna have to go around." Hank was already looking for a different route. He'd had to relinquish the wheel to Michaels, and now he was sitting in the right seat and keeping track of the map.

Fortunately, as rural as Kinmen was, it was well-settled, and there was a considerable grid of roads between fields and farms. There were plenty of alternate routes, provided they didn't get slowed down too much by more bomb craters. The island had been getting plastered for days now.

"Lead, this is Trail. Status?" The other vehicle *looked* like it was okay as some of the dust and smoke cleared, but appearances could be deceptive. He'd seen it happen before.

"We're good." Spencer sounded hoarse. He'd clearly sucked in some dirt and smoke when the clouds had enveloped the truck. "Still mobile, no casualties."

"Roger. We've got lead, taking the east turn directly behind us." He jerked a thumb to the rear and Michaels put the truck in reverse.

"Actual, this is Seven." Without a concrete spot to put Xu, Hank had given him the callsign Tango India Six-Four Seven, just for the section net. Since Six was usually the commander, with the other numbers taken up by Spencer, Shevlin, and the squad leaders, Seven worked. "We need to move west."

Hank could have demanded more details, but Xu was the man in contact with Colonel Tsai. And if they were getting rerouted for the reason he thought, they might not have a lot of time. He nodded to Michaels, who immediately put the truck back in drive and twisted the wheel around, heading for the next turn, only a couple yards ahead. "Give me a sitrep, Seven." They *did* need the details, but they could get them on the move.

"Landings have begun on the beaches north of Ci Hu." The muted, reserved fear that had been in Xu's demeanor since they'd tried to extract was now gone, subsumed in the professionalism of a committed soldier. "They are being heavily opposed, but we have limited anti-armor weapons. Colonel Tsai wants us to move in on the flank and intercept what appears to be a small raiding force that is attempting to penetrate the bunker complex." He paused. "I do not know whether they were already on the ground, or if they came in under cover of the landings, but they were last spotted just north of the causeway."

"I know where that is." Michaels had been studying the map almost obsessively since they'd ended up on Kinmen. "Where do you want to drop?" Just driving right into a possible contact was not going to be a good idea. It *would* be a good way to get shot to doll rags before they even had a chance get out and fight. Neither of their vehicles were armored, or even mounted machineguns. They were just regular transport trucks.

Hank pointed to a patch of woods that stretched southeast from the intersection with the causeway that connected Big Kinmen with Little Kinmen. He wondered if the PLA had gotten their raiders across that way. If they'd pounded the defenders on Little Kinmen hard enough, they might have been able to get a small raid force through. "Let's get in there. They might be using that veg for concealment already, but it's our best bet."

Michaels just nodded, but Hank started calling out the turns anyway. He had the map in front of him, and he didn't want to rely entirely on Michaels' knowledge of the terrain. The younger man had a good sense of direction, but if he missed something—because the map is *never* exactly one-to-one with the reality on the ground, and memory is rarely one-to-one with the map—they could end up turned around and retracing their steps at a point that they really couldn't afford to.

It took only a few minutes to get where they were going. The roads got extremely narrow and quite a bit rougher as they got into the glorified hedgerows between fields, and when they stopped, they had to stop at least partially out in the open, because otherwise they wouldn't have been able to get out without breaking brush.

Fortunately, the sky was clear as they piled out and spread out to take up security positions in the weeds around the trucks. Hank found Xu back by the second vehicle. "Any updates?"

"They were last spotted moving into the woods about five hundred meters northwest of here. The grill owner saw them during a lull in the shelling and called it in. That was fifteen minutes ago, though." Xu sounded uncertain as to how they were going to pull this off.

Hank could fully understand that uncertainty; he felt some of the same thing, himself. There was still a lot of territory to cover, and if nobody had eyes on the bad guys, there was no way of knowing for sure which way they'd gone.

"Where do you think they're going?" Hank kept his voice low as he scanned the thick woods and brush around them. "You know the island a lot better than we do."

Xu thought about it a moment. He didn't live on Kinmen, and Hank mentally kicked himself that Xu might *not* know the island any better than they did. Except that he'd known where to go to get them into the bunkers, so he had to know *something*.

"They are probably going for the northern command post." The frustration in the man's voice was obvious, and the reason was just as evident. If the raiders were heading north, that put the Triarii behind them.

"Would they know where it is?" Hank had some hope, knowing what he did about Taiwanese counterspy operations, that finding their target might slow the PLA commandos down.

"There have been enough tourists on this island that they know where the controlled areas are." Xu's voice was grim. "It should be simple enough to narrow it down from there."

Hank thought about it for a moment. The geometries weren't great, but if the commandos stayed in the woods to cover their approach, then they might have a chance.

"Cole, take Navarro, get back on the trucks, and get back to the main road." Hank pulled out the map and pointed to the intersection to the north. "Get up here, then spread out in a blocking position here. We'll sweep up through the woods and fields here. Either we drive them toward you, or we get them in an L-shape."

Spencer didn't need much more than that. "Roger." He thumped Hank on the shoulder then hustled back to get Navarro and 3rd Squad.

Hank hadn't picked Navarro just because he didn't know the man that well and wanted to stick closer to the squad leaders he'd gone through the Southwest and Mexico with. Navarro's squad had taken the lightest casualties during the fighting in the South China Sea, which meant he had the biggest squad, making him the easiest choice for a blocking position/base of fire.

Even as the truck backed up out of the brush, Hank, Lovell, and LaForce got 1st and 2nd Squads spread out across the fields and the woods and began their sweep toward the north. They didn't wait for 3rd Squad to get into position, but immediately started moving even as they extended their formation out across the landscape.

Hank stayed near the center, close to the road. It put him at least partially out in the open, and left him exposed a lot, but he could keep track of more of the formation that way. If a PLA commando suddenly popped out in front of him, he planned to just hit the deck as fast as gravity would let him.

The sounds of combat echoed across the landscape, despite the buildings and trees. He could hear sustained small arms, heavy machinegun, and cannon fire off to the north, as well as the rumble of more bombs and artillery shells. The ROC Marines on the northern beaches were putting up a hell of a fight, but it sounded like the PLAN marines—or whoever was making the landing—were fighting just as hard for a foothold.

More Chinese fighters growled overhead, and missiles streaked down to slam into targets to the east. They must have stepped up their suppression of enemy air defense missions after losing a bird. Hank could only hope that the ROC SAM units had relocated.

There were only so many places to relocate on an island the size of Kinmen, though. Sooner or later, they were going to run out of places to hide in between airstrikes.

The Triarii continued their sweep, stepping it out about as fast as Hank was remotely comfortable with moving under a combat situation. Several times, the vegetation go so thick in some places that the squads had to split and go around, bunching up in the clearer areas more than he would have liked. Still, though, they took no contact.

Hank had just moved past a small, corrugated aluminum house with a short, brick wall out front when he heard the first shots.

To some people, those shots might have blended in with all the other fire rattling across the island, but Hank had been in combat far too many times, especially over the last year. He knew the difference between near and far gunfire. That was out at the end of 1st Squad, on his left. Which meant the commandos hadn't gotten that far yet. So much the better.

The volume of fire picked up, and Lovell was already moving toward the contact, circling back behind the house and getting into the tall veg for some extra concealment as he moved, flanked by Carrington and Keith. Hank kept going, pushing up to the front of the house as LaForce started to hustle up the treeline to the east, getting into a rough L-shape along with 1st Squad. Navarro's 3rd Squad might not get any action this time, but there'd be plenty of fighting to go around soon, he was sure.

Hank had just gotten to the low strip of brush that cut through the field north of the little house when two men in Chinese green, gray, and brown digis, with high-cut helmets and carrying suppressed QBZ-191s, came out of the trees just ahead, one turning to take a knee and aim back the way they'd come, where the small arms fire was still crackling through the woods, the other watching the open ground between the woods and the road.

He spotted Hank a moment later, but Hank was already on a knee in the damp marsh, already aimed in. His M5 *crack*ed just before the *Jiaolong* commando could bring his own rifle to bear.

It was still a hasty shot, and took the man in the shoulder, knocking him sideways. Hank took a follow up shot a split second later, as soon as the sights had settled again. The bullet smashed into the ChiCom's front plate, staggering him, but it still didn't put him down.

The second man had turned and was spraying rounds at him now, the 5.8mm bullets crackling through the air over his head. Hank dove for the deck, dropping to the soggy ground, suddenly finding he couldn't see through the bush.

LaForce and his boys opened up then, suppressed 7.62 fire tearing through the brush and trees. Evans raked the tree line with short bursts from the Mk 48, and as Hank got up, covered by 2nd Squad's fire, he saw the second man cut down, bullets smashing through his legs and dropping him into the rest of the burst. Several rounds hit his plates, but enough hit him in the shoulders and head that he went down and didn't move.

The man whom Hank had shot first had fallen back into the trees, or maybe that was just another of their squadmates. Hank saw movement, took a second to identify the distinctive PLA camouflage, and fired.

That time he was on target. He'd cranked up the magnification a couple notches on his scope while he'd been down in the mud and the wet grass, and he got a good look at the man's face above the QBZ-191 just before he put a 7.62mm bullet through it. The commando dropped like a puppet with its strings cut and disappeared into the undergrowth.

LaForce and 2nd Squad were bounding forward now, advancing in pairs as they covered each other in well-practiced lanes across the field. Hank held up a hand and dropped it to indicate the narrow line of brush where he was crouched. "Base of fire here!" He keyed his radio. "One, Actual. Two has base, you're maneuver!"

"Roger." Lovell was panting. "Shift fire."

"Shift fire right!" He reconsidered. "Hold your fire, only engage if you have a target!" Without eyes on 1st Squad—and he wasn't ever going to make it SOP that somebody had to advance standing up and on-line so that the base of fire could coordinate. The L-shape was useful for some things, but he'd learned enough real light infantry tactics over the years that he knew that trying to coordinate fire and maneuver too tightly only got men killed or objectives lost. Better to let his shooters adjust to the situation on the fly, using the tools they'd put together in training and a lot of real-world engagements.

All the same, he wasn't willing to just sit there and wait for Lovell and his boys to finish sweeping the kill zone by themselves. They were mobile, they had ammo, and time was short. He signaled LaForce and those of 2nd Squad who could see him to advance toward the trees, fading right as they went to avoid getting behind 1st Squad.

They didn't get up and charge forward. Instead, maintaining their intervals and still bounding to cover each other, they crawled or dashed, bent over, across the open ground toward the trees.

Hank had learned a long time ago that cover and concealment count for even more than body armor and fire superiority.

More gunshots *crack*ed from somewhere inside the strip of forest. Even suppressed, Hank could hear the difference between the Chinese 5.8 and the Triarii 7.62. They were definitely *quieter*, but they weren't *silent*.

Identifying the fire was made easier by the fact that the Chinese were spraying and praying as they tried to break contact, while the Triarii were answering with single shots, controlled pairs, or the occasional burst from Brule's Mk 48.

Reaching the tree line, Hank took a knee and scanned his immediate front, dropping flat again as a burst of fire tore into the trunk just above his head. He couldn't see much, so he had to assume that the Chinese commando had just sprayed bullets into the weeds in an attempt to suppress or hit *anyone* who might be out there. It was a technique, but it also gave Hank a better idea where his adversary was.

Crawling forward, he found himself next to Bishop, who paused just long enough to put his eye to his scope and fire off a controlled pair, the suppressor coughing loudly in the close jungle.

Hank saw foliage move and heard a body hit the ground. He could see blood-spattered Chinese cammies through a gap in the greenery. The man had been a lot closer than he'd expected.

They pressed forward again as more gunfire rattled through the trees, bullets ripping through the air overhead with harsh *snap*s, thudding into tree trunks and dropping shattered branches and shredded leaves down on them.

Another long burst of 5.8 fire sounded, answered and suddenly cut short by the double bark of a 7.62. The woods got quiet, the thunder and crackle of the ferocious battle happening to the north seemingly louder in the sudden pause.

Hank got up to a knee, and almost lost his head. A burst of 5.8 fire smashed into the tree next to him, one passing so close to his cheek that he *felt* it go by, and was almost sure he was probably bleeding, even as he threw himself sideways and snapped his own rifle up, looking for the target.

If the man had stayed still, he might have lived. As it was, he'd fired his covering burst and now he surged to his feet, turning to run.

Hank shot him in the back of the head from twenty yards away, just under the helmet. Blood and brains sprayed on the bushes in front of him as he fell on his face.

The woods suddenly went quiet again.

None of the Triarii were quite ready to assume that the enemy had all been accounted for. If these were *Jiaolong* commandos, then they would have had more training than even the PLAN marines they'd faced in the Philippines. And every once in a while, a certain type of man really *does* manage to overcome his training in times of stress. A Chinese commando who had just seen a bunch of his comrades get slaughtered from ambush might just go to ground and either try to set his own ambush or crawl out of the kill zone.

Movement to his left stirred the bushes, and he turned, raising his muzzle as he recognized Xu. The former ROC Army officer nodded, and they continued the advance, the two squads now having linked up.

Hank got to his feet, though he was still half-crouched, his weapon up and ready. Slowly, step by step, he, Xu, and Bishop swept across their kill zone.

They found three bodies. Hank didn't know how many had inserted, but that made five, counting the two back by the treeline. After continuing several dozen yards past the last dead man, he got on the radio. "This is Actual. Consolidate."

The two squads moved in, carefully linking up in the close vegetation and setting in a rough perimeter. "I counted five enemy KIA back there," Hank said, jerking a thumb over his shoulder. "How many did we have, total?"

"Looked like eight. Three more to the west." Lovell glanced over his shoulder. "I *think* we got 'em all."

"Let's hope so." Hank looked at Xu. "I think we should probably get back on-line and sweep north/northeast toward the intersection. Make sure we didn't miss any."

Just then, however, a massive explosion sounded to the north, echoed by what sounded like tank main gun fire. Xu's radio squawked.

"I think if any got past, they are going to be very lucky." Xu looked up toward the north. "Our lead units are falling back toward the second defensive line at National Quemoy University. I think we had better move to join them, if we do not want to be cut off."

Chapter 11

The dormitories of the National Quemoy University stood five stories tall, built of brick in a strange blend of western and eastern architecture. While they looked like ordinary dormitories, except for the roof lines that echoed traditional Chinese architecture, they were hardened to an extent Hank hadn't seen since he'd last been through a US embassy. The walls were thick and solid, and every window was deeply inset. He didn't think they'd stand up to really intense artillery, missile fire, or bombing, but anything short of a direct hit was only going to do minimal damage.

It was a good spot to hole up and wait for the next phase of the defense of Kinmen. That was probably the reason the buildings had been constructed the way they had been in the first place.

There were ROC Marines everywhere, dug into defensive positions along the perimeter, with covered trenches leading back to the main campus. More were in the buildings, setting up with MAG-58s—the local, Taiwanese-built version was designated the T74—M2 .50 cals, Mk 19s, Javelins, and French APILAS anti-tank missiles. Hank was pretty sure there were more teams with Stingers up top, but then, most of the air defenses were probably concentrated in the half-dozen remaining Humvees with Stinger mounts down below.

The infantry weren't going to be stuck trying to hold the university alone, either. Hank had seen at least two platoons of aging M60A3 tanks set into sandbagged revetments along the northern edge of the campus. He'd also noticed that they weren't dug in in such a way that they couldn't back out and retreat. This wasn't the Alamo.

If there had ever been any doubt in Hank's mind that the Taiwanese intended to make the PLA bleed for Kinmen, but still expected to lose the island, it was clear now. This was defense in depth, with a built-in fallback plan for every line they took up.

He had to approve. If the PLA brought all the weight it could bring to bear on Kinmen, there was no way the ROC Marines were going to hold. Best to make the bastards hurt, even if they came out on top in the end.

Columns of black smoke rose into the sky to the north. Not all of those ugly, oily fires were from PLAAF and PLAN strikes, either. Mines and IEDs had been set in along the routes leading from the beachhead, and it looked like they were reaping their grim harvest as the PLA forces moved slowly south.

Hank watched the rising smoke, seeing another ugly plume fountain skyward only a couple miles away, reflecting that if the Taiwanese had prepared this hard for Kinmen, the main island was going to be a nightmare.

He only hoped that the Chinese got the same message from what was happening here. It might head this off before it got *really* ugly.

If the intel reports about unrest in major Chinese cities, not to mention the burgeoning emergency at Three Gorges, were true, though…

He kinda doubted it.

Why the hell did you volunteer for this *op?*

He knew why. And it was far too late to back out.

***

The lead elements of the PLA assault took their time approaching the university. Hank was up on the top floor, all too aware that he was a lot higher up than he wanted to be if the shelling started in earnest, watching as the first armored vehicles edged out of the trees and began spreading out across the fields to the north of the campus. Mostly painted in the weird blue, green, and gray PLAN marine camouflage, the first ZBD-2000 light tanks and ZBD-05 amphibious assault vehicles crept out onto the open ground, PLAN marines using the vehicles for cover as they advanced.

They were moving more slowly and cautiously than Hank had expected. Maybe they'd taken more losses on landing than they'd anticipated.

That slow, cautious advance wasn't going to help them as much as they might have hoped.

A tank's main gun thundered off to his left as one of the dug-in M60A3s opened fire at what amounted to point-blank range for a tank.

The Taiwanese had been upgrading their aging M60 and M48 tanks over the last few years. That particular M60A3 down there was covered in reactive armor and sported a 120mm main gun, instead of the 105mm gun that it had originally been built with, decades before. At that range, it was more than enough punch for the lightly-armored ZBD-2000 trundling across the muddy fields to the front.

The angular light tank blew up with a spectacular fireball as the penetrator round slammed into it just at the turret ring. The turret itself tumbled skyward on a column of flame and smoke as the tank's magazine brewed up.

It can't have been good for the infantry behind the vehicle when that turret came down.

The Chinese opened fire in response, even though it almost seemed as if they didn't know exactly where their targets were. The ZBD-05s opened fire on the buildings with their 30mm cannons, while the ZBD-2000s tried to target the tanks. One fired, its 105mm main gun blasting the sandbag revetment in front of an M60A3 to dust. It might even have penetrated and struck the front glacis plate.

It sure didn't knock the tank out, though, as that M60 rotated its turret slightly, then a fireball blossomed from the 120mm muzzle, and that ZBD-2000 was smashed to burning scrap.

Small teams of PLAN marines dashed forward, lugging tubes that looked an awful lot like Javelin launchers. They were looking for the tanks and trying to knock them out.

That was a threat Hank and his Triarii could help with. That had struck him when they'd gotten on campus and joined the defenses. He had a couple dozen riflemen and three Mk 48s. No anti-tank missiles or anything fancy like that. Facing a major combined arms offensive, there was only so much they had to offer.

He leaned into his M5, braced atop the sandbags stacked in the little balcony where he'd set up with Shevlin and Xu, and found one of the HJ-11 teams in his scope. It wasn't a long shot. Only about three hundred seventy-five yards. Easy day with a 7.62 battle rifle.

The trigger broke just as the missileer shouldered the launcher, putting his eye to the targeting module. Hank had the rifle clamped down as well as he could, and he didn't just fire a single shot, but dumped three controlled shots at the man with the ATGM. They had to knock those teams out quick, and volume of fire has a quality all its own.

The man with the missile tube fell over sideways, and his support gunner turned and started to run. Xu shot him in the back and dumped him on his face.

Then it was a matter of find a target, hit it, then transition to the next one, as fast as they could shoot and traverse.

The building was getting hammered by machinegun fire and 30mm cannon shells. A ZBD-2000 fired its main gun, and the whole dormitory shook as the northeast corner disintegrated under the impact, fire and smoke billowing up into the sky as smashed brick cascaded toward the ground. That tank didn't last long after, though, as a ROC Marine Javelin team knocked it out with a well-placed missile.

Tank guns thundered repeatedly, and more and more of the lighter amphibious tanks and assault vehicles succumbed to the heavier main gun shells, Javelins, APILAS, and even AT-4s. Heavy machinegun fire and Mk 19 40mm grenades walked across the open ground, tearing men to pieces as they came, even as they tried to bound forward under cover of the heavy fire being laid down by their supporting vehicles.

Then the PLAN marines' response really started in earnest.

Two J-16s roared over at low level, and the eastern dormitory complex was half blown apart by the falling bombs. Smoke rose as two of the Stinger vehicles burned, and a single M60A3 was out of action.

Then the artillery started, as the assault force halted and went to ground.

The sudden halt in the attack was their first warning, followed a moment later by the howl of incoming shells. "We need to get below!" Xu was already falling back from the balcony. The PLA had gotten either PLZ-07Bs or PLL-09s ashore. Which meant those incoming shells were 122mm, best case. Worst case, they were 155s.

They dove into the apartment behind them just in time, as the whole building shook and shuddered as the artillery rained down, hammering at the roof and the north side. A heavier *boom* rocked the ground, probably another tank dying.

"Fall back to the secondary line!" Hank didn't bother with callsigns as he, Shevlin, and Xu ran for the door. There was no time.

Even as they got to the hallway, the balcony where they'd been set up moments before took a direct hit, smoke, dust, and frag billowing into the apartment and the hallway beyond with killing force. Shevlin, who was already limping after the boarding action not long before, jerked and grunted but didn't stop as they raced for the stairs.

The top floor of a building that was coming apart under sustained artillery fire is not where any infantryman wants to be.

Hank could *feel* the building going to pieces as they raced down the stairs, joined by most of 3ʳᵈ Squad, who'd also been spread out along the top floor, as well as most of a platoon of ROC Marines. The shaking was getting worse, and he could hear shattered masonry falling as they ran. Faced with killing resistance, the PLAN marines were going to flatten the building to clear it out.

Too bad for them that had always been part of the plan. Even if it hadn't been, securing an area by sheer firepower never *quite* works out as cleanly as expected.

They hit the bottom floor along with most of 1ˢᵗ Squad. Hank looked around for a moment, even as the building shook again, dust sifting down from the ceiling as the pounding continued. Somewhere behind them, a section of ceiling fell in with a crash, that still seemed almost muted compared to the hammering of the artillery bombardment. "Michaels?"

Lovell just shook his head, his eyes haunted, his jaw tight.

Another one gone.

LaForce and 2ⁿᵈ Squad were already outside, moving rapidly back to the second line of defenses. As soon as the buildup on the mainland had started, the Taiwanese had started excavating trenches, reinforced with sandbags and carefully camouflaged, at least up until recently. Those trenches led from the forward positions back to the next line, giving the defenders some cover while they fell back under fire. Some had even been carved through the sidewalks and roads on campus. The excavators had been busy.

Hank was about to lead the way out when a shell hit the edge of the roof overhead, and half the roof and the wall beneath it blew out and fell to the ground. Lovell grabbed Hank by the arm and yanked him back, stopping him just before he charged out the door and into the cascade of debris.

Smashed brick and twisted metal crashed the ground as the building shuddered. Hardened as it was—far more than any dormitory Hank had ever seen back in the States—it wasn't going to last much longer under the pounding it was taking. The tanks were falling back, too, reversing across the campus, visible through the clouds of dust and smoke, and now the ZBD-2000s were bringing the positions along the north face of the dorm under direct 105mm fire.

As soon as the fall was over, Hank started out. It might feel like he was running first, but he was running *into* a much greater danger. Artillery shells were hitting deeper into the campus now, shattering windows and smashing brick, throwing fountains of mud and debris up into the sky. A tree took a direct hit and exploded, flinging shattered branches and shredded leaves through the air along with the frag from the exploding shell.

Hank dropped into the trench, which was still a morass of mud from the monsoons. He had to hope, nevertheless, that the next storm would come in soon, just so the ChiComs didn't have air or drone support.

Keeping low, he slogged into a side branch of the trench, making room for the others to get past him. He might have been the first man out into the open as the artillery rounds were coming down, but he was going to be the last one off the first line of defense.

The hammering continued as the rest of the section hustled down the trench as fast as the mud and their gear would allow. Another shell hit disturbingly close, and Hank dropped into the ditch, showered with mud and shredded grass a moment later. He could hear the whickering of the shell's fragments overhead.

Then the dormitory collapsed.

It shuddered under multiple impacts, then the north side must have given way. The entire building shifted, then the roof fell in as the entire structure tilted toward the north. More smashed and cracked brick slumped and fell away, massive clouds of dust and smoke rising above the wreckage, until only a hollow, smashed shell remained beneath a rising pall of floating dust and debris.

Spencer passed him. "Last man!" He had to yell to be heard over the thunder of weapons fire and falling artillery. A moment after the last syllable, one of the M60s fired again, the thunderclap washing over the central campus with the force of a physical blow.

The second line wasn't that far back, even with the main university building, a veritable fortress built in a square layout with towers at each corner. Hank rather suspected that it had been built that way deliberately, even after hostilities with the mainland had seemingly eased.

There were other strongpoints set in on the flanks to the northeast and southwest, but this one was going to be the lynchpin. Which meant they could expect one hell of a lot of heat in the near future.

Xu was there ahead of him, already talking to the unit commander. He waved Hank over as another barrage of tank rounds went out through the gaps in the mangled buildings, hammering the oncoming PLA armor and infantry. Another turret was blown sky-high atop a column of smoke and fire as another vehicle moved through the gap.

The initial contact hadn't been meant to stop them. It had slowed them down, and now they were going to have to move through the rubble—along very narrow lanes—to get at the defenders in the main building. Which made it a shooting gallery for the M60A3s that were left, not to mention the AT missile teams.

Not that they were guaranteed to hold. The PLA had far greater numbers than the Taiwanese did, and there had been only so many ROC Marines who could be spared to defend Kinmen.

Hank joined Xu and the young ROC Marine officer running liaison for the defenders. "We have a position on the northeast corner." Xu grinned, though it was a brittle expression. "We even have our own Mk 19."

Hank nodded. The artillery barrage was lifting. "Let's get into position before this really gets nasty."

Chapter 12

The next assault didn't come right away, somewhat to Hank's surprise. The armor behind that latest ZBD-2000 that had gotten smoked by an M60 had pulled back a moment later, and they'd been left watching the damp, crater-pocked quad in the middle of the campus under the lowering clouds while the smoke from burning buildings and blazing vehicles hung over the landscape, making the weather even darker.

Xu headed back toward the command post to see what he could find out. Hank went to find Lovell.

The squad was set up in what had been a lecture hall, at least from the looks of it. There weren't many windows, but firing ports had been knocked through the brick and concrete walls, then sandbagged. The Mk 19 was set up on a tripod behind one of the biggest, positioned where it had a clear field of fire across the eastern half of the quad.

The squad was at about fifty percent security. It had been a long, grueling day already, and it wasn't over. With the lull in the fighting, Lovell had put half the squad down to get some rest. They'd need it, especially if the PLA tried to renew the assault on the campus once it got dark.

Lovell, meanwhile, was sitting at a table just behind where Carrington was posted up on the Mark, staring at nothing.

Hank sat down across from him, folded his hands as he leaned on his elbows, and just waited.

Amos Lovell wasn't generally the most serious of men. He was a notorious tomcat, even for a combat arms soldier. He and LaForce had often gotten along like oil and water, in no small part because of that lack of seriousness. A consummate professional when it came to the job, he never acted like it off duty.

Until now. Despite the losses they'd already taken, he'd always managed to brush it off, maintain the façade. Now, he was sitting slumped at the table, staring at infinity. He didn't even seem to have noticed the blood on his face, or the dust caking every inch of his skin under his helmet.

Finally, after a small eternity, he looked up and met Hank's gaze. His eyes were haunted, dark circles underneath.

"He just fucking disintegrated."

Lovell's voice alone spoke volumes. Those four words told the story in more detail than the man might have been able to summon otherwise. But he still had to get it off his chest.

"We'd just gotten the word to fall back. I held what we had while the rest headed for the door. Michaels was on the other window. I turned and yelled at him to move, as I fell back from my window. He'd just turned to face me when the shell came down past the sandbags and hit right at his feet."

He wasn't looking at Hank. He was reliving that moment. He would again and again, for as long as he lived. Hank knew that from bitter personal experience. Arturo's death had had the same effect.

"I got knocked on my ass. It rung my bell a little. I couldn't see, couldn't even breathe. The apartment was full of dust and smoke. Pretty sure I got a concussion." He glanced down at his rifle, which was as filthy as the rest of him. "When I got up, though, Michaels was just... *gone*. I could see bits of what had been him, and what was left of his rifle, but he was..." He choked. "He was just... pieces. The biggest one I could see through the murk was his hand." He hung his head, his NVGs almost touching the table. It was getting dark enough that everyone had them mounted. When he looked up, his eyes were red. "There wasn't a damn thing I could do, but..."

"But why is he gone, and you're still here?" Hank kept his voice low. He knew what Lovell was going through, because he'd been going through it himself for a long time. Only right now, Lovell didn't need a shoulder to cry on. He needed a rock to lean against and haul himself back onto his feet, because they didn't know how much time they had before they had to fight again.

"Because that's the way it fell out. Maybe God just said it was time for Michaels to go home. Maybe the universe rolled the dice, and it came up snake eyes. I don't know. What I *do* know is, these guys need you to accept that while he's gone, you're still alive, they're still alive, and that you need to keep pushing. *I* need you to cram that vision—and it's gonna be with you until your dying day; I don't need to tell you that—into the back of your head, in the deepest, darkest vault you've got, and get back in the fight. Because the rest of us are counting on you." He leaned in to make sure that he held Lovell's gaze. "I need you to cowboy up and compartmentalize this shit, Amos. And I don't need to tell you why."

He tilted his head slightly, sizing the other man up. "Can I count on you, Amos? Or do I need to put Carrington in charge?" He kept his voice low, not much more than a murmur, only loud enough that he could be sure that his 1st Squad leader could hear him. He didn't want to undermine Lovell's position with the squad, if he was still up to the squad leader position. Didn't want the boys to know that Hank was worried that he wasn't up to the task. That could be devastating for the whole section, especially given what had already gone down. But at the same time, he had to know that he could count on Lovell to keep it together. He'd never seen the man this shaken. He knew a few things that Lovell had been through before he'd even joined the Triarii, including a harrowing rescue mission in South America as a private contractor. Lovell had seen hell before.

But every man has his breaking point, and there's something about watching a squadmate get turned to pink mist right in front of you that has a way of getting to a man.

Still, Lovell shook his head, squeezing his eyes shut. When he opened them, taking a deep breath, he was steady, if not the devil-may-care playboy he'd been before. "I'm good, Hank." Another breath. Some of the steel came back. "I'm good. I need to kill some more of these bastards."

Hank reached out and gripped his hand, and Lovell returned the squeeze, hard. Once again, there was a flash in his eyes, but the man that Lovell had been was gone.

LaForce would probably applaud that fact, though Lovell would promptly throw it back in his face, just because. Hank, as much as he'd often found Lovell the playboy taxing, would have to mourn. A part of the man in front of him had died when Michaels had gotten hit. And that part was never coming back.

There wasn't a single one of them who hadn't lost a piece of himself. Hank knew some of the holes in his own soul, all too well. Lovell himself had broached the subject, back during their ops with the Filipinos.

War tears a bit out of a man, even if he survives to see the end of it.

And Hank didn't think he was going to see the end of this one. Not as big as it had gotten.

Reassured that Lovell was still functional, Hank got up and went to make the rounds.

***

Night fell. The shelling resumed but this barrage didn't last as long as the first one. While it was hard to hear at first, the distant *thump* of artillery began to sound *behind* them, somewhere to the southeast. Moments later, the shells started screaming overhead, heading *north*. The ROC Marines' M109 howitzers were giving the PLAN marines a taste of their own medicine.

Hopefully they were throwing some serious counter-battery fire in there, too.

Hank kept pacing from position to position, forcing himself to take a thirty-minute catnap from time to time. Despite the bone-deep exhaustion that weighed down his limbs, the stress and the anticipation of the next fight kept him awake. He wasn't sure what the ChiComs were waiting for, unless they'd taken enough of a beating that they were reconsidering their strategy going forward. He kind of hoped so. The more of a monkey-wrench got thrown into the PLA's plans, the less likely this was going to completely sideways.

Do I really think that's going to happen? Do I really have that much hope left? He had to admit that he probably didn't. The ChiComs had moved an awful lot of men and materiel into the Eastern Theater Command, committed an awful lot of resources. If they didn't pull this off, the repercussions for the higher commanders could be catastrophic.

Hank had been around long enough that he had no illusions about the propensity for higher leadership to double down on a bad idea, at whatever cost to their subordinates, just because they stood to lose if they admitted it had been a bad idea.

With the ChiComs' demonstrated disregard for human life, the mountain of bodies that could get stacked just to avoid the perception of defeat was probably going to get pretty high.

Still, he hated just sitting there. He'd never been a fan of sitting in defensive positions, even when Squad in the Defense had been a necessary part of any Marine infantry unit's training. To stay in a fixed position, no matter how hardened, just waiting to get hit, went against the grain. Marines are aggressive, at least the infantry Marines are, and Hank had always leaned into that aggressiveness, both as a young hard charger and even later, as an NCO and SNCO. Now, he found that as he got older, he might have tempered it, but he still didn't like sitting still and waiting for the bad guys to make the next move.

He wanted to be out there, in the dark, making the ChiComs' lives hell.

Instead, he had to wait. He wasn't coordinating this op. Appealing to the "Strategic Corporal" concept wouldn't work if it wasn't coordinated with the ROC Marines. And Colonel Tsai was concerned with holding the line, not with the fact that a bunch of wild roundeyes who couldn't speak the language were getting restless.

He entered 2nd Squad's position and found Xu next to LaForce, peering out into the night. Light flickered in the distance as shells fell on positions to the north. He squinted, checking directions. That was probably PLA artillery, hammering ROC Marine positions up by the Jinning Zhong Elementary School.

Xu looked over his shoulder as Hank came in. The room was dark, except for a couple of red lens lights in the corners, where a couple of the men who couldn't sleep were trying to read some of the rare English books that had been in the classroom. Everyone else who was up was on NVGs, watching through their loopholes.

Checking his watch, Hank saw that it was just after midnight. It felt a lot later, but it had been a *long* couple of days. "Xu, what do you think of going to have a talk with Captain Guo, see if there's anything we can do besides sit here?" While Tsai was the overall commander for the island, Guo was responsible for the defenses here at the university.

It was hard to make out the other man's expression in the dark, on NVGs. Things get a little blurry close up, and the image intensifier tubes tend to sort of wash details out, anyway. But he'd gotten to know Xu well enough—though he still couldn't say he really *knew* the other man—that he suspected Xu would be on board.

"We'd have to wait for the artillery to lift." Xu was clearly already thinking along similar lines, which Hank found a little heartening. It meant he wasn't the only crazy bastard who wanted to go out there and slit some throats in the dark. "I don't know about you, but I really don't want to have survived yesterday only to get killed by our own guns."

"Goes without saying." Hank wasn't offended at the Taiwanese spook's statement of the obvious. They were all tired and strung out. If he got his back up whenever someone said something dumb under these circumstances, he'd be pissed at his own guys more than the enemy. "Come on. Let's go find Guo."

They left the room and headed back toward the command post, set up in the main gym, on the south side of the quadrangle. Both men were still geared up, rifles slung across their chests, hands on pistol grips.

The halls were dark, as was the entirety of the campus. Most of the island north and west of Jincheng was blacked out, if only to give the ChiComs as little targeting information as possible.

Two men in filthy ROC Marine tiger stripes, holding their T91s at port arms, stood guard at the entrance to the CP. Xu spoke briefly, giving the challenge and pass, since he didn't have credentials on him. None of the section did, either. They'd been entirely sterile, carrying no identifying materials whatsoever, when they'd embarked on the assault on the *Luck Genius*, just in case.

That had been less than two days ago, but it felt like far, *far* longer.

The ROC Marine guards accepted the password and let them in.

Hank hadn't been in the ROC Marines' TOC yet, but what he saw was perfectly familiar, even if the spoken language and the writing on the maps and the couple of computer screens was all in Mandarin. The maps on easels and walls, the radios stacked on folding tables in the middle of the gym, the laptops running comms, drone feeds, and the local equivalent of Blue Force Trackers… it was all very much like every other TOC he'd ever set foot in. The ROC Marines didn't use exactly the same SOPs that Western militaries did, but it was close enough.

Xu looked around for a moment before leading the way toward where Guo was leaning over a watchstander's shoulder, watching a drone feed. No, not a drone feed, Hank saw as they walked up. It was too low-angle and steady for that, and the monsoon had come in again, grounding drones as well as aircraft. This looked like a camera mounted on top of a tall boom or mast, somewhere inside the main building's quadrangle, looking out over the ruins of the dormitory where they'd made their first stand.

The flashes up there were artillery, going in both directions. And there were a lot of flashes across the dim horizon in the grayscale night vision image.

Guo looked up as they approached and offered Xu a nod. There was a decided amount of respect there. When Xu spoke to him, quietly, in Mandarin, Hank thought he heard some personal concern in Xu's voice. This wasn't just a straphanger speaking to the commander he was momentarily attached to. These men knew each other. Especially as Xu gripped Guo's shoulder, he saw an older veteran speaking to a man who had probably been one of his junior leaders before he'd retired and joined the National Defense Bureau.

Guo led the way to the map and pointed out several of the markers, still speaking in Mandarin. Hank couldn't really follow it, though the map itself still told him something.

It looked like the Taiwanese were holding the line, which extended across the headland from just north of Jincheng to the beaches northeast of Jinning Township. Several red pins indicated attacks elsewhere along the northern shores of the island, but those shores, in addition to being nasty mudflats at low tide, were still littered with landing obstacles left over from the '50s, and while Hank hadn't heard any solid confirmation from the Taiwanese, he was pretty sure they'd been *extensively* mined before the first landings.

There was one red patch up in the north, encompassing Guanao Village. It appeared that the PLAN Marines had forced another landing there. It was a smaller patch than the one they faced along the Jincheng-Jinning line, but still a matter of some concern.

At least it appeared that the ROC Marines still held the airport, though there were a couple of red pins there, too.

Guo pointed out several more detailed markers to their north, then led the way back to the camera feed, having the watchstander adjust the view so he could point out what he was talking about. It was hard to see much. The rain, the slope behind the ruins of the first line of buildings, and the trees meant that there was a lot of crap between the camera and the enemy.

Xu began to translate. "It looks like we destroyed the better part of a company here this afternoon. The initial defense at the beach killed a lot of them, especially since some of the armor started to get bogged down in the mud. The Communists are now being much more cautious, as they've realized that trying to simply blitz our positions is only rushing into the gunfire. They have pulled back to the trees here, at the edge of the fields, and are using their artillery to try to soften us up."

Guo's reached out for a photo map of the area, then traced a finger through the patch of forest—or jungle—between the campus and the Jinning Elementary School. He spoke rapidly, and Xu filled in the translation.

"We have many positions through this strip, but it has been the least touched since the attacks began. The enemy appears to be thinner here." Guo was pointing to the fields between two small, middle-of-nowhere apartment complexes. "There *might* be a command post in one of these buildings. Even if there is not, a small team, moving carefully, might be able to get through with explosives and possibly a few anti-tank rockets. At the very least, in this rain, it might be possible to set in some more mines and IEDs in the enemy's path before they try to move again."

"*If* we can get out there without getting pasted by arty." Hank was thinking about it, though. This was more his speed. Get out there and take the fight to the enemy.

"We can coordinate lifting ours. We could even intensify the counter-battery fire." Guo seemed to be warming to this idea. If it took some of the pressure off the defensive line, Hank could imagine why.

He thought it over, staring at the photo map. He'd need to take one squad. More than that would probably be too large a footprint. He thought about Lovell's 1st Squad but given the losses they'd taken—and Lovell's mindset at the moment, never mind his protestations that he was good now—he figured he needed to take someone else. *Probably Navarro.*

"Give me half an hour."

Chapter 13

The rain was coming down in buckets. It was strangely quiet, the Taiwanese counter-battery fire having slowed, while the PLA seemed to have decided to lift their own bombardment, if only because they couldn't tell if they were actually having any effect in all the murk. It was one of the darkest nights Hank had seen in a long time.

In fact, he couldn't see very far even on NVGs. They needed *some* ambient light to work, and with thick clouds and rain blotting out the stars, and most of the island blacked out, there wasn't much.

This was going to get interesting if they had to fight. Especially since the Triarii—and Xu—had enough experience to know not to go flashing IR around when the bad guys probably—almost certainly—had NVGs of their own. There was a reason every Triarii in Hank's section had an offset red dot mounted in addition to whatever magnified optic he was running on his M5. But when they could barely see a few feet in front of them, just seeing the enemy was going get…interesting.

They moved as quickly as they could, ducking from cover to cover until they were outside the campus, moving through the thick woods as quietly as they could. The darkness and the closeness of the vegetation meant that they had to stay tight, closer together than Hank—or any other experienced infantryman, and they were all experienced infantrymen—really felt comfortable with. But the alternative was to lose each other in the dark, and potentially lose men when they did make contact, simply because they couldn't support each other.

Or couldn't be sure where their bullets were going.

They paced through the trees, so close that it was more like a stack in urban or close quarters combat than a rural patrol. Hank was right behind Navarro, who had taken up right behind Lee Nakato. Hank could barely see the younger Nakato brother in the murk, even though he was only about ten feet ahead of him.

Movement in the jungle, at night, is achingly slow. Even with their NVGs to help, they weren't moving much faster than the old MACV-SOG guys had done in daylight. And those teams might have moved five hundred yards in a day.

Move a few yards. Stop. Scan. Listen. Repeat. As slow as it is, it's also nerve-wracking.

Fuck the jungle. Hank never had enjoyed working in thick brush. He'd usually preferred the desert, despite the lack of cover and concealment there. At least in the desert, they could spread out and *see*.

They might have gotten a hundred yards before Lee put up a fist. *Freeze*. That means stop moving *right now*. Even if you've got one boot up off the ground.

Hank froze, thankful that he had both feet on the ground when he saw the signal, throwing up his own clenched fist to pass it on.

Lee was half-crouched, motionless, his head moving ever so slightly to scan their surroundings. Hank strained his eyes and his ears to try to pick out whatever had caused Navarro's pointman to stop.

The rain deadened his hearing, but after a moment he thought he could just barely hear movement ahead of them. He wished that they had the clip-on thermal attachments for their NVGs, but those were also bulky, heavy, and couldn't see through the rain very well, never mind the veg.

Lee lowered himself to a knee, and then both Navarro and Hank moved up to join him. Navarro leaned in, and he and Lee had a short conversation, subvocalized so low that Hank couldn't hear them even a few feet away. Finally, Navarro turned to Hank, and he leaned in to hear.

"Movement to our ten o'clock, maybe fifteen, twenty yards. Lee thinks he heard a voice."

Hank didn't bother to ask what language Lee thought he'd heard. There weren't many options. The only concern was to make sure that they weren't about to clash with a ROC Marine patrol. Guo hadn't said there were any out, but if one of the adjacent units had a security patrol out, and hadn't coordinated with Guo, this could get bad, quick.

Hank pointed left. While they hadn't been in too many situations in the States that had called for react to contact drills, this was one that they'd practiced, nevertheless. Hank had seen too many units get slack, forget about the fundamentals, and subsequently watched their tactics—and their security, by extension—go to shit. A Triarii infantry section was often off by itself, with just local cops, sheriffs, and militia for support. They had to be on their game.

Hank didn't believe in "conventional" warfare. Didn't believe in the "get on-line and assault through, don't ask too many questions" school of infantry combat. He'd seen what that led to too many times. He wanted his boys to be every bit as capable as the Grex Luporum teams. More capable, if he could swing it.

So, without hesitation or undue noise, the entire column turned left and moved perpendicular to their previous route for about two dozen yards before they halted, almost without needing a signal, turned right, and advanced on-line toward the contact.

They still moved carefully, creeping forward and "swimming" through the bush as much as possible. Since they were all facing the contact, Hank wasn't so concerned with them staying entirely on-line. As long as each man watched his fire— as difficult as that might be under these conditions—they shouldn't need to worry about any blue on blue.

Creeping forward, step by step, Hank started to think he could hear what Lee had picked up. It was faint, and his hearing, brutalized by years of combat, training, and loud heavy equipment, including helicopters, wasn't nearly as good as Lee's. But as he stepped forward, put his weight on his foot, and paused, listening, he could hear rustling up ahead.

Again, the rain was making it difficult. The constant dull roar of water on the foliage overhead, not to mention his helmet, masked a lot of what he might have been able to hear otherwise. But a broken branch under a boot and a muttered curse are pretty distinctive.

He brought his rifle up, sensing more than actually hearing or seeing Navarro and Durand do the same to either side of him. He stepped forward again, weaving past another bundle of fronds, and suddenly he was only about ten feet from the enemy.

The man in front of him wasn't a ROC Marine. While there wasn't that much difference in their equipment, or even their weapons, now that the PLA had shifted mostly to the QBZ-191, there was something about this guy that rang that alarm bell in Hank's head. He wasn't a friendly. The boxy sort of NVGs in front of his face—one of the last details Hank saw—was the final giveaway.

That, and the fact that he looked up, saw Hank, and started to bring his rifle up.

But Hank already had his own red dot right on the man's upper chest.

The suppressor coughed, and the PLAN marine staggered, the bullet hitting his front plate hard enough to knock the wind out of him. The follow up shot, ever so slightly higher, snapped his head back and dropped him.

At almost the same moment, Hank hit the dirt, searching for the next target, but knowing pretty well what was probably coming next. More suppressed gunshots *crack*ed to either side, then the PLAN marines they *hadn't* been able to see opened fire.

None of these guys were running suppressed, and flame flickered in the dark and the wet as they hosed down the jungle at roughly mid-chest level. Which was why the Triarii had trained to hit the dirt as soon as the ball got opened.

Hank spotted a muzzle flash and dumped three rounds at it, as fast as he could squeeze the trigger. He got a glimpse of movement as the body dropped.

Crawling forward, he looked for a target. It was a lot harder to find the enemy while low-crawling through the mud and the undergrowth, in the jungle, in the rain, on NVGs. The limited field of view meant he had to crane his neck a lot more than was comfortable in order to see, but comfort goes out the window fast once the bullets start flying.

Another burst of 5.8mm fire shredded the vegetation over his head, showering him with soggy, shredded vegetable matter along with the rain. That time, he saw the muzzle flash out of the corner of his eye, around his NVGs. He rolled to his side, pivoting to bring his own rifle to bear, but another suppressor spat with a harsh *crack* off to his right, and the man fell, triggering another burst into the mud.

The woods went quiet after that. Hank kept moving, crawling forward a few more yards before levering himself up onto a knee. He was almost within arm's reach of the first man he'd shot.

Movement. He shifted toward it, only to see another PLAN marine on his back in the mud, coughing blood as he shook and spasmed, his face turned to the sky. He was dying. Hank still kept him covered as the rest of the squad moved up.

He was glad that Rossiter hadn't opened up with the Mk 48. There was still a chance that the gunfire might have gone relatively unnoticed. While a major advance hadn't materialized since the first clash at the National Quemoy University, there were still random bursts and pops of gunfire echoing across the landscape, even after dark. This little clash *might* be dismissed as just another defensive position shooting at shadows.

Maybe. As they swept through the remains of the PLAN marine unit, Hank began to have his doubts. This group was bigger than he'd thought, at least a squad in strength, possibly more. There were four bodies along his lane alone, and he knew there had been more off to the flanks. And several of them were carrying assault packs or DZJ-08 80mm recoilless launchers. This wasn't just a security patrol. They'd been carrying that kind of heavy ordnance through the jungle to blast a hole in the ROC defenses, and that meant that there was probably going to be a larger unit either right behind them, or else not far away, waiting for them to report in.

If that follow-on force had heard the gunfire…

He circled his hand above his head. *Assemble.* They'd consolidate here and take stock. He needed to know that everyone was up and up, and then he needed to consider the next move.

They didn't get the time, though.

One of the dead ChiComs' radios squawked. And Hank heard the voice on the other end out in the bush, all too close.

The follow-on force *was* right behind the vanguard, and they'd definitely heard something.

Hank yanked one of his precious frags out of his vest, pulled the pin, and lobbed it into the jungle, toward that voice. "Frag out!" He dropped onto his face as he yelled, and the rest followed suit.

Nobody wanted to be standing or even kneeling that close to a frag grenade. The blast and shrapnel radius tends to be wider than a man can throw it.

The detonation sounded almost muted in the rain and the jungle; a single flash followed a fraction of a second later by the heavy *thud* of the explosion. Shrapnel ripped through the foliage, invisible in the dark and the wet, and judging by the screaming he heard out there in the night, it had torn through flesh, as well.

Rossiter opened up then, the suppressed Mk 48 still chattering loudly enough to warn anyone downrange that they didn't want to stay there. Hank heaved himself to his feet, dumped the rest of his mag into the dark, and ran.

He didn't go far. He'd only run first because he'd been out front. He ran about three seconds before turning and throwing himself down in the prone in the mud and the rotting vegetation. He could see just well enough that he was confident he wasn't about to hit either Navarro or Durand, and he opened fire.

Navarro dashed past him in the dark on one side, Durand on the other. They took up the fire a few seconds later, and then Hank was moving, reloading as he went, confident enough in his section—even if Navarro hadn't been with them more than a few months—that he was sure they'd fall back into the battle drill.

The Chinese were shooting back by then, but they didn't have much to shoot at. It was dark as six feet up a well digger's ass at midnight, it was raining, and all the Triarii were running suppressed, denying them muzzle flashes to shoot at. The ChiComs made up for it by spraying gunfire wildly into the woods around them, effectively shooting a mad minute into the jungle since they couldn't see their targets.

Bullets *snap*ped overhead and thudded into trees or ricocheted off trunks to whine nastily into the night. This time, when Hank turned and dashed between Navarro and Durand, he stayed bent double, trying to make tracks while keeping his head down and away from the bullets.

This time, when he stopped, he dropped prone, getting behind his rifle but holding his fire. Most of the rest were still hammering rounds into the jungle, but they probably didn't have targets. He needed to get them moving back to friendly lines with a quickness, and the longer they stopped to try to suppress bad guys they couldn't see, the harder that was going to get.

They only had a couple dozen yards to go, but they had to do it without getting shot by either side. He knew those ROC Marines were going to be keyed up as hell, because there was no way they were going to miss this.

Xu was on top of it, though, not far away from him, already yelling into the radio.

Mortars started to *thump* behind them. Whistling down out of the sky, the first rounds hit long, hammering into the jungle about six hundred yards away.

The incoming fire slackened considerably, though, as the Chinese hit the dirt. Then Xu was at Hank's elbow. "We need to get back, now!"

"On me! Back to the lines!" The mortars were still falling. They had to run while they were still keeping the enemy's heads down.

The squad started to collapse in on him. He started counting them in, slapping each man on the shoulder and pointing him back toward the campus, making sure they were following Xu. They ran doubled over, staying low and keeping as many tree trunks between them and the enemy as possible.

He and Navarro stayed in place until Bob Nakato went by, all but disappearing into the bush toward the university and friendly lines.

Hank looked at Navarro. "We're short one."

Navarro turned back to head into the teeth of the enemy fire, which was starting to pick up again, though it was still sporadic. "Alexander."

Hank stopped him. "No. You get back to friendly lines. I'll find him." He wasn't sure how he was going to in the dark, the rain, and the jungle, while the ChiComs were out there still taking shots at them, but he was the section leader. He had to try.

Another burst went over his head, but it was high. Keeping his head down, he plunged into the bush.

He didn't need to go far. Alexander had been trying to collapse in when he'd taken a round to the back of the head, just under his helmet. He was face-down in the mud and the undergrowth, not moving.

Hank rolled him over, threw the body over his shoulders in a fireman's carry, and dashed for friendly lines, following the sound of Xu's voice, where he was bellowing the password to keep them from getting shot by their own guys.

Chapter 14

Three days.

They'd held the university for three more days, taking on at least six or seven renewed attacks that Hank could count, not including the constant probes and pot-shots in both directions. Only on the fourth night, as the PLA poured more and more men and materiel onto the island, and airstrikes and cruise missiles hammered the ROC Marines' artillery in the south, no matter how much they maintained their shoot-and-scoot tactics, did they stage a fighting retreat to the next line back.

The ROC Marines were still fighting to hold Jincheng Township, but when a PLA thrust east of Jinning broke through—though at considerable cost to the PLA—Captain Guo got permission to fall back to the airport.

Hank had expected the ChiComs to push harder as soon as the Taiwanese started falling back. Instead, they'd been, if anything, even more hesitant than before. The ROC Marines had still lost two more M60s on the way to the airport perimeter, but it looked like the bodies and the burned out ZBD-05s and ZBD-2000s had a certain chilling effect on the Red Chinese troops' aggressiveness.

Now he stood in a hastily constructed bunker, built of sandbags and logs, staring into the gray sheets of monsoon rain, at the north end of the airport, watching the dark line of trees just on the other side of the highway.

Routes to the airport that Chinese armored vehicles could use were severely limited. Most of the installation was surrounded by thick woods, which gave infantry plenty of concealment, but canalized armor like crazy. The woods had been sowed liberally with mines and punji traps—that was a blast from the past—but there was still a chance that the Chinese might get infiltrators through, if only to try to clear out the anti-tank teams that were set in to watch the roads and ambush the inevitable armored assault. Since Hank and his section didn't have anti-tank weapons, Tsai had put them out on counter-infiltration duty. They had joined several platoons of ROC Marine infantry stationed at points along the highway where they could watch and interdict any enemy forces that tried to cross. Boring duty, but necessary.

Hank sighed and rubbed his eyes. They ached, along with just about all the rest of him. It had been a long week, and he'd gotten very little sleep.

"Hank." Shevlin was at the back of the bunker, on the radio. Despite the weather and the electronic warfare going on, they were still getting sporadic HF comms with Vetter, back on Taiwan. "Boss wants to talk to you."

Hank stepped back from the firing port and joined Shevlin at the back, while Reisinger took his place.

By some miracle, they hadn't lost anyone else since that first night. Michaels and Alexander were gone, their final resting places in the rubble and churned mud of the university, but the rest were still hanging in there.

Hank took the handset from Shevlin. "Six-Four Actual."

"How are you boys hanging in there?" Vetter didn't sound as chipper as he had the last time. He hadn't been in the fighting—at least not that Hank knew, but then, news from anywhere but Kinmen had been less than forthcoming for the last few days—but knowing Vetter, he'd probably been up for most of the last ninety-six hours, as long as he'd had men in the fight. He had to be utterly exhausted to sound remotely tired over the radio.

"We're alive. Most of us." Hank took a deep breath and collected himself. "Only two KIA. A couple of frag wounds, but nothing game-ending. The ROC Marines are keeping us supplied with food, water, and ammo." Most of the 7.62 they'd reloaded with had been de-linked machinegun ammo for the Taiwanese T74s, but it would do. "Right now, we're trying to hold Kinmen Airport and Jincheng. Haven't heard much from the east side of the island lately, so I don't know if they're holding there or not."

"What we're getting back here is that they're getting plastered from offshore. Constant naval gunfire and drone swarms. The weather's giving them a respite from the drones, but the gunships and destroyers are still hammering the shorelines." Vetter probably *was* getting better word, back in Taipei, than Hank was on the ground. "Look, we're launching a strike tonight. It's going to be dicey, given the weather, but the Taiwanese have decided to cut losses and pull everyone they can from Kinmen. Matsu's already fallen."

Hank sighed a little. He hadn't heard that yet. It had probably been inevitable, given the numbers they'd watched the PLA move into the region, but Matsu would have been a tough nut to crack.

Still, the PLA had gotten farther in trying to conquer Kinmen over the last few days than they had the other two times they'd tried it in the past.

"Extract will be on the beach to your south, at 0220. We've got assets moving into position to punch a hole through the cordon. Hopefully we've got enough mass this time to avoid the cluster that happened last week." Vetter sounded almost apologetic.

Hank didn't know enough of what had happened on the previous attempt to get them out to have much of anything to say. He wasn't sure what he *could* say, even if he'd known what had gone wrong. Triarii had died trying to get them off Kinmen. They hadn't just been abandoned.

"If I'm going to be frank, we're banking on the monsoons to cover this op. If the rain lets up, we might not be able to pull it off. Be ready but have a fallback plan." Vetter broke squelch, then was back. "Hank, I can't say what you've been through so far, but

I want to make one thing clear. You're Triarii first. You're Americans first. If there is a chance to get off that island, you take it. You copy? I need every section and every team I've got, and I don't want any brave last stands on Kinmen. If the ROC Marines want to make them, it's their territory. You get off that rock."

Hank suddenly found that he had more mixed feelings about that order than he would have expected. They'd been fighting alongside the ROC Marines for over four days. They'd shed blood and lost brothers, and not only Michaels and Alexander. There was a bond there, even though most of them couldn't understand each other without a terp or crude pointy-talky. It stung, thinking about leaving those boys to their fate.

Yet Vetter was right. They had their own responsibilities and chain of command. And if they could get mobile again, they might have a better chance to really hurt the PLA.

It just sucked to think about.

"Roger that." His voice sounded flat and dead in his own ears.

"It's not like that, Hank." Vetter had to have picked up on his tone, not to mention probably understanding the emotion behind it. Vetter had been around the block, and having been an old Delta hand, he'd probably seen more of this sort of thing than Hank had. In fact, Hank was sure that was the case. "We're going to get as many of the ROC Marines off as we can, too. That's the president's decision. They've bled the PLA, now it's time to get as many off as possible for the defense of the main island. She doesn't want to see her people get slaughtered just to buy a couple more days.

"Don't miss extract. 0220."

***

Hank waded through the mud, Xu by his side, as he headed back through the woods toward the forward command post. Colonel Tsai should be set up there, along with another ROC Marine company commander named Peng.

Even in the woods, somewhat sheltered by the trees, everything was utterly soaked. The carpet of fallen plant matter underfoot made it easier to walk, but the ground underneath was a sea of mud, and anywhere that there *wasn't* undergrowth was worse. That was going to slow the enemy, too, which Hank was grateful for, as much as he hated slogging through the crap.

He'd actually rather be in the desert.

The CP was in a hardened concrete building just off the airport, painted a strange red, black, and gray camouflage pattern, the paint peeling off in most places. The outside windows were all covered with plywood. It looked like it had been there since the initial fights for Kinmen in the late '40s and had been slowly crumbling ever since. Hank hoped it was sturdier than it looked.

The guards, soaked to the bone but not nearly as muddy as the Triarii and the National Security Bureau spook, halted them but let them through after Xu gave their bona fides. There was a soaked, muddy mat on the inside of the door, and both men essentially ignored it. There wasn't time.

The CP itself was buried in the middle of the building, with another set of guards outside the locked door. Apparently, despite the rather intensive counter-intelligence measures that the Taiwanese had put in place, there *had* been some clandestine attacks on Taiwanese military officers and government officials, at least on Kinmen.

It was a good thing they'd evacuated as many of the civilians as they had before this had really clacked off.

The interior of the CP looked like any other office, except for all the uniforms and the fact that everyone inside was armed. Several tables had been set up in neat rows, and if not for the cables connecting military radios to laptops and screens, with more cables snaking up to a hole in the ceiling that led to the antennas on the roof, each one could have been a corporate workstation.

Hank immediately felt muddy and disheveled, but Xu didn't seem bothered, and when they wove through the desks toward the big screen against the back wall, Hank was somewhat surprised to see that Colonel Tsai was in cammies every bit as soaked and muddy as his own.

Tsai looked up as they approached and nodded. "I have good news." Unlike many of his men, Tsai spoke English, and fairly well. "We are preparing to fall back and evacuate. We have hurt the Communists. We have hurt them very badly. But we are outnumbered, and as things stand now, so long as the Americans—except for you Triarii—and the Japanese are more concerned with Korea than Kinmen or Matsu, this island will eventually fall." He pointed to the screen, which currently displayed the map of the island as well as several camera feeds. "The units that have been holding Jincheng are falling back under fire as we speak, and we are nearly finished setting the cratering charges on the airport airstrip." He didn't smile, but there was a note of defiant triumph in his voice. "They will not be able to fly anything on or off this island for some time."

It was a laudable attempt to deny the area to the enemy, Hank had to admit, but all the same, he doubted it would slow the PLA down *that* much.

"We just got word from our command, as well." Hank pointed to the map. "Where do you need us?"

Colonel Tsai studied him for a moment, and Hank started to wonder just what the man was thinking. He had to know that the Triarii had attempted to extract off the island the better part of a week ago and had stayed to fight because they'd been cut off. Was he wondering if the Triarii were just looking to cut and run?

"There is a possibility that the enemy will see that we are falling back and will try to press the offensive harder in an attempt to eliminate us before we can escape. I cannot afford to draw any forces back from the defenses until the very last minute."

Hank nodded. It made sense. It was what he'd do. It still rankled that Tsai was acting as if he thought the Triarii were just trying to get out of harm's way. *Didn't we just sail across the fucking Pacific to fight these assholes? Haven't we already been in combat for months in the South China Sea?*

Tsai didn't seem to notice Hank's bristling. "Except for those setting in charges, every unit will be holding their position until thirty minutes before departure."

Hank had to fight to keep his expression under control. Thirty minutes was a hell of a short window if they were looking at getting *everyone* off the island. He wasn't as tuned in as Tsai was on actual numbers, but judging by the marks on the map, they were looking at trying to evacuate the better part of two battalions.

There was no way they were going to get two battalions to the beach and off the island in thirty minutes, not without it turning into a rout. And as badly as the PLA had done so far, he had little doubt that they'd take full advantage as soon as they figured it out. Even if that just meant shelling the hell out of the beach.

"Sir, I think it's going to take longer than that. Even if we push it, that's going to turn the beach into a clusterfuck." Xu and Peng both gave him a look at his choice of words, but screw it, he was essentially a contractor. There was only so much decorum that was expected of him. "The best bet under these circumstances is going to be a phased withdrawal, pulling units back in bits and pieces, so that the enemy can't immediately tell what's going on."

Tsai studied him coolly. Hank refused to back down, knowing that he was right. He understood Tsai's reasoning. If the PLA noticed that the ROC Marines were falling back, especially as the PLAN out at sea started getting hit, they were probably going to push harder. It could turn into a mess, fast. Hank just couldn't imagine that trying to fall back all at once wasn't going to turn into an epic clusterfuck.

"We have plans in place, and unit commanders are being informed." Tsai wasn't backing down, either. He was a colonel, a *Siōng-hāu*, talking to a foreign contractor. He was the ground commander. "It is under control."

Hank suppressed a sigh. "Roger that. So, you want us to hold on the highway until we get the word?" There was only so much he could do. He'd developed a great deal of respect for Colonel Tsai during the fight for the university, but even some of the best commanders were prone to making a boneheaded call. Tsai had to be just as tired as they were. He wasn't going to agree with every call the man made.

Tsai nodded and turned back to the map. They were dismissed.

Hank just hoped, as he and Xu left the CP, that Tsai turned out to be right.

***

Night fell. The shelling continued, though at least the airstrikes had stopped. The monsoons had made sure of that. Visibility dropped to barely fifty yards, and NVGs didn't really help. Hank could only see the tree line across the highway as a blacker line against the gray of the road and the sky. Sporadic small arms fire rattled off to the left, but Hank couldn't be sure if someone had actually just engaged a probe or was only shooting at shadows.

He watched the trees. There had been an engagement up the road earlier, shortly after his conversation with Tsai. He'd heard the explosions and seen the black smoke rising above the woods. No real word had been passed, but from what he could tell, given the tank losses the ROC Marines had taken so far—and they hadn't had many tanks on the island to begin with—a PLA armored column had probably gotten hit.

It didn't seem likely, given what had already happened, that the Chinese *wouldn't* send infantry support up to try to clear out the AT teams ahead of their main assault on the airport. But he still hadn't seen anything moving in their sector. The woods were still and dark, curtained by rain and black as pitch past the tree line.

Either the Chinese infantry were extremely patient, creeping along inch by inch, or they weren't in there. From what Hank had seen so far, the PLA and PLAN Marine Corps weren't training their guys to be that kind of old-school sneaky. Nothing about the offensive so far had displayed a great deal of operational patience. They'd slowed down once they'd started getting chewed up, but that's not the same thing.

It was almost as if they hadn't expected so many of them to get killed, and they were becoming more hesitant as they took casualties. That might be good.

He wasn't going to get optimistic.

That's when Murphy rears up and kicks you in the ass. Right when you start to think that everything's going swimmingly.

He checked his watch, pulling back the cut-off sock cuff that he'd been using to shield the tritium hands for longer than he cared to think about. It was getting awfully close to extract time, and there had still been no call.

Glancing at Xu, he had to think about it. He had his orders from Vetter, which amounted to being on that beach by 0220. If worse came to worst, could he pull his guys without the call from Tsai, *without* risking the entire alliance between Triarii and ROC Army?

And how would Xu respond?

Xu himself, though, appeared to be getting just as restless, checking his watch in between scans of the highway and the woods beyond. He was keeping his thoughts to himself, but he was clearly feeling the same tension that Hank was.

Everything was broken down and packed up, ready to move. That meant the long-range comms, too, so if Vetter called them, they couldn't immediately answer. Hell, they wouldn't even know. They did still have comms with the CP, though.

Xu's radio crackled, and he answered immediately. He looked up at Hank with what might have been thinly veiled relief in his eyes. "Time to go."

"You heard the man." Hank got on his own radio. "All Tango India Six-Four. We are falling back to the airport. One has point. Three, you're on trail." He looked around the bunker. "We're in the middle, Etienne."

He stayed at the firing port as the rest of the squad rucked up and got ready to move. The absolute last thing he wanted was to start smelling the barn and get shot in the back because they were in a hurry.

Still, nothing. No movement, no gunfire, no sounds but the distant *pop*s of small arms fire and a few distant rumbles of artillery, along with the occasional buzz of a shell going over, in both directions. The ROC Marines' M109s had taken a beating over the last few days, but a few were still hanging in there, though they had to be getting low on munitions by then, given the volume of fire they'd been putting out.

He'd been somewhat surprised to see just how much ordnance the Taiwanese had still had cached on Kinmen, given the general appearance of demilitarization that they'd presented over the last couple of decades. But without constant resupply, those stocks were still limited, and they *were* going to run out.

"We're ready, boss. I see Amos out back." LaForce had his ruck on and already had Faris and Huntsman heading out.

"Let's go."

He just hoped they got there in time and without getting swarmed by the PLA.

And that the extract platforms could actually get through.

***

Getting through the lines and onto the airport was every bit the logistical and communications nightmare Hank had worried that it would be. There were only so many ways onto the installation, and those were guarded. The roads were packed with ROC Marines and their equipment, and Hank quickly found his fears were being realized.

They were hunkered down in the dripping bush next to the Military Airport bus stop, waiting. The entire line to get on the base appeared to be stalled out, the ROC Marines finding any shelter from the incessant rain that they could. That was pretty much the jungle, which was going to be the only thing that saved most of them if the Chinese figured out that the forward positions had been abandoned and came roaring down the road with a few ZBD-2000s. Or even ZBD-05s.

Even so, the assault didn't materialize as the time ticked by. Hank stood up and leaned out into the road, to see the column moving through the gate, if still far too slowly. He checked his watch again. They were going to be late.

Artillery shells screamed in overhead with buzzing, dopplered whines, hitting somewhere on the airport with heavy *crump*s, muted by the constant low roar of the pounding rain.

Hank hoped they weren't hitting anything vital, but there wasn't a whole lot of cover on the airfield. This could get ugly, fast, with the entire remaining garrison—and those civilians who'd stayed to support them—packed onto that open ground.

The ground assault still didn't come yet.

He heard explosions and small arms fire to the north, and looked up that way with a frown, but he couldn't see anything but the darkness of the jungle.

Tsai left a stay-behind element to delay the enemy without telling us. Holy shit. He thought about it for a second. *Damn, I hope those were volunteers.*

The column was moving faster now. Finally, with another look at his watch—0218—Hank got to his feet. "Let's go."

They fell in with the ROC Marines, most of whom were looking back every few seconds, gripping their weapons, which included more than a few MP5s and the older T65K2s, local AR-18 knockoffs, as they watched their surroundings and kept looking up the road, expecting the Communist tracks to come roaring down on them at any moment.

A rippling series of explosions sounded to the north. The Communist armor was coming, but Tsai's rear guard were hammering them.

Hank realized that he hadn't seen any of the remaining M60 tanks on the road. Had the tankers volunteered to hold the line to the last? Or had they just parked the tanks, shown the volunteers how to work the guns, and then joined the exodus?

He wasn't sure he really wanted to know.

It was 0234 by the time they got onto the airport, joining the hustle toward the south fence, which looked like it had been bulldozed through to open a wider gate for the exodus to the beach. A couple of CM21A2s mounting 25mm cannons and a CM25 TOW vehicle were on the airstrip, their weapons trained on the north as the infantry ran toward the beach.

Now that the view out to sea was unhindered by the vegetation, Hank could still see little of the fight that was supposed to be happening out there. He could see a few dim flashes in the distance through the rain, and hear the rumble of explosions and weapons fire, but that was about it.

Then he was at the gate, making sure that 3rd Squad was through before he finally followed, with one last glance at the low, dark line of the island before he did.

The evacuation flotilla would have been one of the most motley assortments of fishing boats, RHIBs, yachts, and other small craft he'd ever seen, had he not just spent several months conducting maritime guerrilla warfare against Chinese forces both regular and irregular in the South China Sea. Clearly, the Taiwanese had mobilized any small craft that they could get across the Straits and that might be able to get past the gunships and frigates out to sea.

"Tango India Six-Four, this is Tango India Seven Two Actual. I've got three RHIBs directly across from the terminal." Hank hadn't heard Michael Chan's voice in what felt like forever, though it had only been about a week. "Holding seats for you."

"This is Six-Four. We are en route." Chan had transmitted on the general Triarii operational freq, so Lovell, LaForce, and Navarro should all have heard.

He saw the formation start to veer toward the terminal and the beach beyond. They'd heard. He jogged to keep up, his knees protesting under the weight of his ruck.

Then the artillery came in again.

122mm rounds came howling out of the murk overhead, the first salvo slamming into the tarmac only about a hundred yards away, throwing up fountains of shattered asphalt and mud with bone-jarring *thud*s. The Triarii picked up the pace. Nobody wanted to be under that, let alone in a RHIB.

The M109s, still stationed at either end of the airstrip, returned fire, their muzzles spewing fire in the dark and the rain. But the enemy arty kept coming. The disparity in numbers and firepower was now too great for the ROC Marines' counter-battery fire to suppress the PLA guns.

Hank saw a platoon of ROC Marines take a direct hit. Half of them just disappeared in the black puff of the impact.

Then they were on the beach, clambering aboard the RHIBs with the help of the skeleton crews that Chan had manned them with. Even with each squad having taken losses, it was still a tight fit to get a squad each aboard the boats. They managed it in record time, though, and then they were pulling off the beach. Though not before Hank had headcounts.

Chan was at the wheel of Hank's boat, turning it as soon as they were off the beach and clear of the tank traps that still lined the sand. As soon as he was pointed back out to sea, he opened the throttle.

Soon, Hank could see one of the Chinese gunboats in the distance, blazing fiercely. The Triarii raiders—probably with ROC Navy support—had avenged themselves for the lost torpedo boats five nights before.

As they raced away from Kinmen, making for the hole that had been blasted through the blockade, Hank glanced back, just in time to see the faint sparks in the darkness as the ROC Marines blew up the last of their vehicles to deny them to the enemy.

Chapter 15

The knock at the door jerked Hank out of his reverie, and he realized that he'd been staring into space for at least the last few minutes. He shook his head, looked down just to make sure he was dressed—he was—and went to answer it.

Vetter, Chan, and Bonifacio were waiting out in the hallway. Hank pulled the door open and ushered them inside.

Chan clapped him on the shoulder as they entered. "I'm surprised to see you conscious, let alone dressed, after Kinmen. If half the stories we heard were true…"

"I haven't been up that long." Truth be told, Hank had been awake far longer than he would have liked. He was still bone-tired, and his eyes felt like there was sand crammed under the lids. The dreams had precluded much sleep after a while.

The door swung shut behind Vetter, and Hank waved them to the chairs or the bed to take a seat. For his part, he stood against the wall, his arms folded. He didn't want to get too comfortable. He was afraid he'd pass out and find himself back in the nightmares again.

Since tourism to Taiwan was essentially extinct for the moment, the Triarii had been put up in the Ambassador Hotel in Taipei, each man getting his own room. It was quite comfortable, and the hotel was still providing meals, but Hank couldn't help but feel a little guilty. He seriously doubted that Tsai's men were in similarly posh accommodations. They had probably been stuck in old barracks across the island, if they weren't already set into bunkers on the defensive lines, waiting for the next hammer blow to fall.

He nodded toward the TV, which was on but muted. "What's it looking like? I don't know enough of the language to be able to glean much from the local news."

Vetter leaned back in the armchair next to the window, though he shifted the chair so that he wasn't right in front of it. They were on the tenth floor, so there wasn't a lot of chance that he'd even be seen, let alone invite an attack, but between the drone threat—and the PRC had drone units on the ground on Taiwan, nobody doubted that—and simple habit, built by years in war zones and a lot of intense training when in secure areas, it was instinctual.

"Well, it's kind of too early to say. The PRC's propaganda arm is going gangbusters to say that Kinmen and Matsu were secured quickly, with very few casualties, and that the residents of Kinmen welcomed the PLA soldiers as liberators, rejoicing at the elimination of the 'imperialist' forces that have occupied Chinese territory for so long, forcibly keeping them separated from their Chinese brothers, blah, blah, blah." He snorted. "They have to be keeping every unit committed on complete comms lockdown, and from what the intel weenies have seen, they keep showing the same couple of scenes from somewhere that didn't get hammered too hard, over and over. Otherwise, it might start to get out how many you boys killed there."

"I know we probably made it a lot longer and more costly than they planned on, but do we have any idea by how much?" Hank knew that there was only so much they could be sure of. The Chinese *had* to have assumed that they'd take casualties capturing an island archipelago that they'd failed to take twice before. The question was, how many casualties would they consider to be too many?

Vetter shook his head. "Guesswork, at best. The Chinese are even more tight-lipped about plans and contingencies than the Russians. Anything they *do* let out has to be taken with a five-pound bag of salt." He shrugged. "We did get a drone over Kinmen during a brief break in the weather a few hours ago. It looks like Colonel Tsai's plan worked. The runway is a cratered mess. They're not landing any fixed wing aircraft there anytime soon. Most of the island's infrastructure is similarly wrecked, either by the bombardment or Taiwanese sabotage. They got rid of the knife at their throats, but at a significant cost and without gaining any of the islands' usefulness. They got rocks, mud, jungle, and a few houses that didn't get destroyed, and that's about it.

"We couldn't get a *really* precise count with the one pass we got with the drone, but it looks like close to a battalion's worth of armored vehicles got destroyed, if not a bit more. I'm sure we missed some, and it's entirely possible that we overcounted, too. But I think it's a fair bet that you and the ROC Marines killed a *lot* of PLA soldiers and PLAN marines. Hopefully, you got some they were counting on for the invasion of the main island."

"On the more strategic level, we seem to be in an operational pause at the moment." Hank didn't know Bonifacio well, but they'd worked together once or twice during the South China Sea ops. "They've stopped launching missiles, though overflights into Taiwanese airspace are a daily thing now. The monsoons are interfering with our recon flights, but what word we're managing to glean from the internet—mostly TikTok, if you'll believe it—shows that their mobilization hasn't stopped. They're still moving units and equipment into staging areas across the Straits.

"So far, we've seen zero reaction from the States, or from the Japanese. They seem to have their hands full with the Norks, who have launched ballistic missile strikes on targets in South Korea as well as Japan and pushed across the DMZ in an attempt to take Paju. It's bogged down, since their bridging operation went sideways as soon as they started. Reporting is spotty, but it sounds like they're basically squatting on the river, pounding the hell out of Paju with artillery, while our guys and the ROK Army move in.

Surprisingly, they haven't opened up on Seoul yet, given the sheer mass of arty they've got pointed at the city."

"Maybe the ChiComs don't want it going that far yet. Then they might have to get involved, and if they just encouraged that fat fuck in Pyongyang to kick this off just to make sure that all eyes are up there, it kinda defeats the purpose, doesn't it?" Hank shrugged. "So, essentially, we're still right where we were before, in the big picture scheme of things."

"Sort of." Vetter clearly wasn't quite that ready to write off what had happened on Kinmen as just a speed bump. "We were expecting the first strikes on Penghu last night, right after Kinmen fell. They've been investing Matsu for the last couple of days. But it's been quiet. The PLAN is still staying outside the median line. They've lobbed a few ballistic missiles into the sea to the north and south, but they haven't actually hit the island of Taiwan yet." He rubbed his chin. "I think Kinmen did give them some pause. They've always known that it was going to be tough, but I suspect that they thought the drawdown in the garrison meant it should fall faster than it did, and with less cost.

"The PLA has a few structural problems that often get overlooked when people just look at the numbers and the sheer weight of equipment and weaponry it has. They haven't really fought a war since 1979, and then, they got their asses kicked. The NVA leadership was all combat hardened, and they kicked the Chinese out of North Vietnam in three weeks, maintaining their own occupation of Cambodia for another ten years. Hardly the victory the ChiComs tried to paint it as. And they really haven't fought a major war since. They've slid into all sorts of flashpoints around the world, but generally in a sneaky, low-key sort of way, letting other people do the bleeding and the dying, then picking up the pieces while everyone else is either pointing fingers or just trying to forget that anything's happened.

"Here, it's different. Here, they don't have proxies they can just give weapons to and let them kill each other until they can start extracting minerals and fuel. And they aren't up against some Podunk militia, either. The ROC Army might be a lot smaller, but they're arguably better-trained than the PLA, and they're dug into this island like a tick. That's *got* to give any ChiCom commander pause."

"You're starting to sound dangerously optimistic, Doug," Chan remarked. "They've got all sorts of reasons to keep pushing this."

"Oh, I know. Especially with the unrest that's been rocking just about every major city for the last few months. The state media organs are denying everything, but demonstrations have been breaking out regularly in Beijing, Shanghai, and Wuhan. *And* if Three Gorges really is in danger of cracking, this could get *way* worse in short order. They can't *afford* to back off now. They're going to need to demonstrate strength, and the PLA leadership's been itching for this fight for a long time now, anyway."

"So, where does that leave *us*?" Hank cracked his neck. "I'm aware of the strategic situation, and while it sounds like we *might* have slowed them down some, we probably didn't stop 'em, and it's only a matter of time before they really do try to come across the Strait."

"Penghu's probably next, but I don't want any of us in that meat-grinder. The ROC Marines might not let us in at this point, anyway." Vetter frowned. "Truth is, we're essentially auxiliaries here, and I *can't* make a serious call without input from the ROC Army. I want to start hitting their staging areas. That's going to slow them down the most, aside from invoking Option Zulu, and while I think Santiago's *thinking* about it—and he's probably been looking at that idea *real* hard ever since you boys clashed with those ChiCom "contractors" in San Diego, Hank— but he hasn't dropped that hammer yet."

The hotel room went pretty quiet for a moment after that. "How likely do you think it is?" Bonifacio asked. "Option Zulu, I mean?"

Vetter didn't respond right away. When he did, his voice was low and thoughtful. "Look around you. How far have we already gone just in the last year and a half? Who would have actually believed, even during the chaos a few years back, that we'd be *actually* fighting a new world war, and against the Germans and the Chinese, for fuck's sake?" He sighed. "I'm not writing *anything* off as impossible, anymore."

"So, we're in a holding pattern for a while?"

"We're in a holding pattern for a while." Vetter nodded. "I'll be up at ROC Army headquarters at least a couple times a day, but it looks like we're in a pause for the moment, at least until I get the go ahead to send you guys raiding again." He stood up. "I just wanted to come by and see how you were doing, Hank. That can't have been fun."

"It wasn't. But I'm all right." Hank wondered how much of that was just a "gotta stay hard" lie. "I'll check on the rest of the boys here in a bit. I don't imagine many of them are up and about yet."

Vetter clapped him on the shoulder. "Get some rest. You've earned it, and if things go the way I think they will, you're gonna need it."

Chapter 16

That night, Hank went out on the town with LaForce, Xu, Xu's wife, his sister, and one of her friends. LaForce was married, but he was gallant as all hell anyway, chatting Liao Ren up and making her giggle, while still keeping his hands off.

Xu Mei-Ling had latched onto Hank almost immediately, somewhat to his discomfiture. Xu and his wife, Shu-Ching, had smiled knowingly. Hank knew when he'd been set up, but Mei-Ling was gorgeous, so he didn't actually mind all that much, after he got over the initial surprise at having a beautiful Taiwanese woman immediately slip her arm inside his and lean against his side as they walked toward the Old Sichuan Nanjing Restaurant.

Given everything that was going on, he might have expected the streets of Taipei to be all but deserted. The threat hanging over the island was something these people had lived with their entire lives, though, and despite the economic relationship that had developed between Taiwan and the mainland over the last couple of decades, they were still expecting an attack, had worked that expectation into their day-to-day lives, and went about their business. The traffic was still lighter than he'd expected in a major city, though. He'd asked Xu if it was normal, and the older man had nodded yes.

Hank was, frankly, somewhat surprised at how polite and orderly the traffic was. He knew he shouldn't be. Taiwan was not a Third World country, and while he'd seen Third World level traffic in the Philippines, the Filipinos and Taiwanese were very different people. Different histories, different cultures. Hank realized he'd gotten used to fighting in Third World hellholes, and even after seeing Kinmen, and the ROC Marines they'd fought beside there, he still hadn't quite wrapped his head all the way around the fact that this was a war in a place arguably every bit as prosperous and civilized as the US.

Compared to some of the places in the Southwest he'd spent a good chunk of the last couple years in, Taiwan was arguably even more civilized.

There were no *Soldados de Aztlan* or MS-13 here.

Granted, that didn't mean they were *safe*. Hank had long ago disabused himself of any belief that anywhere was *safe*.

As if to echo his thoughts, as they crossed the next street, an air raid siren began to wail.

Xu motioned quickly, his face gone grim, and they hurried off the street, quickly running around the small forest of mopeds parked at the curb and into a 7-11. It was hardly the air raid shelter Hank would have preferred, if given the choice, but it was better than being caught in the open.

Taiwanese police and ROC Army had already begun to appear on the streets, quickly stopping traffic and directing the people to get inside. Everyone moved quickly, with a purpose. Hank watched as the locals got off the streets, their faces tight and worried but without panic.

He'd been in enough incidents stateside that he didn't expect most Americans would react that way. Not in the cities, anyway.

The streets cleared fast. Hank, despite his own best instincts, moved to the window and scanned the sky. High clouds, nothing else. The sirens continued to wail, but no missiles came crashing down, no bombers and strike aircraft roared overhead.

A voice called out in Mandarin over the PA system, momentarily drowning out the sirens. Hank looked over at Xu, but it was Mei-Ling who explained.

"It is a drill. We used to have them once or twice a year. Everyone knows what to do. We learn it in school." She stood close to him, watching the streets, now eerily empty except for the uniformed police and a few ROC Army soldiers. The sirens continued to wail. "Now, it is every two weeks, sometimes every week. The last one was only six days ago." Her voice was calm, but there was still a note of something faintly nervous in her demeanor, especially the way she stood even closer to him, holding onto his arm.

Hank looked down at her. He'd just met this woman, but she seemed to have ideas about him. He glanced at Xu, who smiled.

Hank just shook his head, even as the sirens trailed off, the police started to disperse, and people started to come out of the buildings. The drill was over. They stepped back out onto the street and joined the other pedestrians, resuming their walk to dinner.

The rains had paused again, which was the only reason they were walking instead of taking a taxi. It also allowed Hank to see more of what the Taiwanese were doing as they waited for the inevitable.

He looked down at Mei-Ling. She was watching the crowds, still holding onto his arm, and she seemed happy enough. He wondered just what Xu had told her. She seemed awfully enthusiastic about this date, having never met him before.

It took a few more minutes to get to the restaurant. The staff didn't seem to speak English, but since they had Xu with them, that wasn't a problem. Xu spoke with the maître d, and they were ushered to a booth with a round table in the center, bordered by elaborately carved screens and with a traditional lantern with a Chinese dragon twisting in gold around the red cylinder overhead.

The meal was probably the most pleasant time Hank had had in a very, very long time. Mei-Ling was eager to talk, plying him with questions, sitting noticeably closer to him than he would have expected. Xu and his wife were watching with barely concealed amusement. Hank found himself responding to her attention with a lot more interest than he might have expected. She was warm and engaging, and she *was* very attractive.

It was a change, he knew, and he didn't really know where it had come from. One of the female NICA officers they'd worked with in the Philippines, a pretty woman named Althea, had expressed some interest in him, but he'd ignored it. He didn't want to form that kind of personal attachment, not after watching Arturo, a kid who'd latched onto him as a surrogate father, get cut in half by a .50 cal.

But for whatever reason, after that fight for Kinmen, he didn't mind Mei-Ling's attentions that much. At all, really.

They finished the meal and headed back toward the hotel. From the way she was practically crawling under his arm, Hank began to suspect that Mei-Ling expected to be invited in when he got back to his hotel room.

He wasn't sure what he thought about that. But she was soft and warm and vivacious, and for the moment, as they walked back, he was willing to just try to shut his brain off and enjoy the moment. He'd decide what to do when they got back.

Xu and his wife broke off before they got to the hotel. LaForce said his goodbyes at the entrance. He'd explained his situation when they'd first met up, and Liao Ren had been somewhat disappointed, but she'd understood, though Hank might have seen her shooting Mei-Ling a few *what the hell* glances.

Hank paused at the elevator, turning to face her with a deep breath. Mei-Ling stopped him with a finger to his lips. "Whatever you're going to say, I'm not ready for tonight to end yet. Let's go upstairs." She put her hand on his cheek. "Even if it's only to talk."

He wasn't sure what he was getting into, but Hank couldn't quite bring himself to tell her no. He nodded, and they headed into the elevator together.

***

All the way up, Hank was second-guessing himself. *What the hell are you doing? Sure, she's pretty and engaging, and she seems to be genuinely interested. So what? Doesn't change your situation or hers. You do this and get killed next week, what's that going to gain?*

Hank had been a bit of a tomcat in his younger years, like many Marines. Over time, and several interactions that had gone beyond the first drunken night, he'd started to doubt not only the wisdom of it, but also just how harmless it really was. He'd seen a lot of hurt buried under a studied façade of indifference, on both sides of the equation.

It wasn't something that was talked about. Even bringing it up seemed to be an unspoken taboo. It had started to fascinate him, the almost religious faith that sex didn't really mean anything, but at the same time, was a requirement of living, like water, food, or air.

Even so, he still hadn't summoned up the guts to tell Mei-Ling that she should probably go home by the time they got out of the elevator and headed to his hotel room.

He realized, as he unlocked the door and ushered her inside, that he'd left the TV on. And he immediately regretted it.

Scenes of devastation panned across the screen, and it didn't take long to recognize parts of Kinmen. Smoke and fire drifted through the air, despite the rains, and smashed and burning M60s were displayed next to what might have been torn and charred bodies amid shell craters and destroyed fortifications.

Mei-Ling let out a little gasp and turned away, clinging to him tightly. He couldn't understand the Mandarin coming quietly over the speaker, but she could.

"What are they saying?" He had little doubt that this wasn't a Taiwanese broadcast.

It took her a minute to collect herself. There were tears in her eyes as she glanced at the screen, but she quickly looked away.

"They are saying that this is what the leadership of Taiwan has led us to. That this is our fault. That Taipei and the president have forced Chinese into killing Chinese, only for their own gain." She looked up at Hank. "Was that what it was like?"

He stared at the images on the screen, his jaw clenched. "They're being a bit selective for horror, but it was pretty rough, yeah." He sighed, still holding her though his eyes were still fixed on the PRC's propaganda. He knew they weren't showing this to their own people. This was specifically for Taiwanese consumption. "Do they have infiltrators in your media, or did they just hack the TV station?"

"They probably hacked the TV station." Mei-Ling, it had turned out, worked in IT there in Taipei, so it wasn't a question she wouldn't have known the answer to. She buried her face in his chest. "Please turn it off."

He disengaged himself to find the remote. "How often has this been happening?"

"They get something through every couple of days or so now. It never lasts long, before our own people shut down the hack." She sniffed, collecting herself, and met his eyes. "It means they're really getting ready, aren't they?"

Hank nodded grimly. "Propaganda and political warfare are usually part of the prep phase, yeah. Seen it in quite a few places."

She seemed to collect herself as she stepped closer. "There have been some people already talking about how hopeless it is." She slipped her arms around him. "I don't want to talk about that right now."

Hank looked away. "Mei-Ling…"

She stopped him with a kiss. "I don't want to be alone tonight. Not now. We don't have to have sex if you don't want to, but please don't send me away."

With another sigh, Hank could only nod.

Chapter 17

"You *know* they're going to paint this as an escalation."

Chan continued staring at the chart as he spoke. Hank just snorted.

"Right. Because *they* didn't escalate *anything* by assaulting Kinmen and Matsu." He shook his head. "The war's already started, and Vetter's got people prepped to start the counter-narrative as soon as things kick off. Better this than just sitting around, waiting to get hit."

While he and Mei-Ling had spent a lot of time together since that first night, Hank had been getting ever more restless with every passing day. The expected PLA offensive hadn't yet materialized, though the movements from inland to the coast had slowed. Intel thought some of that was due to the weather, but the sheer weight of men and materiel now massed in camps all along the coast of Fujian Province was great enough that everyone on the Taiwanese side of the Strait was starting to wonder just what the PRC was waiting for.

Now the *Jacqueline Q* was staged alongside the *Double Up,* just off the seaward coast of Pengjia Islet, along with two blue-hulled fishing trawlers that still had all of their Chinese markings and even PRC flags aboard. Those would come in handy, where they were going.

So would all the ordnance packed into their holds.

"Besides, unless we get captured or leave a casualty behind, they shouldn't have any concrete evidence they can parade in front of the cameras to prove that it was Taiwanese or Americans." Hank nodded toward the trawler off the starboard side. "Plausible deniability."

"Since when has that mattered to a Communist?" Chan retorted. "They'll say whatever they want, and *make* it be true."

"So much the more reason not to worry about it." Hank picked his helmet up off the console and headed below, to where the rest of the section was already transferring aboard the trawler, originally a spy ship for the PLAN, now crewed by Taiwanese fishermen—all veterans of the ROC Navy—and several officers in the National Security Bureau. "We know the war's already kicked off, so we need to fight it, instead of worrying about how the ChiComs are gonna lie about it."

***

Pingtan Island was a low line of lights against the horizon, the bulk of the island itself invisible in the night. More lights glittered off to the port bow, at the west end of the Pingtan Bridge.

There were also a lot of angular, predatory shapes in the water, most of them still showing running lights, somewhat to Hank's surprise. He would have expected the ChiComs to have started imposing blackouts in anticipation of Taiwanese airstrikes.

Maybe they were a little too confident in their own information operations. After all, as far as he knew, the ROC Air Force still hadn't launched strikes directly on the mainland.

He wondered about that a little, too. Were the Taiwanese still hoping that they could avoid or put off the full-blown kinetic conflict by playing along, just a little? Maybe they were still worried about the lack of American or Japanese interest in the fighting on Kinmen and Matsu. The last intel update, just before they'd gone black on comms, had indicated that there was a Carrier Strike Group hovering off the Senkaku Islands, though so far, their overflights had been limited to Taiwan itself. Hank had seen a few US military personnel on the island but given the irregular legal status of the Triarii in the Western Pacific, they'd steered clear.

The Taiwanese hadn't had any problem with accepting Triarii help, and even helping pay into the logistics requirements of their operations. That technically made them civilian contractors in the employ of the Republic of China, though when the US Government had openly decided to ignore the PRC's role in the attacks on the US mainland over the last year, it still raised questions, questions that the flotilla didn't have answers to. Not even after the USS *Lake Erie* had taken fire from Chinese ships during the fight for the Spratly Islands, not long ago. So, they had to step carefully and stay away from the Navy, Marines, and Army where they could. This wasn't like the arrangement in Europe.

Hank shook off the reverie. They were getting closer to the island, and it was game time. He needed to focus entirely on the situation at hand and worry about the big picture stuff afterward.

Pingtan Island was one of the known staging points for PLA amphibious forces in preparation for an invasion of Taiwan. There were several, but Pingtan seemed to be seeing the most activity, so it had become their target. Hank was sure that other teams and sections were raiding other points that night, or close to it, but they hadn't been read in on those strikes. Too much risk. This kind of operation *had* to be compartmentalized, just in case somebody got caught and turned out not to be quite as tough as they thought they were when dragged in front of an MSS interrogator.

"Five minutes." Xu was passing the word from the captain, whom Hank was pretty sure was National Security Bureau, as well. He'd only met the man, who didn't seem to speak much English, when they'd boarded the trawler. He didn't even know his full name. He was just Captain Zhan.

And that might have been an alias, for all he knew.

Zhan was on the radio, and while Hank couldn't make out the words, the tone sounded tense. More than likely, he was using captured code phrases and challenge and pass, and the question was whether they were still legit, or if the Chinese had figured out that they'd been penetrated and changed the codes.

There was a pause, and then a short reply came over the radio in Mandarin. Zhan opened the throttle again and they began to pick up speed, pushing deeper into the Haitan Strait. Xu let out a long breath.

"I'm guessing that means the code phrase worked." Hank's attention was divided between Zhan and the ships out in the strait.

"Hopefully." Xu still sounded like he was wound as tight as a drum. "Or else they are waiting for us to get closer before they slam the door shut behind us."

Hank hadn't known that that was a Chinese or Taiwanese saying, but maybe Xu was just more Westernized than he'd thought.

"Better get below and get ready for the drop." His section had the first set of targets, so they were splashing first.

Xu nodded, and the two of them turned and left the boathouse.

The trawler was packed. There was no way they'd pass an inspection if the PLAN decided they needed a once-over. That was, of course, why they'd picked the ship they had. This particular trawler, painted blue and crammed with electronic monitoring equipment, had only ever been a fishing boat in outward appearance. In reality, just like the trawler they'd used to get close to the *Luck Genius*, it had been a MSS spy ship, captured by the ROC Navy only a few days before. There was significant risk in using it, since it was always possible that the PRC knew that the trawler had been seized, but so far, their camouflage seemed to be holding.

The ship's provenance also—hopefully—precluded boarding by a PLAN marine inspection team. Nobody messed with the MSS, at least not without a *lot* of Party clout behind them.

Much like the Triarii fishing vessels turned raiders, the Chinese trawler still had its boom, but they weren't going to use it for launching that night. There was too much risk that they might be observed doing it. They couldn't know for sure what kind of optics were focused on the trawler despite the MSS identification.

So, instead, they were launching the Zodiacs by hand, heaving them over the side and into the water, then jumping in after them.

Hank joined LaForce at the side, stepping in to help manhandle the big inflatable raiding craft over the rail. They had picked the darkest side of the trawler, in the hopes that if someone *was* watching—and given the lights and buzz of helicopters over the big island, that was a good bet—they might go unnoticed.

The boat was heavy as hell. The motor wasn't mounted, which made the launch tricky, but they didn't want it getting hooked on the rail when they dropped it. Using the grab lines and sling ropes, they got it out over the side, then let it fall.

Hank watched as the boat dropped, smacking into the water with a splash. It had fallen square, instead of flipping over, and the motor—which had still been carefully tied in, just in case—was still where it was supposed to be.

Stepping up onto the gunwale, he cinched down his rifle sling, crossed his arms over his chest rig, and stepped off.

He scissor kicked as he hit the water, effectively arresting his momentum so that when he went under, he only dipped a few inches below the surface, quickly kicking back into the air. From there, it was only a few strokes to the boat, though he didn't waste time.

Nobody wants to have two hundred plus pounds of man, weapon, and gear fall on their head in the water.

Reaching the boat, which was drifting slowly away from the trawler, rocking on the swell raised by the fishing boat's wake, he hauled himself up, flinging a leg over the gunwale and dragging himself into the bottom of the boat.

The rest of the squad swam over and dragged themselves aboard as they jumped into the water. Hank had already untied the motor and was dragging it toward the stern. It took LaForce's help to get the heavy outboard up over the transom and dogged in place, but by then Bishop and Winkler had the fuel bladder hooked up, and all that was left was to start the motor.

By the time it caught, the trawler had moved on and was lost in the lights and the darkness ahead. They were still far enough away from shore, and any of the other nautical traffic in the bay, that he wasn't that worried about being heard.

The boat was packed solid. The section had taken some serious losses, so the squad wasn't at its full, ten-man strength, but there were still seven men with gear, weapons, and packs crammed into a fifteen-foot boat. The raiding craft, black and low-level, was riding lower in the water than usual. That was going to slow it down, too, and they still had close to six nautical miles to go. They weren't going to be able to use the motor for all of that distance, either, which was going to eat up more of the precious darkness they had to work with.

Keeping as low as he could, after pulling his helmet and NVGs out of their waterproof bag in his assault pack, Hank opened up the throttle and started them moving toward their target.

Chapter 18

Not far from the sandbar that sheltered the entrance to the first inlet south of Jidiao Island, Hank cut the motor. The rest of the squad was already prepped, paddles in their hands, and they started to carefully sit upright on the gunwales, the paddles dipping almost soundlessly into the water, keeping the boat moving north.

Hank had been a regular grunt, but he'd learned in the boat training before they'd left Texas that this was what the Recon bubbas called, "Engine Appreciation."

With most of another nautical mile to go, he was sure they were going to be appreciating the hell out of that outboard in short order.

LaForce and Faris weren't paddling, but were both up in the bow, behind their rifles, watching for the enemy. If they got spotted, this could go bad, fast. They were deep in hostile territory, with zero support. Their only hope was stealth. Get in, set the charges, and get out, all without being detected.

Given the sheer weight of PLAN vessels in the strait, that was going to be interesting. Hank could only imagine how many troops were on shore, if this was really getting ready to kick off.

The paddles dipped and kept the boat moving. Hank watched for lights, keeping an eye on the helicopters still circling above Pingtan Island. All it would take would be one stray spotlight.

They had no eyes on the other boats, but that had been expected. Each squad had their own target, and while Hank had his radio on and his earpiece in, no one was planning on transmitting unless they were compromised and couldn't break out.

Even then, it was probably going to be better to just fight to the end rather than call for help, and they all knew it. The likelihood that any one squad was going to be able to break another out was pretty slim, if the PLA had the numbers on that island that they thought.

As they paddled past the islet at the mouth of the inlet, Hank got a better look at the southern wharf of Pingtan Jinjing Harbor.

It was packed. Ships were docked practically bow to stern at the wharf. Several of them were cargo ships, mostly smaller bulk carriers and what looked like a mid-sized tanker. A lot of the others were PLAN landing ships.

Hank knew the rough profiles, but none of the class names. He didn't especially care at the moment, either. Their mission was to get in there and do as much damage with the charges they were carrying in their assault packs as possible.

Also, if possible, they would set the fuses long enough that they could get clear and link back up with the trawler on the way out *before* things started blowing up.

They didn't have to slow much as they approached the spit of land that thrust out into the strait and sheltered the small cove where the local fishermen moored their boats. The wharf was on the other side.

Infiltration was going to be tough. The wharf was lit up with dozens of sodium lights, casting a bright orange glow over the entire port. Getting in and out without being seen was going to suck.

If there had been a way to hit the local power station, they might have put the lights out. That, however, ran the risk of giving the game away, and they hadn't been able to pinpoint a target guaranteed to knock out *enough* lights. So, they were just going to have to move carefully.

Slowly, cautiously, they paddled toward the wharf, threading their way through the shadows as best they could. As they neared land, Hank saw that despite the glare, there were actually a lot more shadowed areas than it had first appeared. Furthermore, while the helicopters overhead and the ships and patrol boats out in the water were a concern, he couldn't see any foot patrols out. Of course, there was a wall at the top of the wharf, which meant that there very well could be foot patrols on the inside, in the actual loading and unloading yard. Almost certainly there were cameras.

With whispered commands, he got the boat pointed toward the breakwater at the eastern end of the wharf. He'd considered going ashore, but since the ships were their targets, that wasn't really necessary, and staying on the water might well keep them out of the light and help avoid detection. So, they were going to stay in the boat, hugging the hulls—provided they could get close enough without someone on deck spotting them—and do their work.

They'd planted limpet mines before. It wasn't a new process to the Triarii of Tango India Six-Four. This many targets, this deep in enemy territory, right under the noses of the PLAN though…

That was new.

They paddled softly up to the first hull, a landing ship by its lines, and shipped oars, pulling the paddles in as they turned broadside to the target ship, trying to avoid allowing anything hard to impact the steel of the ship's side. The harbor wasn't silent by any stretch of the imagination, especially since it sounded like there was loading or something going on farther up, but hopefully the noise would simply mask their own movements.

With the paddles momentarily stashed inboard, Huntsman and Reisinger started getting the first two charges out. The Triarii flotilla's supply of Texas-built limpets was getting low, but they should have enough for tonight. There were supposed to be resupply and reinforcement ships on the way, but with some of the mutterings about increasing pressure from the Feds back home, Hank wasn't all that confident that any of it was going to come in time.

Huntsman twisted the clockwork fuse, setting it for—hopefully—about six hours, then, very gently, eased the mine against the ship's hull. The magnet was pretty powerful, and if they weren't careful, it was going to latch on with a *clang* that could be heard for miles over the water, never mind aboard the ship itself.

Huntsman knew his business, though, and even as Hank realized he was holding his breath, the big man got the edge of the mine against the hull and slowly eased it flat.

The next part was going to be tricky, and probably was going to make some noise, but not as much as just slapping the mine against the hull would have.

Taking his paddle, bracing himself with his knees against either side of the gunwale, Huntsman put the end of the handle—they'd learned in the train-up that you *never* put the edge of the paddle itself against a hard surface if you can help it—against the mine, and began to slide it down, below the waterline. It scraped against the steel, but the noise was still low enough that Hank didn't think anyone who wasn't right on the other side of the hull could hear it.

Without diving, they couldn't necessarily get the mine as far down as Hank would have liked, but given the size of the charge, it should be sufficient to severely damage the ship if not sink it at the wharf altogether.

Pulling the paddle back onto his lap, Huntsman gave a thumbs up, and they carefully pushed away from the hull, the paddles going back in the water and digging deep to move them toward the next ship.

They'd just reached that one, a smaller bulk carrier, when Hank heard voices above.

He didn't need to tell the squad to freeze. They'd all heard it. Huntsman and Reisinger held the boat off from bumping against the hull with gloved hands, but the attempt to suddenly stop at the sound of voices had the effect of actually forcing the boat into a sideways drift away from the hull, and out from under the shadow of the ship.

Hank had his rifle in his hands, looking up at the rail above them, where he could see the glimmer of flashlights moving around the deck. He could hear his heartbeat in his ears.

Dammit, I do not *want to be the team that gets spotted and throws this entire op in the shitter.* But if they drifted too far out, one of those flashlight beams *was* going to hit them, and then it was game on.

He just hoped he could get the motor restarted and get them moving soon after the first shots were fired, and then get enough distance from the wharf fast enough to get lost in the dark.

Evans and Bishop were on it, though, quickly plying their paddles to force the boat back toward the hull, the push cushioned by Huntsman and Reisinger. Hank let out a breath he hadn't quite realized he'd been holding. Still, he didn't relax. The two men on deck were still up there, and they could look over the side at any moment.

As he watched, his weapon raised, the red dot tracking the glow of the flashlights, he noticed that they weren't really shining them outward, off the side. Not deliberately, anyway. A flicker of light occasionally went over the rail, but the guards seemed to be focused on the deck. Almost as if they were just crew checking the ship one last time on their watch and weren't actually worried about infiltrators.

Why would they be? They were docked at Pingtan Island. This was PRC territory. The PLAN was openly patrolling the waters outside. The US Navy had all but openly declared that they were steering clear of China, and they were all focused on the escalating Korean conflict in the north, anyway. The Taiwanese had lost Kinmen and Matsu and were supposed to be bottled up and cowering on their island, waiting for the inevitable triumphant victory of the PLA.

Hank realized he had little doubt that that was the line the CCP was pursuing. Being realistic about the enemy wasn't generally a Communist trait.

Still, they waited, listening to the faint chatter of the two crewmen overhead and the lapping of the water against rubber and steel, trying not to move or breathe too loudly. Finally, the glow of the lights faded, and the voices receded.

Hank heard Reisinger let out a long sigh as he reached for the next mine.

He got it armed easily enough, but as he leaned out to attach it, he slipped.

The mine clapped against the hull with a *bong*, and everyone on the boat froze. Only the fact that Reisinger had his back to Hank kept his grimace of chagrin and fear hidden.

They waited, rifles pointed up at the top of the hull again. Waited for the lights to stab down to see what had just hit the ship.

Nothing. No movement. No voices. No lights. A ship's horn blared in the distance. Hank started to breathe again.

Pointedly staring at the mine rather than face the rest of the squad, a couple of whom were watching him accusingly, their body language plain even around their NVGs, Reisinger rotated his paddle and started to slowly and carefully push the mine down the hull and under the water.

Every line of his body broadcasting his embarrassment, Reisinger brought the paddle back up, and he and Huntsman pushed them off gently again. Paddles went back in the water, and they kept going.

The next two vessels went smoothly, without incident, aside from a close pass by a Z-9 helicopter that growled past almost directly overhead. Once again, they froze until the bird was some distance away and showed no sign of coming back around.

They were just coming even with the fifth target vessel when the first rattle of gunfire echoed across the water.

Heads came up, eyes scanning through NVGs, looking for the fight. None of the rounds were coming anywhere near them. The telltale *snap* of a bullet's supersonic shockwave couldn't be heard. But the sheer fact of gunfire on an op that was supposed to be executed without detection was a bad sign.

In fact, it was abort criteria.

Huntsman and Reisinger kept paddling, while Evans and Bishop dug their paddles into the water, swinging the boat around until the bow was pointed back at the straits behind them. Then Huntsman and Reisinger dug deep, stroking it out even as they continued to hug the hulls of the ships docked at the wharf, staying in the shadows as long as possible. The gunfight was getting more intense behind them, and Hank twisted around to see if he could spot what was going on.

Even as he turned, the night lit up. A massive fireball rose above the causeway between Haitan Island and Nanqing Islet, and a moment later, the causeway itself fell into the water.

More gunfire rattled in the distance, joined by the heavier *pompompom* of a 30mm. PLAN gunboats were converging on the causeway and the massive mushroom cloud billowing above it.

Hank knew what had happened, even without being able to see more than that. Chan had taken the causeway as his own target. He'd accomplished his mission, but there was no way they were going to be able to go in and get him out. Not if he'd blown his charges early. That told Hank one thing. Chan had seen what was coming, and he was drawing all the heat down on himself to give the others a chance to get away.

Even as they paddled past the sandbar, heading for deeper water, the gunfire was already dying down. There was no cover out there on the water.

Hank had no illusions that Chan or his boys would allow themselves to be taken alive. The Chinese might not be the savages that jihadis or narcos were, but all the same, no one expected anything from the PLA except torture followed by a bullet to the back of the head.

Better to go down fighting.

Hank knew that was what had been going through Chan's head because that was what they'd talked about on the way in. No one had had any illusions about this mission.

The helicopters were spreading out in widening circles around the blast, searchlights stabbing down out of the darkened sky at the water. The Haitan Strait had just become even more hostile than before.

Machinegun fire roared down from one of the helicopters. They'd spotted another boat. Or, at least, they thought they had. Hank hoped and prayed that they were shooting at shadows, even as his own boys hauled for open water.

He didn't dare start the motor yet, as much as every nerve screamed at him to yank the starter cord and get them out. Stealth was their only hope, and as long as they didn't get pinned by a searchlight, there was still a chance.

He hoped and prayed that the other squads were clear and heading for the open ocean. As badly as it stuck in his craw, he knew that Chan and the others were dead. There was nothing they could do for them.

They paddled for their lives, staying as low to the water as they could, and prayed that they—and any other squads still surviving—went unnoticed.

***

Two hours later, Hank was watching the water, just barely able to see the faint glow of the lights around Pingtan Island in the distance. They had been at the emergency rendezvous for about fifteen minutes, and so far, only his and Lovell's boats had linked up.

He was getting worried. Not only had he gotten no contact from Navarro, Lind, or Corrin, but there was no sign of Zhan and the trawler. If they'd all gotten rolled up…

They were only twenty nautical miles from the coast. They didn't have the fuel to go all the way back to Taiwan and trying to bring the *Jacqueline Q* in this close was going to be risky as hell, even if they could get comms.

Nobody was talking. The weight of the losses they knew they'd taken hung over both boats. Spencer and Lovell confirmed that they'd seen Chan take contact, deliberately detonating the charges early. No one knew how many had still been alive after the blast to keep fighting.

The putter of an outboard motor sounded, and Hank turned his NVGs to look. There. It took a moment, but he spotted the low, dark silhouette of a Zodiac off to the west with men in helmets and NVGs low on the gunwales, weapons outboard.

The boat came alongside, the coxswain throttling back as they got closer, the man in the bow triggering three short flashes on his NVGs' IR illuminator. Hank replied with two. Friendlies.

As they came alongside, Hank recognized Durand and Lee Nakato in the bow. It was Navarro's boat.

He felt a rush of relief, followed a moment later by a sickening feeling of guilt, that Navarro's squad had made it. There was still no sign of any of Chan's section.

Had they all been wiped out?

A light shone on the horizon, and as Hank turned toward it, he could just make out the shape of a ship. It appeared to be coming straight for them.

He tensed, even as the others spotted it. "Everybody stay low and stay quiet." He opened the throttle slightly, starting the boat drifting away from the oncoming ship's line of travel.

Still, the ship came on, growing larger as it came. He hoped they could avoid it in the dark. Most commercial ships' crews wouldn't have night vision.

He just hoped it wasn't an MSS trawler.

Keeping eyes on the ship, he kept the Zodiac moving slowly away until the earpiece in his ear crackled with a familiar voice.

"Tango India Six-Four, this is Tango India Seven-Two." Lind sounded like a man walking through a graveyard. "We are approaching the rendezvous point. Showing IR flash."

A second later, a triple flash of IR light blinked in the oncoming ship's bow. Hank let go of the throttle and reached up to return it with a faint sigh of relief. It was Zhan's trawler.

At least, he hoped so.

As they came closer, the Triarii in the boats still alert and keeping their weapons up without needing him to say anything, he saw a familiar profile at the side, and lines were dropped to the men on the Zodiacs. Hank brought the boat up against the hull and the squad started to climb up to the deck, while he and LaForce got the lines hooked up to haul the boat aboard.

Hank was the last one up the ladder as the lines went taut and the winch started to haul the boat up. He swung his leg over the gunwale and met Lind, still geared up and armed. That, at least, told him that the ship hadn't been taken by the MSS.

They shook hands. "Did any of the rest of the section meet you guys out here?" Lind sounded almost painfully hopeful.

Hank had to shake his head. "Just us."

"Fuck." Lind hung his head. "We were the only boat the trawler picked up."

Hank gripped the other man's shoulder. "We can hold station for a little while, see if they catch up." He wasn't confident, but he didn't want to just write off Corrin's boat, either.

He already knew Chan was gone. He didn't know if Lind knew it, or had accepted it yet, but all the same he wasn't just going to pop smoke and leave while there was any chance that that last squad *might* make it to rendezvous.

Lind nodded. Together, they turned to helping get the boats aboard and stowed.

***

Two hours later, Lind admitted defeat. They didn't have much time left to get away from the mainland, anyway. The sun would be up soon, and from the massive pall of smoke that was still rising, lit from beneath, on the horizon to the north, they'd done enough damage that the PLAN was probably going to be searching the surrounding seas soon.

Besides, if Corrin's squad had made it, they should have caught up by then.

With a heavy feeling of failure, despite the damage they'd done to the Chinese, they headed for Pengjia Islet.

Chapter 19

A lot can happen in thirteen hours. Especially when black on comms.

Hank and his boys had had time to clean weapons and dry out a little bit on the way, hidden deep in the trawler's hold. Some had even been able to sleep. Hank had stayed awake for a while, mainly to keep an eye on Lind and what was left of Mack's squad. They were shell-shocked, every one of them—except for Cantor, but Hank had learned on the voyage out from Texas that Cantor was a little off—had that thousand-yard stare that told him they were all getting much too deep in their own heads.

Still, aside from giving them some kind of busy work to divert their minds—which didn't really exist while they were trying to stay out of sight aboard the trawler—he didn't know what to do. He was no counselor. And he knew he was far too damaged to try to talk any of these guys off the ledge himself, either.

Finally, he had to lie down and catch some rest. They hadn't been on the water all *that* long, but the sheer tension of the raid had left him exhausted.

The dreams weren't fun.

By the time they reached Pingjia, the sun was already nearly at the western horizon, the mainland long out of sight behind them. The *Jacqueline Q* was still there, along with the *Double Up* and two of the yachts turned gunships, the *Connie* and the *No Ragrets*. Hank had often wondered just what kind of memelord idiot had named the latter.

Vetter was already on board the *Jacqueline Q* when they crossed over from the trawler. His face was grim. "Hank, meet me in the COC once you guys get everything aboard."

Feeling a creeping sense of dread, as if losing Chan and two of his section's squads in a single night wasn't enough, Hank hurried to get the Zodiacs back aboard their ship, then hustled into the ops compartment, where Vetter was standing with his arms folded, his brow creased.

"What's going on?" He suddenly wondered, just for a moment, if he was about to get bitched out for losing Chan. He started thinking a mile a minute for how he might have gotten the other man and his boys out, past the helicopters and the gunships. Gunships that had been engaging a combat rubber raiding craft with a 30mm cannon.

Despite the look on his face, Vetter didn't seem to want to get to the bad news first. "From what our drones have been able to pick up, it looks like you boys did some good work last night. We counted at least seven ships sunk at the pier, several support structures on fire, and the causeway out to the island collapsed. It won't stop the invasion cold, but it's going to be harder for them to get the mass they need across the Strait."

He glanced over Hank's shoulder. "I can't help but notice that Chan isn't aboard."

Hank let out a long, shuddering breath. He suddenly felt older and far more tired than he ever had. "Chan didn't make it. They got caught setting the charges on the causeway, set them off early, and died fighting." At least, he hoped they had. The alternative didn't bear thinking about. "We didn't see what happened to Corrin's squad."

Vetter nodded and bowed his head. "Damn. I was afraid of that." He looked down at the map table. "It was always a risk, sending you guys that deep into the lion's den. I had nightmares about you boys just disappearing. Frankly, I have a feeling that when Option Zulu gets called in, we're going to see a lot of us just vanish into enemy territory."

Hank gave him a sharp look. "Option Zulu?" That was the absolute last-ditch plan, more of a wild contingency thought up on a dark night when things had looked particularly grim. It meant essentially saying, "Fuck it," and going after a target state or nation's entire infrastructure, effectively turning them into a Stone-Age hellhole where no bridge, railway, power station, dam, or telecommunications center went untouched. It was a doomsday solution for an organization without nuclear weapons. Bonifacio had brought it up when they'd talked in Taipei, but it was something that was often mentioned without anyone necessarily expecting it to go all the way to execution. Something about the way Vetter had said that, though… "Is that next?"

Vetter eyed him coolly. "Hank, it's been on the table since the cyber attack. Or do you think that Santiago didn't know who was most likely behind it and planning for the last year how to give them a taste of their own medicine?" He leaned against the table, both hands flat on the map. "It wasn't just speculation. And there's a reason we haven't kept the plans entirely secret, either. It was *our* deterrent. And I think the big part of the reason why the Feds haven't decided to alter the deal from a year ago—given some of what you and I saw back home—is because there are enough people up top who *know* that we've got that plan on file, and that we *will* use it if necessary.

"But no, it hasn't been called in yet, and we've got more immediate things to worry about."

He reached for a folder, but Hank wasn't done yet. "What *would* trigger Option Zulu?" He had to admit that he'd never thought it was a real plan. It had always sounded a little too…ambitious. Not that he'd thought it was impossible. It was the kind of thing that many an infantryman had mulled over: how small teams of trained, determined men could bring a country to its knees. No, he'd just never figured that it was the kind of thing that would ever *actually* be implemented. It was probably because of too many years of indecisive, risk-averse leadership that would *never* have approved even putting such a plan on paper.

Vetter looked him in the eye. "Nukes. Another hit like they pulled last year. Mass murders and mass graves. Hell, at this point, I kinda expect that if things are going badly enough overall, it conceivably *could* get called in if only to make it clear that fucking with the Triarii and the people we protect is a losing plan."

That was sobering. But it made sense. Hank had been of the growing opinion, over the last several years, that many of the problems of the modern world had metastasized to the point they had because those responsible for drawing the line and bringing utter hell down on anyone who crossed it had refused to do so.

The old rules were making themselves felt again. The fact that so many in his own country still refused to acknowledge that didn't take away from the reality of it. It only made them that much more of a danger to their own people.

In some ways, it was encouraging, knowing that Colonel Santiago took these things seriously, even if he was doing it through what amounted to a paramilitary NGO.

Vetter was moving on, though. He pulled the file over and opened it, revealing several overhead photos. They looked like drone shots, taken at a relatively low angle. And as Hank tilted his head to see them more clearly, he was pretty sure they were a lot deeper into China than he would have expected drones to go. "Isn't that Three Gorges Dam?"

"It is. Or, rather, it was." Vetter was pulling more photos out. "We've been keeping an eye on it, especially since any satellite views have been, shall we say, disrupted." He didn't quite put the new photos down yet. "We're not sure if it's just ASAT attacks, some kind of cyber attack, or what. There are zero readily available satellite overheads of Three Gorges for the last three months." He finally put the new photo down next to the first one. "That one was yesterday. This is today."

Hank let out a low whistle. It wasn't hard to see what had happened.

In the first, the gray, artificial cliff of Three Gorges Dam stood proudly across the Yangtze River, just as it had since 2006. There might have been a little bit more water coming out of the spillway than he remembered from past images.

In the second, a chunk of the dam a quarter mile long was just gone.

"We've always known it could happen. There was so much graft, so much corruption involved in the construction—that we *knew* of—that there was no way it was going to be sound, not indefinitely." Vetter rubbed his square jaw. "I'm frankly astounded it lasted this long. It almost broke in 2020."

"I remember hearing about that." Hank reached out and started checking the other drone overheads. "That probably did some serious damage all by itself. Weakened it." He shook his head as he looked over more of the photos.

It was bad. A massive wall of water had swept down the Yangtze gorge. It didn't look like there was much of anything left of the cities of Yichang, Jingzhou, or Yueyang. Wuhan and Changsha had also been hit, though it looked like the water had spread out enough by then that they hadn't faced nearly the devastation that the higher cities had.

There had to be millions dead. He looked up. "Did they have any warning?"

Vetter shrugged. "Given the PLA units they had up there, they had to have known *something* was coming. Whether they were really ready for how bad it was?" He shook his head. "From what little we're seeing, I doubt it. The CCP was apparently still insisting that the dam had nothing wrong with it, right up until it broke."

He gusted a sigh. "This changes the whole equation. They're already blaming 'separatist' saboteurs for this." He glared down at the map. "They're going to try to take this out on the Taiwanese, and soon, before the shock wears off and the real misery sinks in.

"I don't think we've got a hell of a lot of time left."

Chapter 20

They had less time than they'd thought.

The *Jacqueline Q* was just off Keelung City when the first missiles came in.

A series of flashes and billowing clouds of dust, smoke and debris rippled across the hills. Even from out at sea, Hank could see an apartment building take a hit, the corner of the high-rise collapsing in a cloud of dust and shattered concrete, glass, and steel.

"Well, here we go." Hank stayed where he was in the bow, watching as destruction rained down on Keelung. Most of it was probably supposed to hit the port, but given the general accuracy of Chinese weapons, and the callous disregard for human life that characterized the Chinese Communist Party, the widespread bombardment wasn't exactly a surprise. Add in their scapegoating the Taiwanese for Three Gorges, and this was going to get *ugly*.

Just like every other part of this war he'd seen so far. Only worse.

"We knew it was coming." Spencer stood next to him, along with Lind. With Tango India Seven Two down to one squad—and a seven-man squad, at that—they'd just folded them in with Hank's section. They hadn't even consulted Vetter about it. No point. Lind wasn't going to accomplish much with only seven dudes. If they'd been a Grex Luporum team, that might be one thing, but the infantry sections trained and geared up a bit differently.

Hank suspected, given some of what they'd done over the last year and a half, that there really wasn't as much difference between the SOF vets of the Grex Luporum Teams and the regular infantry guys anymore. It had been that kind of war. Hell, one of the GL dudes they'd worked with in the Southwest, Dale Chang, had said as much. That there was less and less of a division between "conventional" infantry and special operators. In fact, Chang had quietly suggested that that division needed to just go away, given the nature of modern war.

Maybe he was right. Hank didn't feel like this was quite the time to be mixing up how he worked, though.

"What are we going to do now?" Lind wasn't asking out of despair. He watched the warheads fall with blank, dispassionate eyes, his voice even and flat.

Hank was a little worried about Lind. The man seemed to have essentially shut down his emotions entirely after the loss of Chan and the other two squads. Hank had been around long enough that he knew there was a storm brewing behind that blank, dead stare, and he didn't want any of his boys in the crossfire when it finally broke.

Not that he expected Lind to go nuts, but that kind of shutdown rarely boded well. He just hoped that the man kept it together in combat, because they really didn't have the time or the room for counseling right then.

There'd been a time when men had to face death on a daily basis from the day they first really became aware of their surroundings until the day the Reaper finally caught up with them. Modern society had effectively insulated so many in the West from that reality that events like a couple nights back were more traumatizing to modern man than they might have been to their ancestors.

Still, he hoped that Lind had seen enough that he was just compartmentalizing. It was a slim hope. Even seeing as much death as he had, he wasn't sure how *he*'d react to having two out of three of his squads wiped out.

"I suspect I won't have to tell Smythe to hold off heading in." Hank turned toward the stern and the pilot house. "He's not going to want to go wading into that. Maybe once the bombardment eases up. I do need to get in touch with Vetter." That was probably a long shot. As carefully as the Triarii frequencies had been picked out, the electronic warfare over the Taiwan Strait was going to be ferocious in the days ahead.

Fortunately, they'd discussed their contingency plans beforehand, so as much as he wanted to touch base, he didn't *need* to talk to Vetter. Their next move had already been planned.

As he hustled down the length of the ship, he could still hear the missiles falling. The steady rumble of thunder only increased the intensity of the sick feeling of dread in his gut.

It was happening. With the US and the Japanese moving more of their limited forces into the Korean peninsula, the CCP had decided it was time to take care of Taiwan.

It felt awfully lonely out there on the ocean, knowing what was coming and how little they had to face it with.

***

The plan had been for all Triarii units that were not currently on the island to pull off into international waters as soon as the strikes began. It felt shitty, kind of like running away, but as Vetter had pointed out in planning, getting pasted by a Chinese ballistic missile without a chance to fight back wasn't going to do anyone any good. The Taiwanese had an extensive missile defense system—which Hank could see was better spooled up than he'd thought at first—but out on the periphery of that bubble, things got hairier.

The missile bombardment would end eventually. The Chinese were unlikely to attempt an amphibious landing while still dropping ballistic missiles all over the island. For one thing, it was going to make close air support next to impossible outside of very narrow corridors, which could then easily be turned into killing fields by Taiwanese air defenses.

So, all they could do was hunker down if they were on the island or set out to sea if they were on ship, and wait. Hank was all about more raids on the mainland, but if the assault force was already moving, they'd only be of limited use.

Not *no* use, but limited. They could conceivably blunt any reinforcement or resupply, but that first assault was going to hit the island, unless the ROC Navy and the arsenal ships and torpedo boats could put some *serious* hurt on the forces crossing the Strait.

Once the landings had started, and the missile fire had lifted or diminished, they could move in and provide support to the defenders. Until then, they could only wait and watch.

It was dark again. Hank had been keeping an eye on the situation reports coming into the COC, but he needed some air, and he needed to look at the situation with his own eyes. He knew that from this far out at sea, there was only so much he was going to be *able* to see, but he had to try.

Keelung City was still lit up. The *Jacqueline Q* was too far away to tell how much of the illumination was from electric lights and how much was fires from the bombardment.

Even as he watched, streaks of flame rose from the mountains above Keelung, and several sparks ignited into fireballs in the darkened sky above the city. Fire and debris rained down, doubtless to do some damage, but not nearly as much as the warheads themselves would have done.

The anti-missile interceptors didn't get everything, though. It had long been suspected that the Chinese would attempt to overwhelm their adversaries with sheer numbers of missiles, and it looked like that was what they were doing. For every warhead intercepted, at least one more got through. Sometimes two.

He finally turned and headed back inside, no longer able to stomach it. It was bad enough watching the situation reports update the map from out at sea. To watch it happening, unable to lift a finger to stop it…

He swore and spat off the side as he headed back to the COC.

∗∗∗

Hank couldn't see everything that was going on, but the picture was becoming much clearer in the COC than it had out on the bow.

The Taiwanese weren't just sitting there and taking it. As soon as the bombardment had begun, return fire in the form of HF-2E and Yon Feng cruise missiles were winging their way toward the mainland, climbing into the sky on pillars of fire to return the PLA's gifts with interest.

The Communists weren't without their own defenses, and they'd anticipated some return fire. As the HF-2Es descended, HQ-9 SAMs rose to meet them, and almost half the strike was blotted out of the sky.

Unfortunately, the ROC missile forces didn't have quite the numbers that the PLA did. They had just enough, though. And the Russian-based tech of even the HQ-9s weren't quite up to hitting the Yon Fengs.

Several known military installations across Fujian province were hit. Even as smoke and fire rose above those targets, several flights of missiles continued their journey across Central China, skimming the ground, heading for Wuhan and Beijing.

Without satellite reconnaissance, it was hard to determine exactly if those missiles hit their targets. Judging by what happened over the next twenty-four hours, however, the Triarii intel types thought that there was a pretty good possibility that at least one had struck the Eastern Theater Command headquarters.

The missile bombardment lasted most of the night. Just before dawn, the rain of ballistic missiles ceased.

While there had been some strikes on civilian targets—that had been almost inevitable, given the sheer quantity of missiles launched—the majority of the Chinese targets had been Taiwanese military installations. Fortunately for the Taiwanese, most of those had been hardened for a long time. Quite a bit of destruction was still wreaked, but when the missiles stopped falling, the underground hangars opened, even as bulldozers and

173

other heavy equipment came out of cover to clear away the debris on the runways and fill in any craters.

There hadn't been a lot of cratering. The PLA wanted the airstrips intact, so that they could bring in troops by air. In a matter of less than thirty minutes, the first flights of ROC Air Force FC-K-1 Chung Kuo fighters were airborne. Their pilots had ridden out the bombardment in their cockpits, sitting inside the underground hangars.

They found no opposition at first. It was weird, but they maintained their patrols, as more Chung Kuos and F-16s joined them. Until the missile bombardment recommenced, or the inevitable waves of J-10s, J-11s, J-16s, JH-7s, and H-6s started across the strait, they would stay in the air, landing only to refuel and rearm if necessary.

For over an hour, the expected air attack didn't materialize. Finally, just as the ROC Air Force Combatant Command was about to lower the alert level, the first birds appeared on those early warning radars that had survived the bombardment. The jamming was intense, but they still managed to pick out enough to know that the enemy was coming.

Hank and his section had nothing to do with that. They'd already found their target. A small craft dropped off by a Chinese flag freighter was headed in toward the island's east coast, and if Hank had it figured right, it was carrying PLAN *Jiaolong* commandos. Their probable target: Chiashan Airbase.

He wanted to be on shore before them, with a welcoming committee.

Chapter 21

The S70 from the *Bell Challenger* skimmed the waves as it carried Hank and Xu, along with Lovell's and LaForce's squads, toward the Taiwanese coast. Intercepting that boat moving toward the mouth of the Shanzhan River on the surface was going to be next to impossible. The angles had meant it would be a stern chase as the sun was going down, which made things even worse than just the distances. The Chinese would be ashore and into the weeds before the Triarii could catch up with them.

They'd called ahead to the ROC Army, with the understanding that they were going to move to intercept anyway. The bulk of the Army was on alert, and the reserves were poised to reply to any impending PLA landings. They had security forces on the bases on alert, but the Triarii got this one. The Taiwanese weren't going to look a gift horse in the mouth.

With a roar, the bird raced over the fields that covered the narrow strip of flat land between the mountains and the shore, flaring as it came in toward the landing zone. Xu was already on the radio with the Taiwanese police who were their contacts on the ground, coordinating with the pilot over the intercom to spot the IR strobe on the field below. Between the vegetation and the high-tension power lines, there were precious few viable HLZs on the east coast of Taiwan, aside from Hualien Airport or Chiashan Airbase itself.

They could have landed at either Hualien or the airbase, but the boat was heading here, toward the Shanzhan River. Hank suspected that their plan was to get ashore and disappear into the forests and the mountains, so they could strike from an unexpected direction, probably at an unexpected time. Hank wanted to head them off before they could potentially disappear into the bush.

The Taiwanese—and their Triarii allies—were about to have their hands full as it was.

The pilot settled the S70 to the dirt, the rotor wash kicking up a surprisingly small cloud of debris. It was getting toward the end of the monsoons, but the ground was still muddy enough that there wasn't any dust *to* get kicked up.

The figure of a man stood at the end of the field, holding an IR strobe over his head. It was a method. Not the terminal guidance technique Hank would have chosen in the man's place, but it had worked. As the helo settled and the rotors slowed, the side doors slid open, and Hank was the first one out.

Even as he hit the dirt, the other reason for landing at an HLZ against the mountains instead of the airbase roared overhead.

Three H-6s wove their way through the sky over the mountains, while their escort of J-10s tried desperately to fend off the flight of F-16s that was hounding the bombers. Even as Hank looked up past the spinning rotors, he saw one of the Chinese copies of the Tupolev Tu-16 take a missile strike to the wing, folding it over the fuselage as the remains of one engine caught fire. Trailing flame and black smoke, the bomber turned over and began to plunge toward the coast.

The F-16 pilot who'd shot the bomber down paid for it with his aircraft, at least. Two J-10s got behind him and blotted his aircraft out of the sky with four missiles. Hank couldn't see a chute, though that didn't mean it wasn't there. He couldn't stay there, gawking at the sky, anyway.

The other two H-6s survived long enough to drop their bombs on Chiashan Airbase before diving for the ocean, still pursued by those F-16s that weren't occupied with fighting off the J-10s. The Taiwanese pilots knew that the fewer aircraft that made it back to the mainland, the fewer they'd have to deal with in coming days or weeks as the invasion went forward. It was believed that the PLAAF had around 180 of those bombers, but every one that didn't make it back was one less that could return to rain destruction on Taiwan.

Hank tore his eyes away from the life-and-death drama in the skies as the day's light died. He had his own responsibility. The war was too big for any one man to watch it all.

Both squads were off the bird, down on a knee in the muddy field, too many of them watching the dogfight. The rotor was still turning but the bird wasn't taking off yet. The threat of the fight overhead was a little too high. They could afford to hang out on the ground a little bit, rather than run the risk of catching an errant PL-11.

Grabbing Xu, Hank headed forward, toward where the man with the strobe was waiting for them. Dressed entirely in black, the Taiwanese cop was carrying an M4 at the low ready, having already stuffed the strobe back into his chest rig, on top of a rather overlarge armored vest. He spoke quickly to Xu, who replied in rapid-fire Mandarin, and then waved to them to follow.

Hank pointed to Lovell, who nodded and got 1st Squad moving, following the Taiwanese policeman toward the southwest and the river. They immediately got on the road to cover ground more quickly. Hank followed, though he hung back a little to hear the update from Xu.

"He says that they have not made landfall yet, but they are closing in. They seem to think they are still undetected, and they *are* very hard to see from shore in the twilight. He suspects that they will hold off on landing until after dark." Xu spoke quickly as they paced after the Taiwanese cop between 1st and 2nd Squads.

Hank glanced toward the shore. "Still a lot of lights down there."

Xu nodded. "They have increased security around the local power station, but they expect that there are already saboteurs on the ground who are tasked with taking it out. Since they failed to hit it with air or missile strikes."

"I wonder if that was part of the plan, or if the saboteurs are just a contingency." Hank knew that until one showed up, they had no proof that any such saboteurs were actually on the ground, but it was a good bet. The Taiwanese had been awfully good at counter-espionage operations over the years, but they could never have gotten *everybody* the Chinese would have tried to put in place.

Xu shrugged. There was no way to know. They had to focus on their own targets.

Two trucks were waiting next to the road just on the other side of the line of shrubs along the edge of the field. The Taiwanese cop pointed to them with a quick sentence in Mandarin. The Triarii didn't need a translation. They clambered aboard the trucks as Hank and Xu headed for the cab of the lead vehicle.

It was a tight fit, since they had to get three men, all in gear and carrying weapons, into the cab. But it was done quickly, and without much preamble, the Taiwanese cop behind the wheel put the truck in gear and started them moving.

Xu, sitting in the middle, spoke quietly to the driver, who seemed to be of some rank, if not the man in charge. Turning to Hank, he elaborated. "There are several units of police in Xincheng, on both sides of the river, but we are going to be the main effort. The river is high, and if they are moving fast enough, they can get upriver. We suspect that they will try to get under the bridge and into the gorge, past Xiulin. From there…"

"From there they can work their way into the jungle and go after the airbase from the mountainside." Hank nodded. "*If* they manage to get past us."

"The police are not showing lights and have kept a low profile. Inspector Sun wants a clean sweep, and while they are not military as such, they have all had reserve training." Xu sounded slightly defensive. "They know that our best chance to stop them is an ambush."

Hank just nodded and let it go. He hadn't intended the remark to be an aspersion on the Taiwanese cops, but sometimes the language barrier isn't just limited to words and grammar.

It took less than five minutes to get to their staging point, right at the end of the bridge over the Shanzhan River. Hank and Xu piled out as the rest of the two squads joined them. It was dark by then, while most of the houses and buildings in Xincheng Township still had their lights on, somewhat to Hank's surprise and concern. They *were* going to be targets. He would have blacked out the entire island.

Still, he wasn't calling the shots when it came to the big picture. He could only control what he could control. "Amos, set in on this end. Get to where you have eyes on the river." There was a low, concrete guardrail along the side of the bridge, and the banks of the river were thickly carpeted in vegetation. This was going to be tough. "I'll head over to the far side with Etienne. Make sure you've got an element down in the weeds in case we have any squirters."

Lovell gave him a thumbs up, and Hank and LaForce started across the bridge at a run. A look over his shoulder, down the river, showed him only darkness out to sea. The *Jiaolong*—presuming that was who the ChiComs had sent—were still out of sight, either slowing in the hopes that they could move inland unnoticed as the exhausted residents went to sleep, or else waiting for the lights to go out.

Just before the last light pole on the bridge, LaForce slowed, grabbed Bishop, and told him, "Take Evans and Reisinger and get down alongside the bridge to take any squirters."

Bishop looked at the dark mass of vegetation down there. "That's a lot of jungle for three dudes."

Xu pointed to the dark SUV parked at the end of the bridge. "The police will back you up. I just suggest that you try not to lose sight of them. They do not have night vision, and they might make a mistake in the dark."

Bishop gave Hank a look, despite the fact that his eyes were hidden behind his NVGs. "That's comforting." Without any further comment, he turned and jogged toward the police SUV.

At almost that very moment, all the lights in Xincheng went out.

Hank turned to Xu, who was already on his radio. Even in the dark, Hank could see the faint sag of relief when the response came back. "They just caught two men trying to penetrate the power station. Inspector Sun ordered the power shut off anyway, just to fool the enemy."

"Good idea." The roar of more aircraft passing overhead was punctuated by a flash and a *boom* as another plane died, flaming debris tumbling toward the mountains above. The airstrikes hadn't ended yet. Hank wondered if the landing force was already on the way. It was probable. There was too much water to cross for the ChiComs to still be sitting back on the mainland, waiting.

The rest of the squad, minus Bishop, Evans, and Reisinger, got down behind the concrete guardrail, spreading out for the best view of the river. Hank took a knee beside Xu and LaForce, closest to the center of the bridge, laid his rifle over the guardrail, and waited.

Except for the distant rumble and thunder of jet engines, bombs, and missiles, and the even fainter wail of air raid sirens to the south, in Hualien City, it got quiet. Birds, insects, and nocturnal animals made their usual noise in the vegetation down by the river beneath them, but almost all traffic on the roads on the island had halted due to the air threat. Hank remembered the drill he'd witnessed in Taipei. These weren't the Middle Easterners he'd gotten used to in the Corps, with that "Inshallah" mindset that kept them moving around and going about their business while all hell broke loose a block over. This was a disciplined people who had been living under an existential threat for decades.

As he waited, he started to wish that he hadn't quite disdained kneepads as much as he had over the years. He'd known a handful of infantrymen who used them, but he'd always found them more of an annoyance than anything else. They tended to slide down and end up around his ankle. He'd stopped wearing them when he'd been a Lance Corporal.

Now, though, as he knelt on the damp asphalt, he was feeling every one of his years, every mile he'd rucked, and every rock he'd ever knelt on for the last twenty-seven years.

It's easy to be hard, it's hard to be smart.

He was about to shift to the other knee, trying to do it quietly and nonchalantly so that Xu, at least, didn't take notice, when he spotted movement below on the river.

Trying to use the magnified optic with NVGs was a non-starter, but as another plane died somewhere in the air overhead, the fireball lighting up the coastline, it was as good as a flare in his NVGs.

The boat wasn't the rubber inflatable he'd expected. In fact, it looked more like a regular motor launch, painted black or else some dark camouflage that looked black at that distance. The men in it were all crouched along the gunwales, their QBZ-191s trained outboard, scanning the banks of the river.

They were alert, but they must have thought that their saboteurs had done their job. Which had been exactly what Inspector Sun had intended.

Hank canted his weapon and put his red dot on the coxswain, or at least as close as he could get. The dot completely obscured the coxswain and part of the boat's stern. The enemy was still a good distance off, farther than he was comfortable taking a shot under these lighting conditions. He flipped the M5 to "fire" and waited, his finger hovering near the trigger, as the boat chugged closer.

He would open the ball. The rest of the section would open fire on his shot. He could afford to wait until they were well within range to make sure they got all of them in one fusillade.

Unfortunately, the Taiwanese cops hadn't gotten the memo.

A burst of 5.56 fire lanced out from the bridge on the far side, kicking up spray from the swollen river as rounds punched into the water around the boat. A few of them probably even hit, but if Hank was gauging things right, the boat was still a good five hundred yards off, and even if the Taiwanese NPA officers had

NVGs, the odds that they could actually shoot accurately at five hundred yards in the dark were slim to none.

And Slim had left town.

The Chinese commandos immediately returned fire, only the faintest flickers registering in Hank's NVGs as the suppressed gunshots snapped across the river at the NPA muzzle flashes. Some heavier *crack*s sounded, probably suppressed 7.62 shots from Lovell's squad, because they weren't just going to sit there after the NPA had opened the ball.

The coxswain had reacted quickly, hauling the tiller over and turning away from the gunfire, driving the boat into the south bank, as the rest stitched rounds across the bridge. Hank had to duck as several of those 5.8mm bullets smacked off the light pole above him.

Then the Chinese were in the weeds and running, and Hank and the rest of 2nd Squad were moving to try to cut them off before they disappeared into the bush, only to show up at Chiashan Airbase later.

Chapter 22

Xu was on the radio as they ran, practically screaming at the NPA to get units spread out along the highway and down Hai'an Road to cut the commandos off. The roads presented their only advantage at the moment. They could move much more quickly, even on foot, and that NPA SUV at the end of the bridge immediately started up, even as several of the Taiwanese police piled out of the veg at the edge of the road and jumped in, the driver almost immediately pulling a J-turn, the tires squealing as he threw it in gear and went screaming off toward Hai'an Road.

Two more went by, moving fast, lights flashing and sirens wailing, to stake out the highway in case the commandos attempted a crossing.

Hank wasn't sure how much good they were going to do without thermals and belt fed machineguns, but they could hopefully at least slow the bad guys down for the real infantrymen to close in.

Xu was still on the radio. "Tell them to spread out along Hai'an Road and set up blocking positions." Xu might be the liaison officer and a former military man himself, but Hank had been doing this for a *long* time, and his boys hadn't screwed up the ambush by getting buck fever. "We'll get on line and sweep the woods. They just need to keep eyes on the road." He stopped. "And the river. Get some guns and eyes on that boat." He did *not* want those bastards slipping away in the confusion, or worse, heading on up the river while everyone was down by the seashore looking for them.

Lovell's squad had arrived at a run, barely catching up as 2nd Squad kept going past the walled property just off the bridge and onto Hai'an Road. Hank thought, as his boots pounded the pavement and he sucked in the humid air, that they should have hopped a ride with the NPA, or had the trucks carry them.

Just past the walled compound, they cut between houses, spreading out across the strip of jungle between the road and the river, and with only about five yards between each man—less in places—they began their sweep.

It was a nightmare from the first step. Night vision goggles or no, it was pitch black in places under the trees, even as more fire and explosions lit up the sky above the mountains behind them. Even without the darkness, visibility was immediately cut to a matter of yards or mere feet.

Footing sucked. Vines and branches grabbed heads, limbs, gear, and weapons. They had to find a way to "swim" through the vegetation, or else they'd get hung up.

They also had to move carefully to avoid making so much noise that they couldn't hear the enemy. He didn't want to just stumble on the bad guys in the dark. Better to see and hear them first.

It was a slow sweep, and the tension was as thick as the humidity as Hank moved through the vegetation, his rifle up, scanning through his NVGs as much as he could. He was drenched in sweat, though he was starting to think that he'd been in the Western Pacific long enough by now that he was getting used to it.

He stopped, straining his ears, listening. The rustle and snap of men moving to either side continued, but he still thought he could hear something just up ahead.

The years of gunfire, explosions, helicopters, and other damage to his hearing were taking their toll. He couldn't be sure, either of the sounds themselves or how far away or what direction they were coming from.

No movement showed in front of him. If they were up there, he couldn't see them yet, even if he could hear them, and shooting blindly at noises was a recipe for disaster. So, he stalked forward carefully, taking a step before scanning, his muzzle following his eyes, then taking another step.

They'd done just enough jungle fighting down in the Philippines and the South China Sea that he trusted the rest of his section to know what to do. None of them should be shooting at shadows, and they were all going to be keeping mostly the same pace. He could just make out Xu to one side of him, and Faris to the other. If anyone spotted any of the enemy soldiers, the signal would be passed quickly and soundlessly. Even Xu, relative outsider that he was, was schooled in the hand and arm signals the Triarii used. The Taiwanese had mostly been trained by Americans, anyway, so there hadn't been too much difference to get ironed out.

A shot *crack*ed off to the right. It sounded like a suppressed 7.62, which meant it was one of his guys. A moment later, with a hissing crackle, a torrent of bullets tore through the trees and bushes, and the Triarii hit the dirt.

More gunfire roared from up by the road, and Hank was glad that they hadn't advanced that deeply into the woods yet. They would have been within the Taiwanese cops' line of fire if they had.

The Chinese commandos returned fire wildly, as the Triarii crawled forward, continuing their advance under cover of the NPA officers' fire.

Movement rustled just in front of Hank. He'd paused under a tree, coming up to a knee to get a better view of the jungle around him, in a position where he didn't have to crane his neck so much to see. He pivoted slightly, bringing his rifle to bear, just as a man burst out of the vegetation in a high-cut helmet and plate carrier, and carrying a QBZ-191. The commando was still turned halfway to his left, looking up toward the Taiwanese cops.

It had worked out better than Hank had feared. While the NPA officers might have just started spraying somewhat indiscriminately into the bush, they'd had the effect of driving the prey to the hunters.

Hank shot the man in the face from less than ten feet away, his trigger breaking just as the *Jiaolong* commando sensed there was someone ahead of him and turned to look. The enemy soldier hadn't even had his weapon on line, forgetting that where eyes go, muzzles need to go, too. His head snapped back and he went over backward, his back bending like a U as he fell.

More suppressed gunshots barked to his right and left. A wild burst of suppressed 5.8mm fire responded immediately to his left, and Hank pivoted again, searching for the blast.

There. Fronds flapped and waved, barely visible in the dark and past another tree. He moved forward, stepping over the body of the man he'd killed, and spotted the low, slightly lighter shape of the commando leaning around a palm tree. He put his red dot on the man's side and double-tapped him, the bullets tearing through ribs and one arm, punching deep into the man's chest and throwing him to the ground, his last scream quickly dying to a hoarse rattle as his final breath hissed out of his destroyed lungs.

Xu was already on the radio, calling for the Taiwanese cops to cease fire. They'd driven the ChiComs into fleeing, but they were getting close enough that they had to either shift fire or cease altogether, or else risk hitting the Triarii. Slowly, raggedly, the 5.56 fire from up on the road died away.

Several more bursts of 5.8mm fire ripped through the trees, quickly answered by single and paired shots of suppressed 7.62.

Hank held his position for a few moments, trying to figure out the lay of the land and the relative positions of Triarii, NPA, and PLA. It was starting to look like they'd forced the bad guys somewhat back toward the river and east toward the ocean. Those who were still alive were trying to break contact.

As dangerous as it was in that close forest, they had to pursue. Making sure that he still had eye contact with Xu and Faris, he signaled a slow arc toward the sea and the river. They'd have to continue their sweep.

They couldn't do it quite as slowly and quietly, or they ran the risk of letting the survivors get back to the boat. So, he stepped it out, moving from tree to tree, taking just enough time to find the slight gaps in the undergrowth that he could get through without slamming into a wall of brush, weapon up and always looking for the enemy.

He and Xu came out into a small opening at almost the same time, only to see the undergrowth moving where someone had pushed through only moments before. Hank halted for a moment, listening. The gunfire had died down to practically nothing, but he could hear movement through the bush, bodies crashing through the vegetation. A voice was raised nearby, calling out in Mandarin. The survivors were making a run for it.

Run after them, or adopt a more careful pursuit, and call in more support from the bridge? He'd barely thought the question when more gunfire *crack*ed through the night, answered with somewhat quieter suppressed 5.8mm gunshots from a lot closer.

The Taiwanese cops on the bridge had seen the ChiComs come out of the jungle and opened fire. The commandos were returning fire, but they were probably pinned in place, at least for a moment. It was time to close in.

"On me!" There wasn't much point in trying to stay quiet anymore. Keeping his weapon up, he plunged into the bush.

He could barely hear the others to either side of him over the racket he was making. The gunfire ahead continued, and he slowed as it got louder. He didn't want to trip right into the middle of the firefight.

A shot *snap*ped off to his left, and then the commandos were right in front of him.

There was no time to pick targets. He just snapped his rifle up and opened fire.

For a brief few seconds, the two squads dumped a "mad minute" into the boat and the figures crouched behind it, already trading fire with the Taiwanese cops up on the bridge. Dragging muzzles across the huddled forms of the Chinese commandos, they emptied their magazines with a harsh, rolling thunder, until bolts locked back on empty mags.

Hank found he was breathing hard, staring at the cooling pile of meat that had been four men trying to take cover behind the outboard. Almost without thinking about it, he stripped out his empty magazine, dragged a fresh one out of his chest rig, slammed it home, and dropped the bolt.

"Consolidate." He looked over at Xu. "Might want to have those guys up on the road sweep toward the river, make sure we didn't miss any squirters." It was unlikely at that point that any survivors could do anything against Chiashan, but they could probably still do *some* damage.

"They are already moving."

Hank nodded. He wasn't thrilled with some of the cops' fire discipline, but they were still professionals, to some degree.

He looked up at the hills, listening to the distant rumble of heavy ordnance. *It's starting.*

Chapter 23

It was indeed starting, but not quite the way Hank thought.

The air war had begun, with Chinese H-6 bombers and JH-7 strike fighters crossing the Taiwan Strait to hit their assigned targets up and down the island, escorted by Su-30s, J-10s, and J-11s. Strangely, the vaunted J-20s had not yet made an appearance.

Facing them, the ROC Air Force was prepared and dug in. They'd lost a few planes on the ground, but the hardened shelters and underground hangars had done their job. Furthermore, while the initial missile strikes had done their share of damage, including knocking out one battery of Tien Kung "Sky Bow" air defense missiles, the Patriot systems and the surviving Tien Kung missiles were taking their toll.

What was even stranger than the delay in the first airstrikes was the fact that, as far as Triarii and ROC Navy drones could tell, the amphibious landing hadn't started yet. The ships were still in port, from Pingtan Island to Shantou.

Vetter decided to take full advantage, running arsenal ships in close to the mainland to north and south, avoiding the Strait itself. No civilian ships that didn't have vital strategic business were venturing into that channel at the moment, and to do so would be to paint a bullseye on their backs. So, they edged in toward Pingtan Island, Shantou, Zhangpu, and Chihu, staying slow and non-threatening, until they opened their launch cells and sent their drone swarms out.

The drones were the same models that had nearly eviscerated the *Shandong*. They were followed by more multiple-launch rocket systems rippling their "dumb" rockets toward the ports from the outer edge of their range.

The Chinese response was immediate. Anti-ship cruise missiles and coastal defense J-7s arrowed out toward the arsenal ships, even as explosions rippled across the Chinese ships that were waiting to cross the Strait.

Two of the converted bulk carriers were struck by three YJ-18 anti-ship cruise missiles apiece. One took a hit amidships and sank almost immediately, her back broken as her remaining stores of munitions detonated. The other struggled to limp away, massive holes blasted in her hull, her decks afire. She'd make it only a few nautical miles before the captain made the call to abandon ship, two more converted fishing vessels moving in to rescue the surviving crew.

Two of the arsenal ships off Pingtan Island survived the initial missile barrage, only to have a flight of four J-7s—the Chinese version of the MiG-21—drop bombs on them. All eight bombs missed, but two of the J-7s were blotted out of the sky by 30mm fire.

It didn't take long for the PLAN to start broadcasting over just about every available commercial radio channel that there was now a maritime exclusion zone extending for a hundred nautical miles around Taiwan. Any and every ship that was not Chinese would be warned off, and then fired upon if they violated the exclusion zone.

The ROC Navy had so far been hanging back, except for their minelayers. Those ships were working overtime, preparing the seas for the PLAN, while the destroyers, frigates, corvettes, and fast-attack missile boats popped out from behind the island to harass the PLAN where they could before retreating to safer waters.

So far, the US Navy's Carrier Strike Group, centered on the USS *Carl Vinson*, was holding its position off the Senkakus, still declining to intervene. That was a matter of some concern, and Vetter was trying to get in touch with some of his contacts to find out just what was going on. Everyone had expected that the Navy would get involved once strikes on the island of Taiwan itself had begun, and that assumption had worked its way into some of the strategic planning for the defense. Vetter had good intelligence that at least two Virginia-class subs were blockading Hainan Island, but so far, the *Carl Vinson* was staying put.

The news of a new North Korean offensive, including missile strikes on Tokyo and Seoul, and a new salient that had nearly taken Pocheon, might explain some of it. The DPRK was throwing in all the marbles and going for it. And it was drawing all eyes, especially since the Norks had "tested" a nuke just north of the DMZ only a few days before.

The odds were poor that the Norks could manage to maintain an offensive for long without direct support from the PLA, but if it kept the limited American and Japanese resources focused on the Korean peninsula for long enough…

The ROC Navy began to clash with the PLAN north and south of the island. They were still playing it cagey, conducting hit-and-run attacks on PLAN destroyers and frigates. A lot more ordnance was expended than actually hit, but three PLAN destroyers and two ROC Navy frigates were sunk in the first few hours.

After a few hours, it began to appear that the amphibious assault was delayed because the overall commanders were waiting on orders. That lent some credence to the theory that the Yon Feng strikes *had* hit the Eastern Theater Command, and that as a result the orders had gotten mangled or delayed, so that the missile bombardment, airstrikes, and then the final launch of the amphibious assault were all delayed due to communications problems stemming from those strikes.

Whether it was because their cruise missiles had hit PLA headquarters, or simply problems due to Communist inefficiency and the unprecedented disaster of the Three Gorges Dam collapse, it had bought the Taiwanese some time. The strikes on the amphibious staging areas bought them some more. Fueling stations and docked ships were ablaze, and many of the ships and their cargos of troops, munitions, and combat vehicles couldn't depart until those fires were under control.

It was almost forty-eight hours after the first airstrikes that the ships finally started moving.

***

The first amphibious warfare ships and their commercial auxiliaries hadn't made it halfway across the Taiwan Strait before they hit their first check.

The PLAN was already aware of the mining operations off the Taiwanese coast. Repeated airstrikes and even submarine attacks hadn't been able to halt them. What they hadn't been expecting was a belt of mines just off the mainland coast.

The *Yimeng Shan* struck a sea mine just off the coast of Kinmen, ripping open the hull just below the waterline. The amphibious transport dock wallowed on the water for a few minutes, men jumping desperately from her gunwales into the ocean, before she turned over and sank like a stone. Almost eight hundred men died with her.

The *Baxian Shan* and *Dabie Shan*, both Type 072A LSDs, hit mines on the outer reaches of the Haitan Strait. The *Baxian Shan* was blown in half and sank immediately. The *Dabie Shan* managed to come around and limp back to port, though she was taking on water and nearly sank at the wharf, next to one of the other transport ships that had been destroyed with a limpet mine during the raid only a few short nights before.

It was a ragged, somewhat disorganized flotilla, already bloodied, that dragged out to sea from the Chinese coast. To make things worse for the PLA invasion force, timing was shot all to hell by the delays and the breakdowns in communication, so only a fraction of the main force reached the staging point on time. Then they had to hold position, waiting for the rest, lest they attack the beaches piecemeal, which made them stationary targets.

Taiwanese anti-ship missiles raced out across the Strait, followed up by both ROC Air Force Mirage 2000s and F-16s as well as an alpha strike of F/A-18E Super Hornets off the *Carl*

Vinson. The strike was not unopposed, facing both anti-air fire from the PLAN destroyers and frigates escorting the amphibious strike force and also PLAAF J-10s and PLAN J-15s. The Chinese fighters gave a good showing. Though the US Navy and ROC Air Force pilots gave as good as they got, downing six Chinese aircraft all told, they also took losses, with three Mirage 2000s and one Super Hornet shot down. The airstrike did little damage.

The Hsiung Feng III anti-ship cruise missiles, however, took a heavy toll. With ranges that reached nearly all the way to the mainland, they wreaked havoc on the oncoming ships.

Even so, while over a dozen transports and several corvettes and frigates headed for the bottom, leaving little more than smoke and burning oil on the surface, the Russian-built Kashtan CIWS systems mounted on most of the PLAN warships still shot down a lot of missiles.

Finally, almost twelve hours behind schedule, the flotilla was assembled and moving. The tide was against them, and more missiles and airstrikes continued to hammer at them, but they were heading for the shore.

The invasion of Taiwan, put off since 1949, had finally begun.

Chapter 24

Hank watched the coast over a drone feed from a bunker deep in the hills above Keelung City. The ROC Army was dug in around the city, waiting for the coming onslaught, and while Triarii assistance had been welcomed, Colonel Weng had put them in reserve, along the secondary defensive works lining the gorge that formed the one route that any mechanized force could use to get from Keelung City to Taipei.

Against the force steaming toward the island, even with the losses taken to cruise missiles, mines, and airstrikes, defense in depth was a must, and the Taiwanese had been preparing for this for a *long* time. Those preparations had never been abandoned, even during the détente with the mainland that had resulted in considerable economic traffic across the Strait.

Given how much the CCP in Beijing had openly talked about forcibly "returning Taiwan to China," even while trading with the democratically ruled island, that stood to reason.

Smoke hung over the port, and rockets and gunfire from the ships out at sea were still hammering Taiwanese positions. Air superiority still eluded the Chinese, however, and while the drone had a limited field of view, Hank could see a plane fall toward the sea, trailing smoke and fire, crashing just beyond one of the PLAN destroyers in the distance. There was no way to tell whose it was.

The craft moving in toward the port, however…

Swarms of ZBD-05s and ZBD-2000s swam out of the deployment bays of the LPDs and LSDs, driving toward shore as fast as they could. Hovercraft ran ahead of them, even as one disintegrated in a massive fireball as a Taiwanese missile smashed into its bow. Artillery from hardened positions along the shore rained down into the water, sending up geysers of white water where they didn't hit an amphibious armored vehicle or landing craft.

It was going to get worse as they got closer. Hank had some idea of what kind of defenses had been set up on the port, up to and including 30mm cannons in bunkers and sandbagged M48 tanks. Once those landing craft—and they weren't all military landing craft and amphibious vehicles, either; there were quite a few commercial vessels mixed in there, too, pressed into service or already part of the Maritime Militia—got close enough, they were probably going to wish they were out at sea, facing the artillery and airstrikes. The entire harbor and most of the water beyond it was a killing zone.

Hank chewed the inside of his cheek as he watched the little screen in the darkness of the bunker. He understood why Weng had put the Triarii in reserve. They'd demonstrated their capabilities on interdiction and raid missions, making them more valuable in that role than as front-line bullet sponges. They were also Americans, and while Hank wasn't sure that Weng was fully aware of the irregular status the Triarii had in relation to regular US military forces, it was apparent that Weng didn't want to deter further American intervention by losing those American allies he had.

Hank wondered if it had crossed Weng's mind that if Americans *were* killed by Chinese regulars, it *might* mobilize further intervention. Hank doubted that Triarii deaths would have that effect, but if he were Weng, and of a particularly ruthless, pragmatic frame of mind, it certainly would have occurred to him.

The first hovercraft were nearly at the docks, and they were starting to take fire from the revetments where the tanks had set up. Gunboats had moved in along with the landing craft and were returning fire. Even as Hank watched, one of the old M48s took three hits, two deflected by the reactive armor that had been strapped onto the Vietnam-era tank. The third hit penetrated, turning it to burning scrap as it blew the turret off.

No one made it out that Hank could see, though he might have missed something in the relatively low-resolution video feed from the drone, which was hovering just above the hill overhead. He hoped he had.

Two more hovercraft took hits as they neared the wharf. One kept coming, smoke trailing from its superstructure, while the second took a hit to its skirt, deflating the air cushion and dropping the craft to the water. It sank almost immediately, weighed down by the armored vehicles in its hold. That kind of craft wasn't designed to float without its fans holding it up.

Hank shook his head as he watched the bloodbath. Hundreds of men were dying every minute out there.

Vetter was at his shoulder, watching the same screen. "An amphibious assault across open water, in broad daylight, against prepared positions." He mirrored Hank's expression. "I don't know that anything like this has been seen since Inchon, and that had the advantage of much less accurate weaponry and operational surprise."

"Yeah." It was a slaughter. In just the last few minutes, he'd seen ten ZBD-05s go down, smashed by fire from shore and air, along with another four ZBD-2000s.

If the Chinese thought Kinmen had been costly, that island was nothing compared to what they faced on Taiwan itself.

The screen suddenly went dark. Hank checked it, but it appeared that they'd lost signal. Either the drone had been hit, or it had fallen victim to the intense electronic warfare outside.

"Well, I guess now we wait."

***

Night fell. The air battles were *still* going on, and the Patriot batteries were reaping souls among the PLAAF pilots.

Hank couldn't see all the way to the harbor. The terrain was rough, and the jungle was thick. He could see the glow of the fires, however, and the acrid tang of smoke reached them even that high up, five miles inland from the port.

They were getting reports via radio, despite the jamming that had blanketed the coast for the last several hours. It appeared that the PLA had gained a beachhead on the port itself, forcing their way in through sheer mass of numbers. They'd taken horrific losses, and while Hank hadn't been able to tell much from the Mandarin over the radio, Xu had told him quietly that it sounded like some of the ROC Army boys were getting physically sick at the slaughter out there. The PLA had paid a heavy price for the Keelung beachhead.

Unfortunately, they still *had* a beachhead. Which was bad news, no matter how badly they'd bled for it.

Other reports had filtered in over the day, as well. Keelung City had been only the flanking maneuver. Taoyuan had been the main effort. And it had been bad.

The pre-landing bombardment had been ferocious. Entire blocks of Taoyuan City had been flattened. They still hadn't managed to suppress the defenses sufficiently to secure their landing without serious opposition. Between the mine belts out at sea, what appeared to be serious accidents caused by tides and bad seamanship—the invasion force *had* launched late, and the tides were off—and intense fire from deeply entrenched fortifications overlooking the beach, the landing zone was reportedly littered with wrecked and burning vehicles, sunken landing craft and commercial vessels, and thousands of dead bodies, clad in the brown, green, and gray PLA camouflage, slowly bloating or being swept out to sea by the receding tide.

In the south, PLA commandos had attempted to seize Kaohsiung International Airport. The attack had failed bloodily and spectacularly, as their initial assault had been met by armed and ready security forces, and when the survivors had taken hostages and tried to barricade themselves in the terminal, NPA SWAT had stormed their position and killed them to a man.

The assault on the Kaohsiung City port was still ongoing.

And yet, despite the cost they'd already been made to pay, the PLA still had two footholds on the island. They hadn't won, but they hadn't been repulsed, either.

The war was far from over, but the ChiComs seemed determined to swamp Taiwan with a tidal wave of bodies.

Hank looked up at the sky. More sparks of missile fire streaked across the blackness.

It ain't over yet. Maybe, just maybe, we can hurt them badly enough in the next day or two that they'll back off.

He doubted it. With millions dead from the flooding of the Yangtze, and the Forbidden City putting all the blame on the Taiwanese, the ChiComs couldn't *afford* to back off.

This was going to get ever uglier as time went on and the body count went up.

And he couldn't help but think that now that they were on the ground, he probably wasn't going to get off the island of Taiwan alive.

With one more glance at the war in the air above, he ducked back into the bunker to wait for the next mission order.

***

It came sooner than he'd expected. Vetter was waiting for him inside with a map and what looked like a hasty warning order, scribbled on Rite in the Rain paper.

"Get your squad leaders and bring it in, Hank. We've got some hits to do tonight." Vetter was spreading the map out on a couple of ammo crates.

That didn't take long. Hank only had to stick his head into one of the bunkers and call everyone in. Navarro, LaForce, Lind, and Lovell joined them, most of the rest of the section crowding the doors to listen in.

"From the reports we've been getting, the bad guys are holding onto the mouth of the harbor, and while they've brought in reinforcements over the last couple of hours—still under fire, I might add—they haven't attempted to push out into the city itself yet. There are probably a couple of reasons for that. Some observations at the front suggest that they don't have NVGs, at

199

least not in widespread issue, which means that they can't or won't try to advance in the dark. I know, that seems against type, but remember, these kids they're throwing into the meat grinder aren't the hardasses who did the Long March or assaulted Chosin Reservoir. Most of 'em are probably city kids, and they don't have much experience or training in fighting at night."

He traced a route on the map, hastily drawn in with red map pen. "We've got transport down to Baimiweng Fort. The ROC Army's holding that against all comers right now, and they've got the port bottled up from the west. They are concerned about the Xiehe Power Plant, however, which is why we're going into Baimiweng and getting as close as we can to the shore before we move in and hit their flank. If we can, we want to open the way for the guys in Baimiweng to assault the port itself and put the hurt on the ChiComs, destroying as much of their logistics ashore as possible." His finger circled the port itself. "They're still bottled up there, and the more supplies we can destroy before they can push out, the less they're going to have to work with." He looked around at the squad leaders. "We've got several other sections conducting similar strikes around this part of the island." He laughed humorlessly. "Just be glad you're not over in Taoyuan. Word is that's a fucking mess."

Hank could imagine. He didn't expect that the ChiComs had stopped bombarding the city, especially if they'd taken the losses on landing that had been reported.

Vetter checked his watch. "Jump off time is in four hours. I know it's short, but it's what we've got to work with. Get it figured out, get your planning done, and I'm afraid you're going to have to chalk-talk your rehearsals." He glanced up at the concrete ceiling over their heads. "I don't think doing run-throughs is going to work right here."

"We'll figure it out, Doug." Hank nodded as he took the order and the map from Vetter. "It's what we've been doing for years now."

Chapter 25

It was a wild ride to Baimiweng Fort.

With the skies still contested, and continuing exchanges of rocket and artillery fire between shore and sea screaming overhead at irregular intervals, the trucks had to move fast while still being ready to stop suddenly and take cover. Even though the Taiwanese drivers seemed to be really good, it was still hairy.

They raced down the highway as fast as the trucks could go without losing control. They still narrowly dodged a stick of bombs from a formation of H-6s overhead, presumably aimed at the Hsin-shan Reservoir. The bombs hit far off target, but that was to be somewhat expected when the bombers were being harassed constantly by US and Taiwanese fighters. The burning bomber that augered in to crash in a brilliant fireball in the shipping yard just below the reservoir got closer to hitting the dam than the bombs did. The flames were one of the last things Hank saw before the truck plunged into the tunnel through the mountain ahead and into darkness.

A missile strike—who knew where it had been aimed—slammed into the hillside above the tunnel as they came out into the open again. Debris and rocks rained down on the road, and the truck veered dangerously to one side to avoid being crushed.

Hank craned his neck to look through the rear-view mirror, trying to see if the second truck had made it. It looked like it had. They were running blacked out, the drivers as well as the

Triarii all on NVGs. The ChiComs might not have extensive night vision, but the ROC Army did.

So far, the ROC Army appeared to have the PLA outclassed in just about everything but numbers.

Unfortunately, that was still no guarantee of victory.

They continued racing down the slot between the hills, slowing only to take the sharp right turn onto Jijin Road, racing past a darkened 7-11 and the Dawulun Police Station.

There was more damage on the south side of the road than the north, since the hills to the north had sheltered this extension of Keelung City from much of the artillery and missile fire from the sea. The south had taken a hammering, though not nearly as badly as areas closer to the port. Some structures still burned, while others were now little more than blackened, hollow shells.

The destruction got worse as they continued down the road and passed through Zhongshan District. The sheer weight of ordnance that had been flung at the island just on this northern salient was daunting. Entire blocks had been turned to rubble, framed by the broken walls of buildings that somehow still stood.

Hank had been in some rough places, and he'd seen some bad stuff. This was probably the worst he'd ever seen. And he couldn't even see the bodies that were probably still buried in the mountains of often still-smoking debris.

He kept expecting to take fire or get bombed as they headed for Baimiweng, but while several airstrikes came in from the north, and the road was completely deserted except for their trucks, none of the bombs got any closer than the attempted strike on the reservoir. Apparently, the PLAAF had bigger fish to fry than two transport trucks full of infantry.

While he couldn't help but be thankful, all the same, he was hoping they'd show the PLA that night that those two trucks were carrying a lot more hurt than they'd expected.

It was just after 0200 when the trucks pulled up to Baimiweng Fort. They took some fire from PLA positions down close to the port on the way in, but most of it was wild.

Baimiweng Fort had been turned into a tourist destination decades before, but the ROC Army had hastily retrofitted it, and had sandbagged and dug-in positions not only on the grounds of the fort itself and the hill above it, but apparently also around Keelung Lighthouse, overlooking the port. He had no idea if any of the defenders around the lighthouse were still there. If he'd been the PLA commander, he'd have shelled that position to oblivion as soon as he'd had eyes on.

The ROC Army guards weren't posted up at the gate. For one thing, there was no gate. The fort had been a coastal defense battery when it had been built. Instead, they were hunkered down behind sandbagged positions and T74 machineguns.

Hank's driver had been flashing the IR illuminator on his NVGs as soon as they'd come around the corner and into sight of the machinegun positions, despite the fact that Xu, sitting in the middle of the cab, had been on the radio to deconflict well over a mile back. Clearly, the driver, whose name Hank thought was Ma, didn't entirely trust his fellow soldiers not to get trigger happy.

Instead of machinegun fire, however, they got an answering IR flash, and then the trucks were weaving through the hasty serpentine of concrete barriers across the road and into the fort.

Two men in combat gear and carrying T91s rushed out of the white, two-story building just inside, frantically motioning for the trucks to stop. They did, somewhat sheltered behind the building, and Hank and Xu got out. Xu quickly spoke to the first man, and then turned to Hank.

"We need to get to a hardened structure immediately." Hank was pretty sure that the white building with the bars over the windows was probably pretty hardened, since those two had come out of it. "They have been shelling and mortaring the fort regularly." Even as he said it, a series of hollow *thunk*s sounded from higher up the hill, mortar rounds whickering away into the sky, toward the port. The ROC Army were giving as good as they got.

Of course, Hank also hadn't survived as long as he had by waiting around when the locals said there was a threat. "Everybody out!" He banged a fist on the side of the truck, even as Ma, or whatever his name was, piled out and ran for the nearest bunker.

The Triarii got to shelter in the white building just in time, as a barrage of 82mm mortar rounds rained down on the fort, preceded by that telltale whiffling sound that made Hank grit his teeth as soon as he heard it. The hammer blows of the impacts and detonations were almost a relief, if only because none of them had hit their position.

From the glimpse of the craters and rubble lining the narrow street leading down the hill that Hank had gotten as he'd exited the truck, the exchange of mortar fire had been going on for a while.

They had to wait for the mortar fire to slacken. The incoming ended faster than Hank had expected; the PLA was probably stuck counting mortar rounds, since so much of the materiel they'd tried to land with had ended up on the bottom of the ocean.

Don't get cocky. They've still got a lot more where that came from.

As the echoes of the mortar impacts faded, Hank turned to Xu. "As soon as it's clear, we need to move." They only had so much darkness to work with. Before Morning Nautical Twilight started in just about two hours. Hank did not want to still be on target when the sun came up.

Xu spoke quickly with the Taiwanese officer. "It's never entirely 'clear' up here, but we should be able to move in the next five minutes."

"Squad leaders!" Hank looked at the four of them. It felt strange, having four squad leaders plus his assistant section leader, but Lind couldn't very well take one squad into combat like a section, and he hadn't seemed to be that eager to, anyway. "We're moving out in five!"

***

It took slightly longer than that, mainly because another PLAN airstrike came in only a few minutes later. The ChiComs' aircraft were still flying at night. Their ground forces were just holding what they had.

It was possible that they'd taken such a mauling that those forces clinging to the port were just trying to catch their breath.

Instead of going directly down to the port through the close-packed houses below the fort, they slipped over the cliff, past the old gun emplacements, and onto the jungle-swathed slope that led down to the beach. The slope itself might have also provided an attacker a back way onto the fort, and they were alert and ready as they headed down, just in case the PLA commander had had the same idea.

They reached the beach without incident, however. Hank wasn't even sure if they'd have been able to hear Chinese infantry in the jungle, given the artillery and small arms fire that continued to rumble across Keelung City.

Looking out at the ocean beyond, Hank could see more flares of light as the Chinese destroyers launched more missiles at the island. Counter-battery fire and Taiwanese airstrikes streaked out in response.

A vague thought rose in the back of his mind as they patrolled quickly but quietly along the causeway above the rocky beach—fortunately, like much of Taiwan's shoreline, it was utterly unsuitable to landing operations—that neither side's stocks of cruise missiles and other guided munitions could possibly last long at the rate they were getting thrown around.

They slowed down even more as they neared the tunnel at the end of the causeway, opening onto the port. It was going to be gated, since the port was supposed to be a secured facility, but they'd come prepared for that. What Hank was a lot more worried about was if the PLA infantry chose that same time to use it to pull an end run on the fort. It would be just as bad if they'd simply set security on it. A tunnel in the rock would make one hell of a shooting gallery.

The Triarii held up, 1st and 2nd Squads setting in to either side of the tunnel entrance while 3rd Squad and Lind's Straphangers—not a name that Hank had encouraged, but Faris had coined it and it had stuck—covered their six. Everyone was doing their damnedest to stay out of the fatal funnel.

Hank took a knee next to Lovell and scanned the tunnel. It was pitch black inside, and too dark under the blackout that had descended on Keelung City—the power was still on, but the Taiwanese were covering their windows and doors, so it may as well have been out—to see if there was anyone inside near the gate. The gate itself wasn't all that visible. He chewed his lip as he stared at that blackened opening and thought.

The hasty operational plan had been to set up cover on the entrance of the tunnel then send a small element up to get the gate open, with the rest behind them ready to fill the opening with bullets if the PLA tried to stop them. That would probably be mission failure. There'd be no way they'd be able to force the tunnel if it was well and truly held against them. It was a "fatal funnel" times ten.

Now that he was looking at it, though, he had another idea.

There was a small building on top of the hill, directly over the tunnel, only a few yards in front and above them. It was fenced, but it was a cyclone fence. Easy enough to cut through. From up there, provided the PLA didn't have a squad inside the building, they should be able to creep over and get eyes on the far side of the tunnel from a better concealed position. Maybe even neutralize any security that might be holding it. The ChiComs couldn't be so crazy that they'd try to set up *in* the tunnel.

He tapped Lovell, and when the man's NVGs rotated to look at him, he pointed up. "On me."

Lovell looked up, saw the roof above them, and nodded. He got the squad moving a moment later, as Hank clambered up the slope and into the thin bit of jungle below the target building.

With the squad forming a rough and narrow wedge behind him, Hank worked his way up to the fence. It was just a cyclone fence, and while it might have sensors attached, he doubted that the PLA had control of them.

There'd been a time when he would have figured that they'd need bolt cutters or tinsnips to get through the wire. Experience had taught him that a simple pair of side-cutter wire cutters were actually a lot faster, and a lot less bulky.

While Lovell, Carrington, and Keith held security around him, Hank hauled his cutters out of a pouch on his belt and got to work.

They were through in less than a minute. It might have been faster just to go around, but Hank wasn't in so much of a hurry that he was willing to leave that building uncleared behind them.

The windows were dark, but when the only lights nearby were the work lights that the PLA logistics personnel were using to unload ships in between artillery and air strikes, that didn't necessarily mean anything. Hank, Lovell, Carrington, and Keith stacked on the nearest window while Brule and the Rodriguez brothers covered security around the flanks.

Hank wasn't going to take the time to try to breach the door, especially not if it was locked. They'd come for an infantry raid, not a breach and clear mission, and if the bad guys were in there, they'd be expecting the door to be the breach point, anyway. He lifted his rifle and used the suppressor to smash the window, raking the scarred tube around the frame to sweep the glass out of the way while Carrington covered deeper into the room over his shoulder. Then, with one gloved hand on the windowsill, he levered himself up and through, dropping to the floor and immediately moving left, out of the fatal funnel and farther from Carrington's line of fire.

The room was empty, dark, and still. It looked like the place had been a security post of some sort, but there didn't appear to be anyone there at the moment.

In fact, it looked like the PLA had cleared the place by fire.

As he scanned the room, Hank could see that there were bullet holes in the walls and that the papers and furniture had been tossed and partially smashed. The floor was covered with debris, and what might have been blood had been spattered on the doorframe.

When Carrington came in behind him, he advanced on that doorway, toward the second, bigger room, which had definitely been a monitoring center, with two screens that had probably shown CCTV footage mounted on the wall. Both were now dark, and they would remain that way, as their screens were shattered by bullet impacts.

Two bodies lay on the floor, surrounded by brass shell casings. There had been armed security here, but they'd been killed when the PLA had taken the port.

The fact that the bodies had been left where they were didn't surprise Hank. He still checked both of them, just to be sure, but they were cold and stiff. Moving on, he hastily cleared the bathroom beyond, and then they were heading for the door and the fence beyond.

There was no need to cut the fence itself. The gate leading down into the port had been breached, and it was clear going. The approach was also wide open to anyone down below who happened to look up, so they all got down on their bellies and crawled. The work lights were all too far away to illuminate them directly, but while he was *fairly* sure that the majority of the PLA personnel down there didn't have NVGs, Hank wasn't inclined to take chances.

Through the gate, they had only a few yards to go to get to the top of the tunnel entrance. Hank listened, but there was enough noise out in the port area itself that it was impossible to tell if there was anyone below them without getting up and checking visually.

Getting his feet under him, Hank took a deep breath, then lifted himself to one knee, peering over the lip of the tunnel mouth, his red dot just below his line of sight, the rifle already off safe and his finger resting lightly on the trigger. If there were PLA soldiers on security down there, he'd have to kill them fast, before they could raise the alarm. The reports of the shots would probably be lost in the constant background roar of artillery, mortars, missiles, cannon, and small arms fire, not to mention the heavy machinery the ChiComs were operating down on the port, but if this went badly, it would happen fast.

The PLA did have security on the tunnel. He saw the all-too-familiar outline of a Dongfeng CSK-131 sitting just off the tunnel entrance, a mounted QJY-88 machinegun in the turret, with a man in helmet and plate carrier sitting slumped behind it.

It wasn't the first time Hank had seen one of those vehicles on the far side of his weapon. The so-called "contractors" who'd seized the port of San Diego had brought them along on their "humanitarian" mission.

It presented a problem, though. That vehicle was as armored as a JLTV, and their 7.62 rounds weren't going to get through the windows or doors. Which meant, if they were going to pull this off, they were going to have to get close without being detected, get the doors open, and kill the PLA soldiers at bad breath distance.

Scanning the slope beneath him, Hank turned to the left, slowly and carefully pointing out the way down to the inside of the seawall, behind the vehicle. The guy in the turret didn't seem to be all that watchful, though he was clearly awake, as he flinched at every explosion in the distance. That probably accounted for the fact that he was hunched so low in the turret that he really was only barely behind the gun. He'd seen the bloodbath out there and didn't want to die to a random artillery or mortar impact while holding security on some dumb tunnel.

Keeping low, Hank started down the slope, praying that a rock didn't turn or slip out from under his boot. After only a few yards, he was below the turret gunner's line of sight, though if anyone else was inside the vehicle and looking out the windows, they'd probably be able to see him. *If* they had NVGs. It was plenty dark along that seawall. The broken clouds above filtered out some of the starlight, and there was no moon, so the majority of the ambient light was coming from the fires farther inland. That helped, but it also presented some problems, since the Triarii were now looking *toward* those fires, instead of being able to lose themselves in the glare.

Still, they reached the seawall without incident, and while some of the gravel slid as Hank and the others clambered down to the concrete, the noise was lost in the roar as a barrage of 126mm rockets rained down on the port. Hank saw the guy in the turret flinch again, burrowing even deeper down inside the vehicle, and then he was moving.

While Carrington moved to the left rear corner, Hank and Lovell closed on the right-side doors, yanked them both open—the PLA soldiers hadn't bothered to combat lock them, to their very short-lived sorrow—and opened fire.

It was all over very quickly. Only two men had been posted inside the vehicle, one in the driver's seat and the other in the turret. The man in the driver's seat had been dozing with his helmet off, jerked awake by the rocket barrage, and was still looking out toward the main port when Hank pulled the door open and shot him in the back of the head. Blood and brains spattered dark fluid across the inside of the armored glass of the window, and he slumped.

Lovell shot the other man in the pelvis, and then, as he collapsed in agony, screaming in the night, finished him off with a second round through the armpit. The man's wails quickly died away, and he lay crumpled in the middle of the vehicle.

Just to be on the safe side, Hank reached inside and yanked every cable out of the radio before turning back toward the tunnel.

With the rest of 1st Squad holding security on the parking lot and the lines of semi-trucks set up there, using the CSK-131 as cover, Hank and Carrington hustled back into the tunnel and opened the gate. He clicked his radio twice, and then Spencer appeared out of the dark, bringing the rest of the section with him in a tactical column along the sides of the tunnel. Bullets might travel along walls but staying out in the middle of a canalized danger area like that isn't a good idea, either.

Then they were spreading out and heading for their targets, moving through the shadows like malevolent ghosts, weapons up and looking for targets.

Chapter 26

Another ship was steaming into the entrance to the harbor as the rocket barrage ceased. It might have been a conscripted commercial job or one of the PLAN's landing ships. Hank couldn't quite tell in the dark, as good as he'd gotten at Chinese ship recognition in the South China Sea. He didn't think there would be many men on deck, given the amount of ordnance still flying around, but he still led 1st Squad to take cover behind the three massive silos standing over the entrance to the harbor, just in case.

The ship rumbled past, even as 2nd Squad took cover behind the stacks of cargo containers lined up to the north. Hank checked his watch. The artillery was supposed to lift in about ten minutes, giving them a window of about fifteen to twenty minutes to get in, blow up what they could, cause as much havoc as possible, and get out.

It took a second to decide which way to go. Leaning out from around the corner, he could see that there weren't many foot patrols out and about. It looked like the PLA soldiers were trying to stay inside armored vehicles or any other cover they could find, risking exposure in the open only to continue to unload, and then only when the fire had slackened somewhat. They didn't even have much in the way of sandbags to cover the piles of supplies that were stacking up on the wharf, practically unprotected because the shelling was keeping them from moving the pallets except during the short pauses in artillery and rocket fire.

This entire operation was stacking up to be a complete clusterfuck for the PLA, and Hank would only have been happier about it if they'd all been blown to pieces trying to get ashore.

It didn't escape his notice—or his anger—that they'd had a lot easier time invading American ports.

The rumble of artillery—at least, ROC artillery; the PLA was still lobbing missiles inland—faded away. It was time to go.

Setting Brule in with the Mk 48 around the corner, to where he had a reasonably clear field of fire across the wharf and toward the supply ship that had suddenly turned into a flurry of activity as the ChiComs resumed offloading, now that the sky wasn't raining steel and explosives, at least for a few minutes.

Hank was tempted to just open fire and drop as many of the support personnel as possible and run for it. They didn't have a particularly large time window, and the risk was immense. But they'd be able to do a lot more damage if they got in close and placed charges. They might be doing it under fire, but with the bad guys as disorganized and nervous as they appeared to be, he figured they could run the risk.

So, with Brule and Carrington in place as their support by fire position, they slipped around to the other side of the silos and moved in.

Gunfire erupted somewhere off to the south. That would be their diversion. During planning, they'd coordinated with the ROC Army infantry dug into the second line of defense in Keelung City—much of it deliberately rubbled buildings, sandbag bunkers, and roadblocks—for a probing attack to draw eyes and react forces south while they hit from the northwest. It sounded like the Taiwanese were right on time.

They were probably out for blood, after the last two days. The tricky part for their commanders might be getting them not to overextend themselves.

Hank had certainly seen some of that attitude from some of the ROC soldiers over the last thirty-six hours or so. Even those

NPA cops had been eager and bloodthirsty. They'd opened fire early because they couldn't wait to get stuck in. "Better dead than Red" was a slogan most of the Taiwanese fighting men he'd met recently could get behind wholesale.

Moving quickly across the concrete next to the container yard, the Triarii advanced on the loading operation, invisible in the shadows as the ChiComs worked by the illumination of worklights and headlights. The ChiCom support personnel were skittish as hell, ducking and looking to the south as the diversionary attack started, and some of them tried to rush for the ship, but were stopped by what looked like PLAN marines.

Those guys would die first.

They'd just reached the corner of the container yard when gunfire erupted much closer, the initial burst of unsuppressed 5.8mm fire being immediately answered by a crash of suppressed 7.62. One of the other squads had just gotten stuck in.

The PLAN marines were immediately more alert, rushing to covered positions behind some of the stacks of supply crates. Noticing which ones they avoided served to tell Hank which ones probably had munitions in them. They were facing the wrong way, though.

Brule chose that moment to open fire, playing off the sudden gunfire from the south. His first burst tore right into the PLAN marines behind their barricade of supply crates, smashing them to the wharf like bloodied rag dolls.

Hank was already moving, the rest of 1st Squad spreading out in an echelon formation behind and to his right, weapons up and coughing as they rushed the dock.

Two more PLAN marines appeared at the ship's rail, but they ducked below the side quickly, and he didn't really have a shot. A moment later, Brule raked the side of the ship with a burst, and one of them dropped with a finality that was unmistakable, even through NVGs.

Reaching a stack of crates and containers, Hank and Lovell took cover, though they weren't really taking fire. Almost a dozen of the support personnel were sprawled across the wharf in attitudes of violent death, and the unloading had stopped. As Hank peered around the stack of supplies, he saw a small man in body armor and helmet suddenly get up and run toward the bodies of the PLAN marines who had been cut down by Brule's machinegun fire.

It didn't take a genius to see what he was going for. Even as he bent and reached for one of the fallen rifles, Hank's own weapon barked twice and the man dropped, twitching, to the wharf.

Then they were in the clear, at least for the moment.

Brule and Carrington ran up to a new position with a better field of fire on the dock, while the rest of the section closed in, the Rodriguez brothers taking security to the east while the rest moved to the middle of the supply dump and started hauling prepared charges out of assault packs. Gunfire continued to rattle and *crack* out in the sparsely lit darkness of the port beyond, but for the moment, they'd taken their objective, and there weren't enough PLA forces that far in the rear to counterattack quickly.

Hank had no illusions as to how long that would last. They had to move fast. That was also why none of the fuses on the charges were all that long.

Reaching into his own pack, he drew out another limpet mine, one of their last. Slinging his rifle on his back, he ran to the quayside, slapping the mine against the supply ship's hull and cranking the timer over before shoving it down toward the waterline. The quay was too high to get it all the way down to the water, but the mine should blow a big enough hole that it might still sink the ship.

If they could sink enough ships at the quay, it would be that much more difficult for the PLA to bring in supplies or reinforcements. It would be a hell of a mess to clean up after the war, but better to have to raise and salvage a Chinese freighter afterward than lose the war. If they lost anyway, the harder they could make it for the ChiComs, the better.

The crackle and roar to the south intensified. "Six-Four Actual, Six-Four Seven. We're being heavily engaged, falling back to your position." Lind had gotten stuck in, all right.

"This is Two." LaForce sounded slightly out of breath. "We'll hold our position until you pass through. Three's already falling back." Either Navarro had worked fast, or they'd encountered sufficient resistance that they'd had to disengage, which could create some problems for Lind.

A moment later, the tanker docked just a few hundred yards away went up like a roman candle, which told Hank that Navarro had found a big, juicy target and gone after it as hard as he could, then run.

"Actual, Three. Inbound to your position." Navarro was definitely running, but what had he left between his squad and Lind? "We are setting up a delaying position at the warehouses, across from Two."

Hank got back to his feet, but he couldn't answer just yet, since another burst of gunfire sounded from up on deck, as someone on the crew tried to seize control of the wharf again. It was immediately silenced by a roaring burst from Brule's Mk 48.

"Copy. Make it fast. Arty starts back up in about ten minutes." He wanted to be *far* away by then. The Taiwanese gunners were good, but they still weren't exactly lobbing precision munitions following laser designators.

The last of 1st Squad were pulling igniters on charges as Lind's squad came charging down the wharf toward them, pursued by PLA soldiers rushing forward in short dashes, spraying 5.8mm rounds as they came. Several went overhead with faint *crack*s, high enough that they were hardly a threat.

From where he crouched by the quay, Hank could only watch with narrowed eyes, even as 2nd and 3rd Squads opened up with a punishing crossfire, bursts of machinegun fire cutting some off at the knees, aimed rifle fire smashing others off their feet. Still, despite the clutter of supplies and equipment all over the docks, there was only so much cover, and one of Lind's men took a bullet to the back and fell on his face, twisting and writhing in agony. Lind turned and ran back to get him, though Mack was another six feet ahead of him.

Mack took a round to the face and stopped dead, standing up for a brief second before falling limply to the wet concrete.

Hank was already moving. They were only about three hundred yards away. He couldn't leave Lind to try to haul Mack and the other guy who'd gotten hit by himself, and Lind hadn't stopped. He wasn't running so much as he was advancing in a fast combat glide, his weapon in his shoulder, hammering pairs at the oncoming PLA soldiers, driving forward to get his boys.

It was only three hundred yards, but it may as well have been a mile.

He saw Lind take a round to the leg and stumble. The rest of the squad had stopped, finding cover and trying to return fire, but Lind and the others were between them and the PLA soldiers. Hank was forcing himself to move from cover to cover, knowing that the dock had just turned into every bit the bullet funnel that the tunnel behind them would have been. He couldn't save Lind if he was dead.

Lind kept moving, but his knee buckled. He was still shooting, dumping two more ChiCom troops with four shots. Then a burst caught him in the neck, and he went down hard.

Hank killed the man who'd shot him, a long shot in the dark, but right at the edge of his capability with a red dot on NVGs. It was doubtful that the Chinese soldier had gotten anything but a lucky shot, since he still hadn't seen any NVGs, but some more of the fire had been silenced.

Then, as he dashed behind one last bit of cover and grabbed the nearest one of Mack's guys, a skinny dude named Smith, he heard the rumble of diesels and the creak and rattle of tracks.

The bulk of the PLA's infantry was mechanized, and there was a ZBD-04 turning into the lane between the containers and the docks.

"Get moving! Back to the infil point!" They had two LAWs, but that was it, and Lind's squad hadn't been carrying either of them. Shooting 7.62 at an armored fighting vehicle with a 100mm main gun and a 30mm coax would be about as effective as throwing spitballs. "Stay in cover!"

It briefly crossed his mind that if they corked off that 100mm at Triarii in cover, they might destroy some more of their own supplies. It would be small comfort if they turned another one of his dudes into pink mist, though.

LaForce and Navarro were falling back fast, bounding in sprints, sending what fire they could at the PLA infantry that were following the ZBD-04. More rumbling engines and squealing tracks announced that still more vehicles were coming after them. This had just gotten bad. They had over three hundred yards to go to the tunnel.

Then Fuentes corked off his LAW with a *bang*, the recoilless 66mm HEAT round slamming into the lead ZBD-04's side with a flash. It didn't kill the vehicle, but it did break the track, immobilizing it.

Then 2nd Squad was dashing around behind 1st's positions while 3rd fell back toward the tunnel along the mountain, on the other side of another container yard. Hank and 1st Squad stayed in place until the remains of 4th had gone past.

Another *bang* announced the second LAW being fired. Hank couldn't see it, but Huntsman had been carrying that one, and Huntsman was a hell of a shot. He seriously doubted that the man had missed.

"Hank! Turn and go!" Lovell was next to him, firing over his shoulder. Brule had fallen back to the container yard, and was sending short, tight bursts at the enemy.

From where Hank stood, he could see that the PLA wasn't being quite so aggressive anymore. That initial charge hadn't worked out well for them, and while they were still shooting, they weren't moving advancing very quickly.

"GO!" Lovell nodded and sprinted toward Brule's position. Hank fired off the last of his mag then turned and ran after him, reloading as he went.

Somewhere in the distance, almost inaudible over the noise of much closer small arms fire, the first *thump*s of a renewed ROC Army artillery barrage began.

A moment later, the first charges started going off. Explosions thundered around the docks, and the oncoming 5.8mm fire suddenly stuttered, as some of the PLA soldiers found themselves entirely too close to the detonating explosives, especially when those explosives had been set on stacks of munitions.

In moments, half the wharf was on fire, rippling secondaries ripping into containers and men alike.

The Triarii ran for the tunnel, leaving their dead behind.

Chapter 27

The raid had essentially put the Keelung City beachhead on a desperate defensive footing. While the PLAN was still trying to move more men and materiel into the port and had made a brief attempt at taking the Waimushan Fishing Harbor just to the west—mines had ended that before any PLAN marines had set foot on land—they still hadn't established uncontested control of the skies, and they were still taking losses just getting on land. Continued probes and assaults by the ROC Army out of Keelung City itself hadn't succeeded in retaking the port, but the PLA hadn't been able to push out very far, either.

Word from Taoyuan was grim. The PLA still clung to their beachhead, but every attempt to push out had been repulsed from deeply entrenched defensive lines dug into the rock, as well as continued air and artillery strikes. The Taoyuan beachhead was far less sheltered than Keelung City's port, too, which meant that the PLA was taking horrific losses as the artillery batteries farther inland hammered the beach incessantly, and the ships that were still bringing men and materiel in were lucky to make it to shore half the time.

There were more stories circulating about ROC Army soldiers getting physically sick at the slaughter, the sheer horror of it overwhelming even a hardening hatred that is part and parcel of this kind of war. This sort of bloodletting hadn't been seen in a long, long time. And yet, despite the obvious collapse of PLA morale, the PRC kept throwing more of them into the breach.

Hank could only imagine what kind of threats had been leveled against those poor kids' families.

Some of them had to be getting hardened to it, but there were an awful lot of reports coming from the front of PLA units just collapsing and falling back to the beachhead in total disarray, taking even more awful casualties on the way.

The PLAN was getting hammered at sea, too. Another attempt had been made on the harbor at Kaohsiung, and the ChiComs had managed to get some forces inside the harbor, but the losses to mines, airstrikes, artillery, and the one still-surviving Taiwanese submarine had required a withdrawal after six disastrous hours.

Fortunately or unfortunately, from their positions in the hills above Keelung City, the Triarii weren't seeing much of the propaganda and information operations coming out of Beijing. He could only imagine how increasingly ham-fisted it was getting. It had already been pretty bad before the invasion.

It had been relatively quiet for the last couple of days. Even the bombardment had slowed, in both directions. Hank strongly suspected that dwindling supplies accounted for most of the reduction in fires.

He was currently in a command post dug into the mountain above the Xishi Reservoir, along with Vetter, Xu, and a half-dozen other Triarii infantry section leaders and a couple of Grex Luporum Team leaders. Everyone looked haggard and tired, and those who hadn't already been wearing beards were sporting several days' worth of stubble.

Most of them were gathered in the back of the concrete room, mostly lit by the screens that lined the wall. Hank thought he was picking up a few more words of Mandarin, just from being around Xu while the other man communicated with their ROC Army counterparts, but he still couldn't make out enough to understand what was being said.

Xu, however, was giving a running translation.

"The threats from Beijing are getting much more dire. They continue to proclaim that they cannot and will not accept 'separatist' control of sovereign Chinese territory. That this is the endgame, and that the Chinese people will be triumphant against us 'terrorists' and 'agents of imperialism,' no matter the cost." Xu was so tired that he wasn't even being that sarcastic anymore. "And it looks like there is another flotilla gathering around Pingtan Island."

Hank shook his head tiredly. "Second wave?"

Vetter snorted. "Hell, at this point, it's probably more third or fourth. We've certainly killed enough of them already and destroyed what's got to amount to hundreds of millions of dollars' worth of equipment and supplies."

"Do we have *any* reliable intel on what's going on over there on the mainland?" Perloff was one of the Grex Luporum guys, a massive specimen of a man despite the short rations and shorter sleep of the last few days, who looked like a shaved gorilla.

"Not much. They shut the internet down hard, brought the Great Firewall down like the Iron Curtain." Vetter was more up to date than any of the rest of them. "Unfortunately, too much intel collection has shifted to the internet over the years, so what agents the Taiwanese have on the other side of the Strait are having a rough time reporting in. So, aside from CCP propaganda channels aimed at the island, it's kind of a black hole at the moment."

"Would they clamp down that hard if it was going well for them?" Brewster asked.

"It's the ChiComs." Hank snorted. "They might."

"Right now, the concern is what they will do if the invasion continues to go badly." Xu tried to get back to what was being discussed at the front of the room. "There was already a great deal of unrest before Three Gorges collapsed, and while they are almost certainly sending messages to their people telling them about triumphant success against us evil separatists who were somehow responsible for that disaster, sooner or later, they are going to notice that troops keep coming here but not going back."

"And when that happens…" Hank took a deep breath. "I don't expect good things to come from it."

"You're becoming a pessimist, Hank." Carl Norman was another one of the section leaders, a man Hank had known many years before. Norman had always been friendly, but Hank had never especially liked him much. There was something about his forced joviality that had always put Hank's teeth on edge. "If the CCP collapses, then the war's over. What's left of the PLA here will have no choice but to surrender."

"You really think these bastards are just going to roll over and let the same thing happen to them that happened in Russia in the '90s?" Hank shook his head. "They *learned* from that, bud, and they've got a lot of hungry and desperate people. Hell, thanks to Three Gorges falling apart, they've got a lot worse situation on their hands than the Russians had in 1991. No, they're not going to go quietly into the night, and if they can possibly hold onto power at our expense, you'd better believe they will."

The fact that nobody had anything much to say to that was as ominous as what Hank had just said.

***

Unfortunately, while the Triarii arsenal ships were moving toward Pingtan Island, there wasn't much the infantry on the ground could do at the moment. While the PLAN hadn't managed to fully blockade the island, there weren't many gaps when and where anyone could get off, and Vetter had decided that they could probably do the Taiwanese more good as fast-moving auxiliaries on Taiwan itself. Hank didn't really agree with that. The ROC Army was competent and still fairly well-equipped, despite the losses they'd inevitably taken so far. Raiding the PLA's staging areas and hitting the PRC's infrastructure was what he'd rather be doing.

But here they were, still waiting in the gorge above Keelung, while the PLA and the ROC Army kept skirmishing in the blasted hellscape that had been Keelung City.

The airstrikes had gotten more intense again lately, though they'd mostly seemed to be SEAD—Suppression of

Enemy Air Defense—missions, largely aimed at the Patriot batteries. Inevitably, they were slowly whittling away the bubble of defense over Taiwan. The only question at that point was whether or not they could finish the job while they still had enough airframes and pilots left, or if they were going to have to haul the old J-7s and J-8s out of mothballs to fly strike missions. There were already questions as to just how many H-6s were still flying after the last week.

None of that was Hank's concern except as it applied to air support, and that wasn't currently part of the Triarii's bag of tricks. The only drones left were on ships out at sea, and those were generally too far out—to avoid going head-to-head with PLAN destroyers or frigates—to provide close support.

Except that it still nagged at him, intensifying the weight of the sense of dread that had settled on his shoulders since that conversation in the CP. Something was telling him that things weren't about to get better. They were going to get worse.

He stared out at the smoke that never seemed to disperse over Keelung City, his fingers unconsciously tapping on the M5 across his knees, a frown creasing his brow.

Hank had never been given to what he might have called mystical thinking. He'd known some Marines and Triarii who were religious. Some who were downright superstitious. He wasn't against the idea of some sort of spiritual side to life, but it wasn't something he was ever all that comfortable exploring much. He'd always had more practical things to think about.

Yet he couldn't shake this. Maybe it was a premonition. Maybe he was just losing his nerve. He didn't think that was it, though. He wasn't scared of going into combat. In fact, he was sitting there wondering what the hell they were waiting for. No, this was something else. Something that he'd noticed, but his conscious mind hadn't quite put together all the way yet.

He was still turning it over in his mind when the next barrage hit Keelung City.

The PLAN must have massed every missile destroyer and frigate they had left that wasn't occupied with holding off the US

Navy and the Japanese around the Senkaku Islands. Wave after wave of missiles rained down on the city, the thunder becoming a continuous, rippling roar. Shockwaves flickered through the rising plumes of dust, smoke and debris as the warheads kicked up fountains of dirt, frag, and smashed masonry.

Hank sat up a little straighter, as more impacts shuddered through the bunker, more missiles hitting presumed ROC Army positions in the mountains above the city. Fortunately, from what he could tell, they were mostly either pasting abandoned positions that they'd already hit, or else the decoy emplacements that the Taiwanese had built precisely *to* get hit.

It looked like whatever he'd been waiting for was starting.

Chapter 28

The bombardment lasted for what felt like hours, but when Hank checked his watch, it had only been about thirty minutes. But that thirty minutes had been enough to just about completely flatten what was left of Keelung City.

Hank was sure that there were still defenders in there. History had showed over and over that eliminating a dug-in defender by bombardment alone was a fool's errand. But the PLA had one real advantage in all this, and that was numbers and firepower, and they were going to use both.

They still didn't have a clear line of sight down to the port from their positions, and the drone environment had gotten extremely non-permissive, but cameras had been set up on the mountaintops, sending the feeds down to monitors in the bunkers. They weren't wired in, but were broadcasting via wifi, which meant they were still subject to disruption. So far, though, that disruption had mostly just been noise from the constant electronic warfare that had mostly been aimed at the island's commercial internet and military comms. The ChiComs didn't know about this system yet, or at least they hadn't managed to get the assets in place to target it.

Keelung City lay under a heavy pall of dust and smoke. The cloud was so thick that it covered most of the northern coastline, though some of the feeds from the far north and east could see a few of the Chinese ships moving in from around the edge of that cloud. A complete picture was impossible without a drone feed, but there were a lot of them out there.

Despite the flotilla's raids, the next wave was moving in, and it looked like they were hitting Keelung City to try to pull an end run around Taipei and the stalled offensive in Taoyuan.

Which was *a* plan, but not what Hank, who made no bones about not necessarily being a big-picture strategist—not that *they'd* done much better over the last forty years—would have considered a *smart* plan.

After all, they'd still have to get through that gorge. No mechanized force was getting over the mountains between Keelung City and Taipei any other way.

The flashes of heavy weapons fire began to flicker under the dark cloud that hung over Keelung City, as the PLA's next wave sailed into the harbor and began to unload.

***

The fight down in the city took far longer than the PLA had probably hoped it would. For most of the rest of the day, the Triarii and their counterparts in the reserve positions could only wait and watch. The Taiwanese weren't just leaving their guys down there to die; they'd sent reinforcements in to cover the retreat under fire through the rubble, but even with as little as they could see from the distant camera feeds and hear over the radio, it was clear that there were a lot fewer men falling back through the wreckage than anyone had hoped.

They were still bleeding the Chinese as they went. Javelins, APILAS, and AT-4s flashed out of smashed and collapsed buildings to turn ZTZ-96s, ZTZ-99s, ZBD-05s, ZBD-04s, and ZBL-08s to burning scrap, half the time cooking the crews and troops inside. Machinegun nests caught infantry in crossfires that eviscerated entire 7-man dismount squads.

Every time the ROC Army soldiers fell back, they left IEDs behind. The Taiwanese hadn't stocked up on landmines since the '50s, so they'd had to improvise. What they'd built in the lead-up to the invasion was wreaking havoc, though.

Yet as hard as they fought, they were still being forced back. The PLA had landed a massive force in Keelung City under cover of that lengthy bombardment, and they were forcing their way through the surviving resistance by weight of numbers alone.

"Once they hit Phase Line Green, then the ROC guys are going to pop smoke and run for it." Rather than pull everyone in for a brief, Vetter was sending the word over the radio. It was a bit faint and scratchy, given the electronic noise and the sheer violence going on down below, but it was clear enough for an op order. "It's going to be a staged withdrawal from there. Our part in the plan remains the same. Best—and I mean *best*—estimate is that we've got an hour to be in position.

"Good hunting, gents."

***

"Staged withdrawal" in this case meant essentially that the ROC Army was bounding back toward the mountains while killing as many Communists on the way as they could. Judging by the pillars of black smoke rising to the north, they were getting their pound of flesh.

The main thoroughfares out of Keelung City, leading to the only viable route for a mechanized force trying to reach Taipei, almost all went through tunnels, tunnels that had been wired to blow. The PLA had known those weren't a good call, so they'd circled around to the north, weaving through the hills over Maijin Road, paying a hell of a butcher's bill for every yard they advanced. They'd pushed through, though, and now they were coming down the Sun Yat Sen Expressway, not far behind the retreating ROC Army survivors.

Hank moved up next to Spencer and peered through the bunker's firing port. It still amazed him a little just how thoroughly honeycombed this island was with tunnels, bunkers, and fighting positions. Most of them were entirely hidden from casual observation. In retrospect, though, given how long the Taiwanese had been under threat from the mainland, it made sense.

This one was stocked with three AT-4s, but that wasn't the primary weapon at the Triarii's fingertips here.

"Wait for it." Hank really *was* surprised that the Taiwanese had left this particular trigger line to them, but the Triarii had already demonstrated their willingness to fight like hell and kill Communists in job lots, so apparently, they were just another part of the defending force now.

The lead elements were advancing slowly and carefully. Four ZTZ-99 tanks were spread out in a wedge across all four lanes of the Sun Yat Sen Expressway, and from their vantage point, Hank could see several ZBD-04s behind them, with their dismounts out along the flanks, sweeping the sides of the freeway in a Y formation. Dozens more armored vehicles were strung out along the expressway behind them. If the Taiwanese had had A-10s, it would have made for a hell of a target.

As it was, they had to make do with what they had.

Several of the ZBD-04s, ZTZ-99s, and ZTZ-96s down the line were firing into the hills to the west, where PLA infantry was clashing with dug-in ROC Army soldiers, some of whom were still counter-attacking where they could.

Hank's focus was on the vanguard, though, as they crept toward the overpass where Wanrui Expressway crossed over Sun Yat Sen before crossing the Keelung River.

The PLA formation was slowing even more as they got closer to the overpass. They didn't trust it, and after the mauling they'd already received on the way south from Keelung City, they probably shouldn't.

Hank still waited. The PLA column was still only being engaged from the flanks. They'd faced no resistance to the front, yet. Colonel Weng had the same idea in mind that Hank did. He knew that because Xu had told him as much.

His hopes were dashed, however. The armored column didn't just roll right underneath the overpass. They halted just short, more infantry moving up on the hills to the west. They were going to clear the overpass before they tried to charge through.

The PLA was getting even more cautious than they had been after the initial losses they'd taken on the beaches on Kinmen. None of these kids wanted to die for the CCP, no matter how much propaganda had been pumped into their heads since they'd been in diapers, and the gauntlet of dead bodies, sunken ships, and burned-out vehicles behind them had to have been more daunting than had ever been expected.

That didn't make Hank much more sympathetic. He'd seen enough of the damage the Chinese Communist Party had already done. He wasn't going to hesitate when the time came to pull the trigger. If anything, his understanding of just how shitty a deal these soldiers had gotten only made him feel less.

"They're not gonna go for it." Spencer was watching the same view, an AT-4 leaning against the concrete parapet next to his boot.

"No, I don't think they will." He reached for the clacker next to him.

The wires had been set in triple-redundant, with a radio receiver as a backup to those. When he slammed the heel of his hand down on the clacker, he was all but certain that he was going to get results.

He did. With a rippling series of explosions, the overpass cracked and collapsed across the expressway, blocking the road with rubble. At almost the same time, the bridge over the Keelung River shuddered and buckled, falling into the water with a cloud of dust and debris.

It wouldn't stop them cold, but it would slow them down. The rest was up to Triarii and ROC Army infantry.

The dust hadn't cleared yet when some of those ROC Army troops got to work.

A pair of Javelins roared in from the south side of the collapsed overpass, both popping up at the last moment to come crashing down on the top decks of the two lead ZTZ-99s. One shuddered as the missile hit with a flash and a billowing cloud of fire and smoke, then sat there, its turret askew, smoking.

The other's turret blew off, tumbling a hundred feet in the air, and the hull began to burn fiercely, a crackling plume of fire and exploding ordnance shooting up from the top as the ammunition cooked off.

Hank ducked down to grab his rifle and came up looking for targets. The PLA infantry had all run for cover as soon as the missiles had struck, though, and he had nothing but a line of armored vehicles hemmed in by the limits of the expressway in front of him. Not much he could do against that with a rifle. And if any of those tanks or heavily-armed infantry fighting vehicles down there had thermal sights and figured out that they were being shot at from a bunker on the hill, they'd have a pretty clear shot.

More anti-tank missiles streaked in from the western hillsides, hammering into more of the ZTZ-99s and ZBD-04s. More vehicles died quickly, and soon the expressway was a panicked traffic jam of tanks and IFVs trying to get clear while more vehicles burned, belching black smoke into the air. There wasn't enough wind to disperse it, either, and soon a thick, oily black cloud hung over the Keelung River, making it hard to see and biting at the back of the throat.

Hank couldn't just sit there and watch. The thunder of heavy weapons and the crackle of small arms fire echoed across the gorge, and the PLA wasn't just sitting there and taking it, either. They were shooting back, with a volume of fire that was daunting. Even the tanks were hammering main gun rounds into the concealed positions on the western slopes, and Hank was sure a lot of Taiwanese soldiers were dying, despite the mauling they were giving the ChiComs.

He was about to head out the back of the bunker, grabbing either Lovell's or LaForce's squad, to head around the flank and help the Taiwanese, when he spotted movement through the smoke.

The PLA ground commander had spotted a possible route out of the kill zone, and now, with a pair of ZTZ-96s in the lead, followed by some more ZBD-04s, they were pushing off the expressway, crushing the guardrails and some of the vegetation on the side of the expressway, plowing an escape route onto the small industrial area alongside the Sun Yat Sen Expressway and onto the side roads that led up the hill.

Those roads dead-ended at the tank farms up above, but that would be small consolation to the Triarii and their Taiwanese allies if they got overrun.

Grabbing one of the AT-4s in the bunker, Hank headed out the back. If he could stop the lead vehicles, he might be able to bottle the rest up.

He heard Spencer swear behind him, and a moment later, his assistant section leader was following him out, Huntsman, Reisinger, and Bishop flanking him. Hank had just seen the problem and acted, and the rest just had to catch up.

He didn't just charge down the hill. That would have put him into the oncoming ZTZ-96's line of fire almost immediately, not to mention the green, gray, and brown-clad PLA infantry who had taken cover among the buildings and were now starting to bound forward under cover of the advancing tanks. Instead, he kept to the trees, leaning into the steep mountainside that provided some cover to the west. He had to get around on the flank and hit them from a direction they didn't expect, even though it meant losing visual contact for a few minutes.

The hill was not easy going, and it wasn't just because it was so steep. The vegetation was thick, and while the Taiwanese had cut maneuver lanes through the dirt and the jungle, none of them were quite set up for this.

His boot slipped on fallen leaves and he fell, catching himself before he faceplanted on a rock, but he still banged his knee pretty well and the AT-4 slipped off his shoulder, knocking against the palm to his right.

Hauling himself erect, he kept going, pulling himself up by branches and vines where he needed to.

While they were covered from the enemy by a finger of the hill they were currently struggling to climb, that didn't mean they were cut off from the fight. Bullets and heavier stuff *cracked* and buzzed overhead, and the ground shook as a tank main gun round hammered into the hillside not far enough away.

They crested the hill and started working their way down, now in a rough skirmish line, though Hank was still a few paces ahead. The Triarii stayed closer than the combat environment would usually allow, despite the threat that a grenade or heavy-caliber round might take them all out in one go. The jungle was too thick to allow them to spread out enough.

More gunfire rattled and roared just down the hill. Both 5.8 and 5.56 fire from the sounds of it, which meant that some of the PLA soldiers had tried to climb the same mountain and had run into the Taiwanese.

Hank paused, practically sitting back on his haunches on the hillside, and tried to figure out just where the fight was. He didn't want to charge right into the middle of it, but he *did* think that flanking and wiping out that unit of ChiComs on the way to pop some tanks was probably a good idea.

The fight was closer than he'd thought. There was so much noise that his estimate had been off.

A sudden burst of fire tore through the jungle to his left, and then he came out through a bunch of vegetation to find himself face to face with a PLA soldier.

There was no time to notice anything but the cammies and the rifle already very nearly pointed at him. Hank had, fortunately, led with his own weapon, and he had ever so slightly less distance to traverse his muzzle before he shot the PLA soldier three times, really without aiming. The man triggered a burst into the dirt as he fell, spattering red on the leaves around him.

Then Hank was moving, scanning the weeds for movement, looking for targets. He slowed just enough to make sure that the rest of the team was close enough that they could support each other, driving down the hillside in a wedge.

To his right, Bishop blasted a hammer pair into the bush, and he heard a thin scream, quickly dying down into a gurgling wail. Hank couldn't turn to look, as another shadowy figure appeared out of the foliage in front of him, struggling up the hill, and he dumped that one a split second after recognizing the distinctive PLA camouflage.

It was a knife fight in a telephone booth, simply because of how thick the vegetation was.

Hank didn't slow down, but just kept moving. It was risky as hell under those conditions. He knew that rushing through the jungle into unknown enemy forces was asking to stumble into the middle of a crossfire he couldn't win, but if he didn't stop those armored vehicles, they were all fucked.

He saw the black top of one of the big storage tanks through the trees off to his right and adjusted his course that way just a little. There was a finger running down to the road alongside that tank farm, and that meant he could get almost right up to the road without leaving concealment—provided he could avoid stumbling on any more PLA infantry.

More gunfire tore through the jungle down the hill, but as they continued down the finger, it became apparent that they had gotten around the PLA's flank. Still, he could hear the squeal and rattle of tracks just ahead. This was going to be close.

His boot slipped, and he didn't quite catch himself in time. He heard Bishop yell, and then he was sliding down the hill on his ass, narrowly missing getting split in half by a tree. He caught himself a moment later, but he was only a few feet from the tree line, just behind a small industrial building, a warehouse or something.

The others were scrambling down through the jungle after him, but as he turned, he spotted half a dozen or so PLA soldiers working their way between buildings and parked vehicles in the open ground to the north of him.

One of them saw him, pivoting and snapping his QBZ-191 to his shoulder. Hank threw himself behind the building as bullets smacked into concrete and metal, but then one of the team behind him opened up from deeper in the trees, dumping a full mag into the group. Two went down and the rest scattered for cover.

Hank turned and kept going along the side of the building while the team lay down cover fire. He had to get to the road.

He didn't have the greatest or clearest shot between the trees, but that lead tank was already poking its main gun past the corner. He hoped and prayed that the tank commander didn't just decide to blast a 125mm round right through the building, just to be on the safe side.

Given the slaughter that was being wrought on the armored vehicles up and down the Sun Yat Sen Expressway, and presumably across the river on Badu Road, it was only a matter of time before the Chinese Communists started doing just that.

He'd known when he'd grabbed it that the AT-4's 84mm HEAT round wasn't likely to score a catastrophic kill on a modern main battle tank. Yet, as he slung his rifle to his back and jerked the sling tight, then opened the AT-4's sights and yanked back the cocking handle, he saw that while he'd been banking on nothing more than a mobility kill, the skirts and flank of the tank were bare steel, without cages or reactive armor to shield the vehicle against HEAT rounds.

Nothing for it. He put the launcher to his shoulder, lined up the flip-up black plastic sights, bellowed, "Backblast area clear!" gave it a second, and squeezed the trigger, a rubber-encased button on top of the tube.

The recoilless launcher fired with a *bang*. At that range, just barely three times the warhead's arming distance of ten meters, the impact came in an eyeblink.

Hank hadn't expected to be able to do much more than break a track. On that narrow road, it would have been enough. But the Chinese tank's side armor was so thin that the AT-4's High Explosive Anti-Tank warhead punched right through the skirts and into the hull. It hit with a flash and a puff of smoke, and the ZTZ-96 lurched and ground to a stop. Then the driver's hatch opened, and the driver bailed out, as smoke started to pour from the hole punched in the armored behemoth's flank.

A long, ravening burst of machinegun fire sounded from behind him, and then the *whoosh* of a heavier anti-tank missile from higher up the mountain, followed by a *bang* and a shockwave as the next vehicle behind the one Hank had just killed took a warhead to the turret. The follow-on *crash* as that turret slammed back down onto the ground beside the burning hulk seemed almost muted by comparison.

Letting the AT-4's tube fall, Hank turned, brought his rifle around, and went back on the hunt.

Chapter 29

Hank watched FU Jen Sacred Heart High School through his scope, peering around the corner and through a bush from beneath a six-story apartment building of red brick and greenish glass. LaForce and Spencer were behind him. Navarro had, with Xu's assistance to get past the language barrier, gone up to the sixth floor to get a different view. Hank wasn't sure he was really going to get much of a better look even from up there. They already had elevation, and the bad guys weren't showing themselves much.

The air still stank of burning rubber, plastic, diesel, and worse. The faint tang of high explosives and gunpowder mingled with the stench of death that had lingered over Keelung City for days.

Some of the tank hulks along the Sun Yat Sen Expressway were still smoldering, three days after the fight that had stopped the PLA's end run cold before it could even reach the pass leading to Taipei.

As Hank scanned the high school, he could just make out a few vehicles inside the enclosure surrounded by the five- and six-story buildings that formed most of the school's infrastructure. It was a big high school, which was probably why the reinforced platoon of PLA stragglers had gone to ground there, fortifying it as best they could under fire.

Now, cut off from the beachhead in Keelung City—which was still holding, despite the hammering it was still taking from artillery and air power—they were getting desperate. They had hostages in there, and that was why Hank's and Laki's sections were getting ready to move in alongside the ROC Army. The Taiwanese would be focused on the PLA. The Triarii were going for the hostages.

That was a bit of a switch. Hank would have expected the Grex Luporum teams to be better suited for hostage rescue. His boys were still grunts, not high-speed Special Mission Unit operators.

Except that the Triarii infantry had, due to their limited resources and the nature of the shadowy war they'd been fighting for the last several years, had to become special operations forces of their own to a certain extent. Along the way, Hank—and he was sure he wasn't alone in this—had discovered that the over-specialization of such units was an artificial categorization that was really a very new sort of thing. Old-school grunts, the guys who'd fought in the Pacific in World War II and later in Korea, had done stuff that in modern times would have had regular infantry locked down in their FOBs while JSOC swooped in to take care of it.

Now, outside the military's bureaucracy, those specializations were breaking down. The Triarii had to be jacks of all trades, and while Hank could see how that could turn into a disaster if training was neglected—which it all too often was in the regular mil—so far, his boys were doing a pretty good job.

The high school was quiet and still. He could just see the scarred hull of a ZBD-05 past the corner of the nearest building, but there was no movement. The PLA had gone to ground and were trying not to stick their necks out.

Their breakout had turned into a bloodbath. Even as he watched the target area, Hank couldn't help but wonder what the reaction would be. Tens of thousands of PLA soldiers had already died on Taiwan, and they were no closer to overthrowing the Taiwanese government and seizing the island.

Whatever that reaction turned out to be, Hank didn't think it would be good.

That was a consideration for another time, though. Right now, they had a target to assault.

He eased back around the corner. He hadn't seen any bad guys down there, but if the ChiComs had snipers, showing himself would have been a bad idea, even if he didn't have a particularly high opinion of PLA marksmanship.

"Looks like nothing much has changed." The rest of the two Triarii sections were staged in the woods around the north side of the school, but the thickness of the vegetation had precluded running their final reconnaissance from there. "They're still hiding out." He checked his watch. Still about forty-five minutes to go time. "Let's go link back up and get ready to hit 'em." He keyed his radio. "Three, this is Actual. Come on down."

The squad leaders didn't have much to add. They'd all seen the reporting, and they'd seen the hostage video that the PLA soldiers' acting commander had put out. The fact that the internet was still working with all the death and destruction, and that the enemy was using it to try to bluff their way out of a crack was weird, but no weirder than anything else the Triarii had encountered so far in this war.

That video had shaped the plan. It wasn't really something Hank would have thought of, but Vetter had some experience in this sort of thing, and as soon as he'd watched the video, he'd immediately gotten in touch with some of Xu's associates in the NSB. They'd apparently figured out roughly which room of which building the hostages—mostly residents of nearby buildings and the Catholic priest who was the school's chaplain—were being held in by comparing images of interior rooms in the school, talking to those school administration personnel who were still available, and even comparing the position of the whiteboard on the wall. The PLA commander had been smart enough not to allow a view out the window, otherwise, from what Hank had gathered, it would have been even easier.

Navarro came down with Xu a couple minutes later, and without a word, Hank led the way back to the van they'd moved up to their vantage point in.

***

The Triarii crept through the jungle slowly and quietly.

There was a limit to just how much time they could take. There was little radio contact between them and the company of ROC infantry on the other side of the school, and so this was being coordinated by time hack rather than direct communication. So, they had to be in position—in fact, they needed to be inside the compound—in another fifteen minutes.

It was a delicate balance, because they were relying on stealth to get in close and be ready to hit the room with the hostages at the same moment the Taiwanese hit the perimeter.

Ideally, they'd move in on the hostages just before the assault, to sow even more confusion. After the last twenty minutes of moving through the bush, Hank doubted that was going to happen.

He stepped around another bush and found himself facing a mass of foliage. Muttering curses under his breath, he wove his way through, having to get himself and his weapon untangled from fronds and vines twice before he found himself somewhat in the clear again. *Fuck the jungle.*

Then he was moving toward another stand of trees, finally spotting Reisinger ahead of him after far too long without visual contact. The other man was bent down, practically duck-walking under a branch that formed a low arch over the forest floor. Shaking his head, Hank followed.

A few minutes later, barely two minutes before the time hack, they were at the back of the target building. Light tan plaster covered the walls, slightly dingy thanks to the tropical environment, and the windows were framed in gray. Those windows were big, covering most of the entire outer wall on the inside of the balconies that ran along the full length of the building.

This was going to be tricky.

Fortunately, there was a staircase at the end of the building, so they didn't have to cross any of those windows to get up to the target floor.

Of course, the PLA were holding their hostages on the top floor.

LaForce had taken lead with 2nd Squad, and they were now on the ground at the base of the stairwell. A body lay at Reisinger's feet, and since Hank hadn't heard a shot, even suppressed, he had to assume that the man hadn't been as watchful as he should have been. Reisinger had a streak of dark fluid on his trouser leg, probably where he'd wiped his knife blade off before sheathing it.

Hank moved up to join LaForce, who had paused just long enough to get security set before mounting the stairs, rifle aimed up at the next landing.

Keeping close together, the Triarii climbed, muzzles covering every opening as they ascended. Doors, windows, the next landing up…every angle had to be watched. Hank began to feel more and more exposed the higher they climbed, since the stairwell wasn't exactly completely enclosed.

Still, the timing worked out, if not quite as planned. A sudden, hammering storm of machinegun and cannon fire announced the commencement of the assault from Xiding Road, the ROC Army infantry pushing in through the gap in the buildings behind CM-34s armed with 30mm Bushmaster chain guns.

They sped up. With the assault coming in, the chance that the Communists would execute their hostages went up dramatically. No one was under any illusions that they wouldn't do it, either. The ChiComs had a record.

Reaching the top floor, LaForce, Evans, and Hank stacked on the landing. Hank might have pushed his way toward the front, but no one had commented on it. His prerogative.

There was no door, no hallway. The open balcony was it. That was going to be rough, since they'd be exposed the entire time, but there were no other options.

Evans took point, getting low and practically duck-walking down the balcony, staying below the level of the windows. Hank followed, though he high crawled on his knees and one hand rather than try to duck walk. He didn't think his joints could take that anymore.

They could hear raised voices from inside, and what might have been the crackle of a radio. Somewhere on the other side of the wall, a kid was crying. Hank clenched his jaw and tried to shut it out. *Concentrate on the mission. Don't get emotionally involved.*

Evans reached the door and rose more smoothly than Hank thought he could have, keeping his back to the concrete pillar behind him and his presence masked by the door itself. Hank passed him before doing the same, careful to check that he wasn't about to get shot in the back by a ChiCom in the next classroom before turning to join Evans at the door while LaForce covered their backs.

To both men's surprise, the door was unlocked. Evans threw it open, and they went in fast.

There had to be a dozen PLA soldiers in the classroom, along with almost twice as many civilians. The civilian hostages were all on their knees next to the wall, faced by a semicircle of PLA soldiers with weapons while the other four men in ChiCom camouflage stood around a radio, one of them shouting into it.

The man with the handset was the only one facing the door. He looked up as it opened, and Hank looked him right in the eye as he shot him through the upper chest.

Glass shattered under bullet impacts as the rest of the squad rose up into the windows and opened fire, forming an L-shape with the three men who'd just made entry. They kept their shots high to avoid hitting any of the civvies, but it was all over in a moment.

None of the ChiComs had even gotten a shot off.

A bunch of the civilians were screaming, the kids loudest of all. As Hank lowered his rifle, he saw that a young man in black, wearing a Roman collar, had thrown himself in front of the kids, shielding them with his body. He was spattered with gore from the closest two PLA soldiers, one of whom had had half his skull shot away by bullets passing through from two directions, but while he was shaken, the priest seemed to be unharmed.

Xu was on Hank's heels, barking instructions in rapid-fire Mandarin, and one of the civilians, an older man in collared shirt and slacks, quickly got up and started to help usher the hostages out the door. The firefight outside was intensifying, and the whole building shook as something blew up with a heavy *thud*. A black cloud billowed up outside the window and shrapnel whickered through the air, more windows shattering as the Triarii hustled the hostages out, keeping their heads low. Gunfire continued to rattle down below, as the PLA survivors fought tooth and nail. This was a fight for sheer survival for them now.

Hank kept his eye out as they hurried down the steps, expecting at any moment to get in a fight with more of the PLA soldiers who had holed up in classrooms in the big building, but they all seemed to want to stay inside as bullets and frag flew around the cup where the school sat. Xu was on the radio, shouting to make sure the ROC Army watched their fire at the north end of the building.

The descent went as fast as they could get the civilians to move. Speed was security. They reached the bottom just as several PLA soldiers tried to break out into the jungle.

Fortunately, 3rd Squad was on outer cordon, holding security just off the building, as far away as they could get without losing sight of the place. Even as Hank and Bishop popped the corner to cover that flank before letting any of the Triarii or the hostages run out into the trees, the men in green, brown, and gray camouflage started to bolt out of the doors. A storm of gunfire from the jungle cut them down before either Hank or Bishop could get a shot off. Bullets smashed through legs, chests, and skulls, dropping them in a welter of blood and flailing limbs. A few screamed. Most died quickly, falling with an awful, limp finality to the dirt. Some of the hostages started screaming again.

Then they were hustling the hostages into the concealment of the jungle, angling uphill and away from the windows on the west side of the building.

Behind them, the PLA continued to fight and die, as Xu shouted into his radio and the CM-34s started to simply hammer the school building with point-blank 30mm fire.

Chapter 30

"This is weird."

Hank, Spencer, and Xu had joined Colonel Weng in an observation post dug into a hilltop less than a mile from the Keelung City port. They were taking turns on the binoculars, watching the port itself.

The fight had all but ground to a halt over the last couple of days. The ROC Army was still going after pockets of PLA soldiers and vehicles that hadn't made it back to the port, but even those engagements had gotten fewer and farther between. Somewhere off to the east, gunfire popped, and something exploded with an echoing *boom*. But the real front, the Forward Line Of Troops, was a quiet row of dug in bunkers in the ruins of Keelung City, just outside the port.

There were still tanks and infantry fighting vehicles down there. The infantry weren't showing themselves much, instead staying hunkered down inside dug-in fortifications made from some of the sturdier rubbled buildings. They only moved in short dashes, exposing themselves as little as possible. However poor the tactics Hank had seen the PLA use so far, they'd clearly learned.

For the moment, the constant bombardment of the port had stopped. The Taiwanese stocks of artillery shells and rockets were starting to run low. That didn't bode well, not when there were still Communist troops on the island, but it was what it was.

Vetter had gotten word that there were Triarii ships on the way with more rockets, but whether they could get through the blockade was another question. The PLAN had taken a beating, too, but it was still out there, and there were fewer Triarii gunboats and arsenal ships in the Western Pacific, too.

"The Taoyuan beachhead has been reduced by half." Weng spoke good enough English that Xu didn't need to translate. "They have taken terrible losses. The number of vehicles alone that we have destroyed has nearly broken them, and it appears that much of their morale has collapsed. They have been falling back and only fighting when cornered over the last few days." He was watching the FLOT, and despite his words, Hank could *feel* the hatred there. Weng didn't give a shit that the PLA's morale was shot, that they were mostly scared kids who knew they were going to die in a foreign land, no matter how much their masters in Beijing told them that Taiwan was part of China. They were Communists and invaders on *his* land, and he wanted them all dead.

Hank could sympathize. His appreciation for the fear and dead morale of the PLA didn't take away from the fact that they *were* invaders, and many of the same sort of invaders who had tried to steal *his* country's resources and strategic ports, while funneling weapons and munitions to murderous thugs who had been overrunning the Southwest.

This was why he'd come to the Western Pacific, after all.

Still, he didn't feel elated, looking at that threadbare remnant of a force down there, clinging to the port and hiding from sniper and artillery fire. He didn't feel anything.

"This can't be it." Hank was still watching the PLA's tanks, mostly sheltering behind heaps of rubble and in destroyed buildings as much as possible. "They've got millions of people under arms."

"We've killed tens of thousands." Xu's voice was as cold as Weng's. "And our cruise missiles have put half their navy on the bottom of the Straits." That might have been a bit of an overstatement, but Hank didn't bother to comment. It might not be the wisest thing, either. The Taiwanese, despite the hammering they'd given the PLA, were still a people with their backs up against the wall, and the hatred was very real. Contradicting their homegrown propaganda in front of one of their infantry commanders wouldn't be healthy, given where they were.

Still, while things had been quiet, he just couldn't shake the sense of dread, the feeling that they still had the Sword of Damocles hanging over their heads. The Chinese Communist Party was the biggest organized crime syndicate in the world, masquerading as a government, and such men did not simply accept a failure of this magnitude. Even without a disaster like the collapse of the Three Gorges Dam, and the subsequent promise to take the millions of deaths out on the scapegoat of the Taiwanese, to launch an operation of this scale, take these losses, and then just sit back and shrug would be suicide.

He had to assume that the Chinese Communists knew it, too. Which only left the question: *What's next?*

"Are we getting any intel from the mainland?" He knew he had to tread carefully here, but all the same, he couldn't just shrug and assume the ChiComs were finished. "They've sent two major waves already. Are there any signs that they're getting a third together?"

Colonel Weng turned to look at him impassively, and Hank kept his own expression carefully controlled. Not that it was that hard. He was exhausted, even though they'd only conducted a few probing patrols close to the FLOT over the last couple of days. The weight of it all, the months of fighting Stateside, the preparations and the voyage west over the Pacific, more fighting and playing hide-and-seek with the PLAN around the Philippines and the Spratlys, and finally the brutal war for Taiwan itself… He was tired clear down to his bones.

The truth was, if he paused to think about it long enough—which he didn't want to do—he really didn't care that much anymore. He was becoming an automaton, a killing machine that continued on because there was no other choice. Only a sense of responsibility hammered into him during twenty years as a

Marine and close to five years as a Triarius after that kept him asking the questions that he *had* to ask. If only because he owed it to his Triarii.

Weng shook his head as he turned back to the ruined city below. "Most of our sources of information have gone dark since the war began in earnest. We have gotten a few drone flights close to the mainland recently, but they have not reported any more movement of men or materiel." There was a clipped brittleness to his voice, and Hank filled in the blanks.

They haven't gotten enough overflights through to be sure. He was going to have to check with Vetter. Maybe the flotilla had gotten a few drones in, maybe even enough to form some kind of coherent picture.

He didn't need to wait. The PRC's response to the losses they'd taken and the complete failure to hold more than two barely viable beachheads had already begun.

The *boom* that rolled over the mountain behind them sounded different from the explosion that they had heard only a few minutes before. It sounded different from the airstrikes and artillery that had deadened his hearing over the last several weeks.

Everyone else in the OP had noticed it, too. They all looked at each other, then scanned the landscape below. Nothing. No smoke, no sign of an explosion. The cloud of smoke from that fight below had already been swept out to sea by the wind.

Hank was starting to get a bad feeling. That had sounded *big*, somehow, which meant it was a lot farther away.

Weng's radio suddenly went nuts.

Weng and Xu both went white as a sheet.

Hank grabbed his own radio, just as it crackled to life with Vetter's voice. "All Tango elements, this is Tango Charlie. Stand to, I say again, stand to, one hundred percent security. Stand by for an enemy assault." He paused for a moment. "For those who can't see it, there's a mushroom cloud over Taipei. There appears to have been a nuclear detonation somewhere downtown. Take shelter and prepare to defend yourselves if the ChiComs decide to try to push the line while everybody's looking the wrong way."

"I need to get back to my section." Heedless of the fallout that was probably already drifting toward them on the wind, Hank grabbed his rifle and headed out of the bunker.

***

An official for the Chinese Ministry of National Defense gave a statement today declaring that the "separatists" on the island of Taiwan had been planning on launching an attack on the "liberation" forces with weapons of mass destruction, but that the separatists set the nuclear device off prematurely, while still within the city of Taipei. Condemning the attack in the strongest possible terms, the official called for the immediate surrender of the "criminals" calling themselves the government of Taiwan, or else the People's Republic of China will be forced to take drastic measures.

The deadline given for unconditional surrender of Taiwan to the People's Liberation Army was exactly twenty-four hours after the issuance of the statement.

Following the explosion in Taipei, which appears to have been a low-yield ground burst, with a death toll rapidly climbing toward 95,000 people, Chinese missile forces have been put on high alert.

Taiwan still has not issued any response to the Chinese demand, and just what will happen when the deadline runs out in just under four hours remains uncertain.

Part II

Chapter 31

The wheels touched with a faint screech, and we were down.

Kagoshima Airport wasn't a large facility, but it was big enough for us. Granted, it had been a hell of a trip. With the need to avoid Russian and Chinese airspace, never mind the shit-show that was going on up in the Korean peninsula, we'd had to take the polar route to Alaska, then cross to Japan. From what I'd heard, it had still been a pain getting everything cleared, and I didn't imagine the bird had a whole lot of fuel left by the time we touched down. The old Learjet wasn't exactly a 747.

The team got up, stretching and groaning. It had been a long, long trip. We'd been on the bird for almost two days, not even getting off when we landed to refuel. Not every stop had been especially friendly to Triarii, so we'd had to be careful.

Unfortunately, that meant we didn't have a lot of news. I could feel the tension rise as we got ready to get off the plane, waiting to hear just what had happened since we'd left Poland. The last we'd heard, the ChiComs had set off a nuke in Taipei.

None of us had a lot of gear, though it was still more than we'd entered Slovakia with, over a year before. We were still able to heft most of it on our shoulders as we headed down the stairs onto the tarmac.

It was a warm day, and clear, the mountains in the distance standing out green against the blue sky. It almost seemed peaceful, even though this was an international airport in a country at war. There were Japanese Self Defense Force vehicles visible at the fence, presumably there in case the Norks launched an attack. Conventionally, that might seem insane, but the North Koreans were by no means limited to their conventional army, as had been demonstrated already in Tokyo, only a few days before we left Poland. In fact, it looked like the Norks' terrorist arm was far more competent than the rest of the Korean People's Army.

Two buses waited at the base of the stairs. We were all in civilian clothes, though we were still going to stand out in Japan. Given recent events, concealing who we were was unlikely to work. Americans in Japan *were* going to be involved in the war effort, one way or another.

Triarii weren't supposed to be out here, though. To be frank, as far as the US government was concerned, we were back to being borderline outlaws. There was no way they were going to be happy that we were out here at all, much less planning to go in and dismantle the People's Republic of China from the inside out. So, while we apparently had liaison officers with the Japanese, we were going to be steering clear of the Army, Marine Corps, and Navy.

From what we'd been briefed before we'd left Poland, after Western Europe had become non-permissive, since the European Defense Corps was no more, and therefore the powers that be wanted us inconvenient non-state actors out of the way, the Triarii in the Western Pacific had already been doing that for several months, from the South China Sea clear up to Taiwan.

The man standing beside the bus wasn't Japanese, though. I didn't recognize him, but while the redhead with jug ears didn't look like a hardass, he had a nasty scar on his face that practically split his nose, and, more importantly, he had a Triarii patch on the backpack at his feet. This was our pickup.

Nobody said much as we filed aboard the bus. There was a time and a place for the brief, and with most of us more than a little unsure about the Japanese reaction to what we were there to do, best do it in a secure area, where we could be reasonably sure nobody was listening in. There were plenty of places where somebody with a parabolic microphone could pick up at least enough to have some idea what we were up to.

Still, I walked up to the redheaded dude and shook his proffered hand. Us scruffy gingers have to stick together, after all, even if my hair and beard were more red-tinged brown, now peppered with far more gray than I'd ever expected to have at my age. "Matt Bowen."

He returned the handshake firmly. "Taylor Haskins." He looked over my shoulder. "You're one of the guys I'm looking for. Where's Hartrick?"

I turned to see him coming down the steps, the last man off the plane. "That's him. The pissed-off, balding guy." Brian Hartrick would probably try to rip my head off for describing him like that, but I found him a lot less intimidating by then than I had when he'd been chief cadre in the Grex Luporum assessment and selection course.

We'd been through a lot together, Hartrick and I, since he'd also been my first team leader. I'd been through even more over the last year and some change, but there was a big brother bond there, nevertheless. I'd still give him shit, and he'd still get pissed about it, even so.

Hartrick looked up and saw me talking to Haskins, and immediately came over. He shook Haskin's hand. "Brian Hartrick." He glanced at me with narrowed eyes. "I'd like to be able to say that whatever Matt told you was a pack of lies, but he's too damned straight-laced. So, it's probably true." He smirked when my eyebrows went up. "What have you got for us?"

"There's a brief going as soon as we get to the resort." Haskins ushered us onto the bus. "We've got a bit of a boat ride before then, though. First class; we're playing up the tourist angle, even though I don't think any of the locals really buy it." We were the last ones on the bus, so the door shut behind us, and we all grabbed for seats as the vehicle lurched into motion. Apparently, the driver didn't think we had a lot of time to spare. "We've bought out the whole Marine Blue resort on Yakushima. I don't even want to know what it cost, but it seems to be mostly safe from prying eyes." He looked from one to the other of us. "From what little I've heard, though, it might make the first phase a little complicated."

Hartrick shot him a look and he shut up. Vehicles, if they're not yours, are damned poor places to have sensitive conversations.

It wasn't a long drive to the marina from the airport, and we mostly passed it in silence. The driver wasn't Triarii, so he had to be shut out.

We passed through open rice fields for a while before plunging into hills covered in thick, scrubby woods. Occasionally, the woods opened up to reveal more terraced rice fields, but the trip between the airport and Aira was mostly through rural Japan. Even the traffic was light, which was a good thing. Nobody was going to be looking in the windows, which lacked the curtains that probably should have been installed for security purposes.

I supposed, though, that the security curtains might have been a bit of a giveaway if we were trying to get dismissed as nothing more than a bunch of tourists.

I'd never done a Westpac float, so this was my first look at Japan. Aira was a small but modern city, as I generally expected Japanese cities to be, if much less crowded. I didn't see any buildings higher than three stories, and the traffic was still reasonably light.

The driving on the left side of the road thing was still throwing me for a bit of a loop, though. I knew there were places where it was still done, but I'd never been in a modern country that drove that way.

We reached the marina, dominated by the silos and a massive cargo conveyor that made up the port facilities. The bus pulled right up to the pier, and we were ushered off and directed toward the gangplank leading to a good-sized yacht. The boat's name was in Japanese, so I couldn't read it, but it definitely wasn't the standard ferry.

Not that I was going to complain.

It didn't take long to get everyone aboard. Our plane hadn't been the first, and was far from the last, but it had been an entirely Grex Luporum flight. That meant there were fewer of us, with fewer heavy weapons and less gear to load. The heaviest weapon we had was Tony's Mk 48. My back ached just looking at the duffel he was hauling his gear around in, since it was also packed with the suppressed machinegun and about eight hundred rounds of ammunition.

Apparently, we were the last ones to board. A few other guys were already ensconced along the sides and in the main cabin, which was pretty swank. As soon as we boarded, though, the gangplank was being withdrawn, and a moment later, with a thrum of engines, the yacht was pulling away from the pier and out into Kagoshima Bay.

***

It was a long trip, almost four hours. It was dark by the time the yacht docked at the short pier on the west shore of Yakushima Island, but I was wide awake, despite dozing on the voyage. Jet lag is a bear, and I hadn't really experienced it—aside from the general fatigue and schedule whiplash you get from active combat operations—for months. We'd been in the same time zone for over a year, ever since inserting into Slovakia. Suddenly flying halfway around the world was going to make the next week pretty miserable.

Even worse, given what we knew about what we'd flown into, I didn't think we were going to have a week to acclimate.

Filing down off the boat, we dutifully got onto another bus and headed out along the coast of Yakushima, crossing the Nagata River in a few minutes before pulling into the Marine Blue Yakushima resort.

The place didn't look big enough to house the entire Triarii operation, but as we got off the bus, I saw that there were a lot of GP Medium tents down on the beach. I heard a few groans at the thought of racking out on cots in a tent, but we'd certainly slept in worse places recently. Though I had to admit that the last month and a half in Poland had been pretty comfortable.

I had to banish that thought. It brought with it memories of a wedding, a honeymoon, and a farewell to a new wife I didn't know if I'd ever see again.

That's a hard thing to think about, when you're riding a bus through the dark in a country you've never seen before, knowing that in a short time you're going into a hostile country with very little support and the very real possibility that you might not come out.

Not that what we'd done in Europe had been safe. I'd left Klara behind several times to go into France and Germany with almost as little support. I'd pursued the relationship anyway, because to abandon it just because I *might* die was to give up hope, and I was a gloomy enough bastard as it was.

This felt different, though. In Germany, I had been only a couple hundred miles away from her. Here, I was on the other side of the planet. And if I went down in China, the odds were good that no one would ever know what had happened. She'd always have to wonder.

But I couldn't let these guys go in without me. So, I'd done what men have done since time immemorial. I'd kissed my wife goodbye and gotten on the plane. Arrangements to get her to the States had already been set up, so *if* I survived this, we'd meet again at home.

If there was a home left.

Now I just had to focus on the task at hand as much as I could, if only to keep the nightmares at bay.

Somebody had put up signs, out of sight of the road, to direct teams and sections to their berthing areas. There weren't any air or armor assets here, though I expected there would *have* to be air for what we were going to do. Just no Broadswords or Vipers on call, not if we got as deep into China as I expected we would, if we really were doing this.

Option Zulu. It was supposed to be a last-ditch thing. Our equivalent of a nuclear strike. Yet here we were, getting ready to do it.

Haskins saw us to our tent, and we dropped our gear. Nobody was that tired, though Jordan, Chris, and Tony immediately lay down anyway. Always sleep when you get a chance, particularly in a combat environment. And we didn't know when we were going in.

"There's a brief for team leaders and coordinators," Haskins said. "Starts in half an hour."

"Lead the way." Hartrick waved at Haskins to precede us, and he turned and ducked out of the tent. "Where's chow? And when, for that matter?"

"Chow's continuous, and there's a pretty good restaurant in the resort, which is still running. The locals kinda know what we're doing, and they don't give a shit. They're getting paid enough to keep their mouths shut until we're long gone, and with everything going on, the Japanese are pretty eager to see the Chinese get cut down to size." He led the way into the main building. "I think they'd happily use nukes themselves after what happened, even the guys from Hiroshima."

Something about the way he said that drew looks from both of us. "We've been out of the loop for a couple of days," Hartrick said. "But that sounds like something more has happened since they nuked Taipei."

Haskins' eyes widened a little, and he blew a deep breath out. "Yeah, you could say that." He stopped just before entering the main room, that looked like it had been turned into a command center and briefing theater. He lowered his voice. "They blamed the nuke in Taipei on the Taiwanese. Said they were preparing to hit the beachheads with WMDs. Then they gave the Taiwanese twenty-four hours to surrender unconditionally and submit the people who had ordered the nuke strike for trial for crimes against humanity."

He took another deep breath. "Of course, they didn't do that. They couldn't. As near as our intel has been able to determine, the nuke was a Russian suitcase bomb, roughly equivalent to our old W54 warheads, the SADM. It was only about a kiloton or so. Pretty small, as nukes go, but it was enough to kill thousands of people, and since it was a ground burst, it spread fallout all over the north end of the island. It wasn't a Taiwanese bomb. We're about ninety percent certain that the Chinese planted it and detonated it to justify what came next."

"Which we're going to make them pay for." I looked up to see a familiar face. Tom Wallace was well known throughout the ranks of the Triarii. He'd been one of the originals, Colonel Santiago's right hand man. If he was here, then things were serious indeed. "Come on up, Brian. We've got a full brief ready."

I glanced at Hartrick, but he just nodded, and we followed Wallace into the briefing theater. He didn't just leave it at that, though. "What did they do?"

Wallace glanced at us over his shoulder. "They launched five Dong Feng 5s at Taiwan. Hit Hsinchu, Taipei, Taichung, Tainan, and Kaohsiung." His voice was grim. "There's not much left of Taiwan as a country, I'm afraid."

"Holy shit." I'm not usually given to shocked exclamations, but that one just kind of slipped out. "How is Beijing still standing?"

The look that crossed Wallace's face was pure murder. "It seems that DC has decided that since Taiwan isn't really salvageable, there's no good reason to risk a wider nuclear war. 'What's done is done,' or some such shit. They're negotiating, *and* they're still trying to get the ChiComs to rein in the Norks."

"What the fuck?" If Wallace had been broadcasting pure murder, his reaction was pale in comparison to Hartrick's sudden rage. "These fucks already killed how many thousands of Americans, nuked our fucking *allies*, and we're going to just talk nice to them?"

"Does it surprise you?" Wallace's voice was cold. "I was on the convoy into Phoenix after some of our guys found Chinese weapons being shipped directly to narcos under cover of 'humanitarian' assistance, stuff that was suspiciously prepositioned before the cyber attack. Before you boys went to Slovakia, I expect. That's all documented. Hell, even the US mil contributed to retaking parts of the West Coast ports and the West

Texas oilfields, and they saw the same PLA involvement that we did. They still lied and said that it was just 'rogue elements' of 'PMCs,' and that it wasn't *really* the Chinese. The damned Reds have too much of a grip over these bastards, mainly through their fucking portfolios." He got to the screen at the front of the room. "That's why there wasn't a flight of Minuteman missiles heading for Beijing forty-eight hours ago, and currently won't be unless something changes drastically. It's also why we can expect no support from the Army, Marine Corps, Navy, or Air Force."

"How are we getting in, then?"

"We've got air assets." Wallace looked around the room. "Have we got everybody?"

I looked around, too. I recognized a lot of faces, including some other Grex Luporum team leaders I hadn't seen in over a year. I got a few nods, some salutes of recognition, some at whispered conversations that were probably telling the story of the guys who'd gone into Slovakia with only one trail section and some air support from Hungary.

Yeah, we'd done that. Not that I was going to preen over it. We'd survived, that was about the best that could be said about it.

All of us except Dwight.

"All right, gentlemen. Let's get started." Wallace brought up a map of China. "As you are all aware, thanks to the use of nuclear weapons against civilian targets and our own government's refusal to retaliate, Colonel Santiago has authorized Option Zulu against the People's Republic of China. For anyone who needs a refresher, that means we're going to sneak in and systematically dismantle as much of the Chinese Communist Party's infrastructure and political coherence as possible. By the time we're done, provided we do this right, Communist China will cease to be a country."

He looked around one more time before getting down to the meat of the brief. "These motherfuckers tried to do it to us. We've confirmed that Unit 61398 was behind the attack on the grid. The 'contractors' who went 'rogue' on the West Coast were

PLA regulars. The weapons and explosives used against our transportation infrastructure after the cyber attack were almost entirely from the PRC. Now, we're going to return the favor.

"With interest."

Chapter 32

Hank sat on the corner of his cot and stared at the sand scattered on the aluminum flooring. He was exhausted. It felt like he should feel *something* after what had happened, but after the breakneck evacuation from Shen'ao, the mushroom clouds still rising over the mountains behind them, he really couldn't feel anything.

"Hank Foss?" The voice sounded familiar. He looked up to see a figure standing in the tent flap. "Holy shit, I didn't even know you were still alive."

"Bradshaw?" Hank couldn't be sure at first, but the dark-haired man standing in the tent's door sure looked like Tyler Bradshaw. He stood and shook his hand. "Damn. How long has it been?"

"Three years." Bradshaw found an equipment case and sat down on it as Hank sank back down onto his own cot. "Feels like longer, though."

Hank slumped, his elbows resting on his knees. "Brother, you ain't lyin'."

The last time he'd seen Bradshaw had been when they'd both attended the training course that the Triarii had finally put together for their field leaders, several years after both of them had already been doing work. Staged on a ranch in the middle of nowhere, Wyoming, it had almost been less a training school and more a meeting to hash out the organization's Standard Operating Procedures.

They'd been teamed up for most of the course and had gotten to know each other fairly well. He liked Bradshaw. He just hadn't expected to see him here, halfway around the world.

"Were you on Taiwan?" Bradshaw's voice was low, almost as if he had hesitated to pick at the scab if Hank had been.

"Yeah." He was somewhat surprised at how heavy his own voice sounded. "Yeah, we were." He looked around the tent. "Not everybody made it out, either." He wasn't even thinking about the nukes, just then. He was thinking about Michaels, turned to pink mist by an artillery shell, Alexander lying face down in the dirt, a bullet through the back of his skull, Lind going down trying to get to his boys. Even Arturo's death seemed distant, by then.

Bradshaw didn't say anything, though Hank saw him nod out of the corner of his eye. When he turned back to the other man, he saw the same haunted look that he was probably wearing. "I know the feeling." He was looking at something far away, and when he finally snapped out of it, he said, "My section's half replacements at this point."

Hank jerked his head toward the rear of the tent, where half a dozen former ROC Army soldiers sat on their own cots, mostly cleaning T91 rifles that were already spotless. "I got a few reinforcements. They only agreed to come if they could kill more Communists. I told 'em they'd get to kill all they could stomach." He couldn't quite bring himself to grin. Not after everything else. Not after Xu had refused to leave, turning back toward Keelung City with a look in his eye that had told Hank the man was looking for death. When he thought about the fact that Mei-Ling was probably dead, he'd understood. "Most of the others didn't want to leave. Can't say I blame 'em. The rest of us are plenty motivated, though, even without mushroom clouds over our homes."

Bradshaw nodded. "You were Stateside for all that shit?"

"Yeah. Down in the Southwest. We were one of the sections went into San Diego."

Bradshaw's eyebrows went up a little. "No shit? Heard about that from some of the guys who crossed into Poland after the war started."

That raised Hank's eyebrow. He hadn't heard who all had gone to Europe. He'd been a little busy. "You were already over there?"

A nod and a dry, humorless chuckle. "We went into Slovakia with GL Team X. Ended up having to run for our lives with a handful of regular Army survivors when the EDC pulled their end run. Barely made it to Poland alive."

Hank could only shake his head. "Damn, brother. We heard a little about that." He wasn't sure whether he'd rather have been stuck in San Diego or trying to fight his way out of a country with a bunch of Army cats after the EDC had just pulled a sneak attack and was actively trying to wipe out any of the Slovak Nationalists' potential allies. It *almost* made the war on Taiwan seem like a cakewalk…up until the nukes had started dropping.

"I'm guessing you weren't too close to Ground Zero." Bradshaw looked him over. "You don't look like you're dying of radiation sickness."

A sigh escaped Hank's lips. "I don't know." He looked down at his hands. They were still steady. "We were pretty well downwind from the Taipei bomb, and that was a ground burst. Think I remember reading somewhere that those put out a lot more fallout." He looked at the ground and shook his head. "Fuck. Nukes were supposed to be something my *parents* worried about. The bad old days were supposed to be over."

Bradshaw's chuckle sounded like it belonged in a graveyard. "We should have seen enough to put that legend to rest. Ain't no 'end of history' until it *all* goes up in smoke."

"You ain't lyin'." He looked at his hands again. He hadn't felt any nausea, at least none that he couldn't put down to exhaustion and stress. "I don't know. Maybe it'll be better to go down like Sampson, bringing the roof down on our own heads." He hadn't thought about that story in a long, long time. Hadn't thought about the Bible or religion in almost as long. Now that he was pretty sure he was a dead man, one way or another…

He still wasn't sure if he was ready to start thinking that way.

Bradshaw had caught it, though. "Didn't think you were a religious man."

"I'm not. And even now, when I probably should be… I'm not sure God's willing to take a guy like me back."

Bradshaw shrugged, checked his watch, and stood up. "You should talk to the TL of the team I've been working with. Guy's callsign's 'Deacon,' and he damned well earned it. He might have more to say on that subject than I do." He tilted his head to one side, studying Hank for a moment. "You guys hear where you're going yet?"

"Not specifically. We'll be in the south, I know that much, but I haven't gotten a target list yet. You?"

"Still running trail for Team X, I think. We'll be heading up north. Somewhere around Beijing."

Something twisted a little in Hank's gut at that. "I envy you. You get a crack at the big shots themselves."

"Maybe." Bradshaw ran a thumb along his jaw. "First targets are all power stations. I guess we've already got some people on the ground, getting inside the Great Firewall to start hitting their networks, make it harder to coordinate any repairs. Gonna be a lot of people hungry and in the dark by the time this is over."

"Fuck 'em." Hank surprised himself a little at the vehemence of his hate. "They did it to us, then turned around and murdered millions on Taiwan. Let 'em suffer."

Bradshaw watched him a moment, and Hank couldn't quite meet the other man's eyes. They were different men, both of them, from the men they'd been three years before. And right then, after the nightmares he'd seen, Hank didn't feel like apologizing for that.

"Well. Better get going. We're going wheels up a lot sooner than I'd like. Good seeing you again, Hank. Take care of yourself."

"You too, Tyler."

Both men knew full well they'd probably never see each other again.

Chapter 33

Insert was not fun.

While we had some time to work with, ironically due to our own politicians' reticence to do anything about the destruction of Taiwan—though the more I thought about it, the more I had begun to suspect that they didn't have the *capability* after everything that had gone down, which raised some serious questions about how the Armed Forces had performed as well as they had over the last year—we were going to end up using all of it, just to make sure we infiltrated the PRC with some degree of stealth.

Our route covered almost five thousand miles, and the pilots were going to be flying for a while after that. There *were* still airlines flying between Japan and China, strangely enough, though their routes were very tightly constrained by the continued and escalating fighting going on in the Korean peninsula. There were a few teams and infantry sections going in that way, but we were bound to take the long way around.

The stop in the Philippines was too short to do much more than stretch our legs, but at least we could do that. Most of the rest of our refueling stops we'd have to stay on the plane, the windows covered, for security reasons. The Philippines were still a nominal Triarii ally, even though any such arrangement was still mostly on the downlow.

After the Philippines came Bangkok. Some of the other guys on the bird muttered about what they were missing out on. I was sure that if Phil had still been alive, he would have been among them. Most of the rest of us were getting too old to be enticed by the fleshpots of Thailand. I was newly married, and it held zero appeal to me. Just made me think of Klara.

Regardless, we stayed on the bird while it was refueled and checked out. Then we were taking off again, embarked on the last leg. Our last leg, anyway.

The crew had filed a flight plan for New Delhi, but once we were airborne, the pilot shifted course north, tucking the plane in about five hundred feet below and behind the nonstop from Bangkok to Beijing. We wouldn't show up on radar, and our transponder was turned off, so flight trackers wouldn't pick us up, either. From the cockpit, you could have looked up and seen the tail of the other aircraft.

I didn't have all that clear a picture of just how many aircraft and boats were moving in on China, just because of the necessity of OPSEC, but I could imagine. There were thousands of us moving in that night.

Most of us slept as much as we were able as we flew over Laos and Vietnam. I confess I dozed, at best. I was keyed up and while I can't quite say I was worried, I had a lot on my mind.

About an hour before our drop point, I started getting everyone up. We had a lot to do.

While we'd all stayed in civilian clothes for the first couple legs of the flight, now we changed over into field cammies. We weren't wearing Triarii greens for this. Where we'd gotten enough of them, I don't know, but we had enough PLA uniforms for each man. As a disguise, it wouldn't hold up for long, especially not if they got a good look at Jordan, but we were hoping to stay out of sight for the most part. The PLA uniforms were mainly intended to keep anyone from taking that second look at a distance.

Similarly, we weren't going in with our OBRs and Mk 48s. As much as I'd hated to leave that rifle behind, more than I'd hated to leave the SBR Tactical I'd used in Germany most recently, I could understand the reasoning. We had re-outfitted ourselves with captured QBZ-191s, and while we hadn't been able to find enough of the newer QJY-161s or 191s, we had two QJY-88s. They'd do, especially since they used the same 5.8mm ammunition as the rifles.

We weren't even carrying that much ammo. There was only so much we *could* carry, and the explosives intended for our first target accounted for the bulk of the loads in our rucks. That, and hopefully enough water and chow for about four days. After that, we were going to have to forage.

That was part and parcel of Option Zulu, and why we were carrying Chinese Communist weapons. We would have to resupply off the land for food and water, and off the PLA and the People's Armed Police for ammo and explosives. Considering the fact that the PLA and PAP were already targets, we could potentially kill two birds with one stone.

I was under no illusions about what we were about to do. We were jumping into the heart of a hostile nation, almost a hundred and eighty miles from the coast, with only the support we could carry on our backs. Going into Slovakia had been risky as hell. This was exponentially worse.

But it had to be done. The fact that the People's Republic of China had done what it had meant it was an existential threat to everyone around it, as well as to our own country. If none of us ever made it back, it would be a small price to pay.

That's a hard thing to accept, especially when you really do have something to live for.

I crossed myself, put it aside, and focused on the mission. That was the only way I was ever going to possibly get back to see Klara again.

It took most of the next hour to get jocked up and ready to jump. I was the jumpmaster, so I had my hands full. By the time we were ten minutes out, though, I'd finished and was in the rear of the aircraft, helping the crew get the rear door open.

That had taken some retrofitting in Japan. The 727 was an *old* bird, but this one was in pretty good shape. However, after the D.B. Cooper incident, the Cooper vane had been added, to make it impossible to open the aft door and airstair in flight. We'd had to take that off.

Now, as we roared through the night over China, we shut off the cabin lights and cranked down the stairs, the plane buffeted by the airflow, and got ready to jump.

It was far too loud to say much, so I was getting hand signals from the crew chief. Five minutes.

Jumping from an airstair was not something I'd tried before. As risky as it was, as jumpmaster I did my thing, descending partway down the steps to peer out into the night.

To be perfectly honest, I was relying halfway on map study, halfway on guesswork to find our mark. We had some drone shots of the area of the drop zone, but they were iffy. That scared me a lot more than the fact we were about to jump into Communist China.

There. That line of lights had to be the Zhaitang Dam. I breathed a little easier, despite the wind whipping past under my feet and snatching at my trouser legs. We were on course. I hauled myself back up the steps, struggling against both the buffeting of the aircraft and the weight of my ruck, oxygen system, and parachute.

"Thirty seconds!" Nobody could hear me over the roar and through my mask, but I held up my thumb and forefinger, half an inch apart. David shuffled down onto the stairs, Jordan right behind him.

This was going to have to go fast. I hoped nobody got hung up. We had to stay together.

"Go!" I couldn't reach David, but when I pointed down the stairs, my knife hand came out right in front of Jordan's face, and he gave David a hard tap to the shoulder. David promptly dove off the end of the airstair, vanishing into the night.

Jordan was right on his heels, followed by Chris, Reuben, and Steve. Zhao Tsun-han, our former ROC Army straphanger and Chinese translator, followed Steve, right in front of Jim, Lucas, and Tony. As jumpmaster, I was the last one out. I didn't have time to wave goodbye to the crew. Hopefully they made it to Ulan Bator.

Descending the stairs was hairy as hell. They were shaking and rattling a lot in the slipstream, bouncing harder with every step. I had my head ducked, and it still felt like I was about to get scalped on the overhead. The weight of all my gear threatened to trip me up, but I got to the bottom of the stairs and launched myself off into the dark.

My guardian angel must have been looking out for me, because I fell straight, putting my arms and legs back to track toward the rest of the team, all of whom had arched and flattened out to link up. We all had our PS-31s down, and small IR fireflies secured to the backs of our helmets. That was a risk, showing IR these days, but we had to stay together. Getting separated on this jump was probably going to be a death sentence.

I kept streaking downward, the rush of the wind the only sound in my ears, until I was just above the clump of falling figures, at which point I arched and threw my arms out, slowing my descent and falling into formation with the rest. A couple seconds later, we all waved off, swam out to a safe distance, and pulled ripcords.

My chute opened smoothly, and I grabbed the toggles and got it under control, looking around to make sure the rest of the team had full canopies. I counted ten in addition to mine and breathed a sigh of relief.

Looking down at the nav board on top of my ruck, I pulled the left toggle slightly to get on course. We had about forty klicks to go to the DZ.

***

It was a long, cold trip under canopy. We'd bundled up thoroughly in the bird, and it still wasn't enough. It was probably forty or fifty below zero when we'd jumped. It was getting warmer as we descended, but not fast enough. I felt frozen, and the weight of my ruck and weapon crushing me down into the parachute

273

harness hurt. Standing in the bird, feeling it slowly fusing my vertebrae, hadn't been fun, but having those groin straps digging in while I hung under the chute really sucked.

The dark countryside below us was getting closer, and I started looking for landmarks, not just following my compass. There hadn't been a lot of possible DZs in the target area, so this was going to have to be as precise as we could make it. After all, the only viable DZ that wasn't some farmer's field was going to be a road passing through the Gouya Nature Scenic Area, and that wasn't exactly a big target.

Fortunately, my PS-31s gave me a better view than the old green phosphor PVS-14s that I'd used as a Marine. There wasn't a lot of illum—we'd picked that night for a reason, timelines and risk of nuclear war notwithstanding—but there was enough ambient light making it through the scattered clouds overhead that I was picking out a lot more details in the hills below us.

There. The road was a thin, pale ribbon just ahead. The wind was coming out of the southeast, which was going to make this tricky, but we were going to have to do some hairy flying as soon as we dropped below the peaks as it was.

Granted, I wasn't leading. David had jumped first, and he was still acting as the pointman, the lowest jumper under canopy, and he was going to have to figure this out and hopefully not bring us in on the side of a forested mountain.

I saw his strobe vanish as he turned into the wind. A moment later, Jordan followed, with the rest of the stack still tight, only about twenty yards between each of us.

I followed them all down, even as David suddenly banked sharply. No, he hadn't banked, the wind had shifted. I watched what he did, and when I got lower and into that swirling wind in the valley, I was able to compensate more quickly.

Then it was time. I lowered my ruck to the end of its lowering line, watching the road come up to meet me as it hit the end with a tooth-rattling jerk. This was going to suck.

My ruck hit just as I sank the toggles as deep as I could, flaring the chute and slowing my forward rush to almost nothing. The ruck still acted as an anchor, and instead of floating gently to the ground to land on my feet, I crashed to the ground like a sack of rocks. I barely managed a semi-proper parachute landing fall, but fortunately my canopy collapsed almost immediately instead of dragging me along the road.

Quickly shrugging out of my harness, I hauled my rifle around and scanned the darkness around me, reaching up with my off hand to kill the strobe on my helmet. I'd landed only a few yards from Tony. I held my position for a few moments, watching and listening, then quickly started to get my chute packed up before retrieving my ruck.

We were on the ground. We had just invaded the People's Republic of China.

Chapter 34

Hank leaned on the rail as the puttering little fishing boat moved in toward shore. Ahead, he could already see the flames and the faint tang of smoke reached his nostrils. A good number of Guangdong Province's power plants were right on the coast, and the Triarii arsenal ships had taken full advantage of that particular target-rich environment. Already, whole swathes of Guangzhou and its outlying cities and suburbs had gone dark.

That darkness was going to be vital to the night's mission. They had a long way to go, and a lot of targets to hit before sunrise.

In a way, even though he was just a passenger at the moment, Hank was grateful that he'd drawn this particular mission set. They'd get right to work that night, as opposed to some of the teams and squads that were going in deeper, who would have to spend most of the night on insert, going to ground during the day and then moving to their targets the next time the sun went down.

He looked around the hold of the small, rickety vessel. It was no high-end assault craft; in fact, it was little more than a motorized junk. There were a bunch more such vessels out there on the water off the coast of Guangdong Province, all scattering for cover after the drone swarms had hammered the coast. There were too many for the Chinese Coast guard to track all of them, and not all of them were Trojan horses, either.

He wasn't a section leader right then. There were too many targets. Every infantry section had been split up, reinforced as necessary, and was deploying as a squad. In many respects, they were all Grex Luporum Teams now.

Hank didn't worry about the fact that the Grex Luporum Teams had slightly better gear, and training somewhat more geared toward this kind of mission. He didn't envy them. Those boys were going deep, and if anyone involved in Option Zulu had a good chance of never coming back, it was the GL teams.

As numb and hardened as he'd become, he felt a flash of guilt at the thought. *What the hell do you have to live for, huh? Why should those guys go into the lion's den, while you feel relief that you might get to live a little longer? What makes you so fucking special?*

He shook his head. *Little too late for that, ain't it?*

They were passing by Xiaohengquin Island, and the blazing wreck of the Hengqin Thermal Power Station. There were a lot of flashing lights on the ground around the conflagration, as local emergency response tried to put out the fires, but from the looks of things, the plant was fully involved. There wouldn't be any salvaging it for a while.

Even longer than the Chinese probably hoped, if the Triarii had anything to say about it.

They kept their heads down as they motored past, the captain—another Taiwanese refugee, like the three reinforcements Hank had gotten for 2nd Squad, who were down in the bow and currently prepping their first nasty surprise for the night—keeping them close to the center of the channel, away from other boats and vessels. No one on shore seemed to be paying the traffic in the channel much attention. They had more pressing concerns.

The boat wasn't moving all that quickly, so Hank got a pretty good look at the damage the drone swarm had done. None of the drones themselves were that big, so their individual payloads had been pretty small, but put together, they'd devastated the power plant. At least one of the smokestacks was down, and fire was raging through the main building.

The smoke was not going to make life pleasant for those living in the high-rises to the north, either. Especially not with the power out.

More fires became visible as they continued to move up the Xijiang River. Less than an hour later, still somewhat shrouded by evil black smoke, they were approaching their first target.

Hong, the captain, had been gradually drifting the boat to starboard, until they were passing right by one of the sets of pilings holding up the suspension bridge that now loomed overhead. It was one of many that crossed the river over the next fifty miles, and the first inland from the ocean. There was yet another bridge under construction that would pass right over the mouth of the river, but it still hadn't been completed yet.

As they passed, Li and Cai heaved what looked like a 55-gallon drum over the side, shielded from view by the bridge overhead. The drum hit the water with a splash and immediately sank out of sight.

That drum was filled almost to the brim with PETN. There was a *hell* of a lot of boom in that barrel. It needed to be a big charge, if they were going to break the bridge.

The fuse was long enough that they should be at least ten nautical miles up the river before the bomb went off. The drum had, additionally, been weighted so that it should sink straight to the bottom and come to rest immediately, with little risk that it would roll away from the pilings.

Having hardly slowed at all, the boat continued upriver.

***

They dropped four more such charges over the next couple of hours. From what Hank could see just from the river, the countryside of Guangdong Province was either dead quiet or in an uproar. The strikes hadn't hit half the province's power stations yet, but the load on the grid had to be immense. Aside from emergency vehicle lights, Hank couldn't see a single electric light from the river.

Hopefully, losing half the power generation in the province in the space of a half an hour had blown up a few substations. He didn't know for sure that it worked that way, but he could hope.

The drone swarms' targets hadn't limited to just the coast. While he couldn't see or hear them, he knew—even if he didn't know the specifics of numbers or targets, just in case he or any of the others were captured—that there were thousands more quiet, stealthy drones, relatively cheap for what they could do, winging their way inland, heading for known PLA and PAP bases. More would hit power stations in more densely populated areas, where the Triarii couldn't easily get in and out without being spotted.

While the assault on China's power grid would sow plenty of chaos, they still had to step carefully. They were in the country with the most CCTV surveillance in the world, and deniability was vital to the mission. They had to do as much damage as possible without being spotted, so that they collapsed the Chinese ability to retaliate before they realized that the Americans were tearing their country apart from the inside.

The next target was a twofer. The bridge ahead had three spans, which would use up the last of the barrel bombs. And since the bridge was right next to the Nanhai 1st Power Station, they weren't necessarily going to be able to get clear before the charges went off. The power station was the other target.

He still hoped they that they could still get away in the confusion without getting pinned down or identified. The plan was sound, anyway.

They dropped their charges as they went under the bridge and kept moving with hardly a hiccup, angling toward the shore but offset enough that they weren't going to sail right up to the power plant. Getting in and getting out quietly would be next to impossible, as plant security had to be on high alert given what was happening elsewhere that night.

Hank moved to the side, joining LaForce, Huntsman, and Bishop. Like all Triarii entering China that night, they had shed their greens for PLA camouflage, and while the men going deeper into the country had been equipped with more modern QBZ-191s, there had been only so many of those rifles to go around. Hank's squad had the older, bullpup QBZ-95s.

He wished he'd thought to pick up more of the 191s down in the Spratlys. He'd never been a fan of bullpups.

They waited as the boat drifted toward the shore and the quay where tanker ships pumped the fuel into the massive tanks ashore. Originally meant to run on heavy crude, the plant was, apparently, now fueled by coal slurry. That made things a little more complicated.

They stayed low, just in case, but everything was quiet, even though every floodlight on the power station was fully lit and there were several security vehicles speeding around the grounds. Everybody was up that night, and scared stiff.

They probably didn't have night vision, though, judging just by what he'd seen on Taiwan. The PLA had used up so much materiel and men on that island that he didn't expect security guards on a power plant to be their best.

The boat came close enough to shore, and when he was sure they were in deep enough darkness, Hank gave the signal. Two by two, the squad went over the side, splashing into the river and swimming back downstream, toward the shadowed shore just around the point from the pumphouse that provided the plant's cooling towers with water.

It was a short swim, though the water stung a little. Hank didn't want to think about what might be in it. The pollution in China was legendary, and they were close enough to the ocean that *everything* that had washed downstream was probably getting into every crack and crevice.

They came up on shore, guns up and looking for targets. The nearest security vehicle had already turned around, though, and the red brake lights were quickly receding down the riverbank.

The Triarii and their Taiwanese straphangers quickly wormed their way into the brush above the beach, and then they were moving back toward the bridge, far too slowly for Hank's taste, though the creeping pace was necessary, especially with site security being so alert.

It took far too long to reach a spot under the shadow of four large fuel or waste tanks, where there were also trees that might provide some more concealment. Hank almost wanted to just set the charges there, destroy the tanks, and get out. Even if the fire spread, though, that wouldn't necessarily put the plant out of commission for long, and lasting damage was the goal.

There was a solid, sheet metal fence at the top of the bank, which had served to further conceal them as they'd moved toward the conveyor, but now it created a problem. It was a solid wall between them and their objective.

While LaForce put the rest of the squad on security, down in the bushes or along the fence itself, Hank, Bishop, and Evans got to work forcing a breach. Kneeling at the bottom of the barrier, Hank whispered, "Find me a seam."

The three of them spread out, feeling their way along the fence. There wasn't much light down there, which was an oversight Hank was more than willing to take advantage of.

He heard Bishop hiss. Turning back, he saw that the other man was pointing at the fence, about ten feet away. Hank hustled over to join him and saw that Bishop had indeed found a seam. To make matters even easier, it hadn't been nailed into place, but just tied together with baling wire. He'd heard about the "good enough" attitude in Communist China, and right then, he was grateful for it.

It didn't take long to get the wire cut and bend the sheet metal just far enough out of the way to slip a man with gear through. Hank went first. If anyone was going to get spotted by plant security and get shot, it was going to be him.

But the other side of the fence, in deep shadow under the trees, was as quiet and still as the rest of the place. All hell might be breaking loose all over the province, and the security guards might be on their guard, but there were only so many of them.

He carefully checked for CCTV cameras. If they got spotted too soon, this could get hairy. Nothing stood out in his

NVGs, though, somewhat to his surprise. If there was any place in China where he would have *definitely* expected round-the-clock surveillance, it would have been a power plant.

There were probably plenty of cameras around the boilers, but they hoped to pull this off without going all the way in, even though they still had to cross a fair bit of the plant to reach their target.

The rest of the squad slipped through the opening behind him, except for Faris and Huntsman, who stayed on the outside of the fence, holding security, just in case. Faris had gotten real quiet after Taiwan. The man who had been his problem child back in the States had changed, and while it had been for the better for section discipline, Hank doubted it was for the man's own mental well-being.

Now that they were inside the perimeter, they moved fast. Hopefully, if they did get spotted, their PLA weapons and equipment might buy them a few moments. Hopefully enough to break contact and get out.

Staying in the shadows under the trees, they crossed the grounds, passing what looked like a park as they went. They could still see a couple of the plant security guards' vehicles, but this part of the installation was deserted. Nobody was going for a stroll in the park in the middle of the night, particularly not on a night like this.

Hank would have liked to set charges on the boilers themselves. That would have definitely put the plant out of commission for months, if not years. But getting in there without somebody figuring out that they didn't belong there would be extremely difficult, never mind getting out. So, they were going to try to burn the place down by another way.

As they stepped unavoidably into the light and the coverage of several cameras, they slowed and made it look as much as possible like they were just extra security, deployed for the night because of the strikes on other power plants throughout the country. They went unchallenged, for the moment, so it seemed to work. The PLA was probably rushing what forces they could to every intact power station in the country at the moment, and even if they weren't, these guys probably expected them to, and wouldn't want to challenge PLA soldiers, anyway.

Staying away from the security personnel who were hanging out by the gate, trying not to look furtive, they headed toward the main building and the substation beyond it, keeping a second line of trees between them and the other security guards.

The substation had its own border of trees just outside the fence, and while it might have been nice and decorative, it also provided the Triarii with the concealment they needed while they cut a hole in the fence.

There were some CCTV cameras in evidence around the main building now, but no alarm had been raised yet. They probably thought they had to worry more about air attack than saboteurs. More fool them.

It took seconds to get through the fence, and then they were spreading out through the substation. Evans and Bishop took near and far security, accompanied by Cai and Li, while the rest hastily pulled their charges out of assault packs and started to affix them to the transformers with the rare earth magnets taped to them. The fuses were a little short for Hank's comfort, but they should have enough time to get clear before the fire and explosions started.

Except that someone *had* noticed their approach.

A voice called out in Mandarin, and a flashlight shone through the trees. If they hadn't spotted the hole in the fence, they were about to.

Li acted first, stepping out toward the gate, calling out in reply. His voice—if Hank was hearing the Mandarin right—was imperious and demanding, probably just like a PLA officer who'd caught some dirtbag reservist slacking off. Hank eased around the transformer he was prepping for destruction, looking at the confrontation.

The two security men had stiffened to attention, if a sort of sloppy attention. They looked scared, though. They probably hadn't expected a PLA inspection.

Li kept barking imprecations in Mandarin as he got closer, then, just as he leaned into the first man's face, he struck.

Yanking a knife out of his gear, he stabbed the second man in the neck, fast as a striking snake, and then he was on top of the first man, one hand over his mouth as the knife went into the juncture between neck and shoulder, stabbing the man repeatedly as he sank to the ground.

Bishop had already moved in, dashing toward the first man and quickly finishing him off as he gurgled. Then they were dragging the bodies into the shadows of the trees while Hank and the rest collapsed on the hole in the fence, waiting for the alarm to sound.

Nothing happened. Those two must not have called in, and either the CCTV cameras weren't aimed quite right, or whoever was supposed to be watching them was asleep at the switch.

Still struggling to maintain their nonchalance, even though Li was now covered in blood, they hustled back across the grounds. Just before they reached the fence, an alarm started to wail.

"Go!" Hank and LaForce held on the hole in the fence as the rest started ducking through, shielded by the shadows of the trees. Hank could see headlights and flashlights moving on the other side of the grounds, and he knew they didn't have a lot of time left.

Fortunately, neither did the fuses on the charges.

The first explosives went off with flashes and loud reports that were quickly drowned out as the massive transformers exploded. Showers of sparks and roaring blue flames burst into the sky as the surrounding countryside went dark. The fire was soon spreading fast, and more secondary explosions rocked the night.

Hank and the others were already in the water, the junk ready to pick them up for the next leg, just before the charges on the bridge pylons started to go off.

The crew hauled them aboard as spray blew skyward around the bridges, and the nearest span fell into the river with a crash. Several trucks went down with it.

The power plant was now fully involved, several of the trees around the substation blazing as the fire raged. Hank got on deck, dripping and aching, and looked across the water at their handiwork, as Hong kept the boat motoring away.

A decent night's work. There was still a long way to go.

Chapter 35

It took three days to get to our ORP.

Moving through hostile territory takes time. When you're crossing steep hills—I couldn't bring myself to call the two-thousand-foot peaks around Beijing "mountains"—in the bush, it takes even longer. Given where we were, we couldn't take chances, either. Every movement had to be carefully calculated, and every step had to be taken with the assumption that it could be the one that alerted the enemy if we weren't careful.

We were hundreds of miles from support. If we took contact, that was it. We *might* be able to break contact and vanish into the woods, start our E&E for the coast near Tianjin, where we could steal a boat and head out into the Yellow Sea. That was our extract plan, such as it was, anyway. But that would be mission failure, and furthermore, we all knew that even if we managed to break contact cleanly, they'd be hunting us every step of the way after that. We weren't the only units on the ground—I knew that all three of Tyler Bradshaw's squads were out there, *somewhere*—but comm security meant we couldn't afford to do much coordination. We had to assume, based on the intel we had, that any transmission would be picked up. Chinese Communist surveillance was *extensive*, and even if they couldn't listen in, they'd notice something. *Especially* with the wreckage we were making of their infrastructure.

So, we crept through the woods at night and went to ground during the day. It was almost like being back in Germany, before the offensive and the assault on the European Defense Council building, except we were even farther away from friendlies, and except for Zhao, none of us could remotely even try to pass for locals at any close distance.

In retrospect, it *really* wasn't all that different from being back in Slovakia, except that this time we were out for blood. There, we'd just been trying to stay alive.

We were far enough north that we were outside the cloud of smog that hung over Beijing itself, which I was glad of. We were all in pretty good shape but sucking in the putrid air of the most polluted city on earth while humping heavy rucks over steep hills and through scrubby pine woods was not my idea of a good time, and all it could take, in some of the places we had to pass through, would be a single coughing jag and we'd be made. Our route, by necessity, took us through or close to several small villages as we got across the handful of roads that ran through the hills.

Granted, the security forces had other problems, if some of the other teams and squads were on timeline. Intel had fingered ten power stations around Beijing alone, and they were all targets, not to mention the Sinopec refinery off to the southwest. If the hits had already started, then they had to be scrambling.

That could make our mission more difficult than it was already shaping up to be, but that was why we were a Grex Luporum team.

It was only a few hours after dark when I took David and Lucas, leaving the others in the ORP, dug into a thick stand of pines, and headed out on our leader's recon.

We crept along the military crest of the finger that pointed toward the Ming Tombs dam and the Shisanling Pumped Storage power station, staying under the trees as much as we could, keeping an eye not only on the terrain around us but also on the sky above. While we hadn't seen any drones, we knew that the Chinese were using them more and more for surveillance of areas where they didn't have CCTV cameras set up. It was one more threat we had to account for with every step.

Lucas had taken point, doubtless to David's irritation, but while everyone on the team was wound tight as hell, nobody was going to risk our survival by getting into a spat in the hills. We were all too old for that crap, anyway.

He neared the crest of the next hill and slowed down, getting low as he came to the trees at the top. David and I joined him, David taking rear security as Lucas and I got down prone and I hauled out the FSB50-640 fusion binoculars, powered them up, and started scanning.

The upper reservoir of the Shisanling Pumped Storage power station, also known as the "Heaven Pool," was about five hundred thirty yards across, and held up to 4.45 million cubic meters of water. When the grid had excess power, they used it to pump water into the upper reservoir. When they needed to generate more power, then they let it back down toward the Ming Tombs reservoir, almost sixteen hundred feet below, turning the turbines inside Mang Mountain, underneath us, on the way.

There was definitely an elevated security presence. I could just see a pair of 6x6 vehicles below us, stationed at each of the two entrances to the top of the reservoir. There was another road that crossed the front of the concrete dam, halfway down, but that didn't appear, from our vantage point, to be patrolled, at least not by vehicles.

We didn't have anti-vehicle weapons, per se. The rucks had been heavy enough without adding AT-4s or similar launchers. That was going to make this dicey.

The whole target set was dicey. Having only what we could carry in our rucks when we'd parachuted in, we didn't have charges big enough to crack that reservoir by brute force, which would have been the easiest way to put the power station out of commission permanently. Without the reservoir up top, there would be no water source to run the station.

So, we had to handle this more subtly.

I wasn't looking for our target, specifically, at that point. We had a couple of possibilities, but I was looking at the security presence. That was going to largely determine the course of action we decided on.

Those vehicles were a problem. Both were big enough to carry probably a squad each and had mounted QJY-88s in the turrets above the cabs. They were also presumably armored, just judging by the grid cages over the windows, which meant we couldn't scratch them without sneaking up and placing charges, charges we could use elsewhere. If they had night vision or thermals…

Granted, intel from the guys who had been on Taiwan before the ChiComs had nuked it pointed to a lot less use of night vision than we might have expected. It sounded almost like the OWHSC operators we'd clashed with in Germany had been better equipped, in some ways, than the regular PLA. I didn't expect much better from the PAP.

However, underestimating the enemy's capabilities is never a good idea. Still, I wanted those vehicles out of action.

Or, as an idea started to form in the sneaky part of my mind, at least commandeered. After all, if we captured them, they couldn't be used against us, and they might provide us with some transportation and some useful camouflage.

No, it wasn't part of the mission for the night, but we were on our own, with our primary directive being to wreck as much Red Chinese infrastructure as possible. We made our own timelines as much as we could within the strictures of light and dark, as well as enemy movement.

I whispered the idea to Lucas. In the dark, behind our PS-31s, I couldn't make out much of his expression except for the wolfish, feral grin that spread across his stubble-covered features. He liked the idea.

We just had to pull it off without getting compromised and shot to pieces.

After about another hour of observation, spotting and timing out the patrols where I could, and making sure that they weren't using drone support, I powered down the FSB-50s and stashed them in my assault pack, and then we wormed our way back down until we were on the far side of the hill, invisible to the reservoir. Then we were back on our feet and moving. I checked my watch, carefully shielding the tritium hands. We had about six hours of darkness left.

We had to move.

***

Zhao was on point by sheer necessity. We weren't moving on the vehicles first. We were going to waylay one of the mid-level foot patrols instead, so we needed a convincing Mandarin speaker to get us close enough that we could take them down all at once, preferably without any shooting.

That was a new concept that we were kinda having to get used to. Gunfire would attract attention, and even though we had suppressors for the QBZ-191s, if we had to fire a shot, it would still be heard for a *long* way. It was inevitable, with the havoc we were out to create, that the ChiComs would figure out that somebody was in their backyard, blowing stuff up, but the longer we could stay soft, the better.

So, we were going old school, and doing as much with knives as possible. It wasn't a first for any of us, but it was still something that seemed wildly antiquated to most First World militaries anymore.

There were still hellacious risks involved, including the distinct possibility that one of them might raise the alarm if one of us was too slow, but if we were fast, we could do this much more quietly with blades than with bullets.

After a quick, furtive road crossing, we waited in the small draw just behind a hairpin curve in the road. The terrain concealed us and that short stretch of road from the vehicles above, so we would have a short window to do this without being exposed, hopefully without alerting the rest of the security on the reservoir.

We had all set in among the scrubby trees alongside the road and we stayed there, waiting, as the patrol's flashlights came

291

up toward the finger to our right. A moment later, four men in cammies, vests, and what looked an awful lot like old American PASGT helmets, lighting their way with handheld flashlights, with their QBZ-95s slung at their sides, came around the curve. None of them had NVGs.

Zhao stepped out onto the road at the curve and called out in Mandarin. He was immediately pinned by four flashlights, as the PAP officers all grabbed for their rifles. From the way they were scrambling, they hadn't *really* expected anyone up there, not on that side of the mountain, anyway.

We didn't wait around for Zhao to get chatty. He'd timed things perfectly, and our targets were spread out right in front of us.

I lunged for the man at the front as Lucas, David, and Reuben came out of the dark next to me. I hit the guy hard, pinning his rifle to his side as I wrapped an arm around his helmet and wrenched his head back, hooking a leg around his and sweeping his boots out from under him as I brought my knife up under his chin.

He stiffened, and I felt hot fluid run down my hand as the blade transfixed his brain. I twisted it, just to make sure, as the dead body that I was now holding up by the helmet's chinstrap shuddered and twitched, then I wrenched the knife out and dragged the corpse back into the trees.

Reuben and Lucas had done their targets smoothly and quietly. David, however, was still fighting with his, though he was on top of the man, one hand clamped over his mouth as the panicked paramilitary policeman beat at him with his fists. David was still stabbing the guy, ramming his blade over and over into the juncture between his neck and his shoulder. The man was already dying, but he was still fighting.

Zhao closed in as I dumped the body of my man in the bushes, but there wasn't much he could do. The dying man's struggles got steadily weaker, until finally his hands fell away limply, dark fluid pooling on the pavement beneath him. David straightened up, gulping air, then wiped his knife on the dead man's uniform before staggering to his feet.

Without waiting for him, Zhao quickly grabbed the dead man's vest, only to have part of the shoulder strap tear. David had cut it halfway through. Adjusting his grip, Zhao quickly hauled the body off the road.

I had pulled my target's QBZ-95 off his body. None of the PAP were carrying the newer 191s, and there was enough difference between the older bullpup and the newer, more conventional rifle that it would be an immediate giveaway that something weird was going on if we walked up from the isolated far end of the reservoir with the 191s. We'd only need to maintain the illusion for a few minutes—and our bunch of roundeyes weren't going to be *able* to maintain it for any longer than that, anyway—but for those few minutes, allaying the security guards' concerns would be paramount, and that meant carrying the 95s.

Fortunately, the flashlights should blind the guys on the vehicle enough that they wouldn't notice much of anything until we were right on top of them.

Leaving the bodies in the weeds, we picked up the rifles and flashlights and got on our way, hoping that we'd moved fast enough that it wouldn't look like the patrol had stopped. In fact, we stepped it out a little just to make up for any time we'd lost between stabbing those guys to death and hiding the bodies. We'd all stashed our NVGs in our packs before moving on. Those would be a dead giveaway. The packs weren't perfect, but they didn't alter our profile as much as NVGs or openly carried QBZ-191s would.

I knew we all had blood on us, but there was no getting around that. We'd just have to roll with the punches. Maybe we could wash some of it off in the reservoir before we headed down below to do our thing.

The road twisted up the hillside, making another hairpin turn around the crest and leading past a partially completed structure before winding along the top of the mountain toward the near end of the dam that held the reservoir in check. I could see the vehicle ahead, the turret-mounted machinegun pointed at the sky.

Two more PAP officers lounged next to it, smoking. Clearly, despite their superiors' instructions, they didn't really expect anyone to be crazy enough to come up here and mess with the power station. Either that, or they were *really* confident in their early warning setup.

I had to stay nonchalant as we walked up, so I couldn't stop and scope out the security on the other side of the reservoir. They might be more alert.

One set of problems at a time.

The two smokers looked over as we walked up, Zhao shining his flashlight at them. One of them snapped something in Mandarin as we approached. I didn't know the language, but the tone was unmistakably annoyed. I knew I'd be irritated if the patrol came in and shined their light in my face.

Of course, that was all part of the plan.

Now that they couldn't see, we closed in, though we still tried to make it look like we were just on patrol. Only when we were within the last few yards did one of them seem to figure out that not all was quite what it seemed.

One of them straightened, stepping away from the vehicle, and asked a question. In response, Zhao stepped in close and stabbed him in the neck.

The second man opened his mouth to yell, and I charged him, slamming him back against the vehicle and letting go of my captured QBZ-95, pinning both our weapons between us as I snatched out my knife and came in low.

I wasn't trying to stab him in the guts, even though that was probably the easiest target from that angle. I went in lower, cutting deep into his inner thigh and groin, the blade sawing for the femoral artery as he tried to scream past my gloved hand. A sudden hot gush blasted out over my hand, and then he crumpled, his life pumping out onto the ground so fast that he was unconscious before I stepped back and let him fall. He'd be dead in the next couple of minutes.

Lucas already had the door to the vehicle open, and he'd plunged inside. The vic was rocking, and faint, muffled yells were coming from the open door and the open turret up front. They died away quickly, and then Lucas was backing out, dragging a body by its heels.

The rest of the team was coming down off the hill, having seen the hit on the vehicle, and quickly set up security around the vehicle while the rest of us got ready to head back down below and blow a hole in the pressure-relief sluice at the bottom of the dam.

It probably wouldn't be quite as catastrophically damaging as blowing up the turbine, but I wasn't that confident that we'd get out if we went crawling down into the bowels of Mang Mountain to find it. If we made the reservoir unusable, they'd have to at least do some major repairs before they could generate power here again.

Of course, we still had to get past the second vehicle to get out, if we were going to take one or both vehicles. That was Tony's task, though, and I had to trust him to take care of it.

While Tony, Chris, Zhao, and Steve took the captured flashlights and started across the dam, and Jim and Greg held security on the already captured vehicle, Lucas, David, and I re-donned our NVGs and headed back down toward the bottom of the dam.

We moved fast. Even with Zhao in the lead, I wasn't sure that they were going to be able to neutralize the second vehicle and the patrol on the lower road without gunfire. We needed to get the charges placed fast and get back up there to support them, just in case.

It was about a mile and a half down to the small floodgate if we took the road. We headed pretty much straight down the hill, instead.

That was rough going. The brush was nasty, and the hill was steeper than it looked in places. David slipped halfway down, and went skidding down a nearly sheer slope, crashing into the brush at the bottom with a whispered curse that I could have sworn the guards up top had been able to hear.

If they could, though, it was far too late for them.

A pair of suppressed gunshots echoed across the small valley. We didn't have any subsonic 5.8, so the *crack*s were distinctive. A moment later, a storm of suppressed gunfire rattled out above us, and we were pushing hard to get to the bottom.

Scraped, scratched, and sweating, we reached the floodgate a few minutes later. The gunfire had fallen silent, and I had to hope that that meant our guys had come out on top. Otherwise, we were in a hell of a bad spot.

David took up security while Lucas and I got to work. The floodgate was set well back from the maintenance road, but not so far that we couldn't get to it.

I hoped that it wasn't backed up by redundant gates that our charges couldn't reach. We couldn't exactly go spelunking in the depths of the dam.

The gates were a few feet back from the wall, and we had to go wading to set the charges. We had to do it in the dark, inserting the initiation systems by feel, setting in the charges and tamping them as best we could with clay and rocks from outside, then pulling the igniters and sniffing in the cold dampness for the smoke that indicated the time fuse was burning.

We duck-walked out of the narrow space and rejoined David outside. "Fuses are burning. Let's go."

Going right back up the way we'd come was a bit of a non-starter. We could do it, but that hillside was steep enough that it would have taken about the same amount of time to get up to the top of the dam as it would to take the slightly longer route back up. We weren't going to take the road all the way, but where we could, if only to get around the steeper parts, we would.

We still hustled. Right at the moment, the mountain was quiet, but after that exchange of gunfire, I doubted it was going to last. Our plan to hijack those PAP vehicles might not work out.

As we hauled ourselves up the hill, panting and sweating, more gunfire crackled off to the west, both suppressed and unsuppressed. So, somebody had gotten an alert out, and now we were going to have to break contact.

By the time we got to the upper road, the firefight was in full roar, and one of our guys was up on the captured vehicle's machinegun, raking the road below with heavy fire. At almost the same moment, the charges went off.

The *boom* was slightly muffled, but what came next was a little surprising. I'd been hoping that by just knocking out the floodgates, we could drain the reservoir. What we got was a little bit more dramatic.

Just after the initial shock of the explosions, as minor as they were in the scheme of things, the whole structure seemed to shudder. Then it shuddered again, and a deep rumble echoed across the valley below.

Apparently, that dam wasn't quite as structurally sound as it had appeared. There had to have been some deep flaw in its construction, and our explosives had just provided the shock that turned a hidden time bomb into a catastrophic failure.

The entire structure shuddered again, and the dam began to crack. Water started to spurt out of point halfway up the slope, and then all hell broke loose.

A massive chunk of the top of the dam cracked and peeled away, freeing an equally massive wall of water that poured out onto the valley floor below with crushing force, and I was extremely glad that we were up as high as we were. The water continued to chew at the rapidly failing dam, and soon a roaring flood was gushing into the valley beneath the dam, carrying huge chunks of concrete and fill with it.

By the time we got to the top, there was no way across except to go around the long way. And from the volume of fire between the second vehicle and the pagoda that stood above the only road up to the reservoir, there was no way we were forcing our way through that way.

We didn't have a belt-fed with us, but we did have a relatively clear shot at the PAP who were trying to force their way up the road. Spreading out along the treeline, we opened fire.

Fortunately, our QBZ-191s had been captured with red dot sights, and while most of the PLA wasn't equipped with night vision, they did have night vision settings. Which meant we could shoot with our PS-31s, hidden entirely from the enemy, our muzzle flashes suppressed and for all intents and purposes invisible. Five hundred plus yards at night was still a long shot, but we could get close enough to hopefully actually hit some of them, rather than just suppress.

The enemy fire slackened considerably as our bullets started tearing into the PAP from the flank, and the rest of the team immediately started to fall back along the edge of the nearly empty reservoir. There wasn't a lot of cover, but they hugged the buildings against the hillside, and a moment after they'd bailed, the vehicle went up in flames. We'd brought a few thermates, so one of them must have tossed one inside. That would not only give them some cover and concealment, but it would also quite efficiently block the road for a while.

I stopped shooting. The PAP were still spraying fire randomly and indiscriminately at the burning vehicle, but I could see our guys already going over the side, down into the woods on the slope behind the reservoir. "Time to go." We'd gain nothing getting into an extended firefight with the PAP there. Our target was toast and more of the glow of electric lights below and to the south had died away. It was time to fade.

As quickly and quietly as we could move, we disappeared into the darkness of the woods, heading back toward the ORP.

Chapter 36

Once they'd gotten away from the urban sprawl around Guangzhou, leaving collapsed bridges and burning power plants in their wake, Hank's section had found that much of Guangdong Province looked a lot like the tourist pictures of China. Low, rolling hills, covered in forest, were interspersed with hundreds of lakes, rice paddies, villages, and the occasional solar power station. For the first couple of days after hitting the Nanhai 1st power station, the squad had kept their heads down, moving at night and hiding during the day.

They had to strike a certain balance. Option Zulu was intended to bring a country to its knees by wrecking enough of its power, communications, and transportation infrastructure to cause a general collapse. It was a more kinetic, less technologically-oriented version of what had been done to the United States a little over a year before. It relied, to a certain extent, on shock, as well as causing enough damage over a short enough period of time to overwhelm any of the enemy's efforts at damage control. That meant that there couldn't be too much time between strikes.

On the other hand, if they pushed too hard in one place, they were either going to make mistakes or get caught. Or both. They needed to move away, lay low for a couple of days, let some of the heat die down, and then come at it from a different direction.

Hank, however, couldn't just sit on his hands. Rather than holing up and waiting for an opportune time to head back in toward Guangzhou—though he told himself that he'd get there—he was pushing to the northwest, making for one of the major gas pipelines that ran from Guangzhou to Maoming.

If any of the squad—including their Taiwanese reinforcements—had not been on Taiwan, they might have objected to Hank's single-minded drive to do as much damage as possible. But they'd all been there. They'd seen the slaughter, even before the mushroom clouds had risen over five Taiwanese cities. That same cold, driving fury was in every one of them. Even Faris.

Hank eyed the man as they moved through the woods, the cloud cover that had moved in during the day providing even more concealment. Faris had barely uttered a word since they'd left the devastated island. He hadn't slacked, hadn't tried any of his usual tricks to get out of effort or put himself on a different level from the rest. He seemed singularly driven, quiet and dangerous.

LaForce had had a theory on that. Faris had been getting friendly with a Taiwanese girl during the short time they'd been on liberty in Taipei. She, like Mei-Ling, was undoubtedly dead. It looked like she'd taken a part of Faris with her.

That could still be a problem, if he went too far off the reservation. He could put the entire squad and the mission with them at risk in his thirst for revenge. Hank, for all his own bleak outlook on their chances of ever getting out of China—and equally bleak musings about whether or not he really *wanted* to—knew that he couldn't trust Faris's self-control all that far. He still had a mission, and so he'd keep an eye on the younger man. So would LaForce.

Now, as they halted just short of what was supposed to be their target, Hank watched Faris for a moment before making sure that LaForce was getting the rest into security positions, while he moved up to see if he could get eyes on.

So far, this little hunt had been infuriatingly frustrating. The information they'd had before launch on Chinese oil and gas pipelines had proven to be woefully inadequate, where it wasn't outright wrong. He'd already been somewhat aware of the problem, just by looking at the maps, which often boiled down to "new" pipelines being marked by arbitrary lines that crossed the terrain without regard for cities, rivers, roads, railroads, lakes, or mountains. Clearly, most of the intel was sheer guesswork, and lazy guesswork at that.

Two sites that should have given them access to this particular pipeline had already been dry holes, providing neither viable targets nor any indicator of where those targets might be. He was hoping that this one was going to prove otherwise.

Moving carefully through the trees toward the dim lights ahead, he advanced past where he could see the small, tight perimeter, and sank to a knee behind an evergreen that he couldn't have identified even if he'd been interested.

Jackpot.

The terrain had apparently constrained the pipeline's construction such that they'd run it through the hills parallel with the main road, using the existing tunnels and expanding them to accommodate the pipeline. That could end up killing two birds with one stone, if this went right.

The narrow valley held two ponds at the bottom, but a compressor station had been built on the other side of the road, lit by work lights and chugging away, stepping up the pressure of natural gas running through the pipeline. Surrounded on three sides by trees, it was relatively isolated from the surrounding populace, which made it a perfect target.

Furthermore, with the pipeline moving through the tunnel in the hillside, they could move over the hill to get at the compressor station from the woods. They should be able to get in and out quickly.

Provided Murphy didn't stick his oar in.

Creeping back to the squad, he quickly outlined what he'd seen in a low whisper, then sketched out the plan of attack. It was relatively simple. It had to be. They didn't have all night to plan, they had only ten men, and he hadn't seen any guards. That was surprising, and he still added a caveat that there might be PAP or other patrolling security forces on site. He knew, as he looked around at the faces behind NVGs, that he really hadn't needed to. They all expected opposition. None of them were babes in the woods. Even the three Taiwanese were all veterans of the fighting for Taiwan, and Cai, it had turned out, had been on Kinmen, just not where the section had been fighting.

With the plan set and Faris on point, they got up and headed out of their attack position, leaving the rucks in place. Quietly, with a stealth born of experience and necessity more than training, they slipped through the woods, shadows in the dark, staying out of the faint strips of illumination spilling out into the woods from the compressor station's lights.

It took about an hour to move through the forest and over the hill above the tunnel. Just on the other side of that hill, the two elements split, LaForce taking the security element straight down the slope to hold the near side of the compressor station in case anyone came from the road. Hank took the assault element around to the east side and closed in from the woods.

The compressor station sat inside a small, fenced compound, with a central shack where most of the noise was coming from, as well as several pipes running to and from the pipeline itself, and various other bits of machinery that went into filtering, compressing, and cooling the gas as it was pushed back out into the pipeline. The lights bathed the small compound in actinic white light, but that almost seemed like it was for the use of maintenance personnel more than security.

It didn't take long to cut the fence. Then they were moving into the yard, guns up and searching for targets, just in case.

There was a small shed or shack on the side of the main building, and as they came through the fence, the door opened and a man stepped out.

Everyone froze. They *could* shoot him, but that might prove to be counterproductive if there was anyone else in the area with a radio or cell phone. There had been other squads and teams tasked with knocking out cell towers and high-tension power lines, but Hank hadn't gotten any kind of detailed update on the other teams' progress in the short-wave intel dump from Japan. None of them had brought phones, either, for obvious reasons, so they had no immediate way to tell if the local cell network was up or down.

The man lit a cigarette and stared at the sky for a few minutes. He was probably just trying to get away from the compressor's noise for a while. Still, the Triarii couldn't move until he went back inside.

Hank's knees started to ache as he crouched behind a maze of pipes, watching the man. The lights were too bright to use NVGs, so he'd flipped his up as they'd come out of the trees, but he could see well enough. And he was close enough to see the man's every feature.

The guy was short and kinda dumpy. He looked tired and drawn. He was probably worried. The intel dump had indicated that the CCP was trying to assure everyone that nothing was wrong, that there had simply been a few terrorist attacks by separatists, but the ordinary people knew. They saw the lights going out and staying out. They saw the fires. Even if they were out here in the sticks, like this guy, word had to be getting around.

Without power, a lot of things started to go wrong. Without fuel, even more started to grind to a halt. Hank hadn't known whose targets they were, but he'd known that the Maoming and Sinopec Guangzhou Branch refineries had been on the target list. Fuel had to be getting scarce.

His sympathy for the man was pretty minimal, though. *What did you think when you heard that the US had been crippled, huh? Or when you heard that those dirty "separatists" on Taiwan had been nuked? Did you cheer?* He couldn't read the man's mind, but he hardened himself as he watched. The man was an enemy, whether he was bearing arms or not.

Finally, the guy finished his cigarette—it said something about Chinese Communist SOPs when it was perfectly normal for a worker to smoke a cigarette in a natural gas compressor station—stomped it out on the ground, and went back inside. The Triarii were immediately moving again.

They still had some explosives left after the first night, but Hank didn't want to use them. They could do this with other methods that wouldn't immediately point to military sabotage.

Besides, he wanted to save the explosives for bigger targets. He was far from done on mainland China.

Winkler and Reisinger disappeared into the generator shed with a jug they'd swiped from a nearby farm the night before, now full of water. A few moments later, the generator coughed, skipped, and died. The lights went out and the compressor started to wind down.

A gallon of water in the fuel system will do a number on a generator. They weren't done, though.

The man who'd been smoking a cigarette came out of the shed, muttering to himself in the sudden quiet. Bishop had been waiting for him, and snatched him up, wrapping one beefy arm around the man's neck, the other coming down on the back of his skull, driving his neck down into the "V" of his elbow and cutting off the blood to his brain. The man went limp, and Bishop dragged him away from the building. He might just survive the night.

Hank and Evans moved on the shack. It was unoccupied; apparently Cigarette Man had been alone. They must have been getting low on people.

They acted quickly from there. The shack was a mess, and the disarray provided plenty of flammable material. They quickly had a fire burning in the main building, with every valve they could find opened. Hank was the last one out, the rest of the assault element having quickly made tracks as soon as the lighter had come out.

Hank ran to join them. He didn't want to be anywhere near that place when the fire really got going.

They backed off into the woods fast, Hank giving LaForce a quick, double IR flash to let him know that they were clear. LaForce and the security element had a lot more standoff already, but if this went up the way he thought it might…

An explosion shook the hills a moment later, fire quickly raging through the building, belching flame and black smoke into the sky. Hank and the assault element waited just long enough to be sure that the target was fully involved, then they faded into the woods, heading for the rally point to consolidate with LaForce.

They needed to make tracks. This *could* have been an accident, but if the local PAP commander had half a brain and took the time to think about everything else that had been happening lately, he wasn't going to simply dismiss it as such. Better to be far away, circling back toward Guangzhou and their next target, by the time the enemy responded.

Chapter 37

Our next target was a little different.

The day after we blew the upper reservoir of the Shisanling Pumped Storage power station, after we'd broken contact and disappeared into the wooded hills, we set up comms and got our first intel dump.

The setup was similar to what anyone in the resistance in Europe during World War II would have been familiar with. We simply set up to receive, without planning on transmitting at all, and we were using a particular short-wave frequency that wasn't ordinarily used by either commercial or military organizations. The transmitter was on Kyushu, and if you had the right setup, you could probably pick it up in Wyoming.

There were a few different freqs in use, but we only tuned into one. Many of the messages were for other teams, though none of them were all that specific, since there was no way, short of transmitting and potentially giving our positions away, that we could keep the TOC in Japan up to date. So, the data dumps and targeting information were divided up by target area, and we had north Beijing.

Chaos was spreading fast. Because the bulk of the PRC's population was in the east, Han China proper, Option Zulu in China was mostly focused on the coastal provinces. The bulk of the west was open and empty, and where it was inhabited, aside from certain mining and petrochemical resource exploitation operations, it was dirt poor. The coastal provinces formed the bulk of Communist China, so if they collapsed, the rest would follow.

Hell, we might even manage to answer all those "Free Tibet" bumper stickers people used to plaster all over when I was a kid, even if only by default.

Our new target was presented in the form something of a biographical profile. Ronald Bertrand was an American expat who had been living in China for over a decade. He'd started as an English teacher, but his social media presence had exploded to the point that he was now essentially a paid ChiCom propagandist, giving his "real-world" takes on China for young people in the US. He'd rubbed shoulders with half the Central Committee of the Chinese Communist Party, at least judging by his social media videos, and he'd done a lot to influence people in favor of Beijing back home.

He was going to regret all that hobnobbing with the CCP brass.

From where we sat, we could tell that he clearly wasn't hurting. The Changping District, the suburbs north of Beijing, while hardly up to American standards for "suburbs," were still pretty swank for China. Of course, the lights were all out, now, since there might have been one working power station within a hundred miles of Beijing at that point, and half the lines were probably down, presuming the abrupt shifts in load hadn't blown every transformer for miles.

Fortunately, we weren't going to have to go very deep into those close-packed houses. Bertrand might have set himself up as the valued advisor to half the Central Committee, but he was still a "white monkey," a façade for CCP messaging and nothing more. His apartment, provided the intel was on, was in a tiny cottage backed up against the hills and what looked and smelled like a trash heap, on the far side of this particular suburb from the golf course. Apparently, he'd made quite a few videos on that golf course, as if he lived right next to it.

That positioning was perfect. If he'd lived closer to the golf course, we'd have had to take a lot more risks to get to him.

As it was, we were moving cautiously around the trash pit and through the trees toward the back door.

We didn't have a layout of the building's interior, so we were going to have to play this by ear. Fortunately, it was 0330, it was dark as hell, since there was no power, and despite the fact that there were fires all over Beijing, apparently lit by rioters as protests about the government's inability to keep the power on and the food moving turned nasty—no doubt in large part thanks to the PAP and the PLA themselves—nobody in this area was out and about at that hour.

Whether that was just because it was dark, or because they were worried about the rioters was an open question. There was a good chance they were worried about both.

It had occurred to us all in planning that another concern could well be the PLA and the PAP themselves. With the power down, it sounded like a lot of them weren't getting paid. There were reports of units of both arms of the CCP's private military turning into what amounted to roving bandits. Hardly a surprise, given their Communist roots, but an additional threat that we had to take into consideration.

Granted, we'd done some looting ourselves. We'd been on the ground long enough that we'd had to steal some rice, vegetables, and chicken. Living off the land in a hostile country is no picnic.

I'd preferred the stuff we'd found in Slovakia, if we were being honest, but when you're hungry and still have to hump a ruck and fight, beggars can't be choosers.

Fortunately, while the iffy quality of the rations might have slowed us down a little, they hadn't stopped us. Nobody had even gotten the runs, which was a minor miracle.

David, Chris, Greg, and Jim moved in to bracket the house, forming our outer cordon. Lucas, Reuben, Zhao, and I moved to the door. Steve and Tony were behind us, on overwatch up on the hill, just in case.

We had our radios on that night, for the first time since we'd jumped in. If this went sideways, Tony and Steve had to be able to warn us.

Reuben and Lucas covered us as I tested the doorknob. I wasn't worried about alarm systems at this point. The power had been down for too long. But locks and dogs were both still potential problems. None of Bertrand's videos had featured a dog, but it never pays to assume these things.

The door was locked, as I'd expected, but a bump key is a wonderful thing. Two knocks and it was open, and then we were moving inside, on NVGs, rifles up and checking every corner as we moved.

This was very much a "soft" hit. We wanted Bertrand alive, and we didn't want anyone else in the neighborhood to know that we'd been there.

The house, fortunately, was tiny. We found ourselves in a small kitchen that opened onto a living room, though I realized as we swept through that this was actually far larger than most Chinese apartments. Bertrand was a white monkey, but he was the Central Committee's white monkey, so that did come with *some* privileges.

The bottom floor was as dark as expected, quiet and deserted. The bedrooms must be on the top floor.

I pointed Zhao at the front door. He was no slouch, but he didn't have our training and experience in CQB. If any one of us had to peel off to hold security, it was going to have to be Zhao.

If Bertrand had guests, then we might need to pull him to do some translation, but as long as we were clearing, I wanted Reuben and Lucas with me.

We found the stairs, just past the combination bathroom/laundry room. The upstairs was dark, too. I tested the first step, and fortunately it didn't creak. Guns up, we started to climb.

The stairs topped out on a small open room, with two doors to the right and one straight ahead. All were currently closed.

Stepping slowly and carefully across the floor, making hardly a sound, we moved on the nearest door. This could get really interesting, really fast, if Bertrand wasn't alone.

None of his social media had indicated that he had any family in China, but if his content was as carefully curated as intel suspected, then he might have had all sorts of hangers-on that hadn't made it into his videos.

If one of them was in this room and started screaming, we'd have a handful of trouble to deal with.

The door was unlocked. Bertrand probably didn't see the need to lock interior doors when his outer doors were secured. If he even thought of such things. It unlatched with a faint *click* and opened otherwise soundlessly.

The room was filled from wall to wall with a desk, a computer, and a whole lot of audiovisual equipment. This must be where Bertrand did most of his editing and uploading from. No target. We moved on to the next.

That one was a trash heap. Everything that Bertrand wanted to store but couldn't be bothered to sort was piled in there. It was a room to give a neat freak a stroke. Still no target. Unless Bertrand had run for it, we had one more possibility.

The last door opened without a sound, though even if the hinges had creaked, the snoring from inside would have drowned out any noise that we made short of gunfire.

We slipped inside, weapons quickly shifting to cover the corners, then I slung my QBZ-191 on my back and moved to the bed.

It didn't take much to wake Bertrand up. A gloved hand over his mouth and nose interrupted his snoring, and he started awake. There wasn't enough light in there for him to see anything. We could barely see with our PS-31s, it was so dark. So, rather than motion for him to be quiet, I leaned in close.

"If you don't want your throat cut, then keep your mouth shut. Not a whisper, not a whimper, not a cry, until I tell you to talk. Nod if you understand."

He nodded, his eyes wide. I stepped back, letting go of his face to drag him by his arm out of bed. "Get dressed. You've got thirty seconds. We're going for a walk."

Reuben turned on his flashlight, pointed at the floor by his boots, shielded from the window. It gave Bertrand some light to get dressed by, and at the same time gave him a look at the three big men who had just appeared in his room, in filthy cammies, helmets, NVGs, and combat gear, all carrying weapons.

If he'd had any idea of resisting or yelling for help, it died pretty fast when he looked at Reuben, the biggest Texican I've ever known, looming over him, lit from below.

He fumbled and struggled as he got dressed, clearly terrified. I realized that despite our beards and my decidedly non-Chinese accent, he probably still thought we were the PLA, PAP, or even MSS come to take him away.

Shouldn't have been a paid shill for the Communists, you little worm.

He finally got dressed and Reuben took him in hand, grabbing him by the upper arm and steering him out the door. Lucas took point down the stairs, whispering to Zhao that we were coming down, and I took trail, following Reuben and Bertrand.

From there, it didn't take us long to get out the back door. I considered gagging Bertrand, just to be on the safe side, but we should be back into the hills fast enough, and while I wanted to put the fear into him, I also needed him to be conscious enough to cooperate, and if he fainted from sheer terror, one of us was going to have to carry him.

He'd already pissed himself, judging by the acrid smell that overpowered the stench of the trash heap out back when I was close enough to him. Not that any of us were a bed of roses at that point, either.

Lucas went to the back door, pausing just inside, and whispered, "Friendlies coming out."

I couldn't hear the reply from outside, but Lucas headed out, followed by Reuben and our detainee, with Zhao and me taking up the rear. The rest of the team on the cordon collapsed onto us as we headed toward the hills. I flashed my IR illuminator up at Tony and Steve and got a single flash in reply.

We headed back into the woods and the hills, as quietly as we'd arrived.

***

It took several hours, especially since Bertrand was out of shape as well as terrified, to get to our hide site. Fortunately, he was too scared to make much noise, aside from the crashing and stumbling he was doing all the way up the mountain.

The woods gave out partway up, and we had just scrub and low brush to move through, but if we got down flat, that would still allow us to disappear. Fortunately, the Communists seemed to have their hands full down in Beijing proper, as the riots got worse. They weren't looking for us, and even if they were, we had moved a long way since the night we'd hit Shisanling. I was reasonably confident that we were still tougher and faster than the PAP.

Bertrand, unfortunately, wasn't. I'd wanted to get two terrain features away from the Changping District before we stopped, but Bertrand wasn't going to make it. Despite the fact that he'd already gotten more sleep than we had that night, he was dragging within a mile. We finally had to stop short of where I'd intended, burrowing into a high, brush-choked draw, setting security, and getting set to wait out the day.

Bertrand slumped down as soon as we stopped, but Reuben didn't let him rest, manhandling him into a notch in the ground where he could be watched and wouldn't get in trouble.

I was tired as hell myself, but first things first.

I squatted down in front of Bertrand, who already had his eyes closed. I didn't think he was relaxed. I thought he was shutting down. When I slapped him lightly on the cheek, his eyes snapped open, but they were unfocused, scared.

"We're not just lying down for a nap, Bertrand." I didn't have a whole lot of sympathy for the man. He'd willingly made himself a tool of Communist tyrants who had attacked the country of his birth. "You've got some questions to answer."

"I'm just a social media guy." He looked around at us, rubbing his cheek where I'd hit him. "I don't know anything." He'd apparently figured out that we weren't MSS on the hike.

"You know people. Some very powerful people in this country." I held his eyes, even though he was trying to look anywhere else. "We've seen you hobnobbing and rubbing elbows with Zhōu Gang, Hū Jiahao, and Mǎ Zhen. We've seen your little tours of their getaways." I tilted my head slightly. The rising sun was behind me, so he couldn't get that good a look at my face, not that it would do much of anyone any good. When we finally ditched him—I admit to being tempted to put a bullet in the back of his head and leaving him in a draw, but I knew that I'd still have to answer for it, whether I got out of China or not—it was going to be a long way away from here, and he was probably too scared to form much of a detailed mental picture anyway, even if I hadn't been bearded, disheveled, and covered in camouflage face paint. "Unless you're going to tell me that those were all carefully crafted sets." Which was a possibility, but intel didn't think so, judging by some of the tracking information they'd gotten out of the videos. The Chinese were good at using that sort of metadata against us, but they'd gotten sloppy with Bertrand. The locations—as general as they were—didn't line up with any known media offices.

"What…what about them?" He was scared stiff and clearly wasn't getting it. If he'd been one of us, I would have expected that he was playing on his SERE training, pretending to be shell-shocked and too scared to even know what was going on. Unless he was a lot cleverer than his profile indicated, though, he really was that out of it.

"You're buddy-buddy enough with them that you're going to lead us to them." I saw his eyes widen as what I said sank in. "I know you know at least roughly where they might be holed up while everything falls apart."

This might be a wild goose chase, and we'd always known that. There were a few other ways to find our targets, but this had promised to be the fastest…*if* it worked, and *if* Bertrand wasn't more scared of his Chinese pals than he was of us.

He folded like a cheap suit, though. "There's a place in the hills, just above the Changping District. It's practically a palace, but it's got bunkers underneath it. I wasn't supposed to see that, and I was careful not to video that part, but it's there. Zhen told me that all the big names in the Party came there from time to time."

I nodded. "You're going to show us. If you're good, we won't kill you." I got up and moved away, ready to crash for most of the rest of the day. "Believe me, with what the ChiComs have done to your country, it's the least you deserve."

I almost expected some propagandistic defense of how really wonderful the Chinese were, and how the US had deserved everything it got. If he was thinking in those terms, though, he had the good sense to keep it to himself.

Chapter 38

Guangzhou had continued to deteriorate since the night they'd inserted. The lights were still out in most of the city, and fires raged through several blocks in multiple places. Things were getting bad.

Hank's eyes were cold as he watched the flames. He was remembering scenes in Phoenix, San Diego, and Texas. His sympathy was burned out.

Turning back to the hills behind him, Hank looked around at the squad. They were dirty, exhausted, and increasingly leaned out by the local chow they'd been carefully stealing. To be fair, Cai, Li, and Pan had been doing most of the foraging, since they could mostly pass as locals. Better than the Triarii, anyway.

He had no idea whether any of them were going to survive the night. But the potential payoff was worth it. At least, he thought so, and none of the rest had objected.

"You ready for this, boys?" The looks he got spoke volumes.

A couple of them, Huntsman and LaForce, mainly, were looking at the ground. They didn't want to die, they still hoped they could get back to the States, somehow, but they weren't going to crumple, facing death. Faris was as stark and feral as ever he had been lately, staring back at Hank unblinking, the look on his face something close to impatience that they were still sitting there. Evans, Bishop, and Reisinger met his eyes in the dim light under the trees, their faces blank. Winkler didn't hold his gaze for long, but he still nodded. The three Taiwanese were stoic, for the most part, but he could see the glint of bloodlust in their eyes. Their home was gone, probably most of their families dead. They wanted vengeance, and they were going to get some of it that night.

The infrastructure attacks, as effective as they had been, had just been the prelude. They'd thrown the PRC into chaos, at least the small slice of the PRC that they'd seen so far. The shortwave intel dumps had indicated that the collapse was pretty extensive and spreading fast. Even where the Triarii hadn't hit power plants directly, the strain on the system was creating a hell of a crash. It had already been at the breaking point following the disaster of the Three Gorges Dam. Now, the entire Chinese grid was going down, and a lot of their supply chains along with it.

The bridges that had been dropped were helping with that, too, along with acute fuel shortages thanks to the hits on pipelines and refineries.

The riots were spreading as people got hungry and their demands for aid from the Party were met with PLA and PAP violence. The People's Republic of China was unraveling before their eyes.

That didn't mean that it was quite ready to fall, though. The PLA and PAP were still coordinated, and most of them weren't hesitating to crack down on their countrymen, hard. It was Tiananmen all over again, writ large. Meanwhile, the PLAN and PLAAF were still facing off with the US Navy offshore, and daring the Japanese to move, while the North Koreans launched more ballistic missiles into the ROK.

Hopefully, they were going to throw a wrench into some of that coordination tonight.

It had taken over a week to work their way around Guangzhou, watching the chaos spread as they went. Now they had just risked some daylight movement through the woods on the flank of Baiyun Mountain to get into position.

Now, as the sunlight died, replaced by the glow of fires either started by angry Chinese who had finally had their backs pushed to the wall or by the PLA and PAP to crush those same angry Chinese, they started over the last ridge that lay between them and the Southern Theater Command Headquarters of the People's Liberation Army.

The lights in the compound were still on, thanks to the generators they could hear running down the hill. Hank had known a lot of US military bases that had been reliant on the local power grid, but it looked like the PLA had been ready for a grid crash. Given the fact that it was a communist country, that made sense, though Hank wondered if whoever had set it up had put a bullseye on his back by suggesting that the Party couldn't guarantee a constant flow of electricity.

More likely, it just hadn't been mentioned. The PLA was an arm of the Party, after all.

They spread out into a loose skirmish line as they descended on the base. Identifying it had been a bear, and if the coordinates hadn't been included in the last shortwave broadcast, they never would have found it. It wasn't as if the PLA had signs up.

The broadcast hadn't actually specified an assault. It was conceivably possible that they could simply confirm and then break radio silence for the first time since landing to call in a strike from offshore. Hank hadn't been confident that a strike at that range would actually hit, given the terrain, though. The base was set in a narrow valley in the hills, and anything but a direct hit from directly above was unlikely to do enough damage. And he wanted those PLA officers dead.

They moved carefully from tree to tree, getting slower and more cautious as they got closer. They hadn't seen any sign of patrols in the woods so far, and it looked like those PLA units that hadn't already deserted—there were definitely indicators and reports that some had, either to join the rioters, just avoid the violence, or turn bandit—had their hands full in the city proper.

So much the better.

Nearing the tree line at the bottom of the hill, they slowed even more. LaForce, once again, took his support by fire element around to the flank, slipping through the trees under cover of what darkness they could find that close to the lights that were still blazing around the U-shaped, red-roofed building that Hank hoped was the headquarters building. If it was a barracks, this was about to get rough, though *if* things went according to plan, they should have confirmation one way or another shortly. They settled in to watch. Meanwhile, Huntsman and Faris went looking for the generator. They just had to follow the noise.

As he sank to a knee and studied the building, though, the guards at the side doors and the small forest of antennas sprouting from another building at the back told him that they were probably in the right place. Still, he waited. It was the middle of the night, and there were probably only watchstanders inside. They needed to wait for the impetus that they hoped was going to get the command staff on site.

Clearing that monster of a structure was going to suck. He really wished he had 1st and 3rd Squads with him. And Chan's section.

He really wished Chan were still alive.

The plan had been laid out via the shortwave broadcast. Only the broad strokes, of course; micromanaging a small unit's planning from miles away was not the Triarii way. It had been the only way to coordinate disparate elements that weren't in contact, however, so Hank had listened carefully when their code identifier had come up.

His squad had gotten the hit on the Theater Command headquarters. Lovell had gotten the diversionary strike. Again, the transmission had really only given commander's intent, leaving the execution up to the respective units on the ground, but there had been a drop-dead time for the diversion, if only to give Hank and his boys time to execute the actual hit.

There was a chance that Lovell and his squad had been rolled up, killed, or were otherwise unable to execute. If that was the case, Hank would know only because of the activity—or lack thereof—on the ground. It was a hell of an imperfect way to run a coordinated hit, but in an environment where strict communications security was a must, there were certain uncertainties baked in.

He hoped that Huntsman and Faris found those generators quickly, though they were supposed to hold off until they saw the beehive get stirred up. Or they heard gunfire.

Whatever Lovell had in mind, it was too far away for Hank to hear or see it, but after about an hour, a car came roaring down from higher up the valley, stopping in front of the presumed headquarters building. A man in camouflage utilities got out and quickly disappeared into the front of the building as more cars, a couple of BJ2022s, and even a CSK-131 pulled up, coming from the southwest, closer to the city. More officers in various degrees of uniform piled out and rushed inside.

Lovell had, apparently, come through. Whatever he'd blown up or attacked, it was important enough to get the brass out of bed.

The last vehicle to arrive was a shiny black Hongqi sedan, and two PLA soldiers in body armor, helmets, and carrying QCQ-171 submachineguns got out first. That had to be General Sòng Cheng, commanding officer of the Southern Theater Command.

Jackpot.

LaForce saw it, too. A moment later, as the general stepped unhurriedly out of the sedan, the tree line to the southwest erupted with muzzle flashes and the stuttering roar of gunfire.

The guards were smashed off their feet, and Sòng took three rounds through the chest and neck, spinning halfway around and slamming against the side of the sedan, leaving a smear of blood on the glass and metal of the side just before the lights went out.

Hank was up and moving, sprinting from the tree line toward the side door and the still-twitching bodies of the guards where they lay slumped against the wall, the light-colored plaster splashed with blood.

Cai hit the door, yanking it open—it had been left unlocked; the PLA must have felt plenty secure up here in their relatively isolated base with checkpoints controlling the road below—and holding it as the rest of the assault element flowed inside.

There were still several officers and their entourages milling around on the ground floor, staring out at the front of the building in shock at the carnage that LaForce had wrought, and Hank didn't hesitate. Snapping his QBZ-95 to his shoulder, he dumped the entire magazine into the knot of milling men down the hall. At his elbow, Li did the same, bullets chopping through flesh and bone and knocking dead and dying men into others who were still trying to figure out what the hell was happening, just before they got shot, too.

In a matter of seconds, the hallway and the foyer were an abattoir. They advanced through the blood and the bodies and headed for the stairs. Cai got there first.

And died.

One of the officers' bodyguards had seen the slaughter in the foyer, and as soon as they'd seen a figure appear at the bottom of the stairs, they'd sprayed bullets at it.

Cai flopped to the floor in a spreading pool of blood, and while it went against every trained instinct he had, Hank stuck his own rifle around the corner and dumped half his magazine up the stairs without exposing himself. He heard a scream, faint over the thunder of the weapon, and then he hooked around the corner, stepping over Cai's body and shouldering his rifle.

There was a single corpse on the landing above him, and he heard clattering footsteps above, as the remaining officers and their guards tried to get to safety. Hank pursued, feeling more than seeing Bishop at his elbow.

Hank hadn't really known what to expect in a PLA Theater Command headquarters, but what he saw next wasn't it.

Most of the entire second floor was one big, open room, divided up into cheap, industrial cubicles. It looked like a call center—at least, it would when the lights were on.

A few flashlights shone around the big room, as bodyguards hustled officers toward the doors at the far end. That only made targeting easier.

There was no hesitation. The odds were good that only the bodyguards were armed, but this was a military target, and everyone in it was thereby fair game. Rifles barked deafeningly in the echoing space, and bodies went down, torn and smashed by bullets. The guys with the flashlights went first.

Another weapon barked, aimed roughly at a muzzle flash, and Hank felt the bullet pluck at the top of his helmet. He shifted, finding the man who had leveled his QCQ-05 submachinegun over the top of a cubicle. The next three rounds burst the man's skull like a melon, sending him crashing over backward and taking the cubicle wall with him.

The rest of the assault element was spread out across the room now, moving between the cubicles. More gunshots clapped in the dark as they advanced.

Officers were the primary targets, but anyone who looked like they were going to try to fight was fair game. Even if they only moved just a little bit.

If Hank had had the time or the energy to think about it, he would have seen how feral he and his boys were getting. They'd seen an awful lot of slaughter since this had all started, and now they all figured they were dead men, anyway.

Hank pressed on toward the doors at the far end of the room. They were both shut, the last of the officers having fled into the somewhat more secure offices. A man lunged at him from one of the last cubicles, or maybe he was just trying to run. His timing sucked, though, and Hank put a bullet through his skull from about two feet away.

He reached the door and kicked it open. The room was as dark as the rest, dimly lit by the little bit of moonlight and reflected firelight coming through the window. A good-sized desk dominated the middle of the room, with several PLA flags standing behind it, along with an "I Love Me" wall beyond that put most general officers Hank had ever encountered to shame.

There was movement behind the desk. Hank started to work his way around, his rifle leveled.

Three officers were huddled behind the desk. None of their bodyguards had made it inside. They'd probably shoved them out the door to face the gunfire alone.

One of the officers looked up at the sound of his approach, a pistol in his hand. He couldn't see as well as Hank could, though, and he died fast, a bullet through his teeth from six feet away.

Hank didn't wait for either of the others to do something. He was there to kill Chinese officers. He dumped both of them with a hammer pair each, the reports smacking painfully off the walls as the muzzle flash lit up the room with a flickering stutter of flame.

Only a couple more gunshots sounded from out in the main room. He stepped out and started to take stock.

Killing the officers was a vital part of the plan, but if they could wreck the comms equipment, that would be an added bonus.

As he stepped out, however, he heard sustained gunfire coming from outside.

Moving to the window, he peered out. "Fuck."

An eight-wheeled ZBL-08 was rolling up the road, spitting machinegun fire into the trees from its turret, flanked by what looked like PLA infantry. Behind it came two six-wheeled ZSL-92/Bs. It was time to go.

Even as he thought it, though, a Z-8 helicopter roared overhead, banking to circle around toward the athletic field up the hill, near the top end of the base. General Sòng had had quite a react force ready.

They could still break out. He turned and headed for the stairs. "Let's go."

More gunfire echoed from the stairs, and he stopped. They'd been too slow, and the PLA had moved faster than he'd expected. "Get on the doors before we get flanked!"

He wasn't going to give up. Not yet. But it looked like they might be cornered.

The ZBL-08 was out front now. Hank couldn't tell for sure, but there didn't seem to be any more gunfire coming from the trees, which meant that the support by fire position had either been forced back or had been overrun.

A moment later, he heard a hoarse voice shout, "Friendlies coming in!" His heart sank. That was LaForce, out of breath and ragged, bleeding from his shoulder. The only one behind him, who stopped to lob one of the last of their grenades down the stairs, was Reisinger.

"Where's Evans?" Hank was already barricading on the doorway, with an oddly calm certainty that he already knew the answer.

The frag shook the building with its detonation. "Dead. Huntsman and Faris, too. They got cut in fuckin' half, man." LaForce was more rattled than Hank had ever seen him. "Just before they got to us."

Hank looked around. He had two Taiwanese and five Americans left. And the charges they'd brought with them.

He eyed the packs, heavy with their last explosives. Just for a moment, he just felt tired.

Can't start thinking that way. Got to fight to the last. Got to at least try *to get out.*

Even as he thought it, though, Winkler opened fire down the far staircase. They were getting hit from both sides.

Maybe they could still force their way through and get out the back. Yanking his own last frag out of his vest, he pulled the pin, cooked it for a three-count, and hooked it down the steps. He heard a yell, and then the building shook again, smoke and dust billowing up the stairs. "On me." Weapon up, he started down the steps, careful to pop the corner as he reached the landing, leading with his muzzle instead of his head.

Two crumpled bodies lay at the bottom of the stairs. He took two steps down and heard a barked order in Mandarin.

He shot the first man before he could bring his rifle to bear, quickly shifting to the next one he could see. He felt a fiery blow in his side as he shot at the second shape, and then his knee started to buckle.

A hand closed on the back of his vest and dragged him back up the steps, even as he felt two more bullets shatter his shin.

He coughed painfully and felt warm liquid gush out of the hole in his torso. It was higher up and more to the centerline than he'd thought.

He couldn't get up. LaForce was dragging him out of the fatal funnel as Reisinger kept pumping bullets down the stairs.

Time was doing something weird. It seemed to be starting and stopping. After a moment, as he coughed again, tasting blood, he realized he was drifting in and out of consciousness, waking up to gunfire every time he passed out. Strangely, he didn't feel that much pain, while a part of his mind knew that he really should.

He saw Winkler go down in a storm of gunfire, still shooting back until the last. Bishop kept up the fire on the far staircase, backed up by Pan, while Reisinger and Li held down the near staircase. LaForce was still trying to patch Hank up.

He gasped in pain and blacked out again for a moment. He could *feel* his life ebbing away. "Etienne. The charges."

"No, man. I'm gonna get you out of here."

Hank grabbed LaForce's wrist. "We're not getting out of here, brother. You know that as well as I do." Another burst of gunfire cut him off. "We can't be captured. This has to…" He gasped as a stab of agony went through him, and LaForce actually winced a little at the grip on his arm. "We've got to stay deniable. We're cornered. Before we all go down, those fuses have to be burning."

A long burst of gunfire crackled up the stairs, and Reisinger hit the floor, hard. He didn't move.

LaForce lunged for the pack just as a grenade bounced onto the floor next to Reisinger's body.

The last thing Hank ever saw was LaForce pulling the igniter on the satchel.

Chapter 39

Bertrand definitely slowed us down the next night. We didn't even have that far to go, once we figured out where exactly the target was. He wasn't all that helpful on that count, and Jordan was about ready to start breaking his fingers until it became obvious that he had mostly been driven around to these places by Party functionaries. Then we had to do some careful reconstruction of his memories, which eventually revealed that our target was less than two miles away from our hide site.

Serendipitous? Maybe. I wasn't going to complain.

Greg got the radio up for the daily brief. There was nothing specific in it for us, but the picture was getting interesting. And grim.

Most of the coastal provinces were now in an outright state of emergency. Power was out across the board. Apparently, night overheads of the country looked like North Korea. Somebody had even blown up the Southern Theater Command headquarters, killing most of their staff, and the PLA was in utter disarray across the south.

Some of the wider disruption was because of the rampant physical destruction that we'd been wreaking on Chinese infrastructure. Power plants, pipelines, bridges, high-tension power lines, oil refineries, substations…they were all targets, and Triarii infiltration teams and squads were getting ever more inventive in taking them down, as the supplies we'd inserted with dwindled. Some of the destruction, however, we couldn't quite take credit for.

The advance teams that had preceded us had been much more unassuming, and probably were going to have a lot easier time getting clear. Santiago had been recruiting ethnically Chinese hackers ever since the cyber attack on the American power grid. I suspected that some of them had been inside the PRC since before things had gotten really bad, even before the battle for Gdansk.

Once inside the Great Firewall, they'd gone to work. Not only had they shut down a lot by themselves, but they'd also been spreading all sorts of "official" government information that was blatantly wrong and had the MSS chasing their tails while a lot of the little people—who had already been somewhat twisted by over seventy years of Communist rule—were getting increasingly froggy.

The drone swarms had also done a fair bit of damage. But everything we'd done had just been putting more strain on an already teetering edifice.

The Chinese economy had been in trouble for a long time. Triarii hits in the South China Sea had worsened the situation, but the entire thing was propped up by graft, bribes, and the kind of shell game that led to dozens of high-rise apartment buildings being built and then leveled without anyone to live in them. The collapse of the Three Gorges Dam had been emblematic of the rot behind the gilt façade.

It was becoming obvious, as I listened to the brief, that the floods alone might have been enough, over time, to do what we had set out to do. Half the country had been devastated, and the effects were still rippling through the rest, with north-south supply lines cut and refugees flooding the rest of the country, not to mention the fact that almost a third of the PRC's energy sector had been gutted weeks before we started blowing up power stations.

Now the power was out, even fewer supplies were moving, and riots were spreading. Communications were increasingly confused and getting worse.

Unfortunately, as far as I knew—and it hadn't been mentioned in the briefs so far—no one had gotten a solid strike on any of the PLA's missile forces. That bothered me. We'd gone in precisely *because* the PRC had nuked Taiwan, and once the nukes had flown, it had become evident that the PRC was too dangerous to be allowed to exist anymore. But the nukes were the real threat. We'd already gone after the French nukes for exactly the same reason. Why weren't we doing it here?

I had my theories. The French nuclear arsenal had been far smaller than the PRC's, and much more easy to find. The Chinese didn't call a chunk of their missile forces "The Underground Great Wall" for nothing.

I was beginning to suspect that we were sneaking around and destroying the PRC from the inside out precisely *because* we didn't know where the nukes were, so we were on Plan B. And that was to destroy the country and the CCP deniably, before they could figure out that it was Americans who were tearing their guts out.

There was something about that that still bothered me. As if we were expendable, poor man's substitutes for nukes.

I knew that was what Option Zulu had always been, essentially. Now that we were executing, and the sheer logistical nightmare of it had become obvious, I wondered if we'd ever really thought it was practical, up until the time it had become necessary.

That didn't bode well for the future. Especially not given the sheer number of Triarii who'd entered the country. We were all utterly sterile, carrying no ID, no phones, nothing that was overtly American, aside from a few bits of gear that could be fairly easily destroyed. Our uniforms—which were getting sketchy the longer we wore them; the Chinese didn't make high-quality cammies any more than they made high-quality anything else— our weapons, even our radios were all Chinese.

But *we* weren't. And it was only a matter of time before somebody got rolled up, try as they might to evade. We were some of the best-trained light infantrymen in the world, if not *the* best-trained and motivated light infantrymen in the world, but everyone makes mistakes. Everyone gets tired. And we were all scattered and vastly outnumbered, with no local support network. There hadn't been time to build one.

Our only hope, I realized, as we patrolled through the brush, across the road, and up into the hills above the target, was to kill enough of the CCP leadership that it all fell apart before they could figure out what had been done to them and launched on the US.

It made sense against a country like ours. Even when it had become obvious who had been behind the cyber attack—regardless of the EDC's involvement, which had been crucial to the timing—Washington still hadn't wanted to do anything about it. That was why the Triarii had borne the brunt of the war in the Pacific.

Against the ChiComs? They didn't give a damn about their own people, let alone ours. I had no doubt that as soon as they had Americans or American bodies to parade in front of their people, they'd launch in a heartbeat and use it to regain control.

So far, they'd had their hands full. Hopefully it would stay that way.

If we were lucky, tonight would add to that load, if only a little.

It felt a little off, hoping that we'd get a chance to kill a bunch of CCP officials. It seemed wrong, asking God for help in what amounted to an assassination. I decided I should just ask Him for help in protecting what was left of my country and my teammates.

We worked our way up into the hills above the target site, which was still lit up like a Christmas tree, unlike most of the rest of the environs around Beijing. That was as good an indicator as any that we'd found a Party stronghold.

It was fancy as hell. Gardens, pools, and fountains surrounded the buildings, which were all built with a lot of modern steel and glass, but along vaguely traditional Chinese lines.

And there were an awful lot of vehicles down there.

An *awful* lot of vehicles.

None of them were obviously PLA. I couldn't see any tactical vehicles at all, for that matter. There were definitely PLA guards though, and those were just the guys in uniform.

Whatever was going on, though, either Zhen had a hell of a party going on, or the bigwigs were gathering.

That could mean they were running scared. It could also mean that they were getting ready to do something drastic.

The trouble was, the longer I watched, as even more sedans and armored SUVs pulled up, it was looking more and more like we were far too few to pull off a hit on the place, as long as there were that many people, all with their own PSDs, on site.

"Is that who I think it is?" I was the man with the binoculars, so I was probably in a better position to answer the question than anyone else, but Bertrand was behind me, and we were close enough that even if he couldn't recognize people, he could recognize vehicles.

"Holy shit." He sounded terrified. "That's the Chairman's limousine."

"Really." Sure enough, the dead-eyed, fat-faced man who got out of the limousine was either the Chairman of the Chinese Communist Party and President for life, or else a damned convincing body double. He nodded to accept the snappy salutes from the scared-looking kids with QBZ-191s at present arms who flanked the walkway leading up to the main building, then followed the small crowd of sycophants toward the building, disappearing behind the hedges.

"Holy hell." We had the Number One target in the country right below us, and not enough shooters to be sure we got him.

I glanced at Lucas, who was watching the compound through a smaller pair of binoculars. "Did you see that?"

"Yeah, I did. That was him, all right." It wasn't as if any of us would fail to recognize the man. He lowered the binos. "What the hell are we going to do now?"

I scowled down at the collection of cars and SUVs. It was a good question. This wasn't a target we could afford to pass up.

And yet, I wasn't keen on a suicide mission, especially since we'd never get close enough before we got horribly murdered.

"Keep an eye on them." I moved back toward the sheltered little hollow where the rest of the team was set in. Finding Tony, I hunkered down next to him.

Tony glanced over at me. We were all getting long-haired, filthy, and bearded. My mustache kept getting in my mouth, and I didn't have a good way to trim it. Tony's beard was a lot patchier, though it was still better than Greg's.

True to his callsign of "Chatty," Tony didn't say anything, but just waited for me to tell him what was up.

"The Chairman's down there. Along with what looks like a meeting of every CCP bigwig that could make it to Beijing." I scratched my beard. It didn't really itch anymore, as dirty and greasy as it was, but I was thinking. "Too many of them to hit the whole meeting. We'd never get to them, let alone get out alive."

"But we *could* cut off the head of the snake if we hit them." Tony had turned back to his sector, watching the ridgeline above and behind us. He chewed on it for a while, in that slow, quiet way Tony had. As much as I missed Scott, Tony was a good ATL.

Finally, he turned and looked me in the eye, as best he could in the dark. "Maybe we need to break radio silence."

He knew what he was suggesting. There was no guarantee that we'd get DFed as soon as we transmitted, but we'd have to make tracks fast, just to be on the safe side. Still, this was a target that was worth the risk.

I still hesitated, and silently cursed myself for it. I had no doubt that we'd lost guys already. Guys who would never be seen or heard from again, who had just disappeared. Missing, presumed dead. We weren't special.

But as vital as the mission was, I was the team leader, and I didn't want to lead my guys to their deaths.

We'd all always known that it might come to that. It very nearly had in Slovakia. It really had for Dwight, Phil, and Scott. None of us live forever.

And risking a transmission was a lot better, chance-wise, than trying to go in there and shoot the Chairman in the head. It's not so much of a heroic sacrifice if you die before you even get a shot at the target.

"Greg, get the radio set up. We've got a fire mission to call in."

***

It took Greg a few minutes to get the HF radio and antenna set up, and even longer to get a link. I continued to watch the palatial compound below, trying not to get too worked up. Time was against us, and I didn't even know for sure that the receiver was even within range. Greg was deploying the antenna to point roughly at Kyushu, but it was a bit of a long shot.

Greg hissed at me, and I backed downhill again, leaving Lucas and Zhao to watch the target. Zhao accepted the binoculars without tearing his eyes away from the target. That man had vengeance on his mind, and the men who had nuked his country were right there, a bare seven hundred yards away.

I reached the ORP again, and Greg held out the handset. Throwing a poncho—even the PLA ponchos were cheap, but at least this one had gotten beat up enough that it didn't rustle like paper anymore—over me, I turned on my red lens flashlight and pulled out my map.

It wasn't nearly as detailed as I would have liked. A lot of the topo maps we'd had in the Marine Corps had been inaccurate enough that they even included the warning not to use them for call for fire. We had what we had, though, and fortunately, I had target reference points in and around Beijing to use. The nearest one was, unfortunately, about ten miles away, so I was going to have to be *very* careful and precise in my scientific wild-ass guess as to the coordinates.

Those calculations took longer than I'd hoped, but I didn't want to get our own position hit or waste the ordnance on the hills above us. Finally, with a deep breath, I keyed the handset.

"Tango Foxtrot Charlie Seven-Three, this is Golf Lima Ten."

There was no reply initially. Greg had gotten a link, but was anyone listening? I repeated the transmission after a moment, feeling my palms sweat as I held the handset to my ear.

"Golf Lima Ten, Tango Foxtrot Charlie Seven-Three. Send your traffic." Despite how faint and scratchy the transmission was, the voice on the other end sounded tense. We were only supposed to break radio silence for something extremely important, after all.

Something like this.

"We have eyes on the Ace of Spades and multiple other high value targets inside a compound at four nine four eight, five six zero five. Approximately company-sized security element, unable to engage. Request fire mission." I let off the handset and tried not to hold my breath.

There were a lot of things that could go wrong here. I was as sure of my target coordinates as I could be, but even if I was dead on, there was no way this was going to work if the assets weren't in place or were simply too far away. And I did *not* want that asshole to get away. I was already trying to plan an ambush on the road below in my head, but it would be difficult to get all the way down there in time. Almost impossible.

"Copy all. Ace of Spades confirmed present at four nine four eight, five six zero five. Stand by."

I waited. I hoped like hell that this wasn't just a quick meeting. I doubted there was any such thing, given how advanced the come-apart had apparently gotten, but there was always that chance. If the Chairman or his entourage were worried enough about his safety, they might not allow him to stay in one place for long.

"Golf Lima Ten, Tango Foxtrot Charlie Seven-Three. Confirm target coordinates."

"This is Golf Lima Ten, I confirm four nine four eight, five six zero five." I prayed I was right.

"Good copy, Golf Lima Ten. Five Rubicons inbound, time on target, five six minutes."

I let out a breath. Five Rubicon cruise missiles. That should do the trick, provided the targets didn't move before they hit.

The Rubicon was a product of the growing Triarii weapons industry in the heartland states. I'd only found out about it after we'd gotten to Japan. It hadn't been deployed in Europe, and the flotilla in the Pacific had been keeping it close to the vest. It was no Tomahawk. If it could be compared to any US cruise missile, it would probably be the old Matador-A. It could still carry a three-thousand-pound warhead, and it had a range of around six hundred fifty miles. It didn't use GPS for navigation, but instead an inertial navigation system with a pre-programmed flight path.

The timeline meant that the launch platform, one of our disguised arsenal ships, was right at the edge of its range. I got off the radio and handed it back to Greg, whispering a brief explanation of what was coming, and then started back toward the OP proper.

We were inside danger close. Five three-thousand-pound warheads made for a *lot* of boom. But all the same, I didn't think anyone wanted to miss this.

I passed the word to Lucas and Zhao. Both simply nodded and kept watching. "Any movement?" I asked, as I took the binoculars back from Zhao and settled in.

"Nothing." Lucas hadn't taken his own eyes off the target. "No new guests have showed up, and nobody's left. From the way security's acting, they're expecting to be here a while."

I focused on one of the knots of security men, standing near one of the fountains that flanked the hedge-lined lane that led up to the main buildings. Sure enough, they had noticeably relaxed, talking quietly, their weapons slung or leaned against the concrete, several of them smoking. I could only imagine how valuable cigarettes were getting in China these days, as the supply chains broke down.

There had to be more security farther down the road, then. Possibly even armored vehicles holding a checkpoint. Given the growing chaos, I would have expected the close in security to be a lot more nervous, otherwise.

Fortunately, there was no sign that our transmission had been detected, let alone triangulated. I had to assume that they were looking. There was no way the ChiComs thought that all this chaos was just happening on its own. But if they were, they hadn't picked up on us. Not yet.

We settled in to watch and wait.

***

The strike was almost too late.

We saw the security men suddenly scramble to grab their weapons and get into position, stiffening as they spread out across the entryway. I wondered, as my pulse sped up, whether we had finally been detected, and word had just gotten to them that there was a foreign transmitter somewhere nearby.

But soon several groups of men in suits started to come out of the buildings, and several of the security men ran to the vehicles and started them up. The meeting was ending. Whatever was going on, they weren't going to ground, they had just had a meeting and were dispersing.

I gripped the binoculars. To be this close… I started to wonder if I could manage a seven-hundred-yard shot with the QBZ-191 and its red dot. It wasn't likely, but maybe if I dumped the mag, *something* would at least hit the Chairman.

Then I heard the faint roar in the distance.

Turning my head, I still couldn't quite make out the incoming Rubicon missiles. They were jet-propelled cruise missiles, not rockets, and that made them all but invisible in the dark.

A few heads came up as the security men heard the sound. They were ever so slightly too late, though.

The Chairman looked up from where he was speaking to half a dozen of his Central Committee toadies, just before the first Rubicon hit.

The fireball eclipsed the center of the compound for just a moment, before a roiling black cloud started to billow up toward

336

the night sky, disrupted an eyeblink later by the second hit. Then the third, fourth, and fifth all struck within a couple seconds of each other.

In moments, the entire compound had gone dark, as a thunderous pillar of smoke, dust, and debris rose into the night sky, some of that detritus already starting to rain down on us where we hunkered down in the dirt, hoping and praying that something solid didn't punch right through one of us.

The rolling thunder of the *boom*s was still echoing off the hills.

The Central Committee of the Chinese Communist Party had just been obliterated.

We held in place for a few minutes, at least until the shrapnel stopped falling out of the sky. We'd been far too close to fifteen thousand pounds of explosives, and my head hurt from the shockwaves, even though we'd all gotten as low and as small as we could as they'd washed over us. When I finally looked up over the ridge again, all I could see was smoke and devastation. Some of the vehicles were burning, adding a certain hellish light to the cratered field of death that had been the Central Committee's getaway.

Prying myself up off the ground, I turned to the rear. "Time to make tracks."

Chapter 40

We loitered in the area for the next week, though we stayed in the hills above the suburbs around Beijing, watching and listening. Zhao had figured out how to tune our shortwave into some of the local radio stations—not that radio was all that widely used these days, but with the internet largely down, radio was about all the Communists had left to communicate with their subjects—but even those weren't all that informative. Either the stations themselves had no idea what was going on, or they were afraid to publicize it.

There had been no mention of the deaths of the Chairman and most of the Central Committee. After the first few days, we stopped bothering. All we could hear, according to Zhao, was assurances that everything was under control, and that things would get better soon.

Perhaps tellingly, even those assurances stopped just before we quit listening, replaced largely with dead air or Chinese music.

We watched the shit-show for hours from an OP on the top of a hill where we had a view of most of Beijing.

Fires raged unchecked through entire sections of the city. No air traffic came in or out of Beijing Capitol International Airport. And, if I was judging what I was seeing through the binoculars right, there were actual firefights happening in places down below. Without the Central Committee, things were really starting to fall apart.

Actually, I wasn't so naïve as to believe that just cutting the head off the snake had necessarily led to this chaos all by itself. The briefing materials had been clear that the Chinese Communist Party was a hydra, made up of dozens, if not hundreds, of bureaucracies that functioned as independent and rival fiefdoms, with their directors often ignoring the Central Committee altogether when it suited them. The Chairman had been cracking down on a lot of them, of course, which might have only aided our mission.

But the most powerful weapon we'd possessed in this attack had been the innate corruption of the Communist Party itself, and the way that corruption had leached out into every facet of Chinese society.

Reserves of fuel, food, and materials had been wasted or sold for graft. Repairs to infrastructure had been put off or, once again, the materials had either been sold or never bought, because the Party functionaries had pocketed the funds. The destruction we had wrought had been amplified immensely by that very corruption.

And that meant that people were getting increasingly desperate down below. They had no power, no gas, nothing to cook with, and increasingly nothing to cook. And the PLA, what was left of it, wasn't sympathetic. They took what they wanted and crushed anyone who resisted. Everyone, including the remaining authorities, was in survival mode, looking out for Number One and to hell with the rest.

We didn't have powerful enough optics to see a whole lot of detail from up there, but what we could see was looking increasingly post-apocalyptic.

I took stock mentally as I watched. We'd wrought a hell of a lot of destruction. I didn't want to guess at how many people were dead or dying because we'd destroyed the infrastructure that kept them fed, never mind the destruction wrought by the riots and the crackdowns. It was disturbing, if I let myself think about it.

Not all of these people had had any say in what had been done to the US. Most of them had had no say whatsoever.

Nor had any of those who had died in the US or Eastern Europe.

War is hell.

While the plan had been to wreak as much havoc as possible, using not only the munitions and weapons we'd brought in with us, but also anything and everything we could take from the enemy, we were out of explosives, and still didn't have all that much ammo. Enough to win a couple fights, sure, especially given the fact that our marksmanship was far better than the PLA's, on average. But we hadn't yet managed to get close enough to a small enough PLA unit to raid them for supplies.

I was starting to wonder if we really needed to anymore.

There was no hard and fast drop-dead time or end point for extract. That was a failing that I'd hoped the Triarii would have avoided, but all the same, the nature of the beast meant that we had to rely on our own discretion.

As grim as the whole business was, we had to remember that as harsh as he could be, Colonel Santiago wouldn't have intended any of us to turn this into a suicide mission. That wasn't the Triarii way. We were supposed to use our judgement and our training to make the other poor dumb bastard die for *his* country.

Watching the chaos, still lit only by the fires scattered across the darkened cityscape, thinking over the last shortwave broadcast, which hadn't indicated that much more was happening, I made my decision. Zhao might object, but Zhao had a vendetta that probably wouldn't be satisfied as long as he was still alive. But I thought that we'd done about all we could do, at least near Beijing. It was time to fade and head for the coast.

If more targets presented themselves along the way, we'd see if we could take them. But we had eighty miles to cover, give or take, to get to the coast and steal a boat that *might* get us out to a Triarii vessel in the Yellow Sea. Staying undetected was going to remain our chief priority, though, especially since the route from here was going to take us through the fields and rice paddies, weaving between the villages between Beijing and Tianjin. We wouldn't have the hills and woods to hide in for much longer.

Falling back from the OP, I rejoined the rest of the team and told them what we were going to do. We still had an hour until sunset, and from what we'd seen so far, few people ventured out after dark. The bandits, the PLA, and the PAP—though that was a somewhat redundant set of categories—all operated more openly after the sun went down.

Hopefully, we'd be able to make good time.

***

Unfortunately, we still had Bertrand with us. The man was not in good shape, and he was pretty shell-shocked by everything that had happened. Watching the Central Committee get turned to pink mist and black smoke hadn't helped his mental state.

He had already been dragging for the last week. We were all strung out and exhausted, and the diet of foraged rice and the occasional chicken wasn't helping our endurance much, but the most worn-down of us was still doing better than Bertrand, and it was becoming a problem.

I could tell, just by the looks he was giving our unwelcome cargo, that Jordan was about ready to stab Bertrand in the neck and leave him to bleed out. On some level, the more feral part of me wouldn't have minded. I had to remind myself that it was still entirely possible that I was going to die before ever getting out of China, and I didn't want Bertrand's blood on my conscience if that happened.

As opposed to all the others you've killed over the last year and a half?

That's different. That was combat.

Still, by the time we had to go to ground, after crossing two arterial roads—fortunately deserted as fuel became almost as precious as diamonds—we'd barely made five miles. And we were far too close to both the highway and the two villages nearby for comfort.

"He's gonna get us caught and killed." Jordan's voice was a low hiss in the twilight just before dawn. We were set into a strip of trees between farmers' fields, and I was more than a little nervous that we were going to have to break contact before noon. This was not a great hiding place.

"What do you want to do?" I already knew the answer to that question, but I needed to let Jordan say it himself. Sometimes he backed down when he had to face the reality of what his temper was demanding.

"You know damned well, Matt." He wasn't playing the game. "This isn't like back in the States, or even Eastern Europe. He's a fucking ChiCom propagandist, and you know it."

He was right, in a way. Bertrand had willingly and eagerly given aid and comfort to the Chinese Communist Party and worked against his own country in the process.

That still didn't give me the right to cut his throat just because he was a burden.

"And what happens when somebody finds his body?" I knew that I was looking for a practical explanation to get Jordan off my back, but it was still a solid consideration.

"Who gives a shit? These people are shooting, beating, and stabbing each other for a ball of rice. What's one more corpse?"

"And if it's an American? An obvious round-eye?" I thought of the argument even as I started to make it. "What might get the PLA or PAP off their backs faster than a foreign infiltrator found dead in their field?" That was a risk if we got walked on during the day, too, but there were only so many risks we really could mitigate.

He chewed on that for a moment. "Damn it." He really wanted Bertrand dead, and I couldn't entirely blame him.

"We've got relatively flat ground to cover from here on out. We might even be able to steal a truck, if we can find one with gas in it." That didn't seem all that likely, but it was still possible.

"What about the river?" Greg was, as usual, trying to defuse the situation, though he was also bringing up a decent point. "Could we commandeer a boat?"

I shook my head slightly, though any movement had to be minimal in this sketchy hiding place. "These rivers are all dammed every few miles. There's no clear way to float down any of them." I was pretty sure that none of these little dams had been hit. There were just too many targets, and most of them were for flood control anyway, not hydroelectric power.

"It might be an idea, though, even if we can't float it." Jordan had, to Greg's relief, left the idea of cutting Bertrand's throat behind, and now he was thinking about route planning instead. "Sure, the footing's going to suck, but if we got down on the riverbank, we might be able to make tracks with some good cover and concealment. Might make for better hide sites than some farmer's orchard, too."

It was a good point. It would add a couple nights, minimum, to get to the coast, since the river didn't exactly follow a straight line. But the potential to be able to move with more concealment was an inviting option.

"We'll try it." I glanced at Bertrand, who was passed out. He hadn't snored, so far, which was good. None of us had a gas mask, which had been the old school solution to snoring in a hide site. If he started, whoever was on watch would have to wake him up.

None of us had snored since we'd landed, which was a little bit weird, since I knew for a fact that Tony could snore like a sawmill. I could only guess that somehow the strain of being this far behind enemy lines had put us on a knife edge of alertness that meant none of us ever slept soundly enough to *start* snoring.

That was another reason to get out. The sheer adrenaline overload was going to start to take a toll soon. I was exhausted, but even after that long in the weeds, I was still keyed up and alert.

Still not so keyed up and alert that I couldn't fall asleep when my turn finally came, even as the sun burned through the faint veil of smoke that hung over the entire valley, still drifting in from Beijing.

***

It was a long, restless day. We didn't get walked on or compromised, though from what I could see when I was on watch, that was mainly because the local farmer was being furtive as hell, trying to avoid being seen from the road. The banditry must have been worse than I'd thought. At any rate, he didn't come near our hide site, which was good. As soon as the sun was all the way down, we were up and moving.

Getting across the next major road was going to be the hardest part, if I was reading the map right. Fortunately, there was enough of a gap between villages, shadowed by trees, that we might be able to cross there without being detected from a nearby house. There still wasn't a lot of traffic on the roads, so that gave us an even better chance.

David and I crouched in the shadows under the low-hanging boughs, watching for any foot or vehicle traffic. So far, the area seemed pretty dead.

I was about to get up and move when I froze. Headlights had just appeared down the road to the west, heading toward us.

As I dropped flat next to David, the first truck roared by. Fortunately, it was on the other side of the road, and we were down behind an embankment, but I could see just well enough to take stock.

It was a blocky, six-wheeled transport truck with an open bed. Half a dozen men with rifles rode in the back. I couldn't see well enough to tell if they were PLA, PAP, or bandits, or some amalgamation of all three. Whoever they were, there was no doubt in my mind getting spotted would be bad.

They weren't looking around all that much, fortunately, and the trucks weren't exactly moving at patrol speeds. They sped past as fast as they could presumably go, but they'd already slowed as they neared the intersection at the edge of the village immediately to our east.

That wasn't good. Worse, they started to stop and spread out around the intersection, and the men with rifles started to get out.

I didn't think they were after us. If they had been, they'd have gone right to the farm where we'd laid up for the day. No, this was something different.

The gunmen quickly spread out around the intersection, two men moving to the middle of the intersection, seemingly barking orders. Four or five of the gunmen took up security positions on our end of the intersection, while the rest spread out into the village in groups of five or six.

I knew what we were looking at, then. This was a shakedown. They probably were still using some sort of "enemy of the State" rhetoric, but they were going to take what they wanted and kill anyone who resisted.

A part of me wanted to do something about it. The more rational part of my brain knew that there wasn't anything we *could* do. Not without bringing all sorts of hell down on our heads. That was at least a company-strength unit, and we had twelve men, one of whom was completely useless.

Fortunately, we were too far away to hear any screams. I heard the gunshots, though, sporadic enough that I was sure that the shooting was only going one way.

Getting to my feet, I tapped David. He got up, his weapon ready, and with a quick nod, barely visible on NVGs, we both scrambled up the embankment and dashed across the road, vaulting the concrete median, and sprinting as fast as our tired and undernourished legs could carry us to the trees on the far side, skidding and slipping down the embankment and into the trees. I quickly covered down the road, while David took the other direction, back toward the west and Beijing.

The rest of the team didn't waste time, sprinting across in pairs, Tony dragging Bertrand with him. More gunshots echoed through the night. Somewhere, a dog started barking, though it was apparently far enough away from the bandits that it wasn't immediately answered with more gunfire.

Dogs had been a major concern. They might alert someone of our presence, no matter how careful we were. So far, though, we'd had no problems. We were going to have to cross a lot more farmland, though, and with these kind of raiding parties out and about, people were going to be nervous.

We just had to hope that the regular people were too afraid of the PLA and PAP to willingly call on them.

Cloaked in the darkness, disguised by the bandits' own headlights, we slipped into the fields and headed south as fast and as quietly as we could.

Chapter 41

We saw more of that sort of thing as we kept going south and east, toward the north edge of Tianjin. Not that often, since we were doing our damnedest to stay away from towns and villages, but we still saw it enough to see that it was endemic.

One of my old NCOs had always said that if you scratch a Communist, you'll find a gangster. We were seeing just how true that was, as the wheels fell off and everyone with a gun scrambled to take what they could before it all completely fell apart.

It took almost two weeks to work our way along the rivers and canals to the outskirts of Tianjin. We kept setting up for the shortwave broadcasts, but by the third night, instructions were essentially to head to extract. Things were unraveling fast, and it looked like a civil war was brewing between PLA generals for who was going to be top dog. Apparently, the Russians had even stopped talking to the PLA, and while the situation was still extremely dangerous, there wasn't much more we could do to help it along. We still didn't have solid targeting data for the Chinese nukes, either, at least not that was being transmitted on our freqs.

So far, there'd been no launch. There had been, apparently, plenty of threats, but there was a real question about who had control of those nukes. We could hope that things had been disrupted enough that *nobody* had control, but that dread that had been weighing on me for a while just got worse as I listened to the intel reports.

We'd done about all we could. But would it be enough?

There was no answer, and nothing much more that twelve of us, short on supplies as we were, could do about it.

So, we kept moving, trying to keep our heads down as China came apart at the seams around us.

As we got closer to Tianjin and the Bohai Bay, things started to get more complicated.

There were some lights still on in Tianjin. It was impossible to say if there were more working generators around, or if the teams or squads assigned to the area hadn't hit the grid hard enough. There were also a lot more organized PAP checkpoints, and those promised to be a problem. They were patrolling the major roads, and whether they were doing it for loot or for security, either way they presented the same threat to us.

To make matters worse, it was starting to look like we were going to have to get past them to get to the shore, where we could hopefully steal a boat. Or a junk. Or something that floated and had a motor that could get us out into the Yellow Sea, preferably without getting shot to pieces on the way.

It was the night before everything really went to hell that we made our move.

Even miles outside of Tianjin, the coast was still a lot more built-up than I would have hoped. There were still a fair number of lights on there, too, suggesting that whoever was in control in Tianjin had extended their miniature electrical grid out that way. There was a marina on the mouth of the Tanghe River, though, and that was our destination.

We just had to get across six miles of open salt marsh, studded with the remains of smashed wind turbines—the drone swarms must have had a field day here—and get past the patrols on the main coastal highway.

That last was going to be the worst part, and hiking through salt marshes at the pace we'd need to set to get to the marina before sunrise wouldn't have been a picnic even without Bertrand.

We moved out of our hiding place—essentially a handful of Ranger graves dug into a fallow field to the north in the desperate last hour before sunrise that morning—before it was even fully dark. Bertrand was *dragging,* practically stumbling from a combination of hunger and exhaustion, but Tony was always right behind him as we stepped it out across the fields, forming a loose Ranger file as we went.

If you've never hiked across a bog, trust me, you don't want to. Not only was the footing treacherous, and we were soaked to the knees in pretty short order, but we had to keep clambering over the elevated service roads between the wind turbine pylons. They weren't high, but they were high enough that it got tiring after the first six or so. Furthermore, we had to treat each one as a linear danger area, which slowed us down each time we had to cross one.

Bertrand tripped going over the second and faceplanted in the mud. Tony hauled him up with that long-suffering way Tony had, and we kept going.

No matter how hard we pushed, it still took a good chunk of the night to get across, especially since we had to go to ground several times to avoid the patrols that were still randomly moving along some of those service roads, not to mention when we had to backtrack—twice—because there was just too much water in the field. Finally, though, we were less than a mile from our target.

Unfortunately, there was a three-vehicle patrol sitting on the side of the coastal highway, right in front of us.

They looked like regular PAP, equipped with the same six-wheelers that we'd seen up on the Shisanling upper reservoir. The vehicles were running, and they had their headlights on, sitting just off the road, in the parking lot at what looked like a rest stop. That wouldn't have been too bad an issue if they'd been either facing the blasted and burned-out remains of the refinery to the east, or back toward Tianjin, but they were covering down both directions, and those headlights were pretty bright. With powerful enough optics, even if they didn't have NVGs, they'd probably spot us crossing the highway.

I knew what that meant. And as I crouched in the muck and the shadows north of that checkpoint, I mentally braced myself for what was coming.

I was tired. Not just down to my bones, but down to my soul. The rage that had fueled me across miles of Chinese territory and through close calls, fights, and strikes on infrastructure had faded to ash from sheer exhaustion and the horror that was the collapse of the People's Republic of China. They'd struck first. They'd been so corrupt that they had no safety net. The CCP had brought this on their own people, and most of them had paid the ultimate price, since we'd been in the right place at the right time to bring hell down on their heads.

None of that made it any easier.

Now, though, if we were going to get out, we were going to have to kill these guys, and I had to put aside the weariness and the dark shadow that had been weighing on my mind for months and get to work.

It was game time. I took a deep breath, said an almost wordless prayer for strength, speed, accuracy, and forgiveness of my sins if I was killed in the next few minutes, and then I got up and headed over the road and into the open marsh between me and the back of the rest stop buildings.

I didn't run. That would have worn me out faster, and there was no way to keep from splashing and potentially alerting the enemy. That building stood between me and the vehicles, and I didn't have line of sight on any of the bad guys, so I had cover, as long as I moved carefully. David was right behind me, probably cussing me again for jumping the stack.

We got to the back of the building and stacked up. I looked over at Tony and nodded. He returned it. He and Reuben would hold down the west end of the building, covering our backs while the rest of us assaulted from the east and cleared through.

That was the plan, anyway.

Bertrand suddenly broke away from Tony and ran around the corner, yelling in Mandarin.

With a curse, Tony hooked around the corner and opened fire, laying down a long, stuttering burst of fire from his QJY-88. I didn't pause to wonder if he'd killed Bertrand or not. I just went around the other corner and attacked.

Every eye was momentarily on the west end of the building, where Tony was still raking the western vehicle with long bursts of 5.8mm. That gave me just enough of an edge.

I shot the first man from about seventy-five yards, double-tapping him on the move while I dragged my rifle toward the next. That one got a double pair, just to be on the safe side.

I set up on the corner of the building, dropping to a knee while David and Chris dashed toward the nearest vehicle and Greg leaned out over my head, adding his own muzzle to mine. In seconds, we had every one of the PAP shooters in a crossfire, at least the ones on the north side of the vehicles.

Motion caught my eye, at the very edge of my PS-31s' field of view. Shifting my gaze, I saw a man clambering up into the eastern truck's turret, reaching for the QJY-88 mounted in it. I put my QBZ-191's red dot on his head and dumped him with three rounds. His head snapped back, and he slumped, bonelessly, into the turret.

Then I was moving on that vehicle while Jim and Steve took up the corner I'd just vacated.

Moving around behind David and Chris, I slowed as I neared the front corner of the truck. I popped it fast, leading with my muzzle, and found myself face to face with a man wearing PAP camouflage and a black balaclava, his QBZ-95 pointed at me.

I shot first, but I felt a fiery impact along my upper arm even as I blasted him onto his ass with a five-shot group. I kept moving, driving along the side of the vehicle and dumping the rest of the magazine into the figures that were still taking cover behind the other two. Greg had moved with me, and he was shooting over my shoulder, adding his fire to mine.

A moment later, we had no more targets. We consolidated around the vehicles.

We hadn't come through unscathed.

Bertrand had been practically cut in half. As hard as I tried not to think about it, he was no great loss.

Zhao had died shortly thereafter. He'd gone for one of the other trucks and had been shot in the face. He lay in an unnatural tangle of limbs on the concrete in front of the building.

Jim was limping. He'd taken a round to the leg. "You need to stop getting shot." Jordan was already wrapping a bandage around it, Jim's own tourniquet already high and tight. "What is this, the fifth time since you joined the team?"

"Something like that." Even Jim's exuberant sense of humor was gone, after all we'd seen and been through over the last month.

"Get him in the vehicle." I pointed to one of the six-wheeled trucks. "We're going to drive right to the marina and take a boat." I'd been shot too, but it was only a graze, a bloody trough dug into the side of my shoulder but not much else. It hurt, and infection was going to be an issue soon, but I'd probably live long enough to worry about that later.

I held security until everyone else except for Tony was loaded up. So far, there didn't appear to be any response on the way, but it was only a matter of time. Fortunately, while the PAP appeared to be much more on the ball down here than they had been up in Beijing, they were still moving slowly, since their comms and power weren't exactly all that reliable.

We clambered in and headed for the marina.

***

Things actually went pretty quickly from there.

There were a few fishermen already setting up for work in the pre-dawn dimness when we pulled up. They all cowered at the sight of a PAP vehicle, and having just heard gunfire, they probably figured that staying out of the way was the best path to maintaining a heartbeat.

We drove down to the end of the marina, hoping that we could find a boat that still had some fuel in it. We finally stopped and unloaded next to a green-hulled fishing boat that looked like it might have just enough legs. Tony stayed in the truck's turret to cover us, while David and I climbed aboard to check it out.

There was no one aboard, but the fishing gear all appeared to have been recently used, and while everything was labeled in Mandarin, we were able to make sure that it did have a full bunker of fuel, and the engine actually started, though it took several tries and belched an unhealthy amount of smoke once it finally caught.

Greg and Jordan hit the deck above us. "We've got company coming. We need to go, now."

I scrambled up on deck, to see that while the PAP vehicles were indeed on their way, they were still up on the highway, and appeared to have stopped where we'd slaughtered the first group. Our lights were off, so they hadn't seen us yet. "Tony! Get everybody on board!"

That took a pretty short amount of time. Nobody wanted to stay on that shore by then. Not long after, we were puttering out into the bay, trying to lose ourselves in the morning fishing fleet while we kept our distance from those poor bastards who were still going out to catch fish to feed their families, even as their country unraveled.

No pursuit materialized. In three hours, we were out of the bay and heading deeper into the Yellow Sea, Greg already setting up the radio to call for a Triarii ship to come get us, even as the Chinese coast dwindled to our stern.

Our part in Option Zulu was over.

Epilogue

It took two days before we made rendezvous. A lot happened in that time.

While we were trying to navigate with a crap chart labeled in Mandarin, maintaining radio contact with the *Hostile Dancer*, things had started to shake out in China. Most dangerously, General Xiè Guanting got control of at least a part of the Chinese nuclear arsenal.

Issuing a statement via internet and shortwave radio, he declared that the United States had conducted an unprovoked campaign of terrorism against the People's Republic of China, and therefore, the PRC would respond in the only way appropriate.

Those nukes he had control of were flying before he'd stopped talking.

Fortunately, most of them turned out to be duds. They still blew a lot of radioactive material around, but about two thirds of them fizzled.

The one launched from a submarine off the coast of Norfolk wasn't one of the duds.

Washington DC had gotten about five minutes of warning. Word that reached us on the *Hostile Dancer* was that the President and about three quarters of Congress were all dead, along with millions of Beltway residents, and about five million more on the east and west coasts from the warheads that actually went off. The sub was sunk, but the damage was done.

There was enough continuity in the chain of command that the response was quick and devastating.

What was left of Beijing, Guangzhou, Jinan, Shenzhen, and half a dozen other cities, along with every known military target in China was hit by Minuteman ballistic missiles and nuclear-armed Tomahawk cruise missiles launched by B-21 bombers over the next thirty-six hours. The damage we'd done was finalized. China would not rise again for a long, long time.

Apparently, comms had been established with Moscow, and the Kremlin had been assured that we had plenty more where that had come from, if they wanted to get froggy. So far, there had been no response.

We listened to the news aboard the *Hostile Dancer* in a sort of numb shock. Almost as bad, we were getting some idea of just how many Triarii had made it out of China. It was grim.

Of the nearly three thousand men who'd gone in, maybe seven hundred fifty were accounted for.

Option Zulu had failed. Oh, we'd wrecked the PRC, there was no doubt about that. What we'd failed to do, however, had been to head off the nuclear exchange that had followed. We'd had to move too fast, on too little intel. Several teams *had* gotten to some of the Chinese nuclear forces, but not enough.

And a whole lot of men had paid the ultimate price for our revenge.

***

Three months later, we sailed into Port Arthur.

There wasn't a big reception. There were maybe two dozen people waiting on the quay. The Triarii were far too busy for parades or anything like it. It wasn't as if we had a lot to celebrate, anyway.

Klara was waiting on the dock with her parents. They'd made their way to the States about the same time I was leaving for Japan. I came down the gangplank and went to her, then stopped in some shock.

She was smiling, cradling the bump of her belly with both hands.

I think I might have collapsed then, if I hadn't folded her in my arms as Mr. Mikolajczak, my father-in-law, gripped my shoulder.

I just held her for a while, feeling the faint stirring of my child between us. We were still alive, and we still had a future to fight for.

***

After a very long time in the confessional, I got back to work.

Brian Hartrick was among those missing, presumed dead. Colonel Santiago, who was headquartered there in Texas, informed me that Hartrick had told him that he was recommending me to take his place as a Grex Luporum commander/training chief.

I was surprised, but I'd do it. We still had a lot of work to do.

Most of the Chinese nuclear targets had been cities outside of the Triarii "Fortress Zone." The extensive work our organization had already put into decentralization and local self-sufficiency in power generation, food production, and manufacturing had already put the heartland, a good chunk of the south, and the mountain states on a solid road to recovery. Some of those places that had been trouble zones before the war were still trouble zones, but they'd taken a hit, and a lot of the locals were getting fed up. There were apparently talks already going on between the Triarii and the remnants of the federal government to normalize our organization's legal status and end the on-again-off-again civil war that had been simmering for years.

It was still going to take a long time. The PRA wasn't nearly the threat that it had been, but there were entire swathes of major cities and even states that had fallen under gang control. That was why I was busy training new Grex Luporum Triarii, many of them former Army who'd fought in Europe. That, and the fact that the foreign wars weren't all over, either. The Norks had pulled back after the nuclear strikes, but the Russians were positioning themselves in a renewed push for empire.

I pulled up the driveway in the dark, my headlights momentarily illuminating the small timber frame house that we'd bought just outside our new training facility on the east slope of the Crazy Mountains. I'd been ready to settle in Texas, but when Wallace had told me that the new Grex Luporum base was going to be in Montana, I hadn't objected.

The house wasn't new. The board siding was gray with age, and the covered porch out front creaked under my boots as I stepped up and went to the door. I was still in my greens, wearing my Triarii patch on my shoulder for the first time Stateside since I'd gotten it. My OBR and gear bag were slung over one shoulder.

I stopped at the door. Was that…?

I snatched the door open and rushed inside. The lusty yell of a crying baby sounded from the bedroom.

Klara lay on our bed, surrounded by her parents and the midwife. She looked up at me, beaming, holding our son in her arms. "I'm sorry, Mateusz." She always liked to use the Polish version of my name. "We couldn't wait."

I went to her side, setting my rifle and gear on the floor. I looked down at the red, wrinkled, screaming bundle that was my son.

A lot of people were dead. The country—the world— would never be the same. In many ways, the wars weren't over. They'd never be over. But life goes on.

The only other option was to lie down and die.

I kissed my wife and took my son in my arms.

From the Author

So, we come to the end. Three years, nine books, and a lot has happened since I began this little project in speculation on the next world war. It's a very different world than it was when this began, and if this series ended on a grimmer note than it started, it perhaps reflects the reality that we all hesitate to look too closely at. War is hell, and World Wars are worse. As I write this, the war in Ukraine continues, with entire cities nearly flattened. Let us all hope that the Maelstrom Rising series remains fiction.

Much like the American Praetorians series, it was time to wrap this up. There will be more military/paramilitary fiction coming, with a new series launching hopefully near the end of this year. To keep up-to-date, I hope that you'll sign up for my newsletter—you get a free American Praetorians novella, *Drawing the Line*, when you do.

If you've enjoyed this novel, I hope that you'll go leave a review on Amazon or Goodreads. Reviews matter a lot to independent authors, so I appreciate the effort.

If you'd like to connect, I have a Facebook page at https://www.facebook.com/PeteNealenAuthor. For those who have departed FB, I'm also on MeWe at www.mewe.com/i/peternealen. You can also contact me, or just read my musings and occasional samples on the blog, at https://www.americanpraetorians.com. I look forward to hearing from you.

Also By Peter Nealen

<u>The Maelstrom Rising Series</u>
<u>Escalation</u>
<u>Holding Action</u>
<u>Crimson Star</u>
<u>Strategic Assets</u>
<u>Fortress Doctrine</u>
<u>Thunder Run</u>
<u>Area Denial</u>
<u>Power Vacuum</u>
<u>Option Zulu</u>
<u>SPOTREPS – A Maelstrom Rising Anthology</u>

<u>The Brannigan's Blackhearts Universe</u>
<u>Kill Yuan</u>
<u>The Colonel Has A Plan (Online Short)</u>
<u>Fury in the Gulf</u>
<u>Burmese Crossfire</u>
<u>Enemy Unidentified</u>
<u>Frozen Conflict</u>
<u>High Desert Vengeance</u>
<u>Doctors of Death</u>
<u>Kill or Capture</u>
<u>Enemy of My Enemy</u>
<u>War to the Knife</u>
<u>Blood Debt</u>

<u>The Unity Wars Series</u>
<u>The Fall of Valdek</u>
<u>The Defense of Provenia</u>
<u>The Alliance Rises</u>

<u>The Lost Series</u>
<u>Ice and Monsters</u>
<u>Shadows and Crows</u>